"Good evening, Carole."

The deep male voice came from just over her shoulder, causing Carole to whirl with a start. Her heart thundered to a gallop as she spotted R.J.

"I was beginning to think you weren't coming."

"What?" R.J. asked in a cutting tone. "Miss my own brother's engagement party? Surely you jest. Family ties are strong, Carole, particularly among the fine old families of Charleston." His look turned uncontrollably harsh. "You'll learn that as Mrs. Curt Morrisson."

"Mrs. Curt Morrisson," she repeated in a dull voice. "I guess it's really going to happen."

"Of course it is," R.J. returned with mounting irritation. "It's what you want, isn't it?"

Carole glanced away. "We've already been over that."

"Yes, we've been over it," R.J. said. "I don't want to make things any harder for you," he added softly. "So, if this is the way it's going to be . . . Welcome to the family."

His free hand moved to cup the other side of her face as he bent to press a kiss on her forehead. His lips lingered against her skin, his nostrils picking up the scent of gardenia. Of their own accord, his lips began trailing between her brows, along the bridge of her nose to the very tip, where they hovered in midair just above her.

When R.J. gave in to the irresistible urge, Carole's mouth was open and waiting.

CHARLESTON

Margaret Ann Reid

IVY BOOKS • NEW YORK

Ivy Books
Published by Ballantine Books

Produced by Butterfield Press, Inc.
133 Fifth Avenue
New York, New York 10003

Library of Congress Catalog Card Number: 88-91141

ISBN 0-8041-0247-3

Manufactured in the United States of America

First Edition: October 1988

CHARLESTON

PART I

Chapter One

CAROLE GOSSETT STEPPED onto the corner balcony of her second-floor townhouse apartment. Before her to the south was the Ashley River, still sleeping in a shroud of gray mist the dawn had yet to dissolve. To the east, in the distance, was the blue Atlantic, stretching all the way to a horizon that slowly gave up a brilliant sunrise. And the dark water streaked with color as the sun melted an orangy gold path back to the shore.

Carole took a deep breath of the familiar air, laden with the unique, blending scents of ocean salt and flowers. Her gaze left the Atlantic and traveled inland, past the sea-facing wall of the Battery and across the quaint, irregular roofline of the Historic District, coming to rest irresistibly on the tall, brick chimneys of the family home on Tradd Street.

Home. She considered the word, finding once again that it had a hollow ring. The Gossett house hadn't seemed like home since her mother deserted the place a dozen years ago.

Below, the dawn-lit streets were quiet. It was too early for the noisy throngs of tourists, the humming flow of traffic, or even the rhythmic, rattling sounds of horse-drawn carriages making their way along the

3

cobblestones. Now, it seemed, all of Charleston slept except for her. It was peaceful and beautiful—and lonely.

Leaning against the wrought-iron balcony railing, Carole surrendered herself to a melancholy train of thought. She had been only eleven—her sister April, twelve—when their mother had left. April had seemed to take it in stride, but Carole had suffered nightmares for years, clinging to her sister as her father became increasingly irritated by his younger daughter's pitiful wails for "Mommy."

Gradually, as Carole entered her teens and began to blossom into womanhood, she'd discovered that she was rewarded with indulgence, and even a rare embrace from the master of the house when she behaved cleverly. A witty comment here, a flirtatious flutter of lashes there, and her father smiled on her warmly, glowing with pride when she managed to captivate his business associates and guests with her winsome way.

And so, as April pursued her studies, becoming ever more dedicated to the idea of a career in medicine, Carole became the coquette. She hostessed all of her father's business dinners—or at least those that took place in between his marriages. And she gradually gained the reputation of Tradd Street's blond femme fatale. All the boys chased after her, and their families looked on in understanding. After all, Carole Gossett was everything a boy could want—rich, pretty, charming, and not bent on that newfangled, career-minded rot like that sister of hers.

True, Carole had completed her studies at the College of Charleston and received a degree in fashion design, but she had spent most of her time socializing, passing her courses by the skin of her teeth. Everybody knew that it was James Gossett's influence that had secured her a position at that ex-

4

clusive salon on King Street. Everybody knew Carole Gossett hadn't a serious bone in her body.

Everybody would be surprised if they could now see the solemn, thoughtful look on the face they could only picture with a pretty pout or a seductive smile.

At twenty-four, April was in her second year of medical school, well on her way to becoming a doctor. At twenty-three, Carole was in her second year of work at Carlotta's fashion salon.

But it meant nothing. Carole dabbled with design, but when she felt like leaving work, she left. When she felt like staying home, she stayed. Her father had done too much to help Carlotta get started in business, and Carole knew that however she behaved, she was in no danger of being fired.

It seemed that April had always found it so easy to commit herself, to establish a direction and follow it doggedly. Now, in her dismal mood, Carole thought that she herself had never had a direction, a purpose, a meaning. She felt like an empty shell, a pretty ornament to her father's success that would one day be passed along to some appropriate, successful young man. Perhaps Curtis Morrisson, the golden boy at Gossett Enterprises.

It must be two—no, three months since her father invited Curtis home to supper and commanded Carole's presence. She had known who Curt was, of course. Everyone knew of the Morrissons. They were an institution on Tradd Street, one of the first and most elite families in the city. But they didn't mix with anyone who hadn't been in Charleston for at least four generations, so Carole had observed them only from a distance. There were the daughters, Camille and Margaret, and the sons, Curt, and an older brother who had moved away and whose name she couldn't recall.

She had expected Curtis Morrisson to be a bit taken with himself, a bit uppity to anyone without a family history as illustrious as his own—the Morrissons claimed one of the founders of Charleston, as well as a number of dignitaries and officials. But Curt had surprised her. His congenial manner and blond good looks were a match to her own. He wasn't conceited, simply accustomed to his attractiveness; not superior, simply at ease with his social position. Curt was quick, witty, and—Carole had swiftly surmised—completely vulnerable to the feminine wiles she wielded so well.

If he had a fault, it was his ambition, which shone as clear and strong from his pale blue eyes as from her father's dark ones. Curt was bound and determined to make a success of himself outside the powerful Ashley River Shipping Company which had come down through his family. An admirable enough aim, but after years of experience with her father, Carole knew just how cold and destructive such ambition could be.

Still, she had enjoyed Curt's tasteful courtship. Dinners, flowers—he did all the right things at the right times, never rushing her, never pushing for sexual payoffs the way many men did. Carole had thought at first that his constraint was simply the good manners of breeding. But lately she had begun to sense a strategy in Curt's romancing. He was wooing her in the slow, deliberate way that smacked of marital intentions. And her father seemed to be giving his every blessing. Odd reaction from a man who had always applauded Carole's conquests of vast numbers of men but deftly reprimanded her if she narrowed to just one.

And that was exactly what had happened in the past month or so. Curt Morrisson was the only man she was dating, and he had made her believe she was the only woman in his life. He was good looking, wealthy, socially prominent, probably *the* most eligible bachelor in town. So . . . why wasn't she ecstatic?

Because he doesn't really know you. Because

6

you've only shown him the coquettish face you've shown your father all these years. Because if you marry Curt, you'll lose the last tenuous link with the secret person inside you who seems to be shrinking by the day.

It had been so long since she had been truly herself, Carole hardly knew if she even *could* be anymore. That was what she envied about April. That was what had her standing out on her balcony, watching a breathtaking spring sunrise and feeling like she'd lost her best friend.

The first car of the day, a silver Mercedes, purred quietly past, followed by a gusty breeze that rustled the palmetto leaves below, then danced up to the balcony to pluck at Carole's dressing gown.

The breeze was already warm. Her eyes thoughtful, Carole looked up at the cloudless dawn sky. It would be a clear, hot, summery day, though it was not yet the end of May.

A sound pricked at Randall Judd Morrisson's ears. Running water. Vicki. In the bathroom.

As R.J. came slowly awake he could still feel her body wrapped around him, and a half-smile came to his lips. He cracked an eyelid. Soft, shuttered light told him it was morning.

Then his vision lit on the ornate, inlaid, antique chifforobe across the room, and a host of unfamiliar surroundings burst into clarity. Lurching groggily to a sitting position, he thought, What the hell? . . .

"The papers are being served today," came a muffled male voice, confusing R.J. even more. "That means the old man will be gone, and work can begin next month. I hope that satisfies your New York boys."

R.J.'s head swiveled toward the sound, which came from behind a nearby closed door. The running water stopped.

7

"It will," said another male. "Ever since they got an idea of the profit margin in this deal, they've been extremely cooperative."

R.J. knew those voices. He blinked in the dim light that barely disclosed the tall door to the washroom. And then everything fell into place. He was home.

It was his father and Curt he heard, washing up in the bath adjoining the large study that was Robert Morrisson's private domain.

"But no one knows I'm involved, right?" his father demanded.

"I've told you, Dad. No one knows. We're completely screened. No one will bother to look into the affairs of a daft old geezer like Stuckey. . . ."

As the voices receded, R.J. sank back on the pillows. It had been two in the morning when he'd arrived, and he'd made it no farther than the rarely used downstairs guest room, even though he knew full well his mother would be disappointed. She would want him to be in his own room, as if he'd never left.

He hadn't lived in the house on Tradd Street for nearly eight years. First, there had been Vanderbilt, then his position at the state capital in Columbia. Still, Charlotte Morrisson kept her eldest's bedroom freshly changed and immaculate, ready and waiting in hopes that he might drop in unannounced.

And that was exactly what he had done. Folding his arms behind his head, R.J. grinned. No one even knew he was here.

It had come on him suddenly, the urge to return to Charleston. Well, maybe not *too* suddenly. Since spring had arrived, he'd been feeling a pull to return home to the sunny streets and palm-shaded lanes, to the gardens, brilliant with azaleas, to the smell of the sea mixing with honeysuckle. Then yesterday, he'd remembered that the Spoleto Festival would be in town, and that had cinched it.

8

Nowhere he'd lived in the past eight years could stir his blood like Charleston.

Climbing out of bed, he crossed the room to his bags and devoted a little time to thinking about Vicki. Tall, slender, chic Vicki. A vision of her materialized in his head, wearing an expectant look on her face that turned harsh and angry when he announced he was going to Charleston alone. She had been furious that he refused to take her with him, though he had tried to assuage her, explaining that it was, "just some family business."

Vicki's temper was as hot as that short-cropped, flaming hair of hers. She had been irresistibly sexy, standing there in nothing but a short emerald kimono, challenging him to explain himself or call her "a damned cab!" At the time, it had almost made him wish she were coming along.

But now . . . now he remembered. Being away from her reminded him that he was growing tired of Vicki. They had been together nearly four months now. And why not? She was intelligent, attractive, and polished from head to toe.

But there was something hard about her, something he occasionally caught sight of in her eyes. It made him wonder if she'd be with him at all, if not for the fact that he had a position of prestige and all the perks that went with it.

Ah, hell! Hadn't he found something wrong with all the women he'd been involved with? They had all been attractive. They had all been fun in bed. But somehow, they didn't keep his interest beyond a few months. They just didn't seem to have the allure, the soft, constant seductiveness of the females he'd grown up with. For him, there were no women like the beguiling, consumingly feminine belles of Charleston.

By the time he'd washed and dressed, and was stepping out of the guest room, R.J. was convinced he should break up with Vicki when he returned to Columbia.

A bejeweled hand flew to Charlotte Morrisson's throat as she looked up from the dining table. And then she was on her feet, running to the arched entrance.

"Randall!" she exclaimed, folding herself about the tall man. Tears started to her brown eyes. But then she recovered herself, and stepped back to look at her son.

"Of all the nerve!" she accused with a playful slap against his arm. "Giving your own mother such a start on a Saturday morning. What are you doing here?"

R.J. grinned. "Just decided to come on the spur of the moment. I got in early this morning and crashed in the guest room."

"The guest room . . . Why, of all things. You know perfectly well I keep your room ready."

"I know, Mother. I know," he sighed cheerfully. As his mother resumed her place at the table, he meandered toward the silver coffee service on the cherry wood sideboard.

"How long can you stay? And please don't say you're here just for the weekend."

R.J. poured a cup of the chicoried brew, added cream, then slouched familiarly against the antique serving table that had been in the family for generations.

"Just the weekend," he admitted. "But I'm here, aren't I?"

Charlotte eyed her firstborn with pride, her eyes soaking up the tall, athletic form clad in richly understated slacks and shirt, the facial features that could have been carved from the model of a Greek god, the consistently ruddy coloring that made the blond hair and white smile so startlingly bright. He looked wonderful.

10

And then there were the eyes. Heavily lined with dark lashes, their color was the deep blue-gray she laughingly referred to "Morrisson blue." When they were warm and attentive, those eyes could melt a heart in a snap. Charlotte knew, for her husband had them too—though it had been a long time since they held the warm, exciting light that had conquered her the first time she'd met Robert Morrisson, III.

Pushing the thought away, Charlotte swept her attention back to her son. Having stuffed his free hand into his pants pocket, he was sipping his coffee and glancing nonchalantly about, seeming to reacquaint himself with the elegant furnishings of the room where he had taken meals all his life.

He was breathtakingly handsome, her son, but there was more to Randall than his looks. He had a natural air of aristocracy one could only be born with, an aura of breeding that could not be feigned. Charlotte adored all four of her children, but there was something special about her eldest. Perhaps it was the calm, unwavering strength he radiated. God, how she had missed him!

"What made you decide to come now?" she asked. "You haven't been home since Christmas."

"It's spring, Mother. No one who's lived here can resist Charleston in the spring. Besides, the Spoleto Festival is in town. I plan to go out and take a look around."

"So you want to take in the sights," she said. "One might think you miss Charleston a bit after all."

"You know I miss it," her son returned, looking at her fondly.

"But last year you decided on Columbia so abruptly. A good attorney could make a perfectly respectable living here . . . where it's civilized. For goodness's sake, Randall, you graduated from Vanderbilt in the top ten of your class. Why, you could practice anywhere! I always said, and I still say, you could do just as well here at home as you do in the capital, even if you *are* working with that supreme-court judge.''

R.J. grinned behind his coffee cup. It hadn't taken her long to start making the same old pitch.

''It's not a question of doing 'just as well,' Mother. I *like* working in conjunction with the supreme court.''

''But must you live in Columbia? Really, Randall!''

He thought of the shapely redhead he had left warming his bed, of the many other eager women he'd courted at the capital.

''Columbia has its strong points,'' he murmured. ''And please, Mother . . . everyone but you has called me R.J. for more than ten years. How about it?''

He smiled over his shoulder as he discarded the coffee cup, and then came to stand before her.

''I'll make you a deal,'' she suggested spiritedly. ''I'll consent to call you R.J. if you'll consent to move back to Charleston.''

R.J. studied his mother. The chestnut, silver-streaked hair was pulled back with a pink ribbon, the slender face fresh-scrubbed and devoid of make-up. The heavy champagne lace of her dressing gown flopped away from her wrist as she curled her fingers beneath her chin and looked up at him coquettishly, a mischievous gleam dancing in her dark eyes. At forty-eight, Charlotte Morrisson was still a damned attractive woman.

''You look very pretty, Mother,'' he said.

She blushed in surprise, and then a warm feeling of maternal love washed through her. For an instant Charlotte felt as though she would cry, wail against the element of time that wrenched children into independent adults who deserted their mothers.

''Sure,'' she quipped. ''You're just trying to get around the deal.''

12

He grinned but still didn't answer. "By the way, where is everybody? Where's Dad? I heard him earlier."

"Oh, he and Curt have gone into town on some business or other. You know, a businessman's work is never done."

"How about Margaret and Camille?"

His mother took a quick glance at her watch. "What time is it? Nearly nine? Oh, the girls won't be stirring before ten on a Saturday."

Bending down, R.J. pressed a quick kiss to Charlotte's cheek. "I'm going to head on out and look around the festival. Tell the rest of my lazy family I'll see them later."

"All right. Oh, and be sure you're not terribly late. Curtis has invited his girl friend and her family for supper!"

"I'll be back!" R.J. called from the foyer.

As Charlotte watched his retreating form, she was swamped with a flood of memories of a tot, a boy, and a teenager, running out the front door with those very words.

"Yes . . . Randall," she said with a wistful smile.

By the time Carole finished her shower, shampoo, and a painstaking toilette of makeup and hair curling, she had buried her solemn mood behind the effervescent mask everyone knew as Carole Gossett.

Two hours before, she had glanced into the mirror and beheld an entirely ordinary-looking girl with straight, nondescript hair. Now, she saw the persona she had cultivated for years—a woman with golden, flamboyant curls cascading about a rosy, dimpled face with vivid blue-green eyes. Testing a smile on the mirror, she confirmed that the comfortable, dazzling guise was firmly in place.

A single brow arched mischievously as she searched her wardrobe, finally selecting a clinging, yellow sheath of her own design. It had been fun to do. One of the occasional creative bursts had hit, and she had dashed off the provocative drawing, using her influence to manipulate fabric and dressmaker so that the sketch became reality in only a matter of days.

Discarding her robe, Carole wriggled into the buttonless, zipperless thing. The buttery yellow jersey had just enough substance to hide the line of panties, the only undergarment she wore. Other than that, the dress clung mercilessly, conforming to her well-shaped hips and hugging her round breasts into a voluptuous cleavage between which the neckline dipped teasingly, daringly—seeming to be held together only by narrow, flanking straps which lined the plunging V—then reached over bare shoulders to join a square-cut back.

It would not have looked well on April, who had grown tall and thin, her figure as straight as a model's. No, the bright, clinging dress would only complement a wearer with a shape as curvaceous as Carole's.

This ought to make 'em sit up and take notice, she thought with satisfaction. She'd show those simpering spinsters at Carlotta's who could sell T-shirts!

At first, Carole had refused Carlotta's request that she help staff the shop-front booth that would offer exclusively designed T-shirts imprinted with the Spoleto logo.

"The festival lasts for two weeks," Carlotta had said. "If each of us here in the shop takes a turn, we'll only be out there for a couple of days each."

Carole had pleaded an excuse about helping her father host some out-of-town business guests, but then she'd overheard her fellow workers, Elsa and Cathy, gossiping in the storeroom.

"Of course, *she's* too good to help with anything like selling T-shirts at the Spoleto Festival!"

14

"Well, it's probably for the best anyway. She's never had to put in a full day's work in her life. She wouldn't know what to do. The only thing she knows how to sell is herself. Other than that, I'll bet she couldn't sell water to a thirsty man."

We'll just see about that, Carole now thought. And with a final confident grin at her reflection she grabbed her purse and jaunted out the door of the apartment.

It was Saturday. The Spoleto Festival had been in full swing for nearly a week, and banners and bunting hung everywhere in honor of the event. For two weeks every year, Charleston became a different place as the American Spoleto Festival embraced it with a celebration of the arts. Ballet, symphony, and theater performances. Showings of the work of every type artist imaginable. By the time the festival concluded, there would have been more than one hundred performances and shows by artists, dancers, actors, and musicians from around the world. *And* there would be thousands of tourists who would flock to the shops of the Historic District in search of a memento.

The T-shirt Elsa had come up with was somewhat attractive, Carole had to admit. The sleeveless design was made all the more striking by a brilliant, peacock blue material printed with white.

It wouldn't be so bad, Carole decided, spending a day on the sunny street, flirting her way through dozens of sales. Her spirits high, she put an enticing swing in her step and began to enjoy the beautiful walk through the District.

She always took the long way around. From her townhouse apartment on the corner of Broad Street and Rutledge Avenue, it would be more direct to walk along Broad, turn at King, and simply proceed to Carlotta's shop. But Carole always pursued a path that took her along Tradd Street.

It was silly, she often told herself. And yet, it felt

15

good to walk along the well-known street in the morning sunshine, passing the familiar, great houses, waving to neighbors she had known all her life, imagining that she must look the very picture of an attractive young woman of great promise.

That Carole Gossett, they would say. You know, she's very talented and has a post at that exclusive salon. Why, she could have her pick of any man in Charleston. It will be interesting to see whom she chooses.

And so, as Carole strolled saucily along, she had no eye for the historic buildings dripping lavender wisteria, the ancient, twisted oaks draped with silvery Spanish moss, nor for the tall palms that lined her way. She was lost in her own flattering daydreams as she turned onto Tradd, where quaint turned opulent, and pretty flowerbeds became lush courtyards guarded by garden walls and ornate wrought-iron gates.

Most of them meant something. It was an old tradition in the District. People had their gates designed to represent a quality about themselves: the year they established roots there, an element from the family coat of arms, or a symbol of a business or sporting interest.

As Carole approached the Gossett house, her eye was drawn to its courtyard gate, which was elegantly fashioned in the shape of a phoenix, the legendary bird which rises to new life from its own ashes. It had nothing to do with the Gossetts, of course. *They* hadn't come to Charleston until the 1920s, a hundred years after the house with the phoenix gate had been built.

Yankees, some would sniff. Carpetbaggers, old-timers would sneer.

No, the phoenix had been the emblem of the Tarletons, an old plantation family which had settled in the Carolina low country in colonial times. But the phoenix had proven an ironic symbol for the Tarle-

16

tons. Their Ashley River plantation had been burned to the ground during the War Between the States. And later, in the hard Reconstruction years, they had lost all their holdings and fled—case victims of the northern "carpetbagging" opportunists who flooded the South when the bloody war ended.

Lyle Gossett, Carole's grandfather, had been a jazz-age example of one of those. The rumor was that he had made a fortune bootlegging illegal spirits during Prohibition, that it was this vulgar money— much to Charleston's horror—which had purchased the Tarleton house on Tradd Street. But that had been years ago. You'd think people would forget. But Charleston didn't.

For as long as Carole could remember, her father had been trying to overcome the tainted Gossett reputation. And to a degree, he had succeeded. Dynamic business success had gone a long way toward mollifying the southern aristocrats. But James Gossett realized that the many invitations to dinners and social fêtes were extended in deference to his wealth, not his social standing. Even the most kind of Charleston's old guard would still consider the Gossetts no better than *nouveau riche*, and Carole knew that fact tormented her father. It seemed to be his one weakness, in fact, this obsession to be accepted by the blue bloods.

Her gaze drifted beyond the phoenix gate, past the dark magnolias and hot-pink camellias, up the massive, white-columned facade of the brick mansion— and the familiar tugging began at her heart. Even after all these years, she still half-hoped to see the radiant face of her mother smiling down from the master-bedroom balcony when she looked up at the house. But the curtains at both sets of French doors were drawn. All was quiet. And for a moment Carole's morning solemnity threatened to return.

Once, so long ago, she had been part of a family in that house. Perhaps that was why it continued to draw her like a magnet, teasing her with memories of loving security, with echoes of childhood laughter and a mother's lilting, with bedtime lullabies.

Carole shook herself, sternly reminding herself that that time was gone. Now, the great house was comparatively empty. Two years ago when April had moved into an apartment near the Medical University, Carole had quickly followed in her wake, leasing the expensive townhouse loft and telling herself it was all right that Daddy footed the bill.

Now, but for the servants, the Gossett mansion on Tradd Street was inhabited only by her father and his wife. That was the only way Carole could bring herself to think of Kathleen—his wife. She was in no way, shape, or form anything like a mother.

The mere thought of her father's third wife propelled Carole down the street. One block. Two blocks of tall garden walls and taller palms, and then she was alongside the Morrisson property. She eyed it covertly. The white brick wall was interspersed with black iron bars that by their mere presence made passersby believe that the folks within were far too good to be broached by "the likes of you." The gate, a splendid wrought-iron design of the sailing ship that represented the centuries-old Ashley River Shipping Company, opened onto a courtyard which was hidden from view and beyond which towered the white mansion, its tile roof lifting a half-dozen chimneys to a dizzying height.

Carole cringed. When dusk fell, she would be inside that imposing structure, dining with the illustrious Morrisson family. After months of dating, Curt had finally invited her home. She should feel honored and excited, she supposed, but as Carole accelerated her pace, she felt only a vague sense of dread. It was as if this meeting were a necessary step in Curt's unfolding design, the billowing plan that seemed to be gaining force and velocity with

18

every passing evening, threatening to sweep her up with its momentum.

She wished she had the power, like some ancient pagan goddess, to reach out her hand and stop the whole thing.

But she didn't. Something made the urge stick in her throat, an old, overpowering need that drove other considerations into the shadows. Her father. He had never been more warm, more attentive, more openly proud of his younger daughter than he was now. Carole thrived on it, drank it in like heady draughts of champagne that eventually dulled her pangs of panic.

And so tonight, when she met the Morrissons, she would shine—just as her father and Curt expected.

She was halfway past the great house when she heard something. A door was opening, a screen door slamming shut.

R.J. stepped out onto the veranda and took a sweeping look along the familiar, grandiose street. That was when he saw her—a bombshell in a clinging yellow dress, swinging along so that her breasts bounced, and her fair hair danced in the morning sun.

Now *that* was worth driving to Charleston for! Stepping to the front of the porch, he leaned against a massive Doric column and watched her fluid, swaying walk. Before he knew what hit him, his lips drew together, and a long, low whistle escaped.

Carole's head snapped up, though she continued to stare straight ahead. Who the hell was that? No matter. She had stopped turning for whistles when she was fifteen. Tilting her nose disdainfully toward the sky, she maintained a steady pace along the walk.

19

Ahead was the home of the Trippley sisters. And at the sight of it, Carole surrendered a faint smile, the whistler forgotten. They were a pair, Constance and Aurora Trippley. Neither of the old ladies had ever married, and each was eccentric in her own way. Constance—her short, white hair nearly always covered by a comical straw hat—was completely wrapped up in her flowers and birds, while Aurora, of the ample bosom and silver-blue hair, was immersed in the fashions and customs of an era gone by.

Yet, though eccentric, the Trippley sisters were a powerful institution on Tradd. Born and bred in the antebellum mansion that was their home, they were the last of the street's most longstanding family.

As Carole looked beyond the lacy, iron wall that admitted much more of a view than any other courtyard along Tradd, she could see that both elderly ladies were already out in the morning sunshine. Aurora, of course, was on the shaded porch. A staunch upholder of the ancient southern belle traditions, she wore a frilly, floral dress and avoided any ray of sunlight that sought to touch her skin. On the other hand, Constance, dressed in slacks and shaded only by the ever-present straw Panama, was out in the full sun, bent to some task in the beloved garden that had brought her top honors in the annual Garden Tour of Homes for as long as anyone could remember.

"Mornin', Miss Constance . . . Miss Aurora," Carole called as she swung cheerily past.

Constance looked up, her kindly weathered face wreathed in a smile. "Why, good mornin', Carole. And hasn't the Lord blessed us with a splendid day?"

"Yes, ma'am," Carole returned.

"Mornin'," Aurora bestowed succinctly. She watched disapprovingly as the voluptuous young blonde strolled past.

20

"Can you imagine?" Aurora Trippley whispered harshly when Carole was beyond earshot. "Parading through town in such a disgracefully revealing costume, and it barely past breakfast time? Well, of course, that's just like one of those Gossett people. They don't belong on Tradd Street and never did. Don't have the first notion of what's proper!"

Rising to her feet with a sigh, Constance brushed the dirt absently from her hands as she looked over her shoulder at her younger sister.

"Now, Aurora. Don't be too hard on the girl. Times have changed, you know. The young people of today have their own standards. Many of ours, sad to say, have passed out of fashion."

"*Hmph!*" Aurora snorted primly. "Taste and breeding *never* pass out of fashion!"

Her eyes, though seventy years old, were bright with conviction as she turned them to the street, where Carole's form was but a yellow splash in the distance.

"Brazen little hussy," Aurora Trippley hissed under her breath.

Jonah Stuckey sat on the creek bank and dangled his dark, bare feet in the cold water. Down the way, the creek emptied into the Ashley River and the water turned murky. But here, in the pine-shaded hills, the sun-dappled water ran clear and sparkling. It was his favorite spot in all the forest.

Laying back on the carpet of pine needles, Jonah rested his palm on the mound of dirt that held Mama's favorite thing. He had taken it out, just to look at it and touch it, then covered it reverently once more. It was safe and sound. Just like everyone at church said Mama was.

He turned rheumy, hazel eyes toward the sky. Above, the pine branches crisscrossed, forming a green and brown pattern against the clear blue. The

21

wind whistled through the trees. The creek gurgled. The birds sang. The sounds of his forest. He loved those sounds, had loved them for as long as he could remember. And that was more than fifty years, though for Jonah, the concept of time had no meaning. There were only the warm times and the cold times, when Mama made him wear a jacket and shoes.

He liked the warm times best. That was when the flowers came out, and the animals and birds. Jonah fed them. It would have been fair to say that the wild creatures in the forest surrounding the plantation house were Jonah's pets. He had been feeding some of them for years, but it would never have crossed his mind to name them or claim them in any way. He only thought of them as friends, never questioning that they felt the same.

"It's remarkable," people said. "The way he has with wild things."

Some said it was his gentle nature. Most thought it was the work of God, bestowing a special gift to make up for what He left out. For though the older folks could put Jonah at about fifty-six or -seven years old, his mind had never grown beyond the age of six.

But, thank the Lord, he had had a good life. It was Mr. Thomas, who died more than forty years ago, who had provided Jonah and his mother with Belmont Pines, the rambling plantation along the Ashley which—though dilapidated—was still considered grand. Everybody knew it was because he was Jonah's father.

Years ago, the fact that Louise Stuckey had been the lover of a white man had caused quite a stir in First Baptist Church, a major black institution in Charleston for more than a hundred years. But if there were those who resented the secluded plantation Louise had been given, they got over it. Louise Stuckey was too faithful a church supporter to hold a grudge against. She tithed, donating one-tenth of all the money from a successful handmade quilt business. And she brought Jonah to service every Sunday of his life.

"She has her cross to bear," church folks would say, shaking their heads. And besides, Louise was a close friend of Cecile Laroche, a pillar of the church and the black community.

Cecile had been the unquestioned choice to deliver the eulogy. It had been a couple of months since Louise Stuckey suffered a fatal heart attack. The rumor was that one of her customers had come by to collect a quilt and found her sprawled on the floor in the kitchen. Jonah was sitting with her—holding her hand, talking to her as if she would soon wake up.

No one was quite sure what would happen to Jonah now. His mother had taken complete care of him all his life, and—mysteriously—her will was nowhere to be found. For now, the ladies' church auxiliary was taking charge, making sure he was bathed and fed and tended to.

Jonah's eyes fastened on the bulky shape near the knot of an overhead pine branch. The robin's nest! He had forgotten all about it. Lurching to his feet, he strained his ears and picked up the faint sound. Cheeping! The eggs had hatched!

"Babies!" Jonah chortled, and a quick image of his mother flashed through his mind.

She would be standing there in her apron, at her place at the kitchen sink, peeling carrots or snapping beans. He had to tell her. The robin had babies!

The forest was the same as it had always been. The pine needles whispered beneath his feet, the sun poured down in golden shafts on the clearings. It never occurred to Jonah, as he dashed along the well-known path, that anything had changed. He burst into the house and trotted joyfully into the kitchen looking for Mama. But there was no one there. He had forgotten that she was gone, that she would never be at her place at the sink again.

Sitting down in the middle of the floor, Jonah began to cry, his blubbering sobs echoing through the empty house. Then he looked up at the counter, saw the basket of apples and remembered. Miss Cecile would be comin' soon. Miss Cecile came every day, and she always brought him somethin'. Yesterday, it was the shiny red apples in the basket.

His sobbing subsided, and he came to his feet. That was when he heard the noise—a car coming up the drive.

He ambled into the living room and peeped out the window. It was a big black car and when it came to a stop by the porch, a white man got out.

Jonah looked at him curiously. The man reached back into the car, brought out a case and took some papers out of it. Then he smoothed his shiny hair and looked toward the house. He was wearing a blue suit and a smile.

He looked nice, Jonah decided. Company. Mama always liked company! He started toward the door, but then whirled back to the kitchen and selected one of the biggest apples.

A sloppy grin came to his face as he hurried to meet the stranger. It was always nice to have somethin' for company. Mama would be proud.

Chapter Two

BY THE TIME two o'clock rolled around, Carole was hot and starving. Carlotta had not shown up, and Elsa—who had shop duty—had been gone since half past twelve, leaving Carole the double duty of managing the shop as well as the T-shirt sales.

Bitch! Carole thought for the hundredth time. Still, it had been almost worth the running back and forth to see the look of shock on Elsa's face when Carole handed her the receipts from the morning sales. In half a Saturday, Carole had sold nearly as many T-shirts as in the preceding week altogether.

With a smile and a wave, she had flagged down every passerby she knew and many she didn't. All the men stopped. Let's see, there had been Andy and Ward Hall, Greg Dunning, a bunch of guys who hung around Myskyn's, the bar she used to patronize. And that group of cadets from the Citadel. All of them had left with a Spoleto T-shirt from Carlotta's!

And then, just an hour ago, a surprising visitor had put Carole in a daze. He was nothing to look at—a slight, effeminate man in his thirties, sporting avant-garde clothes and a Yankee accent. But he was from New York, and he worked for one of the top

25

design houses. He had come down for the festival, he'd said in a nasal, clipped voice. But so far, the designer had continued, the most interesting thing he had seen was the yellow frock she was wearing.

Uncharacteristically, Carole had blushed as she admitted she had designed the dress. And then her heart had leaped to her throat.

"South Carolina is hardly the place I'd have expected to find a fresh designing mind," Jack Levy said. "But you have indisputable talent. Undoubtedly, your work is very important to you."

"Oh, yes," Carole replied with a blank look. "Undoubtedly."

"You're a free agent?"

"Free?"

"You're not under contract with anyone?"

"Oh . . . no. No, I'm not under contract."

"And have you an up-to-date portfolio?"

"Well, I . . . uh . . . In fact, I'm working on some new things right now," she lied.

The man's narrow eyes swept down her body. "If they have the same freshness as this little creation, I'd like to see them. Are you interested in representation in New York?"

By the time Jack Levy had left the booth, she had promised to send a collection of sketches to his office within the month.

Her mind was reeling. A collection in only a few weeks? You must be mad!

Yet she didn't feel mad. She felt wild and exhilarated, daring and reckless, as if she'd just been let in on a delicious secret.

Talent! A scout for Haut Nouveau of New York thought she had talent! Never would she have guessed that such a thing could mean so much to her. Yet at that very moment, all she could think about was getting home to the expensive, dust-covered drawing table she hadn't touched in months.

Oh yes, Carole was tired and hungry, and her

right shoe was working a blister on her heel. And when she saw loud, overbearing Tom Creighton loping toward her, it was all she could do to stifle a grimace. But she had Jack Levy's business card in her purse and a warm, soaring feeling in her heart. The sense of pride that was pumping through her was more powerful than any adrenaline.

As Tom Creighton loomed close, she flashed him a sparkling smile and determined she'd sell him a shirt for each of his four sisters. It would be wickedly satisfying to see just how far she could cram Elsa and Cathy's insults down their fleshy throats.

R.J. was finishing his third beer. He'd been sitting there in the sidewalk cafe for more than an hour—mesmerized.

He had seen her the moment he turned onto King Street. The blonde from that morning, working outside some dress shop. He had kept a discreet eye on her as he strolled along, and when he came to the cafe that was almost directly across the street from her shop-front display, he ducked into the shade of the awning and took a table. He hadn't really had anything in particular in mind. Just curiosity. Just something to look at while he had lunch. But then he had ordered another beer. And another.

R.J. was a student of people. You had to be, in order to perform successfully as an attorney. It seemed to him that anyone with eyes could see that this woman was putting on a show. The dazzling smile, the provocative, one-hip stance, the light, airy laugh with a toss of blond curls.

Anyone could see she was using her charm the same way a soldier wields a weapon. And yet the men he watched seemed oblivious. They drifted into range and were drawn into her web like witless insects, eventually buzzing away from the shop-front with silly grins and packages under their arms. In the time he had watched, she must have sold a hundred of those blasted blue shirts, and all to besotted men. Once again, R.J. surreptitiously ran his eyes over her. Now, *there* was a southern belle.

Of course, there were different kinds of belles. Those like his mother were bred from generations of Charleston aristocracy; they were the beneficent, all-knowing caretakers of southern society, active in the arts and charities. There were also those like his sister Margaret, who—unless she had changed—was the quintessence of propriety; she wore only the right clothes, made the right small talk, associated with the right people. Cool and aloof, she was quick to turn on a superior air if an unsuitable male approached.

And then there were the rare ones like this blonde. Irresistible to all men and reveling in her power, she was Scarlett O'Hara from head to toe.

R.J. called for his check, then stepped to the curb and peered blatantly across the sun-drenched street. The shop front was a blazing white, the outdoor display of shirts, a brilliant splash of turquoise. And the girl, a stroke of gold. For a moment the colors across the way blurred in the blinding sunlight, and he was struck with the impression of a bright yellow butterfly darting among cornflowers.

That settled it. A crooked grin dragged at one corner of R.J.'s mouth. He was going to enjoy this.

Carole's attention lit on the solitary man strolling toward her from across the street. Tall and blond, he was dressed in casual gray slacks and a white shirt that, on him, looked as if they were tailormade. He was ambling along nonchalantly, his hands tucked carelessly in his pockets, and yet she was instantly aware that his eyes were on her. Something deep within her lurched, an unknown sensation that spurred her pulse to a galloping pace.

The feeling surprised her. Carole was practiced, expert when it came to dealing with men, no matter

28

how attractive they might be. This reaction, on the other hand, was instinctive and unexpected. But Carole Gossett was no babe in the woods. By the time he drew near to tower over her like some fair-haired, Nordic god, she had recovered herself.

"Hi there," she greeted him with her best smile. "Taking in the festival?"

"Not at the moment," he replied with a bold sweep of his eyes.

Close up, she was even more attractive than he had imagined. Her dynamic body was topped with an angelic, blue-eyed face. She wore too much make-up, but it only made him long to see what she'd look like in the raw—fresh out of bed on a morning after.

His blue eyes settled on hers, holding them with a steady, silent look. And as Carole felt herself being drawn farther and farther into them, she thought they must be the deepest blue she'd ever seen. An uncomfortable wave of heat rose to her face. Breaking the intense look, she turned suddenly away.

"May I interest you in one of our T-shirts?" she inquired, glancing over her shoulder as she crossed to the display. "They're one of a kind, designed and offered exclusively by Carlotta's!" Upon reaching a panel where a number of shirts were tacked up for display, Carole extended a hand to her merchandise with a smooth flourish.

R.J. watched her fluid movements with appreciation, and when she turned to look at him expectantly, he smiled in a friendly, deceptive fashion. She would not find him so easy a sell.

"Yes, I might be interested. In fact, I might be interested in purchasing the entire display."

Carole's mouth gaped open. "The entire . . ." Her words drifted away as she considered it. If she could sell all the inventory in one day . . . What a coup!

"But we have dozens of shirts in stock," she cautioned.

"Don't worry. I can afford it . . . *if* the deal is right." Strolling to her side, his eyes on her all the while, R.J. reached over her shoulder and stroked one of the T-shirts as if to test the fabric. Then he spread his fingers against the solid panel, propping himself over her so that when he looked down he was close enough to catch the rich, floral scent of her perfume.

But then she sidestepped and looked up with coquettish admonition. God, she played the game well. Withdrawing his arm from the panel, R.J. took a step toward her. The hunt was on. And he was tracking.

"Tell me about these shirts," he said with a baiting smile. "Who designed them? Not you, I'll wager."

"Well, no . . ."

"I didn't think so. You don't look much like a designer."

Carole took another step back and raised one brow. "Oh really, sir? And what *do* I look like, if I might ask?"

He folded his arms over his chest, cocking his head to the side as if to study her. "A shopgirl, maybe?"

"Shopgirl!"

He chuckled. "No, I take that back. I wasn't being completely honest. If I really had to say, truthfully, what you look like, I'd have to say a courtesan."

Her hands plopped at her hips as spots of color jumped to her cheeks. "I beg your pardon!"

"Yes, definitely," he continued outrageously. "A beautiful courtesan out to hawk her wares. Never a shopgirl . . . or a designer, for that matter."

Without warning, Carole's steadfast, beguiling facade shattered, and she gave the man a scathing once-over. "I'll have you know, sir, that I am indeed a designer. And a damned good one!"

Somehow, he wasn't surprised that beneath all that syrupy veneer was a spitfire. Stifling a grin, R.J. stroked his chin as if considering her words.

"A designer? Really?"

"Yes, *really*. It just so happens that a scout for one of the biggest design houses in New York came by today. He was so taken with the dress I'm wearing, *which I designed*, that he asked me to send him some sketches."

"No denying it's a nice dress," R.J. offered, his gaze dropping to her bosom. "And it fits so well."

Carole ignored his risqué sarcasm and tossed her head huffily. "As Mr. Levy put it, I have 'indisputable talent.' "

"You don't say."

"I *do* say!"

She glared up at the impudent man, who proceeded to infuriate her by laughing heartily.

"What's so funny?" she demanded angrily.

His laughter subsided, and then he shook his head and looked at her in a curious way that seemed to suggest fondness.

"You're funny," he said. "You don't have to get so mad, just because I don't think you look like a designer. Does this mean you don't want to sell me the T-shirt display?"

A sinking feeling rocked Carole's stomach. She'd forgotten all about the sale. But damn! There was something about him that made her lose her temper, lose touch with the polished, charming Carole Gossett who always dealt so successfully with men.

"Of course," she managed to say in a courteous tone. "If you'd like to buy us out, I'll be more than happy to take you money."

"If the deal is right, I said."

"Well, I'm sorry I don't have the authority to give you any sort of discount. It's not my shop. I'm just a *designer* here."

31

"So you've said," R.J. returned. "But the deal I'm proposing has nothing to do with discounts."

Carole looked at him with exasperated puzzlement. "Then what? . . ."

"You," he replied calmly.

Carole's hand fluttered to her breast as she regarded him with wide eyes. Me? Unable to find her voice, she mouthed the word.

"What's the matter?" R.J. challenged with a smile. "Hasn't anyone ever called your bluff before?"

The angry spots of color flared anew in her cheeks. "I have no idea what you're talking about."

"Sure you do. The way you dress, the way you move. You play with men, tease them into doing exactly what you want, and then send them on their way with nothing but a smile. Well, I'm happy to join your little game, but I want something for my trouble. I'll buy out your whole damned display, but only if you have dinner with me tonight."

Carole's emotions careened from incredulity to excitement to self-recriminating outrage. She swept him a haughty look. "I find your comments positively insulting. I do not play with men, and I do not pick up with perfect strangers on the street. As for your invitation, I'm happy to say I have irrevocable plans for dinner."

R.J. was more disappointed than he showed. He studied her and thought for a moment. "All right, then," he said at last. "If they're 'irrevocable,' as you say . . . I'll settle for a kiss."

For the second time in their conversation, Carole's mouth gaped open. "I beg your pardon!"

"Come on, now," R.J. said with a placating smile. "Just think for a minute. One little kiss, and you're through with having to stand out here in the hot street. Hell, you could take the rest of the day off!"

Carole was shocked. The man was a perfect stranger! She stared at him in disbelief, her eyes traveling over the fair hair, sculpted features, and devastating smile. And suddenly, she was no longer thinking of T-shirt sales, or of showing off to her co-workers, or that this was one male with whom she seemed unable to hold her own. She was thinking of those ruddy lips, and how they would feel.

With a start, she realized that she was slipping into surrender.

He must have read it on her face, for he stepped over to her, his cool hands coming to rest on her sun-warmed, bare shoulders. The touch sent shivers along her arms. This man was dangerous.

Looking down at her, R.J. thought she grew more beautiful with each passing second. Her eyes. They weren't just blue, as he had first thought; they were more a shifting blue-green, like the shallows of a tropical sea.

"One little kiss," he urged softly.

As if hypnotized, Carole stared mutely up at him.

He lowered his head ever so slowly. Yet, to Carole, it seemed that everything happened quickly. His palms were on each side of her face, cupping it, and then his lips were on hers. His arms dropped around her waist, lifting her on tiptoe. And then she was in another world, where there was nothing but the starchy feel of his shirt against her cheek, his clean, masculine scent in her nostrils, his seductive tongue within her mouth.

Of its own accord, her body answered him—her tongue matching his lunges, her hips pressing close, her body, turning to fire so that something within her melted and pooled between her legs. For several long moments, she was completely swept away.

And then suddenly, without warning, she was outside herself with the small crowd of tittering tourists who were passing by, watching the woman's yellow dress climb up her thighs, watching Carole Gossett lose control. It was the strangest, most overwhelming feeling she'd ever experienced. It frightened her. And *that* made her mad. She began to push him away, but the stranger would have none of it. He simply launched into a fresh embrace that left her head reeling and her body aching. Finally, she wrenched free and stumbled back.

R.J.'s eyes had turned as dark as a moonlit sky. "So *that's* the woman beneath all the 'sirs' and 'I beg your pardons.'"

"You took unfair advantage," Carole accused breathlessly.

"And you loved it," he countered.

She couldn't bear it. It seemed the arrogant beast could see right through her. As if it were her last line of defense, her hand whipped through the air, connecting with his cheek in a whack that drew a chorus of gasps from some passing ladies.

"I release you from the deal!" Carole spat. "Now, please go!"

The blow hadn't made R.J. stumble, but it sure as hell had turned his head. Now, slowly, with a look of shock on his face, he turned back to her. Her breasts were heaving against the meager neckline of the dress. Her face was crimson, her blue-green eyes flashing. If he had been momentarily angry, the anger fled as soon as he focused on the womanly spectacle before him. By God, but she had fire! R.J. had a hunch that she had no idea just how hot she could burn. That was what had her in such a stew.

Carole was horrified to see a slow, lazy smile come to his face.

"A deal's a deal," he said huskily. "What time do you close?"

She tilted her nose to the heavens. "Five o'clock."

"I'll buy your damned T-shirts, but I have to get my checkbook."

"Don't bother to get your damnable checkbook! Or to come back here!"

"Oh, I'll be back," he assured her. "You can count on that, and I think you know it."

Carole's eyes darted back and forth between his serious ones. He'd be back, all right. He'd be back, and he'd make good on his word. It was something she could sense.

R.J. feasted his eyes a moment longer. This woman compelled him like no woman in a long time. He'd have her, by God. He'd know the full range of the passion he had just tasted, a passion she was so desperate to deny that she'd strike him before she'd admit to it.

"You've got a good, strong, solid right there," he taunted. "But it's got nothing on your lips."

Before she could think of a retort, he backed away with a grin. And to her horror, Carole found herself watching his smooth, cocky walk until he disappeared from view.

A short time later, Elsa returned with smirking excuses that stumbled into silence when Carole announced she had sold the entire inventory and was going home. She added that a tall, blond man would be bringing a check before five o'clock and started to walk away.

But then she had a brainstorm. Hurrying back, she instructed Elsa that for no reason should she divulge Carole's name or address or anything about her. Only when she was convinced that the wide-eyed Elsa was properly impressed into silence did Carole depart in the opposite direction from the blond stranger.

She was tired. Her blistered heel was killing her. And she'd never been in such a ragged mood. The last thing she wanted was to hang around the shop and watch that guy make his grandstand play.

Besides, she didn't want to see him again. He was too unsettling, upsetting her careful control of things and making her feel shameful sensations that, even now, she was hard at work discrediting. Telling herself that he was simply the rudest, most outrageous rogue she'd ever come across, Carole limped her

35

way crossly to the townhouse at the corner of Broad and Rutledge.

"If I never lay eyes on the man, it will be too soon!" she huffed to no one.

Yet, as she climbed the stairs to her apartment, she couldn't ignore the sense of quivering, newborn arousal that had her blood still racing.

Charlotte stood in the spacious, white-tiled bath connecting her daughters' rooms. Peering into the wall of mirrors above the basins, she checked her hair, coiled in a sedate mahogany bun at the back of her head, her makeup, which was generously, but deftly applied, and her ensemble, a conservative dress of navy blue crepe and the perfectly matched pearls Robert had given her for Christmas.

Everything was right, just as always. "Elegance with understatement," her mother had always advised. And over the years, the attitude had become as much a part of Charlotte as breathing.

It was just a small thing, a tiny part of what southern ladies of breeding had passed down from generation to generation for two hundred years— from impeccable taste and manners in all things, to a lofty sense of position within society that verged on *noblesse oblige*. These were things that Charlotte had tried to instill in her own daughters. Perhaps too much so in Margaret—and not nearly enough in Camille.

Stepping back, Charlotte glanced first into Margaret's room, where her elder daughter was slipping into a new Laura Ashley dress, and then in the opposite direction, toward Camille, who was trying her best to pull on a pair of skintight black jeans.

They were both lovely—Margaret, with her classical features and glossy, chestnut hair, and Camille, with her raucous, coppery curls and impish face.

Both were lovely, but that was absolutely *all* the sisters had in common.

"So, neither of my girls is going to help me through dinner this evening?" Charlotte queried.

"Sorry, Mother," Margaret said. "After all, it's Saturday night. I've made other plans."

"Me, too!" Camille chimed.

"If I may be so bold, I'd like to know where you two are going. After all, your brother Randall will be here, not to mention the Gossetts."

Margaret stepped into Pappagallo flats and strolled to the bathroom doorway. She was the only one of the children who had inherited her mother's dark coloring, and she looked very pretty with her rosy cheeks and dancing brown eyes.

"Mother, I *love* seeing R.J., but he doesn't expect me to sit home on a Saturday night. And as for the Gossetts . . . from what I've heard, Carole is nothing but a cheap little flirt. I'm simply appalled that Curt has taken up with her. Besides," she concluded with a dreamy smile, "I've been looking forward to tonight. Clifford is taking me down the coast to a new seafood restaurant."

Ignoring the snobbish comment about the Gossett girl, Charlotte asked, "Clifford? I thought you were going out with Fitzhugh Ames."

Margaret rolled her eyes. "Really, Mother!" she said scoldingly. "You could keep up. Fitzhugh was *last* week."

Charlotte shrugged and turned her attention to Camille. "And how about you, young lady?"

Camille kept her eyes on the cheval mirror as she fastened long, dangling earrings at her lobes. "Rehearsal, Mom," she tossed, and then began to turn before the mirror, assessing her very modern, punk image.

Charlotte watched for a moment longer, then took her leave.

"Rehearsal, huh?" Margaret snapped once their

mother was safely gone. "Since when do you have choir rehearsal on a Saturday night? You're going to that sleazy club again, aren't you? That black club down in the jazz district!"

Camille turned a feral look on her older sister. "So? What do you care? I don't try to keep tabs on *you*, do I?"

"Well, I don't go parading around dingy bars, making a spectacle of myself."

"I don't make a spectacle of myself. I sing. And whether you choose to believe it or not, people actually applaud."

Margaret's face took on a smug look. "Yes, but what sort of people?"

"People who know a hell of a lot more about good music than you ever will. Look, Margaret. Mother had a beautiful voice, and she wasted it. Just because it wasn't considered 'ladylike' for her to sing in public is no reason for me to give it up. Well, *I* intend to sing, and I'll give you fair warning. You'd better not get in my way!"

And with that, Camille slammed the bathroom door closed on her side. In a split second, the sound was repeated with Margaret's door.

Down below in the kitchen, Charlotte told her housekeeper, Cecile, to set two fewer places for dinner.

Several blocks along Tradd, the prospective dinner party shrank by one more.

James Gossett walked into his wife's dressing room and looked at her with disgust. The strap of her silk slip had fallen off her shoulder, her hair was disheveled, and she was making a mess of her lipstick as she wobbled in front of the mirror. On the vanity stood a nearly empty bottle of brandy.

When he had met her two years before, Kathleen had been young, lively, and exciting. An amateur dancer, she had captivated him when he'd dropped in at one of the fashionable clubs. James had intended to stay for only one drink, but had become mesmerized by the dark-haired siren who unquestionably owned the dance floor. Dark eyes snapping, long, black hair flying, body gyrating, Kathleen had been irresistible.

Now twenty-six, at the moment she looked forty. The very sight of her sickened him.

"You may as well stop," he thundered. "You're in no condition to go anywhere, much less to the home of the Morrissons."

Kathleen tried to straighten up and focus on his reflection. "Ah, yes. The mighty, wonderful Morrissons." Despite her efforts, the words came out in a slur. "The *crème de la crème*. I'm in *perfect* condition to meet the Morrissons."

Without a word, James shrugged into his dark, impeccably tailored jacket, straightening the lapels and cuffs with short, jerky movements. Then, turning on his heel, he ordered, "You're staying here."

"Where ya goin'?" Kathleen managed.

He paused at the doorway, impaled her with a sour look. "I'm going to drop by Henry's . . . for *one cocktail* before dinner. It seems I'm the only one in this family who knows his limit!"

Kathleen listened to his stomping footsteps recede down the stairs. Her eyes were leaden. They portrayed none of the relief she felt as her husband stormed out of the house.

Carole stared thoughtfully at her reflection. She had never looked quite this way before. She had planned to wear red but had somehow ended up donning this simple black dress with the cowl neck that dipped elegantly in front and back. And then, of all things, she had put up her hair, restraining it from its usual, curling abandon except for a few wisps across her forehead.

Perhaps it had something to do with Jack Levy's startling praise of her designing ability, this urge to look sophisticated rather than seductive, capable rather than coquettish.

But then an image of the blond stranger burst into her mind. Perhaps it had more to do with avoiding the look of a "courtesan." Carole's pretty mouth took on a firm set as she busied herself with last-minute details before Curt arrived.

"Hi, doll," he greeted Carole as she opened the door.

He looked the same. As good-looking as ever, he had the same boyish features and the same athletic build, now clad in a fashionable pinstripe suit. Curt was an excellent tennis player, and he possessed a tennis player's attractive, tensile physique. Top that with the confident, smiling *savoir faire* that bespoke vintage wealth and position, and you had a man that would make just about any woman's heart flutter.

Yes, Carole thought, he's just the same as always. The difference was that for some reason she wasn't very happy to see him.

He was looking her over with an ambiguous expression. And then he commented, "My, my. Don't we look grown up this evening?"

"I'm grown up every evening, Curt," she replied snappishly. And latching her bottom lip between her teeth, she hurried away on the pretense of fetching her bag.

"Is something wrong?" he asked as they drove the short distance from her apartment to the Morrisson home.

Carole studied his handsome profile, the way the passing headlights glinted off his honey-blond hair. But it was not as blond as . . .

"No. Nothing's wrong," she answered quickly, wishing she meant it. "I'm sorry if I snapped at you

40

earlier. I'm just a little tired after selling T-shirts all day at the festival. But don't worry. I'll revive.''

"Poor doll," he said with a smile.

Carole felt as though she could throttle him. Funny. His calling her "doll" had always seemed rather sweet. But tonight, for some reason, it only grated on her nerves.

R.J. climbed out of the shower and began to towel down. He had needed something to improve his humor. Ever since he raced back to Carlotta's! and found the blond girl gone, he'd been spitting nails. And the shrewish witch who had taken his check but refused to give him any information hadn't helped.

He couldn't believe he had misread the girl. Damn it, he knew women! The fireworks had gone off for her the same as for him. He was sure of it.

Then, why the hell did she take off? he asked himself, even as his ego urged. She wasn't that special. But something inside him told R.J. she was—that she was the most special thing he'd come across in a long time.

And when Curt and his father got home, and Curt began a rampant explanation of the virtues of his girl friend, his mood had darkened even more.

"She's a doll," Curt had said. "That's what I call her, my little doll. Between you and me, R.J., this girl could make me want to take the plunge. She's everything I want in a woman. Charming, pretty . . . not too smart, not too stubborn. And sexy as hell. You'll see when you meet her tonight at dinner.''

R.J. was not up for dinner with the Gossetts. But he couldn't duck out. He came home too rarely for that. And so, he'd taken solace in a long shower, deciding to take his own sweet time getting ready. When he heard the doorbell ring at seven, he was still in the middle of shaving.

Her father was already there when they arrived, and to Carole's relief, Kathleen was "home with a headache." As she'd expected, the Morrisson home was grand, and Curt seemed immensely proud as he led her into the beautiful antique-studded drawing room and presented her to his parents. From their warm reception of her, they seemed to be two of the most gracious people she'd ever met. And Carole only felt more guilty for having wished she could avoid the evening.

"I'm so terribly sorry Margaret and Camille couldn't be here, Carole," Charlotte Morrisson was saying. "Both of them had prior commitments. But I'm sure that if Curt has anything to do with it, the girls will have *plenty* of opportunity to meet you." She raised a teasing brow at Curt, but finished with a smile for Carole.

Her father and Curt and Robert Morrisson had gathered by an extensive marble fireplace, sipping scotch and talking business. It was an old custom, the separating of males and females at social gatherings, still upheld in the Morrisson family.

As Carole perused the group, she saw that the dark hair and eyes of her father stood out as if he were a different breed next to the light coloring of Curt and his father. Hearing her father laugh at something Mr. Morrisson said, she had the sudden, uncomfortable feeling that he was trying to impress him.

Carole was left in the hands of the hostess, but she didn't mind. Mrs. Morrisson was a lovely woman—graceful and hospitable beyond words, with an aura of good taste fairly glowing about her. She was perhaps *the* most prominent woman in Charleston, and Carole had expected her to have an air of superiority, but she felt only welcome.

It was when a black woman, introduced as Cecile

Laroche, stepped in to announce dinner, that Mrs. Morrisson mentioned her other son.

"Cecile," Charlotte said, "would you mind stepping to the stairs and letting Randall know we're ready to go in to supper?"

"There's no need, Mother." A familiar voice sounded from the doorway behind Carole. "I'm here."

Carole's heart skipped, and when she turned to verify what she couldn't believe, the blood drained from her face. He was dressed more formally, in a striped silk tie and white shirt that was blinding against his navy blazer and trousers—but it was him.

R.J. halted in midstride. His eyes widened. Her! *She* was Carole Gossett? *She* was the girl of Curt's dreams?

Unknowingly, Charlotte Morrisson took on a bright smile and steered Carole directly to him. "Carole, dear, this is my elder son, Randall. Randall, Carole Gossett."

His eyes raced over her. The rosy face testified to the day she'd spent in the sun. The blond hair was swept back and up, and the formfitting black dress was understated. But on her, the effect was devastating. Somehow, she seemed to have matured in just the past few hours.

"Hello," he said.

"Hello . . . Randall," Carole returned blankly. Looking up the vast height of him, she offered a lifeless hand.

He grasped it, held on firmly. "Everyone calls me R.J."

After what seemed an eternal moment of looking into those incredibly blue eyes—filled with all the things he wasn't saying—Carole withdrew her hand and turned away. Thankfully, the others chose that moment to broach them.

Curt's arm went round Carole, pulling her back

43

around. "See, R.J. ? Didn't I tell you? Isn't she everything I said?"

R.J. sought eye contact, but she wouldn't give it. "And more," he answered.

"Here you go, big brother," Curt said.

And to her horror, Carole found that he was handing her to R.J. to be escorted into the dining room.

"You can have the honors," Curt said, placing Carole's hand in the crook of his brother's elbow, adding, "But just remember. It's only for tonight. I have prior claim on this one!"

Curt was in high spirits. He chuckled as Carole's breath stopped in her chest. And then she was walking toward the foyer, her arm linked with R.J.'s. Behind them, Curt offered his arm to his mother, and the two older men trailed the group.

After a moment, Carole felt R.J. look down at her, and she couldn't restrain herself from meeting his gaze. He was wearing a forced smile, but even that looked good on his face.

"You might have said someone had 'prior claim,' " he murmured through stiff, smiling lips.

"I hardly had the chance," she smiled in return.

R.J. studied her at close range for a moment, his face gradually taking on that odd look of fondness she remembered from earlier in the afternoon. "Know anyone interested in a truckload of T-shirts?" he asked quietly.

Carole felt an unwanted rush of response to the man, and her fake smile slipped into a real one. But then she caught herself and looked away, refusing to meet those hypnotic blue eyes for the remainder of the sedate stroll along the foyer.

The Morrisson dining room was a place of splendor, decorated in rich brocades and velvets, glistening silver, and gleaming dark wood. A tremendous crystal chandelier presided over the Chippendale

44

dining suite. The table sat twelve, but of course they used only one end.

And as fate would have it, Carole was seated directly across from R.J. Through all the courses, he sent her ambiguous looks—sometimes questioning, sometimes accusing. Doing her best to ignore him, Carole joined in the dinner-table conversation. Everyone said the chicken divan was excellent, but she couldn't have told it from cardboard.

Her father was enjoying himself thoroughly with Robert Morrisson, and by the time the pecan pie arrived, the two men had sunk into their own discussion—business or politics, Carole supposed. Charlotte, who was seated next to R.J., kept the talk lively among the rest of them. And every now and then, Curt reached under the table to stroke Carole's leg or squeeze the hand in her lap. It seemed to take forever for the meal to be over and the after-dinner coffee to arrive.

It was then that James Gossett decided to play his trump card.

"I suppose you know, Robert, that you have an extremely bright son here." Turning a fond look on Curt, James spoke loudly enough that all other conversation at the table drifted into silence. "He's just masterminded a very complex property deal."

"Indeed?" Robert Morrisson commented with a proud smile.

As Carole studied the man, she realized how like him R.J. looked. The older man's blond hair was gray at the temples, but everything else was the same—coloring, bone structure, and particularly the dark-lashed eyes, which were that unusual, deep blue gray. This would be R.J. in twenty-five years or so.

She shifted her gaze to Curt, whose paler blue eyes were upon her. He had similar fair coloring, but Curt's rakish good looks were different from the distinguished, chiseled features of his father and

45

brother. At the moment, he was the center of attention, but Carole had the sudden impression that among the three Morrisson men, Curt was odd man out.

"Yes, Curt has made great strides," James went on. "In the next two years, Charleston will have a theme park that will rival Carowinds or Six Flags Over Georgia, or any park in the country for that matter. And it's all because Curt managed to find and secure the ideal location."

Curt was regarding his boss with a lazy grin that masked his true sense of elation. That he should be singled out for praise in this particular company! Nothing could have pleased him more.

And then his father said, "Well, well, son. I always knew you had it in you."

Curt's eyes jumped to the revered face of Robert Morrisson. And there it was—a warm look of pride all over his father's face, the look he'd always thought reserved for R.J. Something deep in Curt's chest swelled, and he thought, It was worth it. The late nights of planning, the occasional stab of conscience—it was all worth it.

"Just kept my eyes open," he managed to answer modestly. "It wasn't so much."

"I beg to differ," James said. "Your good thinking will pay off quite handsomely for Gossett Enterprises, and such valuable work does not go unnoticed at my company. In fact, I can think of no better time to make a happy announcement . . . *particularly*," he added with a meaningful glance toward Carole, "when it seems our families are becoming so close."

A hush fell over the table as James rose to his feet, deposited a hand on Curt's shoulder, then swept the party with an authoritative look. "I invite all of you to join me in congratulating Curt Morrisson, Gossett Enterprises' new vice-president of investments."

"Good heavens," Charlotte whispered, her fingers clasping excitedly together, her face a picture of maternal pride.

"Congratulations, son," Robert said, leaning over to shake his son's hand.

"Way to go, brother," R.J. offered.

"That's wonderful," Carole whispered, following Curt's gaze to stare up at James; he was wearing the most beneficent expression Carole had ever seen.

"Come on, Curt," James urged. "Let's have a few words from the new VP." And as he sat down and Robert Morrisson gave him a comradely nod, James felt as if he were on top of the world.

Everyone smiled and applauded politely until Curt stood. "Okay, okay," he said. "Whew!" He loosened his collar with one finger as if somewhat embarrassed, but there was no doubt that he was thrilled.

"I'm not very good at speechmaking . . . especially when I've just been rendered speechless," Curt began, prompting a few chuckles. "Let me just say that I appreciate this opportunity, particularly when it comes from such a corporate legend as James Gossett."

He looked admiringly at his boss. It was difficult for Carole to tell which of them was enjoying the moment more.

"You can be sure I'll do my best to live up to his faith in me," Curt said seriously. But then his clean-cut face took on a brighter look as he turned toward Carole. "There are many good things which could grow out of this promotion. It's the kind of thing on which a man can build his future. Wouldn't you agree, Carole?"

The heat rushed to her face so suddenly that it stung Carole's eyes. "Of course," she answered agreeably, her calm voice belying the jitters that rocked her stomach. As she caught R.J.'s morose stare from the corner of her eye, Carole forced a bright smile that bounced from Curt to her beaming father to the regal countenances of Robert and Charlotte Morrisson.

"Who knows?" Curt concluded as he resumed his seat. "This announcement could very well lead to another happy announcement in the not-too-distant future."

Knowing glances went around the table as Curt took Carole's ice-cold hand into his own and sought her eyes. The pit in her stomach swelled threateningly, but Carole Gossett was a consummate actress. No one at the dinner table guessed her turmoil as she smiled so charmingly at Curt that it removed the need for words.

Eventually, diplomatically, she retrieved her hand on the pretense of replenishing their coffee. The older adults fell into quiet conversation at the head of the table as Carole offered to refill Curt's and then R.J.'s cup from an exquisite silver service. When she had finished, a rather awkward silence fell.

"So, tell us about the festival today, doll," Curt said finally. "How did it go at the shop? Did you sell many T-shirts?"

Carole's eyes flickered to R.J., then to her coffee cup. "You could say that."

"Oh, are you a shopgirl?" R.J. broke in with wickedly feigned innocence.

"No," she said with an equally feigned sweet look. "I'm a fashion designer."

Leaning back in his chair, R.J. folded his arms across his chest. "You don't look like a designer."

"Ah, well, perhaps it takes a pro to spot one. As it happens, a representative from a very reputable house in New York has asked me to send him some sketches."

"What?" Curt said with surprise. "What did you say?"

"A Mr. Jack Levy came by the display today and

48

asked me to send him a collection of sketches," she explained.

"Why on earth would he want you to do that?"

"Because he thinks I'm talented."

Curt sputtered a chuckle. "Honey, don't get me wrong, but don't you think he was probably after something else?"

Carole turned to look him full in the face, startling Curt with the icy look in her blue-green eyes.

"How could I get you wrong, Curt? I'm sure everyone here knows exactly what you mean."

That got everyone's attention.

"Now, what's this all about?" her father broke in. "What did you say, Carole?"

She glanced nervously back to her coffee. She knew he would be against this. "I said I'm going to do some new designs and send them to New York."

"New York? You've got a job at Carlotta's! Why would you be sending something to New York?"

Carole didn't dare look at her father. The feeling of rebellion that had been brewing all evening boiled up to her throat. Perhaps it was the influence of R.J., who sat so watchfully across the table, but suddenly she couldn't bear to be cowed by her father, to be led and cajoled and shamed into smiling submission. She was *not* the empty-headed "doll" that he imagined. And in that instant she felt that she would strangle if she played the part one second longer.

"I was just explaining that I met a talent scout today at the festival," she said to her cup. "It would be a great opportunity."

"That would mean a lot of extra work, wouldn't it?" James said in a lighter tone.

"I can handle it."

"But why bother with it?" her father pursued. "After all, you've got Curt here, to take care of. I'm betting he wouldn't be willing to give you up to something like that."

Curt began to grin like a silly, macho boy, but

49

Carole shot a look past him, down the table to her father. "I told the man I'd send him the sketches within the month, and that's exactly what I intend to do."

Her voice, more shrill than she'd intended, rang through the quiet room. Across the table, R.J. smiled behind his linen napkin. What was it Curt had said about her? Not too smart? Not too stubborn? Hell, he didn't know the first thing about this woman.

James Gossett stared at his daughter, his eyes turning darker by the second. "What's the matter with you, Carole? Are you feeling all right?"

"I'm fine, Daddy. Maybe a little tired." And a little sick. It was the first time in her life she had defied her father. "In fact," she added, rising to her feet, "if Curt would be so kind as to take me home, I think I'll call it an early night."

Trying to cover the sudden pall on the dinner party, everyone sprang to their feet and bustled into the foyer to retrieve wraps and bid farewell, as if Carole had just announced she was the queen and everyone would now depart. She knew she'd catch hell from her father later, but for now he was putting on a mannerly show for the Morrissons. It was one of the most awkward times of Carole's life, and yet she felt suddenly buoyant.

Only when she had donned her cape and was ready to walk out did she glance in R.J.'s direction, and then she saw that he'd been waiting to catch her eye.

"It's been a pleasure meeting you, Carole," he said. "A real pleasure."

His expression was sincere, reminding her of the intense look that had characterized him that afternoon when he'd vowed, "I'll be back."

From several feet away, his eyes reached out and locked with hers once again. And again Carole felt the warm, sensual awareness rise within her. Tear-

50

ing away from the sensation, she said nothing to him, and turned toward Curt to leave.

Later, when Curt pressed to come in for a while, she turned him away. He looked a little hurt, and immensely puzzled.

"Is it because of that design business?" he asked. "Hell, I didn't know it meant that much to you, Carole."

"It's not that, Curt," she said, although that was part of it. "I'm just tired. Maybe standing out in the sun all day took more out of me than I realized."

She couldn't explain that there was no reason for him to come in, that he couldn't possibly share the lightheaded sense of euphoria that even she didn't understand. And she certainly couldn't tell Curt that none of his romantic efforts would matter anyway—that in months of dating, he'd never once caused the wild response his brother had managed to stir with one kiss.

And so she sent Curt on his way and sought the solitude of her apartment.

Two men, two strangers, had walked into her life that day. And somehow, Carole Gossett knew she'd never be the same.

Chapter Three

CURT SAT IN his quietly purring BMW, watching the mottled brick face of Carole's townhouse long after he saw her apartment lights flash on. She had been different tonight, her sparkling gaiety and wit replaced by an almost solemn courtesy. And he'd found it disquieting.

She had paid scant attention to his impressive promotion, but had nearly caused a scene about sending some damned dress designs to New York! Curt didn't like it. Something wasn't right.

It irked him that there should be a shadow on his limelight. Vice-president. He'd been promoted to vice-president, right there in front of R.J. and his father! Curt knew the position would carry, in addition to prestige, a sizable raise. That was how James Gossett operated when he was safeguarding something he wanted.

And he wanted Curt. Curt had known it all along. Even before he met Carole, he'd picked up the impression that James Gossett—who was seemingly intimidated by nothing—was intimidated by the Morrisson name. Something about James's own social standing made him covet that of Curt's family.

Conveniently, James offered a daughter of the

right age to be courted by Curt. Thankfully, she turned out to be a beautiful, entertaining, desirable woman who made Curt's mouth water.

Curt had been able to have his cake and eat it, too. Not only was his boss's daughter a knockout, but his courtship had been rewarded with advancement, too. Many times, Curt had wondered just how much his quick rise up the Gossett Enterprises ladder had to do with Carole. Now, having been given a vice-presidency, he had no doubt. In fact, he wouldn't doubt that upon marriage, an eventual presidency might be guaranteed by the man who was both father of the bride and chairman of the board.

More than likely, Curt hypothesized, it was his dazzling success at G.E., as Gossett's employees referred to the firm, that had prompted his father to take him seriously. Never before had Robert Morrisson dealt with his younger son like an equal. And when Curt approached him weeks before with the investment idea, he'd been pleasantly shocked at his father's attentive response. With relish, he conjured up the memory of his father's dark blue eyes, fastened intently on him as he outlined the profitable plan.

For the first time in Curt's adulthood, he sensed his life coming together in a way that would make even his brother envious. He was involved in confidential business with his father, he was rising like a comet at G.E., and he was romancing one of the most desirable women in Charleston.

Curt's wistful thoughts shifted, and within the dark cab of the car, his absent smile faded. Tonight, he had felt all his dreams threatened by Carole's sudden distance. She'd been a different person, one he didn't know how to reach. Even when he'd kissed her good night, deftly reaching inside her cloak to cup one of those perfect breasts, she'd seemed preoccupied, almost uninterested.

He, on the other hand, was hungry and hard. Carole excited him tremendously, and yet when he occasionally lost his resolve not to press her, she managed ingeniously to keep him at bay. It had been more than a month since he'd had sex—and never with Carole.

Of its own accord, his memory turned to Laura Murphy, the brunette he'd picked up at a waterfront bar. They'd shared a brief, torrid affair for a few weeks before Curt had met Carole. And even afterward he had managed to keep up a discreet, sexual relationship going with Laura. But a month ago, he'd decided to go exclusive with Carole; he hadn't seen Laura since.

Her flat was twenty minutes away—in a less fashionable section in the north of town. It was nearly eleven on a Saturday night, and she hadn't seen him in more than a month.

Gunning his engine, Curt screeched away from the curb. Laura Murphy was no Carole Gossett—but she wouldn't turn him away.

The taillights of Curt's white BMW had barely faded up Broad Street when James's Seville pulled slowly alongside the townhouse. James wasted no time. His strides were long as he banged his way through the courtyard and took two steps at a time to his daughter's apartment.

"Who is it?" Carole called in response to his knock.

James gritted his teeth, his ire blossoming anew. "Your father!" he bellowed succinctly.

Behind the portal, Carole's heart fell to her feet. Still, as she opened the door, she was surprisingly calm.

"Hello, Daddy."

He stepped inside, drilling her with a sour look. "What the hell is going on?"

"Nothing." Sighing, she shuffled into the living room.

She had stepped out of her black pumps, but still wore the cocktail dress—odd attire for the task she'd attacked as soon as she'd gotten home. Now, the once neglected drawing table stood clean and shining, and a straightbacked dining chair was pulled up before it. Utensils, pads, and swatch books were on a neighboring Queen Anne sideboard, aiong with an antique porcelain lamp.

The odd, modern work area now monopolized the formal, old-fashioned receiving room. It was almost symbolic, Carole thought. Then she flashed on how the scene must look to her father, and glancing over her shoulder, she found him staring stonily at the drawing table as if it were a Medusa.

"What the hell are you up to, Carole?" he demanded.

"Nothing, I said. I've just been doing a little cleaning."

He came to stand beside her, rested his hands on the back of the dining-turned-work-table chair. There would be no touching. That, Carole knew. No matter how her father might long to reach out—if, in fact, he ever did—there were never any comforting touches.

"I paid for this damned contraption," he said with a vicious nod to the table. "I paid for this whole setup. So I think I deserve some answers. You and Curt are made for each other. He gets a big promotion, practically proposes to you in front of his whole family . . . and you sit there like a stump, hardly opening your mouth until you make a big to-do about some damned designs!

"And then I come over here, hoping you've come to your senses, and I find you setting up shop in the middle of your living room! And you say nothing's going on?"

He was in a fine rage now—dark eyes flashing, an immaculately groomed lock of hair fallen forward on his forehead, fists clenched below the ornate gold links on his stiff shirt cuffs. Carole had seen the look many times before, and it had never failed to cower her into quick submission. But this time was different. This time she had the feeling that if she succumbed, she would be under his thumb for all time.

"I told you at supper, Daddy. I'm going to do a collection and send them to New York. I need a place to work. I can't do my own stuff at Carlotta's!."

"Your own stuff! Since when have you cared about your own stuff? *I'm* the one who got you through school when you didn't care enough to turn in your assignments. *I'm* the one who got you that job at Carlotta's!. You've never cared about your 'own stuff' before! What's gotten into you?"

Tears started to form in her eyes. "I don't know," Carole managed, her lips beginning to tremble. She spun away from the table, wandered to the French doors that opened onto the balcony. Yet as she peered through the small, square panes, she could see only blackness—and the reflection of her father standing forever over her shoulder.

"I only know," she explained quietly, "that I need to do this. Maybe I need to prove something to myself. Maybe I need to see that, for once in my life, I can do something on my own . . . without your paving the way or paying the ticket."

"And to hell with Curt?" he demanded.

"I didn't say that."

"You didn't have to," James Gossett accused harshly. "It was there for anyone to see, especially Curt. Have you forgotten who you're toying with? He's a Morrisson, for God's sake!"

Carole continued to gaze unseeingly out the French door. "I don't mean to hurt anyone. Not Curt . . . or you." She turned to look at him, unaware of the pleading look that had crept to her face. "But I'm going to do this, Daddy. At least I'm going to try."

A warning sounded in James's head. He'd gone

56

as far as he could go. She would not come around—not as a result of any direct pressure he could exert. This was new for Carole. He had seen it before in her sister, April, but Carole had never reacted this way. She was sad, pleading, but hard as a rock in her resolve.

A sudden picture of Marion leapt unbidden to his mind. James hadn't seen his first wife in a dozen years, not since that shocking day when he'd come home to find she was gone without a trace. But he well remembered her blond beauty. She had passed on her coloring to both the girls, but where April had grown tall and lanky like her father, Carole had developed Marion's eye-catching curves. Now, as James studied his younger daughter, he realized she was the very image of her mother—and was, therefore, totally unpredictable.

"I simply want to do this for myself," Carole said softly. "Is that so wrong?"

An instinctive transformation slid over his face—an attractive, beguiling countenance that came as close to offering warmth as anything James Gossett could conjure up.

"No," he replied. "That's not wrong." And then, not trusting himself to maintain the amicable facade, he turned on his heel and left.

Carole jumped as the door slammed behind him, but then the curious, unfamiliar sense of pride she'd been feeling all day swelled anew within her breast. On sudden impulse, she stepped to the phone and called April.

"Hi, honey," came her sister's smooth voice. "You're lucky you caught me. I was just on my way to make rounds. I've got the late shift this week."

Carole imagined the serene face, the solemn blue eyes. "How are things at the hospital?"

"The same. How are things with you?"

"Not the same."

"What do you mean?"

"Oh, April!" Carole gushed, and then related the story of Jack Levy's interest in her work, and his invitation for her to send samples to his fashion house, Haut Nouveau.

"I always knew you were talented, Carole. You were the one who had doubts. Does Daddy know?"

"He knows."

"I imagine he's thrilled," April commented sarcastically.

"Thrilled is hardly the word," Carole replied. "But you know? I did the most amazing thing just now. Daddy came by to try and convince me I should give it up, that I should be thinking only of Curt. But April . . . I held my own. I actually told him I was going to do it anyway."

"I'm proud of you, honey." April told her. "Like I always said, he's not God."

Carole's eyes shifted to the door, where her father had just exited in frustrated anger. "Maybe not," she murmured.

On the street below, James Gossett's black Seville lurched into motion and shot away from Carole's curb and into the night. Driving north two miles, he pulled to a stop beside the building which was both the home and offices of J.A. Horton, private investigator.

And as Curt Morrisson embraced Laura Murphy, and James Gossett shook the hand of Joey Horton, both were thinking of the blond woman in the townhouse at Broad and Rutledge.

R.J. leaned against the column on the front veranda, soaking up the Charleston night. It was cool, but mellow, promising the humid heat of summer with a last, teasing taste of spring mildness.

He should have been thinking of Vicki, of how to break up with her the following day when he returned to Columbia. But he wasn't. He was thinking

58

of Carole Gossett. There was something electric between them, whether she admitted it or not. It was a cruel twist of fate for Curt to have her when he so obviously didn't know what he had.

The front screen door closed quietly behind him, and R.J. glanced over his shoulder to find Cecile Laroche. It was past eleven, late for Cecile to be here. But then, her hours had always been erratic. She was as much a part of their household as any Morrisson. It raised no eyebrows for her to be in the house at any time.

She was an attractive black woman of about fifty, though as she approached, R.J. judged she had grown a bit plump in the past year. Probably from eating her own delicious cooking, he thought with a smile.

"The dinner was superb, Cecile," he said.

Her face lit up with the wide, white smile he had known since adolescence. But then the smile disappeared, and she took a step closer. "I need a minute of your time, R.J."

"Sure. What is it?"

"Somethin's weighin' might heavy on me, son. Mighty heavy. And when you showed up here today, I thanked the Lord. You're a lawyer, and a smart one, your mama says. Maybe you can help."

R.J. peered down at her intently. "You know I'll help if I can. Tell me about it."

"Well, you see. It's about my friend, Louise. She just died a couple of months ago, and she left behind this poor old boy." Cecile's voice wavered at the mere thought of what Jonah had told her that afternoon.

"What's his name?" R.J. asked.

"Jonah Stuckey," she replied with a sniffle.

Stuckey . . . For some reason, the name rang a bell.

* * *

Three weeks later, on an early morning clouded by lingering sleep, R.J. heard the sound of running water. Suddenly a voice rang in his mind.

His eyes snapped open, and for a split second he thought he was in Charleston. But as he bolted up in the king-sized bed, he realized he was in his Columbia apartment. He must have been dreaming.

R.J. climbed out of bed, the dream echoing elusively. Mindless of his nakedness, he wandered into the den. Now fully awake, he realized that Vicki was in the shower. That was the sound that had waked him from the dream. It *was* a dream, wasn't it? He couldn't get a grasp on it, but it had left him prickling with unease.

Thinking of Charleston, a wave of guilt washed over R.J. He hadn't done a damn thing about the Stuckey affair Cecile had mentioned that last night.

Returning to Columbia, he'd sunk right back into the life he'd been living for the past year—hobnobbing with associates on the state supreme court by day, socializing in fast-lane clubs and restaurants by night. For months, he'd found the capital city exciting, his playboy life exhilarating. But at the moment, it seemed the days and nights had run together in one meaningless stream.

He found Vicki's Aigner purse and rummaged through it for cigarettes. He'd given up the habit years ago, but had a sudden, odd longing for a smoke. Stretching out on the tan, corduroy-upholstered sofa, R.J. puffed away, allowing his thoughts to drift.

Since his return, he hadn't looked into the Stuckey case, hadn't broken up with Vicki, hadn't accomplished a single thing he'd planned to do when he was standing in the Charleston moonlight—except maybe to dull his memory of Carole Gossett. In retrospect, he realized he'd been so preoccupied with the blonde that he'd paid little heed to Cecile Laroche when she approached him on the veranda that night to plead the case of her destitute friend.

What had gotten into him? In the old days he never would have brushed off such a request. Nowadays, it seemed all he had time for was fancy court cases and fancier parties.

Cecile was a damn good woman, a good friend. She'd never asked him for anything before. And yet when she came to him with tears in her eyes, all he could do was focus on his own high-powered concerns. R.J. felt suddenly self-centered and hollow.

But then, he had been anxious to wipe the Charleston visit from his mind. Carole Gossett belonged to his brother, would very probably marry Curt. It would do R.J. no good to dwell on how good she'd felt when he'd held her, or how curiously proud he'd been when she stood up to everyone that night at supper.

With relentless clarity, the stilted evening came back. She was sitting across from him, reserved and irresistible in that black dress, her father was making some political-sounding speech about an ideal location for a park, Curt, blushing at being promoted to vice-president.

Then Carole made a simple statement about some designs and New York. You'd have thought she'd announced she wanted a divorce before she'd even married Curt. That father of hers was none to pleased about it, that was sure. It was clear he wanted no interference in the match he obviously approved. Gossett's voice had been quiet, but R.J. hadn't missed the firm undertone of authority when he spoke to his daughter—nor the man's surprise when, cool as a cucumber, Carole had told him she intended to do as she pleased.

And like a fool, R.J. had sat across the table and felt a stupid, warm rush of pride. As if he had a right to feel *anything* for Carole Gossett. What had drawn him was her sexy southern charm; what captivated him was the fiery woman beneath. And yes, he'd done everything he could to forget her. Maybe that was why he'd forgotten all about Stuckey, too.

A shiver ran up R.J.'s spine, and he stubbed out the cigarette with a vengeance as Vicki waltzed in, clad only in a white towel.

"Good morning, darling," she purred. "I didn't know you smoked."

Her short red hair was wet and shining, her long limbs gleaming beneath the inconsequential towel. And yet, the sight of her left him cold.

"Morning, Vicki," he said. And with quick recollection of the automatic coffeemaker he kept programmed, R.J. added, "There's coffee. Why don't you get us some?"

As the tall, slender redhead made her way obediently to the kitchen, R.J.'s mind clicked away.

Today is Thursday, he thought. Tomorrow, I have to be in court in the morning. . . . But then I could leave. I could be in Charleston before supper. And it wouldn't be for Carole, damn it! It would be for Cecile . . . and Stuckey, whoever the hell he is.

Vicki glided back into the den bearing two mugs of steaming black coffee, and handed one to R.J.

"You know I take cream," he accused, taking a quick look at the black depths in the cup.

She curled into the chair opposite him. "No . . . I didn't know."

She was attractive, curled up there in one of his towels, sipping morning coffee from one of his mugs.

"Well, I guess that just goes to show how little we know about each other," he baited.

A wary look leapt to her face. At least, it wasn't a hurt look, he thought.

"What are you trying to say, R.J. ?" she asked him.

An hour later Vicki Monroe was on her way out

of R.J. Morrisson's life. And the next day, he was on his way home—to Charleston.

Joey Horton sat on the plush sofa, sipping coffee from the china cup the secretary had offered him. Glancing around at the rich fabrics and glowing antiques that furnished the Gossett Enterprises receiving office, he thought once again that James Gossett had class.

Joey was impressed by expensive things. It showed in his own custom-made suits. Absently, he reached up to straighten his flawless silk Hermès tie, then rested his hand once again on the manila folder in his lap. All the papers were there. Signed, sealed, delivered. Quick and quiet. Just the way Gossett always demanded.

The matronly secretary swept over to announce, "Mr. Gossett will see you now."

He was dressed in a silk-blend suit not unlike Joey's. In fact, as he grasped James Gossett's hand in a firm shake, he thought they looked rather alike—same dark hair and wiry build, although Gossett was taller, his facial features sharper. Joey smiled. He liked comparing himself with the tycoon.

"Good to see you, Mr. Gossett." He handed over the folder. "I've just come from the attorneys. It's all there. Gossett Enterprises now owns controlling interest in the fashion house, Haut Nouveau of New York."

Taking the folder, James turned his back on Horton and ambled toward the great mahogany desk from which he ruled his empire. The papers were, in fact, all there. A rather expensive little deal—but then, the investment would be worth it.

He turned, drilled Horton with an expectant look. "And a Mr. Jack Levy?"

Joey rocked on his heels confidently. "I don't believe you have an employee by that name, sir."

A moment later, Joey stepped quietly out of Gossett's inner sanctum. A wide smile lit his face as he patted the silk jacket's inner pocket, which now contained three thousand in cash.

He liked doing jobs for James Gossett. The man had style.

R.J. stopped in at the house long enough to drop off his bags and give his mother a joyous start that sent her scurrying up to freshen—not that it needed it—his old room. Then he called Cecile Laroche, confirmed that she would be home that evening and he was welcome to stop by. It was just past suppertime when he drove to the black section north of Calhoun Street.

He hadn't been there in years, but R.J. well remembered the way to the home of the Laroches, a family occupying the same position of leadership in the black community as the Morrissons did on Tradd Street. The line between black and white was strong in Charleston, but there were times when it was crossed. His mother and Cecile—active counterparts in their own social circles and causes—had known, liked, and worked with each other long before Cecile's husband was killed in a car accident and she'd decided to take a job as the Morrissons' housekeeper.

R.J. had known the family since he was just a kid—Cecile, her sons, Stephen and Cameron, and her scrappy grandmother-in-law, the formidable, white-haired Olivia Laroche.

As he turned his car onto Juniper Street, R.J. decided the neighborhood looked pretty much the same. The yards, though sparse, were neat, the modest frame houses well-kept. It was a mild June twilight, and a number of old folks were rocking and fanning themselves on front porches. R.J. drove slowly past, and as their dark eyes fastened on his flashy car, the silver Corvette that had always brought him such pleasure seemed suddenly gaudy and ostentatious. Once again, he was swept with the uncomfortable feeling of vulgar social supremacy that had smacked him the day before when he'd realized he'd forgotten all about Cecile's plea.

Thankfully, the feeling evaporated when he saw Cecile's beaming face. Behind her stood her younger son, Cameron. And as R.J. stepped into the small, tidy living room, he spotted Cecile's grandmother-in-law, her slight, snowy-capped frame huddled into the couch with a shawl, and looking no more and no less ancient than ever.

"Mrs. Laroche," he greeted the old matriarch. "It's nice to see you looking so fit."

"Eight years back," the nearly blind woman croaked surprisingly. "Last time I saw you was at that party your mama gave 'fore you went away to Vanderbilt College. You give your mama my regards, now, ya hear?" she dismissed and went back to watching the small TV in the corner.

Impressed and smiling at the old lady's sharpness, R.J. looked to Cameron. Damn, had it been that long? The gangly boy had grown into a man of twenty, maybe twenty-one. And instead of a basketball, he was holding a carefully polished saxophone.

"Cameron, is that you?" R.J. asked with a grin.

Cameron's face split widely into a smile. He'd always liked R.J. "How ya doin'?" he asked, offering his free hand. "It's been a long time."

"Long is right." R.J.'s eyes fell to the saxophone. "You into music now?"

"Oh, Lord!" Cecile moaned with mock complaint. "That and nothin' else." Then her face took on a typically proud, maternal glow. "Cameron is quite the musician nowadays, R.J. He tends bar at that Myskyn's place over by the college, but he plays every weekend at The River Club. I must admit I was a bit leery at first, but he's stuck with it. Now it seems he's about to get himself a full-time job with a band."

"Maybe, Mom," Cameron hedged. "I said 'maybe' we'd be able to put together a band . . . if we can get a good singer." Thoughtlessly, he turned an admiring grin on R.J. "Now, if R.J. could talk to that sister of his—"

Cameron stopped in mid-sentence, a feeling of horror gripping his gut. What was he thinking? The one thing Camille had always emphasized was that no one *ever* know she sang at The River Club.

"What you talkin' 'bout, boy?" his mother demanded as R.J. looked at him curiously.

"Aw, nothin'," Cameron covered quickly. "It's just that I've heard Camille's got a great voice."

With a quick good-bye, Cameron made fast tracks out of the house he shared with his mother and great-grandmother. He would probably see Camille that very night. If she could manage to slip away from that fancy house of hers, the young redhead would sweep into the hottest jazz club in town and take it by storm the way she always did, the way no white woman ever had before her.

Cameron had come to admire her more than any singer he knew. And some day . . . *some day* . . . he hoped she'd join the band of his dreams. Out front, he gave R.J.'s sleek car a quick, admiring look, then leaped into his old Chevy and sped away, the familiar musical hopes drumming in his head.

Inside the house, Cecile poured freshly made iced tea and settled with R.J. around the small dining table.

"I can't believe that was Cameron," R.J. offered. "The last time I saw him, he came to my shoulder. And that," he pointed to the photograph hanging neatly. "Is that Stephen?"

Cecile's face again took on that ethereal glow. "That was taken last year. Stephen is two years older than you, ya know. He's a third-year intern at the Medical University now."

R.J. shook his head pensively. "Time flies, doesn't it, Cecile?"

"It does, at that." Cecile's look turned inquisitive. "You know, you surprised me, R.J. Always figured you for one that would end up back here in Charleston. Thought you had it in your blood."

Her words triggered a series of comparisons—Charleston's tangy salt air versus the dry, scorching heat of Columbia, antebellum homes and gardens versus modern high-rises. Of course, the legal work with Judge Harper and the supreme court was rewarding, but more and more often, life at the capital seemed to be measuring up short.

"I think I do," he said thoughtfully. "Lately, I've been comparing Columbia to this place. And when I came home a few weeks ago, it really hit me—how special it is here." The "Morrisson-blue" eyes darkened solemnly. "I've got a lot going for me at the capital, Cecile. But you're right . . . Charleston is in my blood."

Cecile gazed fondly at the handsome young man. "It'd make your mama mighty happy if you came home, R.J. Can't think of anything that would make her happier. You know your mama. She's a great lady. She don't let on or complain, but she gets mighty lonesome sometimes. Seems like the happiest times I've seen her, its' been when you're home. You're her firstborn. She counts on you in a different way from the others."

"Well," R.J. hedged, "at least she's got Dad. She can always count on him."

A puzzling, sad look came to Cecile's dark eyes. "Of course," she said, and then briskly changed the subject. "But now, I reckon we ought to get to the reason you came by. . . ."

"Jonah Stuckey," R.J. finished for her, leaning back in his chair. "Okay. I need to know everything about him you can tell me, Cecile. Everything."

Jonah Stuckey was a retarded black man in his

fifties, Cecile told him, who had lived his entire life with his mother at Belmont Pines, a dilapidated plantation on the Ashley River. When Louise Stuckey died intestate, her son had been removed to an institution, his property taken over by a court-appointed guardian. It all sounded very ordinary.

"But there *was* a will," Cecile insisted. "I ought to know. I witnessed it. But I've searched that house from top to bottom, and I can't find it. Louise wanted the property to go to the church, as long as Jonah had a home there for life. She would never have wanted him in that hospital, no matter how fancy it is!"

"But if the will can't be found, the normal course of events has simply taken place," R.J. suggested. "I don't know what I can do, not if Jonah's guardian—"

"And that's another thing," Cecile broke in. "I never heard of no cousin down in Savannah. Louise never mentioned any Geraldine Stuckey."

"Well, apparently the county clerk approved the woman. Otherwise, he never would have appointed her guardian."

Folding her arms across her breast, Cecile looked at R.J. firmly. "Maybe I just don't have the same faith in the county that you do."

He leaned forward, looked at her intently. "What are you saying, Cecile? You think there's been foul play?"

"I'm just saying things are fishy, mighty fishy."

"*Hmph!* 'Taint fishy a'tall," Olivia Laroche announced from the sofa, surprising them with her attentive remark.

"What do you mean, Miss Livie?" Cecile returned. "You know that things ain't right about Jonah."

"Right and wrong ain't got nothin' to do with it," the old woman's voice crackled. "Don't know why you're surprised, Cecile. Same as always, the big white man saw somethin' he wanted, and he stepped in and took it. Simple as that. Just the way it's always been."

R.J. got to his feet, ambled over to the wizened figure that was so paradoxically forceful. "It doesn't have to be that way, Mrs. Laroche," he said.

"Shoot!" the old woman huffed up at him. "A dog ain't got to have fleas, but it do! Nothin's changed in a hundred years, and nothin's goin' to. You listen to me, boy. I know what I'm talkin' 'bout. If the white folks done decided there's somethin' they want, ain't nobody gonna care 'bout an old nigger like Jonah!"

The derogatory word startled him. A strangely familiar tingle shot through R.J. as he looked down on the incredibly wrinkled, brown face of Olivia Laroche. There was something about the old woman's words. . . .

"Now, Miss Livie, watch your tongue," Cecile interrupted scoldingly. Then, drawing R.J.'s eyes to her own, she went on, "Listen, R.J. I don't want to presume too much. But I'm going up to that hospital to see Jonah on Sunday afternoon. Maybe if you've got the time, you'd care to come along."

"Ain't nobody gonna care," Olivia Laroche muttered again.

R.J. took a deep breath, his chin coming up a notch. "Maybe I will," he said. And somewhere deep inside, he realized he *did* care. It felt good.

"What time on Sunday would you like me to pick you up, Cecile?" he asked, and was rewarded with a white smile that split the woman's black face from ear to ear.

On Saturday mornings, the Gossett household was typically quiet. All the servants were away, save Henry and Cora Denning who lived in the servants' cottage behind the screen of magnolias out back. But Henry had already served coffee and Cora's inimi-

69

table homemade biscuits. Now, even the elderly couple had retired until supper.

For a while, James sat alone at the ornately carved, baroque dining table, leafing through the *Post and Courier*. Then, on impulse, he reached for the phone on the sideboard and dialed Joey Horton's number.

"Horton? It's Gossett. . . . No, nothing's wrong with the papers. Everything's in order, and I'm sure the strictest confidentiality has been observed. . . . Good. Listen, I've been thinking. This little maneuver ought to dissuade Carole from her farfetched notions, but just the same, I'd like you to keep an eye on her for me. . . . Yeah, just let me know what she's up to. Particularly if she spends time with anyone but Curt Morrisson . . . Other men, Horton. Other men! Just call me if you have anything."

The phone clicked off in his ear, and James experienced that familiar, sweeping sensation of satisfaction, the same one that hit when he pulled off a particularly lucrative business deal. Then, hearing a noise, he looked with a start toward the entryway.

He was surprised to see Kathleen standing just inside the room, garbed in fashionable exercise attire, her long black hair caught in a tight knot at the back of her head.

"My, my," he crooned, settling back in the plush chair. "Already up and dressed? And it's nowhere *near* noon."

Inwardly, Kathleen trembled. It was a habit that had become chronic in the past year. The only thing that seemed to steady her these days was the numbness of alcohol.

"I'm going to dance class, James," she announced.

His eyes swept over her. In the lavender tights and black midrift that fit like a second skin, her body was shown off to perfection—the lithe, long-legged one of a dancer. For the first time in a long while,

70

he saw the ghost of the sexy young woman who had made him want a third wife. But the illusion was spoiled when he caught her tremulous expression.

"Good," he grunted. "Glad you're going. I pay that fancy studio enough for you to go every day, much less the odd week when you decide to show up." That said, James retrieved the newspaper and turned aside.

"I need the car," she murmured.

He glanced her way. "What's wrong with your Mercedes?"

"Nothing. I just need the keys. You took them two days ago, remember?"

James's lips twisted grimly. "Ah, yes. The afternoon you nearly sideswiped me in the drive." He drilled her with a harsh look. "You haven't been drinking this morning, have you?"

Like no one she'd ever known, this man could make her feel utterly worthless. "Of course not," Kathleen replied quietly.

"Well, then, the keys are over there. . . ," he gestured vaguely, "in the middle drawer of the breakfront."

Hurrying to the towering, china-filled cabinet, she grabbed the keys and started swiftly out of the room.

"When will you be back?" he demanded.

"Around two," Kathleen tossed over her shoulder.

"See that you are!" he called.

A shudder ran through her. He was insanely possessive. He may not want her, but he'd make damned sure no one else had her. Still, Kathleen hadn't missed his fleeting look of interest. There were times, even now, when he came to her and demanded his husbandly rights. She fervently hoped she wouldn't have to pay for her comfortable, but scant, dance attire with an afternoon round of sex that left her feeling, once again, like a nameless, faceless object. And as she made a hasty retreat out of the brick house, Kathleen Gossett shivered in the warm sunshine, wondering at the massive amount of hatred her slim body could hold.

Once out on the street, she floored the gas pedal and sped the red Mercedes convertible along Tradd Street, caring little for the scenic gardens and great houses that had once impressed her. Without so much as a sidelong glance, she roared past the white, cloistered mansion many considered to be the grandest in Charleston.

Behind that impressive front, the Morrisson family—all together for the first time in a long while—lingered over a late breakfast. Charlotte's heart swelled as she looked beyond her four beautiful children to where her husband sat at the head of the table. She would have caught his eye, smiled her contentment at the wonderful life he'd provided her. But as usual these days, Robert was preoccupied with something. This time it was the newspaper. With a sigh, Charlotte turned her attention to the children and picked up on their conversation.

"Really, R.J. I think you'd love this crowd," Margaret was saying. "And the Isle of Palms, if you remember, is simply too beautiful for words. Clifford had to pull some strings to get a permit for the fire, and he's hired a bluegrass band. We're going to spend the day swimming and boating, and then have the barbecue when the sun goes down. I wish you'd come with us."

R.J. grinned, glanced down at his empty plate, then across the table to the youngest member of the family. "How about you, Camille? Are you going to this clambake?"

The impish face took on a look of distaste. "Hardly! Margaret's yuppie friends aren't my cup of tea, and neither is folk music!"

Margaret raised a brow, her brown eyes taking on a caustic gleam. "No, *you* prefer blacks and jazz!"

"So? There's nothing wrong with that!" Camille

returned flippantly. "I wouldn't be caught dead at your dumb old barbecue . . . even if I didn't have choir practice!"

"Girls," Robert cautioned. The single word from the head of the house was sufficient for both Margaret and Camille to still their tongues, although their silent glare continued.

Robert set aside the *Post and Courier*, holding his daughters with a warning look as Curt and R.J. exchanged a comradely grin at their sisters' continuing, long-waged battle.

Margaret tilted her nose to the ceiling. "May I be excused?" she asked.

"I, also?" Camille mocked in a similar disdainful tone.

Helplessly, Robert took on a look of amusement as he considered the two lovely, completely different young women who had sprung from his loins. He nodded in acquiescence, and they came to their feet simultaneously—maintaining a polite silence until they were out the door. But then they sank immediately into heated whispering that became inaudible as they hurried up the stairs toward their respective chambers.

"Charlotte, my dear," Robert said smilingly. "I don't know where your daughters got their argumentative ways. Surely not from the Morrisson side!"

As always, Charlotte melted at the the warm look in her husband's gray eyes. "Surely not!" she rejoined in good humor.

"By the way, R.J. What brings you back to Charleston so soon?" Curt asked. "You were here just a few weeks ago."

"Am I wearing out my welcome?"

"Don't be silly, Randall!" Charlotte scolded.

R.J. glanced to his mother, then back to Curt. "No reason. Guess I'm just homesick."

Curt's eyes were on his brother, but he was

thinking of Carole. They used to spend every Saturday together, but she had turned him down the past two weeks. Well, he'd be damned if he was about to make it three!

"Wanna get together later?" he asked R.J. "Dad and I have a few things to do this morning, but you and I could meet for lunch."

Charlotte rose from her chair, collecting a selection of tablewear to carry into the kitchen.

"Lately, you two have been thick as thieves," she commented, a pleasant look darting from Curt to her husband and back. "Whatever in the world are you and your father up to?"

"That's none of your concern, Charlotte," Robert broke in.

Stunned, she turned her eyes quickly to her husband. The warm look was gone, replaced by the tense, unreadable expression which so often marked his features these past months. A blush stained her high cheekbones as she squared her shoulders.

"Of course," she murmured as she left the room with a regal step.

R.J. looked at Robert Morrisson in surprise. He'd never heard his father speak to his mother in that fashion, never seen the firm, chastising expression turned her way. He shifted his questioning look toward Curt, but his brother merely shrugged and sought to change the subject.

"So, what do you say, R.J. ? Wanna meet for lunch at our old stomping grounds? How about The White Stag at one o'clock?"

R.J. nodded in silent agreement. But as the three men got to their feet and meandered from the opulent dining room, R.J. was still puzzling over his father's odd, discourteous behavior.

Chapter Four

CAROLE RIPPED THE sketch off the pad, crumpled it into a tight ball, and sent it sailing toward the trash can, where it joined a dozen other crumpled sheets—all in various degrees of closeness to the receptacle.

"God help me," she whispered into the palms that covered her eyes and mouth.

Three weeks had passed—three delirious, manic-depressive weeks. At first, she'd been so high, she'd stayed up all night—working into the wee hours, then showing up at six A.M. at the nearby doughnut shop to celebrate her newest creation with a pastry, before heading to Carlotta's! to put in a day's work.

But lately, she'd been struggling to foster even a creative impulse. Damn! She'd come up with her theme. Her pad was now full of fresh, eye-catching day wear, sportswear, swim wear—all on a safari theme. So why couldn't she finish? Jack Levy would be sure to expect the inclusion of evening wear, but she couldn't come up with a single, worthy idea!

Her forearms sank to the surface of the expensive drawing table, and then her head followed, her eyes closing briefly in a semblance of repose. It was nearly eleven o'clock. She'd been working fruitlessly since seven.

When Carole's eyes drifted open a moment later, her gaze strayed across the room to the uncurtained French doors. It was a beautiful, clear morning, the sky as blue as a robin's egg. In the old days, she'd have spent such a Saturday out at the Isle of Palms. She'd be basking in the sun and developing a heart-stopping tan, playing tennis on the famed, competition-ready courts, or dancing on the club patio under the summer stars.

No more. Now, she sat amongst the clutter of an apartment she hadn't cleaned in weeks. Now, as she rested her head on one elbow-propped hand, she perused a pallorous arm that hadn't even seen the light of summer sun.

Wearily, Carole came to her feet and made her way to the kitchen. Coffee would help, coffee always helped. And as the machine perked away, she dove into the shower, seeking some additional source of alertness, some energy beyond a caffeine hype.

When she emerged, she still felt loath to return to her drawing board. Perhaps a change of scene might do her good, Carole thought. The fresh air would clear her head. Yes, she'd take a walk. Throwing on jeans and a sleeveless sweater, Carole went to the bathroom to inspect her reflection in the mirror above the sink. Her hair was straight, her face unmade. Three weeks ago, she wouldn't have ventured outside her door looking like this, much less parade through the District. But it was just going to be a short break from her work, Carole told herself. She didn't have time to really do herself up.

If things had been different, she'd have expected Curt to call. But he'd called the two previous Saturdays, and she'd turned him down. The thought of him brought the uninvited memory of his brother rushing into her mind. Irritated at the man's lingering impressiveness, Carole began to thrash the brush through her fine hair with a vengeance.

Like no man she'd ever met, R.J. Morrisson had managed to snake his way into her thoughts, even during the harried days and nights she'd been spending lately. It debased her, she'd decided, this primitive attraction to the cocky, strutting buck. Yet even when she succeeded at blocking him from conscious thought, he showed up in her dreams, waking her with the remembered sensation of his mouth and body close to her, so that she sat up with a start in bed, damp and aching.

Now, of all times, she wanted no man on her mind. Yet R.J., the phantom she barely knew, had been more successful at sidetracking her than his brother had been in the flesh. In the past three weeks, she'd consented to see Curt only a few times, excusing herself with the firm explanation that it wouldn't be much longer, but that she simply had to work!

She'd not seen her father since his late-night visitation after the Morrissons' dinner party. He was probably mad as a wet hen, but he'd kept his distance. Over the course of the past few weeks, Carole had figured that the uncharacteristic silence from James Gossett was his way of stepping back—of finally allowing his younger daughter the freedom to pursue her own dream.

The thought warmed her heart, for she knew that her romance with Curt—the probable linking of the Gossett name with the Morrissons—was of utmost importance to her father. For him to be giving her such free rein was a real first.

Carole supposed it would be the appropriate thing to call and ask if Curt would like to come along for a walk, maybe lunch.

But she didn't. When she set out a half hour later, she was alone.

* * *

Kathleen had worked off much of her abysmal hostility in dance class. Now she patted her perspiring face with a towel and hung it absently about her neck, perusing the departing members of the class. Patty, Jason, Anne, Sheila . . . There were a dozen of them, all part of the performing company of the renowned instructor and choreographer, Gay Templeton. Kathleen's gaze lingered on the regal, silver-haired Gay as the older woman swept out the door across the room amidst a covey of her talented pupils.

Turning, Kathleen approached the barre. Staring into the wall of mirrors, she extended and began stretching the tight muscles of her right calf and thigh along the deserted barre.

You could be one of them, Kathleen silently accused the reflection. You performed with them a few years ago, and you could do it again . . . if only you had the dedication.

Thoughtfully, Kathleen retrieved her right leg, extended the left. Fan the leg, straighten the back, bend from the hip. Years of ballet training, though sadly unused in the past months, made the disciplines automatic. Kathleen completed the stretch and assumed first position by the barre.

Demi plié . . . grand plié. It's a lack of drive, she told herself. That's the only thing standing between you and the dance. You've got the talent. Gay said so years ago.

Second position . . . demi plié . . . grand plié. Kathleen loved the dance, had loved it since she was a child. And although by the time she was seventeen she realized she would never be world-class material, she nonetheless could hold her own in a local performing company.

She loved the people, the music, the feel of her body as she moved, her blood beating with instinctive timing. She loved everything about the world of dance. Yet lately, she had found herself staying compulsively away from the studio. It was as if she were punishing herself for something.

It was James's fault, she decided ultimately. There was something about him that sapped the will, the very being, of a woman. Only April—cool, dedicated, medicinal April—seemed immune.

Third position . . . demi plié . . . plié. Certainly, Carole was just as much one of James's pawns as Kathleen herself had become. She had seen the way James used his younger daughter. Over the course of her lifetime, he must have taken gradual control until Carole didn't even realize that she was nothing but her father's emissary. Sent here, sent there . . . "Smile now, this man is important to G.E." Kathleen could well imagine the unrelenting, insidious game plan.

Fourth position . . . demi plié . . . plié. If Carole had ever shown her one bit of kindness, Kathleen would have pitied her. Perhaps they could even have been friends. After all, they were only three years apart in age, and their roles with James Gossett were identical. Both were objects to be used.

Fifth position . . . demi plié . . . plié. But Kathleen had discerned early on that Carole resented her. It had something to do with Marion. Perhaps Carole simply couldn't abide the notion of anyone trying to take the place of her mother.

Back to first position . . . demi plié . . . plié. And now, James was having Carole followed by that Horton man—the same one Kathleen had discovered was watching her some months ago when she had dallied, quite innocently with André, a dancer with an Atlanta company.

Second position . . . It had been nothing. Kathleen had been lonely, and André was attractive and complimentary. They'd had a few drinks together, nothing more—and always in the chaperoning presence of the ballet crowd. Kathleen had refused his further innuendos firmly, if somewhat flirtatiously. Even then, she'd been afraid of James, afraid that if she entertained *even the notion* of an affair, he'd somehow know, like some omniscient creature of Olympus.

Third position . . . And then she had noticed the dark young man who was following her. His mere, quiet presence—like some shadow she couldn't shake—had terrified her. More than ever, she'd felt then that behind those ebony eyes of his, James Gossett had a dark power that allowed him to know everything she was doing or thinking.

Fourth position . . . At least she never gave him the satisfaction of knowing he'd frightened her. She simply stopped going to the studio, halted even the chance of running into André when his company occasionally came in from Atlanta for a joint performance. A month or so after that, she realized the shadow was gone. And it had been only a few weeks ago, when she'd glimpsed James talking discreetly with someone in the study, that she learned the dark young man was one Joey Horton, private investigator.

Fifth position . . . And now, James had put the bloodhound on Carole's trail. Curiously, Kathleen turned her memory to the one-sided conversation she'd overheard that morning. "This ought to dissuade Carole from her farfetched notions . . . ," James had said. "Just keep an eye on her. . . . "

Having finished the cool-down exercises, Kathleen meandered to her bag, wondering what Carole had done to displease his majesty. And suddenly, the resentment toward her husband flared anew. What right had he to spy on people, to manipulate and twist them to his own purpose?

Kathleen's emotions banged about noisily within her. Yet the usually bustling studio was quiet and empty as she changed shoes and donned a light sweater over her still-damp dance clothing. She was nearly to the door when she heard a group approaching. And then some dancers strolled in—and she recognized them as part of the Atlanta company.

"Hi, Kathleen," a few of them called.

Her cheeks began to burn as she spotted André. Young and virile, he was as attractive as ever. His longish brown hair was pulled back with a headband; his black tights and tunic flaunted the gracefully muscular build of a dancer. As soon as he noticed her standing steadfast across the room, he started over.

And the instant she saw his sparking, welcoming smile, Kathleen knew. This time, she wouldn't say no.

R.J. nudged his silver Corvette into a tight parking space and hurried into The White Stag. He was late.

His eyes gradually adjusted to the dim light of the popular gathering place that was so like an English pub. The darkly burnished, antique bar was crowded, and a group was huddled round the dartboard, too. Looking around, he spotted Curt already seated at a window booth.

"Hi, brother," R.J. greeted, sliding onto the burgundy leather seat. "Sorry I'm late."

"Oh, that's all right," Curt offered agreeably, swallowing the remainder of the beer in his mug. "I'm just two ahead of you, that's all. Where have you been, anyway?"

Ever since he visited the Laroches the night before, R.J.'s thoughts had been monopolized by the things Cecile told him. Since he couldn't get into the county offices on a Saturday, he'd spent the past few hours in a frustrated search for Stuckey's deserted plantation home, Belmont Pines. But about the time he finally found the grown-over road that led to the secluded place, he remembered he was due to meet Curt. Allowing himself only a quick, distant look at the old house, R.J. had maneuvered a skillful, narrow turn, screeched along the dirt road back to the highway, and raced back to Charleston.

That was where he'd been, Belmont Pines. But he decided not to mention anything about Jonah Stuckey. It might just be a goose chase, anyway. No reason to get everyone alarmed before he knew for sure.

"Oh, I've just been around," R.J. said lightly. "Lost track of the time. You ordered yet?"

They'd finished two of the half-pound burgers for which the pub was famous when Curt ordered another pitcher of beer and brought up the subject of Carole.

"I don't know what's going on, R.J.," he said. "She's changed. I've hardly seen her the past few weeks. She's always 'working,' as she puts it. Here I am, ready to marry the girl, and Carole Gossett can't give me the time of day."

At the mere mention of her name, R.J. felt a guilty warmth climb up his face. "Well," he began, "that night at supper, no one seemed to take her very seriously. But she was pretty fired up about that design business. Maybe it's something she needs to get out of her system. Maybe you should give her a little time." Here he was, giving his brother advice about the very woman he wanted for himself.

"Maybe I've given her too *much* time," Curt returned, a serious look on his good-natured face. "You know the old saying: 'Out of sight, out of mind.' With any other girl, I'd simply lay down the law: 'Look, honey. We're going out tonight, and that's it.' But somehow, I can't do that with Carole."

"Why not?" R.J. asked.

The truth? I'm not so sure she wouldn't end the whole thing if I pushed her. Hell, I've handled her with kid gloves since the very beginning! There's something she can do with those eyes of hers, a look she can give . . . " Curt leaned forward, his voice falling confidentially. "I've never even made it with her, for Christ's sake, and here I am talking about marrying her!"

A flood of relief washed through R.J. Loyal or not, honorable or not, he was relieved that the haunting blonde hadn't been to bed with his brother.

"What makes you want to marry her?" he challenged. "What makes her so special?"

The many dreams that were tied up in Carole Gossett flashed through Curt's mind. "Lots of things," he muttered, turning his gaze morosely out the window.

The afternoon street was drenched with sunlight, and the summer throngs of tourists were out. But as the passing crowd gapped, Curt's eye fell on a figure across the street.

"Damn! There she is!" he whispered. But then another group filed past the window. "At least, I think it's her."

R.J. pivoted to look. The solitary woman was studying a shop-front display. It was Carole, all right. The blond hair was straight, the clothes uncharacteristically low key. But he'd know that shape anywhere.

"What should I do?" Curt asked. "I didn't call her today. Didn't think there was any point."

R.J. sighed discreetly as his eyes lingered across the way. "Why don't you go over and say hello?"

"What? Just say hello?"

"Why not? You happened to spot her, didn't you? It's not as if she's a stranger."

"Lately, she has been," Curt said dismally. "All right, I'll go. But you come with me. That way, it will seem more casual."

"What?!" R.J. sputtered incredulously. "Since when do you need me along for a nursemaid?"

Still, despite his objections, R.J. found himself

drawn to his feet and pulled along by his brother. He was both relieved and disappointed when, after they'd settled their tab, they stepped outside to find Carole had disappeared.

"Come on," Curt urged. "I'll bet she's going home. It's not far. We'll take my car."

R.J. stopped dead in his tracks, his palms coming up as he shook his head. "Hold on, Curt. I agreed to come out here with you and say hello to Carole, but I'm not about to go with you and track her down."

Curt's boyish face turned up to peer innocently at his taller brother. "Why not? I couldn't count the number of women we've gone after together in the past. What's the matter? Don't you like Carole? That's it, isn't it? You don't like her. . . . You don't think I should marry her."

R.J. cringed as he recognized a chance to turn Curt away from Carole, to lead his brother out of the picture so that he himself would be free to step in. His words came angrily.

"I think you should do whatever you want. Drop her. Marry her. But leave me out of it!"

R.J. spun, stomped the short distance to the pub front, and then exploded with an oath. Some jerk had blocked his Corvette in. In angry exasperation, he paced around the long station wagon from Pennsylvania, confirming there was no way he could back his car out without a sideswipe.

"Damn it!" he raged, as Curt strolled up behind him. "Some damned tourist has got me blocked!"

"Gee, that's too bad, R.J."

R.J. nearly wrenched his neck, so fast did he whirl around to confront his calmly smiling brother.

"But don't worry," Curt went on with infuriating good humor. "My car is parked just down the block, free and clear. Guess it's fate. You're meant to come with me."

Months later, R.J. would marvel at his brother's hapless insight.

The June sun was high and hot, washing the white Charleston streets with golden light. Carole ambled along aimlessly, noting the sunburns of passing vacationers and feeling the perilous, warning heat on her own unaccustomed arms and face.

It was after two o'clock, and whatever tourists had ducked into the District eateries for lunch, were now back on the streets in full force. Usually she disliked the summer crowds, but today she found comfort in the anonymity of the hordes. Already, she had passed the "Four Corners of Law" at Broad and Meeting, lollygagged among the black street vendors selling flowers and handwoven baskets across from St. Michael's Church, and window-shopped "the Market," that extensive stretch of restaurants and shops along Market Street from Meeting to East Bay.

Now she shot an uninterested look down the cobblestones of Chalmers Street, home of the Old Slave Mart which currently sported flea-market stalls. Her sneakers moved surely along the old, uneven stones—which had come to Charleston as ballast on sailing ships centuries before—and then left the churning marketplace behind. Of their own volition, her footsteps turned toward Tradd.

Constance Trippley was out in her yard, Carole noted. Nothing surprising about that. Miss Constance was *always* out in her yard. As Carole approached, she smiled fondly. The elder of the Trippley sisters had been her favorite ever since she was just a child, when Miss Constance would often make a bouquet for Carole to take home to her mother. Since she was in no hurry, Carole paused to speak to the old lady.

"Your garden's looking mighty pretty, Miss Constance," she said through the wrought-iron court-yard wall. "You'll be sure to win the Garden Tour, just like always."

It was true. The Trippley gardens were a study in floral beauty. The spring azaleas had faded, but some of Miss Constance's roses were already in bloom, while others were showing first buds. By the time of the Tour's annual competition, the judges would view a panorama of jonquils, hydrangea, roses and camellias—all carefully blended within a framework of dark green magnolia, lavender wisteria, and twisting live oak draped with Spanish moss.

Now as Miss Constance came to her feet, she took a break from planting a row of white geraniums by the brick walkway already lined with waves of purple thrift. The smiling, weathered face peered out from under the straw Panama.

"Why, I thank you for your kind words, Carole. Gardens are like people, you know. When you love them, they most often love you back."

Carole smiled. "Is that what you feed your roses, Miss Constance? Love?"

"Oh, yes," the old lady returned. "In large, daily doses."

Their attention was drawn for a moment by the sound of an approaching vehicle, and when Carole glanced over her shoulder, she recognized Kathleen's red convertible Mercedes. She ought to recognize it. There was one just like it in the garage at her townhouse.

The familiar, sour taste gurgled up her throat and into her mouth as she peered into the cab of the car and made out the dark shape of Kathleen's head. And then she saw Kathleen do the oddest thing. Pulling to a stop, she leaned forward until she could catch Carole's eye.

It was a sort of silent invitation to step over, but naturally, Carole didn't make a move to join Kathleen. Their stiff, estranged relationship was too long instilled for that. From across the curbside, she eyed her stepmother warily. A few seconds passed, and it seemed that Kathleen was about to speak. But she apparently changed her mind, pulling the Mercedes back out into the street and roaringup Tradd Street. Curiously, Carole watched the receding red convertible until it slowed and turned into the drive to the Gossett home further along down Tradd.

"Now, there's a sad young woman for you," Constance offered.

Carole's head snapped round, and forgetting her manners, she demanded, "Why do you say that?"

"You moved away two years ago, Carole. Just after your father married Kathleen. I don't think you ever really got to know her. Of course, I can't claim to *really* know her myself—Aurora won't hear of inviting her to the house. But I've talked with Kathleen often enough. She used to take a walk every day, and oftentimes, if I was out here in the yard, she'd stop by the gate for a moment."

The elderly, but still-bright hazel eyes of Constance Trippley fastened on the young blond woman. "I'm sure I've no need to tell you that your father is a strong man, Carole . . . that he can be rather overwhelming at times."

Carole's expression turned solemn. "Overwhelming is the perfect word."

"Well, surely my dear, you don't think that James is that way only with his daughters. I've seen him and Kathleen at a few benefits and social functions. It's clear that he admires her and enjoys showing her off. It's also quite clear that she stands in complete awe of him . . . perhaps even fear."

"Fear?" Carole repeated, surprised at the old lady's perception of a feeling she thought she alone harbored for James Gossett.

Constance nodded, smoothing the dirt from the

knees of her saggy britches. "I'm not a gossip, Carole."

And Carole knew it to be true. It was Aurora who claimed that distinction.

"I've brought up this subject for a reason," Constance went on. "There were times when you were a child that I spotted the same reaction to James in you. Now you're all grown up. But perhaps not so grown that you can't remember how tormenting those fearful feelings could be. I know that you and your stepmother have never been friends, but I have the feeling she needs one . . . one who can truly understand what she's going through."

Carole sniffed. "I think the main thing she's going through is Daddy's money."

"Carole!" the old lady said scoldingly. "There's nothing wrong with living a luxurious life when you can afford to. You know that. Kathleen shouldn't be taken to task because of your father's money . . . ," Constance paused, knowing she trod on thin ice. "Or because of your mother."

Carole's blue-green eyes snapped warningly, but as she looked into the kindly face, something within her softened. Still, she regarded her elderly companion piercingly.

"Kathleen has nothing whatever to do with my mother, Miss Constance."

"I agree," Constance responded. "That's exactly what I've just said. Marion made her own painful decision many years ago. Kathleen is in no way responsible for the fact that your mother is gone, and I'm certain you're too fair a person to blame her."

The old ache had leapt to Carole's heart, the one that always accompanied thoughts of her mother. As she stared wordlessly at Constance Trippley, Carole recognized the truth in the old lady's gentle accusation. Carole *had* blamed Kathleen, had reviled her as a usurper ever since James Gossett started courting her.

Constance took in the pained expression that had climbed over the young woman's pretty face. And when she next spoke, her voice was tender.

"Ever since you were a baby, I've liked you, Carole. You, your sister . . . your mother, too. I used to flatter myself that I understood Marion. Now don't get in a huff, but sometimes she talked in a way that reminds me of your father's current wife. Kind of quiet and . . . yes, afraid. Sometimes when I look at Kathleen, it saddens me. So young she is; yet those dark eyes of hers can look so old and beaten. As I said, she could use a good friend. Maybe you could, too."

Carole searched the wrinkled face, found only good intentions and a certain look of ancient wisdom. "You're very astute, Miss Constance," she finally admitted.

"Ah, well," the old lady laughed. "When you spend all your time with flowers, you have a lot of time to think."

Constance Trippley went back to her puttering, but as Carole strolled away, the old lady's words were ringing in her mind. Miss Constance was right; she'd never given Kathleen a chance. And suddenly she remembered a number of occasions just after the marriage, when Kathleen had tried to be friendly and Carole had brushed her off.

As she passed the massive Gossett house, Carole glanced up at the French doors of the master bedroom. Perhaps it had something to do with her new, independent frame of mind. For instead of the remembered image of her mother on the balcony outside those doors, she imagined the dark-eyed face of Kathleen.

By the time Carole reached Rutledge Avenue, however, her thoughts had returned to Jack Levy and the unfinished sketches that lay on her drawing table. It had been good to get out of the apartment. She'd gotten a little exercise, a little sun. Still, the inspiration she'd sought had not materialized. As she neared the townhouse, she was wondering if she should simply send what she had to Jack Levy at Haut Nouveau. Maybe it would be best to get something to the man, even if the collection wasn't complete.

She saw the familiar white BMW before she noticed the two men leaning against the courtyard gate. Curt, at least, was leaning. R.J. was pacing like a caged cat.

R.J. Carole's heart began to pound, her steps to slow, as memories burst like fireworks in her mind: the deep blue-gray eyes, the blazing kiss, the white, teasing smile. *Know anyone interested in a truckload of T-shirts?* he had asked. She could almost hear his suave, drawling voice.

Then Curt spotted her. His frame straightened from the gate, and she could make out his face — so open, so hopeful. Without a thought, she brought forth a happy smile from some hidden well, and he took a few steps to meet her, arms outstretched, as R.J. came to a sudden halt in the background.

With the best of intentions, she allowed Curt to enfold her against his softly knit Lacoste shirt. He was so attractive, so bright and promising. She made herself recall all his good points and knew that she was truly, genuinely fond of Curt. At another time in her life, she could perhaps have loved him. But, as if they had a will of their own, her hooded eyes looked around Curt's shoulder to R.J.

"It feels damned good to hold you, doll," Curt whispered as Carole surreptitiously perused the taller figure of his brother.

As before, her willful, pulse-racing response to the blonder, taller man startled her—then irritated her.

"I've been worried about you," Curt went on, pulling away just enough to gaze down into her eyes. "Let me have a look at you." His face took on

90

a concerned look. "Have you been sick?" he asked finally.

Carole chuckled lightheartedly. "Flattery will get you everywhere, Curt."

"You know I think you're a knockout anytime, Carole," he admonished. "But you look different . . . pale."

"Just haven't had much time to spend on things like suntans and makeup," she explained. Then, nodding in R.J.'s direction, she commented, "I see you've brought your brother."

"Yeah," Curt grinned. "He seems to be showing up in Charleston every time I turn around these days."

The only acceptable, hospitable thing to do was invite them up. "Would y'all like to come in for a cool drink?" she asked. At last, her eyes turned openly to R.J., where he stood so solidly several yards away.

"I've got some beer," she added. "And a little . . ."

Her words died away as she took note of it—the sort of shirt-jacket with upturned collar that R.J. was wearing. It looked to be made of fine, cream-colored linen; it was lightweight, but elegant. The same was true of the styling, which was reminiscent of safari wear. Her eyes lingered on the garment, but what she was seeing was a bare-shouldered evening gown with a crisp collar, belted at the waist and extending to the ankle in straight lines.

R.J. was instantly aware that her attention had fixed on him. He just didn't know why. As if in a daze, Carole left Curt behind and meandered in his direction, looking him over intently as if he were some odd, fascinating specimen.

She stopped just before him, and he couldn't prevent his eyes from devouring the sight of her, roving over the jeans and sweater molding to her shapely body, the fine, blond hair falling unhindered to her

91

shoulders, the heart-shaped face. This was how he'd pictured her, natural and unadorned, as if she'd just stepped out of the shower. A powerful heat rushed to his loins, and R.J. shifted his weight uncomfortably as he recalled that Curt looked on.

"Hello, Carole," he offered.

"R.J.," she acknowledged succinctly. She was circling him, looking him over at close range from head to toe.

R.J. glanced at his brother to find him looking puzzled—and then somewhat alarmed. Quickly, Curt crossed the short distance to join his intended and interrupt her quiet study of his brother.

"Carole has invited us up for a drink," Curt said, drilling R.J. with an imploring look. "What do you say?"

Over Carole's head, R.J.'s dark eyes met Curt's pale ones. He should leave, he should get the hell away from the girl. But as her blue-green gaze fastened on him, he found himself acquiescing, covering his conflicting emotions with a show of bravado.

"Sure, why not?" he said, his expression teasing as he glanced to Curt, then looked down again at Carole. "After all, it seems your girl friend can't take her eyes off me."

Curt's face reddened as one of Carole's brows shot up.

"Gee, Curt," she said in a syrupy tone. "I hope your brother's tender ego can take it when I tell him it's his shirt, and *not him*, that has captured my interest."

"His shirt!" Curt repeated with a bewildered look.

R.J. only smiled one of his bedazzling smiles and grasped comically at his chest, as if her barb had pierced him through.

"I'll explain later," she said to Curt and, with a sweet smile, linked her arm in his. "For now, why don't we go upstairs and get something to drink? I must admit I've walked up quite a thirst. You know, Curt, I almost called you this morning"

"I wish you had," he replied eagerly.

"Well, I just needed a break. Thought I'd take a walk . . ."

And away they went, leaving R.J. to follow in their trail, feeling like the proverbial third wheel and knowing instinctively that that was exactly what Carole had intended.

Carole stepped into her apartment and gasped. She'd forgotten what a mess the place was. Normally, she kept it reasonably tidy. But today . . . Wadded up sketches littered the floor, forgotten coffee cups crowded the Queen Anne sideboard, discarded clothing was draped across the back of the velveteen loveseat, and the whole of the room was scattered with colorful fabric samples.

"Nice place, Carole," R.J. drawled, offering her an insulting grin. "Do you have a maid come in?"

"Oh no" she replied huffily. "I did it all for you, R.J. Just on the hope you might drop by."

"I knew you two would get along," Curt supplied with unknowing good humor as Carole flew around the living room, filling her arms with extraneous belongings she quickly dumped in the bedroom. Closing the bedroom door firmly behind her, she regarded her guests brightly.

"Now, what would you two like to drink?"

When she returned from the kitchen with a beer for each of them, Curt had meandered to her makeshift work area. As she handed him the bottle, he looked at her with a somewhat dubious expression.

"So *this* is the infamous workplace?"

"This is it," she confirmed, crossing the room to where R.J. was standing by the French doors, looking out across the patio.

"Here you go, R.J.," she said, extending the beer.

"Thank you, ma'am." He couldn't stop himself from shooting a private, heart-stopping look.

Carole whirled uneasily back in Curt's direction. "So . . . what have you been up to?" she asked conversationally.

Curt turned slowly away from the drawing table. His attractive face had gone serious—his mood, sour—as he studied the table and saw bits and pieces of what Carole had been working on. Concealed, professional-looking drawings peeked out from under a sketch pad. And the longer he had looked at them, the more threatened he had felt.

"Not much," he muttered. "More importantly, what have you been up to? How's the work going?"

"Slow," Carole admitted. "I came up against a brick wall a few days ago." She turned a bright look toward R.J. as he mosied over to join them. "That's why I was so glad to see your brother's shirt. I think it's given me an idea that will allow me to finish up the collection."

"Glad to be of service, Madame Designer," R.J. said with a mock bow.

"I knew you were *bound* to come in handy for something." she responded, a grin taking the bite out of her words.

R.J. would have liked to win a round, but Carole matched him quip for quip. She was damned quick, and he was in a state of wonderment, remembering Curt's comment that she was "not too smart." He propped an arm on the back of the drawing table chair and asked, "So . . . what exactly *is* this brainstorm my shirt has triggered?" His eyes swept uncontrollably down and up her body, noting that Carole was actually blushing—whether to his question or his heated look, he wasn't sure.

"Do you really want to know?" she asked shyly.

"Sure," R.J. replied with a half-turn so he could glance at his brother. "Don't we, Curt?"

"Sure," Curt repeated in a cutting tone.

But R.J. missed it, so enthralled was he by the look of childlike pride that climbed to Carole's face.

"When I met Mr. Levy at the festival, I told him I was working on some new things," she began, pulling forth a selection of sketches that had been hidden in a stack on the artist's table. "But it was a lie. I've done these in just the past three weeks." She began pointing at the designs. "As you see, all the designs . . . sportswear, swim wear, everything . . . reflect the safari look. But the thing that had me stymied was evening wear."

The vivid eyes settled on R.J. "But when I saw your shirt, I got this sudden image of a tailored, ivory gown with a high collar. I think I can come up with several variations that will round out the collection."

R.J. perused the drawings with surprise. The girl had talent. He emitted a low, quiet whistle. "Well, I'll be the first to admit I don't know anything about fashion design," he said, with a look toward his brother. "But these look damned good to me. Don't you agree, Curt?"

That was when he realized Curt's temper was brewing. Whenever Curt was mad, or scared, his face went bright with color. And at the moment, it was red as a beet.

"They look fine," Curt said, his eyes locked on Carole. "What happens now?"

One look at Curt told Carole he was angry. Resignedly, she began to stack the work away, out of his sight.

"Now I finish and send the drawings to New York."

"And then?" Curt pressed.

"And then I wait to hear from Jack Levy."

"And then?"

She whirled to Curt with a frustrated look. "And then? I don't know what happens then. I guess I hope they'll accept my work and want to buy it."

R.J. saw the quarrel about to erupt and—though

he damned himself for playing peacemaker between *any* man and Carole Gossett—he broke in.

"I think you've got a good shot at New York, Carole. I wish you the best." Trying to get his brother's attention, he raised his brows warningly. "Any fool could see this means a lot to you. Isn't that right, brother?"

But Curt's vision was clouded. All he could see was his future boarding a plane to New York. "Apparently, it means more to her than anything," he choked. "Carole, we've got to talk."

She sighed tiredly, feeling as if she were on a see-saw—flying up with every kind word from R.J. plummeting with each dark look from Curt.

"About what?" she said.

"About us," Curt returned.

"Okay, we can talk . . . as soon as I get this work out of the way."

"What do I need to do?" he sneered. "Make an appointment? You know, Carole, I've been planning to ask you to marry me. But seeing how your work schedule is so tight, maybe I should just drop the diamond in the mail!"

"Look, Curt—," R.J. attempted, but Carole cut him off.

"I don't deserve this, Curt," she stated flatly. "I don't have to make excuses to you or anyone for trying to make something of myself."

"You already are something!" Curt exploded. "Or at least you were . . . something beautiful and charming and soft. But these days, I don't know what you are!"

"Now is not the time to discuss this, Curt," she warned, with a glance in R.J.'s direction.

"Well, when the hell *is* the time?"

Her eyes ignited and were burning with blue-green fire by the time she swept them from R.J. to his brother. "When I say," she managed in a deadly, quiet voice.

Curt was speechless with fury. It was obvious he didn't expect her to stand up to him.

"Fine!" he sputtered finally. "Just don't expect me to be waiting around like some lackey by the phone." And then he spun on his heel, his athletic legs carrying him swiftly across the room.

"Coming, brother?" he added without turning. And a second later, the door slammed behind him.

R.J. thought he'd never been so uncomfortable in his life. A cacophony of emotions were sounding off in his head. He was both irritated by and sorry for his brother. He was proud of Carole, he wanted Carole. . . . He must keep his distance from Carole.

"Well," he muttered, grinning in an attempt at lightheartedness. "That's my little brother."

"Little is right," Carole replied, her temper still bristling. "And chauvanistic. I mean, pardon me, but women have actually had the freedom to pursue their own careers for quite some time now!"

"Come on, Carole," R.J. urged, taking her by the shoulders and turning her to face him. "I'll admit Curt is not exactly a liberated male, but he's a good guy."

R.J.'s voice dropped off as he sank into the warming depths of her eyes. How long the silent, charged look raged between them, he didn't know. But suddenly, he realized the hands that still held her shoulders were pulling her closer.

"Hell, if I were in his shoes, I might be acting the same way," he murmured.

"I doubt that," Carole returned huskily. "As I remember, you said some pretty nice things about my work. You seem fairly liberated to me."

The inexplicable magnetism was drawing her like never before—mentally, spiritually, physically. Now, as she stared up into R.J.'s dark-lashed eyes, her breasts strained against the thin sweater, her nipples tightening as they brushed against his chest.

R.J. lowered his head another notch, and they

were nearly nose to nose. "Not so liberated. Like right now . . . I can see merit in the old saying about a woman's place being in the home. Right now, that's where I see *you*. In the home . . . In one particular room of the home . . ."

His eyes were nearly closed, his voice barely audible. R.J. lifted her chin with his finger, and then his mouth was on hers. The remembered taste of him burst across her palate. His arms went around her, a hand sliding to her hip, and Carole went limp. It was as though her body had never before known the touch of a man—so new and quivering was the feeling.

R.J. hardened so quickly his knees went weak. His hands roved along her back to the hips, then up the sides until they encountered the swell of her breasts. Somewhere in the back of his head, a voice began whispering a name. And suddenly the voice barreled to the forefront of his mind, ending in a shriek that left his ears ringing.

Curt! R.J. released Carole abruptly, stumbling back a few steps.

What kind of power did the vixen possess that she could make him forget so quickly that she belonged to Curt? Make him forget that to touch her, to covet her, was a vile betrayal of the values he was raised on, the code of honor which bound him to his brother in a thousand ways?

R.J. was staring at her with shock as she opened her eyes to regard him dazedly.

"Curt's outside waiting," he mumbled, slowly recovering his wits.

At that moment he almost resented Carole as she stood there breathlessly, making him want to take her. He searched his mind and found no graceful way out of the situation. Yet, the callousness of the escape that sprang from his addled brain surprised even him.

"Curt hasn't lost his touch," he commented. "He always *did* have good taste in women."

R. J. slouched to one leg, feigned an arrogant grin. Now that he'd begun the charade, there was no turning back.

"Guess I haven't lost mine, either," he added boastfully. "I can still manage to steal them away from him."

Carole's warmly roiling insides seemed to congeal as she backed away in horror. He had fooled her completely! She, the ultimate coquette, had been swept away so suddenly she hadn't stopped to consider that this man might not be feeling the same mindless explosion as she. Apparently, the earth-shattering kiss they'd just shared was nothing more than a macho proving ground for R.J. Morrisson.

"Get out," she hissed.

And as he took in her blazing look of fury, R.J. felt something within him die. He didn't move.

"Get out, I said!" And in her trembling desperation, Carole began to scan her surroundings for something to throw at him.

There was no outward show of the regret that enshrouded him as R.J. made for the doorway.

"Yes ma'am!" he tossed over his shoulder. And as the door closed behind him, he heard something splatter against the other side.

R.J.'s eyes closed as he leaned briefly against the solid-oak panel, pulling himself together for a moment before hurrying down to the street and climbing into the car.

"What took you so damned long?" Curt fired.

"I was trying to smooth over the damage you'd done!" R.J. lied.

Curt snorted as as the BMW careened around the corner onto Broad Street. "There's no smoothing it over!" he spat, slamming his palm against the steering wheel. "Damn it, R.J., I *care* for this woman! Why else would I come back to her time after time when she turns me away? But I'll be damned if I know how to reach her anymore. Carole has changed. All she's got on her mind is that design stuff. And New York. She couldn't care less about becoming my wife. Did you see the way she looked at me? She hates my guts!"

R.J.'s already grim expression turned thunderous. "If it's any consolation," he muttered. "She hates mine, too."

It was a mild June night. Streetlamps blinked on throughout the Historic District as folks turned out to enjoy the scented breezes that were uniquely Charleston.

On such a night it was easy to think of the city as timeless. But for the modern habiliments of the couple strolling the Battery, they could have been two antebellum lovers out on the pretense of viewing the distant towers of Fort Sumter, or even two rebels, swearing their love despite the British ships that threatened on the horizon. There was a vintage aura about the place—not just in the carefully preserved buildings and gardens, but in the spirit of generations who had fought and loved, lived and died, all in the arms of Charleston.

And this June night was no different from those hundreds of years before. People laughed and cried, rejoiced and sorrowed. . . .

In room number seven of a discreet coastal motel, Kathleen moaned with ecstasy in the arms of her young lover. . . .

In the jazz district, Camille delivered a gutsy performance that brought her black audience to its feet with crashing applause. . . .

In the townhouse at Broad and Rutledge, Carole swiped angrily at nagging tears and attacked her vision of an evening gown with vengeful determination. . . .

And in a succession of dingy bars, the Morrisson brothers tied one on that the waterfront crowd would not soon forget.

A gibbous moon brushed the streets with silver as, across the city, people went on with their lives, adding yet another chapter to the ongoing saga of Charleston.

PART II

Chapter Five

JONAH STUCKEY WAS sitting motionless on the floor—a rather pudgy, brown lump in a white institutional gown. At the sight of him, Cecile gasped, a hand flying to her mouth, tears starting to her eyes. But then she brought herself under control, and when she knelt beside the man, her voice was steady, unwavering.

"Hello, Jonah. My, but I'm glad to see you. Look! I've brought you the biggest, shiniest red apple in all of Charleston."

R.J. had been glancing about the room, taking in its sterile appointments of bed, chair, wash basin . . . and an unused set of elementary building blocks in the corner. Now he turned his full attention to Jonah. The man was more than fifty years old, R.J. knew, but the face that turned up to Cecile was the sad, confused one of a child.

"Miss Cecile?" came a thick whisper.

"Yes, honey. It's me."

"Miss Cecile!" And then the boy-man threw himself into the woman's waiting arms.

"No trees," he whimpered. "No friends." He dissolved into tears, adding, "Take Jonah home. Take Jonah home now!"

Behind Cecile, R.J.'s hands fidgeted within the pockets of his finely creased trousers. Jonah Stuckey was sobbing freely now, as Cecile cradled him like a baby, rocking back and forth on the floor and murmuring soothingly.

Something wrenched in R.J.'s gut. How long had things like this been going on? The poor and defenseless being crushed under the heel of the uncaring, indomitable giant that everyone politely referred to as, ''the system''?

And yet he knew the answer. Such things had been going on as long as there had been the powerful and the weak, the victor and the victim. As long as man had walked the earth.

Jonah's sobbing had calmed, but steady tears continued to roll from between his tightly shut eyes, streaming down his unlined, ageless face.

R.J. watched the pitiful sight until he could do so no longer; then he stepped out into the hallway, the institutional door closing behind him in a soft whoosh. There would be no interrogation of Jonah Stuckey today. The man was in bad enough shape as it was. R.J. rubbed at his eyes, where the dull ache of a hangover had lingered all day. But it did no good. The scene he'd just witnessed, emblazoned on his brain, could not be erased.

The stabbing pang of pity bloomed suddenly into anger. Nothing's ever going to change unless somebody starts somewhere, he thought vehemently. And R.J.'s face took on a look of determination as—like a knight of old—he mentally took up a gauntlet.

Thoughtfully, he meandered along the hospital corridor, past the efficient looking matrons at the nurses' station. There was no doubt the facility was well managed, but it was a medical institution. And from what R.J. knew of Jonah Stuckey, the man didn't need medical treatment, or confinement. And besides, why had he been sent so far away—an hour and a half's drive—when there were several reputable institutions in Charleston?

Unless . . . unless someone was trying to get him out of the way?

R.J. was beginning to sense a method behind the circumstances surrounding Jonah Stuckey. Recalling Cecile's suspicions, he wondered if there really *were* some unknown force at work.

He came to the end of the corridor, turned, and walked slowly back in the direction of Jonah's room. The first thing to determine was who would benefit most by the placing of Jonah Stuckey in a distant institution. The mysterious guardian from Savannah? The relative Cecile disclaimed?

There was only one way to find out: the county records. If Louise Stuckey died intestate, the county clerk would have conducted an incompetency proceeding regarding Jonah, and then a guardianship proceeding. The first step in unraveling the mystery—if, in fact, there *was* a mystery—was the examination of those documents.

It would be easy enough to do. In fact, R.J. even had a contact in the county offices. The clerk of county, Dan Shriver, was a long-standing friend of his father. But it had to be done on a weekday, during business hours, and R.J. was due in state supreme court in Columbia the next morning.

By the time Cecile came out of Jonah's room, he had decided to call Dan from Columbia and ask him to send transcript copies of both proceedings involving Jonah Stuckey. It was a small enough favor, considering all the backing the Morrisson family had given Shriver during his election campaign.

On the lengthy drive back to Charleston, Cecile talked only of Jonah. His mother had brought him to church every Sunday, Cecile told him. He was the kindest, most gentle soul on earth, and he had a legendary way with wild animals and birds.

''That's what he meant in there when he said,

'no friends,' " Cecile explained. "He's been taking care of the animals around Belmont Pines for years. They're his best friends, especially now that his mama is gone. Louise would *never* have stood for him ending up in a place like that hospital. I don't care *how* fancy it is! She must be turning in her grave."

R.J. glanced at her. Cecile was a strong woman. She was looking calmly ahead, but the rigid set of her features hinted at her inner turmoil and despair. "I've never seen Jonah look so lost," she finally said. "He'll die in there."

The image of the helpless man flared across R.J.'s memory.

"Not if I can help it," he returned firmly, and the two of them sank into their own silent thoughts as the silver Corvette sped neatly through the pastoral, South Carolina low country.

It was dusk when R.J. dropped Cecile off at her house on Juniper Street. His luggage was already in the trunk. After lunch, he'd bidden farewell to his family, letting them assume he was on his way back to Columbia. He was puzzled by his inclination to keep the Stuckey matter private, but R.J. had long ago stopped going against his instincts. It seemed that whenever he did, he was sorry in the long run.

Now, he should simply hit the road. He had to be in court bright and early the next morning. Yet he wasn't really surprised when he found himself cruising through the District, pulling up beside the fashionable townhouse at Broad and Rutledge.

Lights were glowing warmly in the penthouse suite, and as he watched, he saw a shadow pass by the window in the front room he remembered as the kitchen. It was Carole, and at the mere sight of her silhouette, R.J. felt the blood begin to pound at his hangover-ridden temples.

It had been a long time since he and Curt had gotten drunk together. But last night had been a justifiable occasion—although just how justifiable on R.J.'s part, Curt hadn't a clue.

In the midst of his slurred ravings, his younger brother had divulged much about his current life and aspirations. Success at "G.E.," as Curt had called it, was about to enable him to buy a house. He had been eyeing a beachfront resort home on the Isle of Palms, and when he'd mentioned the price tag, R.J. had turned to him in disbelief. Where the hell did Curt expect to get *that* kind of money?

And then, of course, there was Carole. She would be the sparkling gem in the setting of Curt's ritzy life. Although right now Curt was mad as hell about her sudden preoccupation with a career—so mad that he'd begun taking his sexual release with an old flame, Laura Murphy. Hell, Curt had even gone off to Laura's place late last night. Though how he expected to perform when we got there, R.J. had no idea!

It was Carole who had driven them both to drink. *Guess I haven't lost my touch*, he had bragged disgustingly to her. *I can still manage to steal Curt's women.*

The memory knocked relentlessly about in R.J.'s mind. In the dark privacy of his car, he rubbed his fingers across his forehead as if to ease the pain.

Carole must think he was a perfect ass, he thought. And suddenly the drive to set her straight became overwhelming. Climbing out of the Corvette, R.J. took long, purposeful strides across the walk, through the courtyard, and up the brick stairs leading to her apartment.

He paused on the stoop, his hand halfway to the brass knocker. What would he say? That he was sorry? That he hadn't meant what he'd said? Couldn't she understand that he was in a difficult position because of Curt?

Standing there, outside Carole's door, the thought of his brother was a sobering slap across the face. Laura Murphy or no Laura Murphy, it was Carole Gossett who possessed Curt's heart. And R.J.

knew it. So, what the hell was he doing standing outside her door, hoping, like some lovesick schoolboy, to make amends?

With a snort, he turned and hurried back down to the silver car. Starting up the purring engine, he took a last look at the bright townhouse windows, imagined the woman who dwelled behind them, remembered the last time he'd seen her face and the look of bitter fury it was wearing.

Shifting into gear, R.J. laid rubber several yards down Rutledge. It's better this way, he assured himself. Yet the thought did nothing to quell his reluctance to leave Carole—and Charleston—behind.

Even if R.J. hadn't been preoccupied, he wouldn't have noticed the stealthy figure that lingered in the alleyway across from the brick townhouse. Joey Horton was too good at what he did to be noticed.

But now, in the safe, dark solitude of the empty street, Horton lit a cigarette, the glow of the match briefly illuminating his twisted smile. Reaching inside his breast pocket, he retrieved the ever-present pad and pen, leaned swiftly beyond the shadow line of the streetlamp, and made note of the Corvette's South Carolina license-plate number.

The late June afternoon was unseasonably hot, and the air-conditioning in the plush new office was faulty. Irritably, Curt drew a finger around the inside of his collar, hoping to loosen it from his chafed throat. He never liked Mondays anyway, and today was worse than usual as he'd had to pay the lingering, aching price for his debauchery of Saturday night.

He glanced at his watch and, seeing that it was after three, he began to toy with the idea of skipping out early. But at that precise moment, James popped his head through the half-open door of the office.

"So, how do you like your new digs?" his boss asked with a satisfied glance at the rich furnishings decorating the office. The place had the sedate, expensive look befitting his corporation's newest vice-president, James reflected, however young he might be.

"Very nice," Curt replied with a grin. "If they can ever get the air-conditioning to work."

"I'm sure that will be taken care of." James shrugged and, strolling to the oak desk, took a seat in one of the overstuffed chairs before it. "Seen Carole lately?" he asked with feigned casualness.

Heat raced to Curt's face. "I saw her Saturday, over at her place."

"How is she?"

"Fine!" Curt exclaimed angrily. "Just fine. If you call locking herself up in that apartment and becoming obsessed by those damned designs 'fine'! "

Leaping from his leather chair, Curt stalked around the desk. Silently, James studied the young man as he brought himself under control, stuffed his hands in his pockets, and slumped his weight onto the desktop. James's face betrayed nothing, but within he was overjoyed. The boy was more besotted with Carole than he'd realized.

Curt's expression was pained as he confided, "I don't know what to do. I think I'm losing her."

James's black eyes were sparkling. "We'll see about that," he said quietly. "Right now, I want to make you aware of a little acquisition I pulled off last week."

A warning sounded in Curt's mind. "What kind of acquisition?"

"Gossett Enterprises just purchased controlling interest in a New York fashion house by the name of Haut Nouveau."

Red color flooded Curt's face all the way to the tips of his ears. As vice-president of investments, *he* should be calling the shots on something like this. And besides, he liked to keep Gossett's vast finances as much as possible in the Charleston area. Bring the profits *into* the area, not dole them out!

First, Carole. Now, this encroachment on his authority. Suddenly, Curt wondered if the two were connected. He eyed James Gossett suspiciously, then drew from the well of Morrisson standing that put him on equal terms with *anybody*, including his boss.

"I really wish you had consulted with me on this, James," he said evenly.

Gossett waved away his objection as one would shoo a pesky fly. "Shall I tell you why Haut Nouveau is a good investment, Curt? A very good investment, indeed?"

As his boss continued, Curt's expression changed from stony anger to enlightened surprise.

"It's just a passing fancy," James was saying. "Carole has been like this all her life. One time it was horses; another time, dancing lessons. She grows tired of all her little hobbies after a while. Still, I think it's best to nip this thing in the bud."

Curt regarded his boss with mounting relief. Granted, the whole thing was underhanded, and he was sure Carole would be disappointed. But she would get over it. And—best of all—he'd have her back! As he sat there looking into James Gossett's black eyes, Curt vowed that he'd make it up to Carole. He'd make her so happy she'd forget all about a career, and anything else that would take her away from the luxurious life he intended to give her.

"Now that I think of it," Curt said ultimately, his pale eyes twinkling, "being on top of the fashion industry could prove *very* rewarding." His old charm had returned. "Guess that's why you're the boss . . . *boss*."

James grinned in a comradely way that suggested, Don't worry, boy. As long as I'm around, you don't need to worry about a thing.

Gossett came to his feet. "Guess I'll let you get back to work." He was almost out the door when he stuck his head back in. "By the way, what would your brother be wanting with Carole?"

"My brother?" Curt repeated.

"Yeah. He was in town this weekend, right?"

"Right."

"Well, it seems he stopped by Carole's place last night."

"He went to Carole's?" Curt questioned in confusion. "How do you know?"

James's grin was sardonic. "I have my ways," he said cryptically and, flinging up a hand in farewell, he was gone.

R.J. went to Carole's? Last night?

Curt meandered to one of the front windows that looked across the quaint rooftops of Old Charleston. The bulk of Gossett Enterprises was located in an industrial section off the interstate highway, but corporate headquarters were housed in the downtown business area that offered the inspiring views of wrought-iron-trimmed buildings, palms, and beyond them, the dark blue waters of Charleston Harbor.

Curt gazed out to sea, scarcely taking in the post-cardlike beauty of colorful sailboats against the deep blue water and sky.

But R.J. left for Columbia yesterday afternoon, Curt reflected. Surely James was mistaken. But as soon as the thought was born, Curt dismissed it. James Gossett didn't make mistakes.

R.J. . . . at Carole's? For a moment, Curt's expression relaxed into one of trust, as he thought, oh well, there must be an explanation. Maybe he went over there to try and patch things up for me.

But he said he was leaving town just after lunch.

And at the back of Curt Morrisson's mind, a spark of jealous suspicion flickered into being.

It was nearly a hundred degrees in Columbia. R.J. had doffed his jacket and loosened his tie, but still he was perspiring profusely as he raced down the courthouse steps and hopped into his car.

113

Checking his watch as he drove toward the apartment, he confirmed that it was nearly four o'clock. He'd meant to call Dan Shriver earlier in the day, but he simply hadn't had the opportunity.

The supreme court had lingered and dawdled, and R.J. had found himself becoming exasperated as the day wore on. The distinguished counselors and judges were so damned caught up with legal language, it would take them a month before they could even agree on how the defendant should be charged! And through all the impersonal harangues, R.J. had squirmed in his seat on the bench, trying to clear his mind of the image of a black man sitting hopelessly on a hospital floor.

It was an odd feeling. R.J. had always found the elevated talk of the supreme court interesting. Today, it had seemed like so much hot air.

By the time he got home and called Charleston information for the number, he was afraid Dan Shriver might already have left for the day. But then, after he was kept holding for a moment, the familiar voice came on the line.

"R.J.! Glad to hear from you, my boy. How long has it been? Two or three years?"

"It's been a while," R.J. returned. "How are you, Dan?"

"Can't complain. But your dad says you're up in Columbia these days. Going big time at the supreme court, huh?"

"I can't exactly claim to be big time," R.J. said with a chuckle.

"Not to hear your mom and dad tell it. They're mighty proud of you, son. And, of course, it's always nice for the rest of us to hear about a hometown boy making good at the capital. . . . Well, tell me. What can I do for you?"

"I'm looking into a case for a friend, Dan, and I

114

was hoping you could help me with some information."

"Sure. You know I'll help if I can, R.J."

"I'd like you to send me a couple of transcripts if it's not too much trouble."

"County transcripts?"

"Incompetency and guardianship proceedings." There was a silence at the end of the wire.

"Dan? Are you there?"

Dan Shriver cleared his throat nervously. "Yeah . . . yeah. I'm here. Sorry. Somebody just stepped in for a minute. Now, what was that? Incompetency and guardianship? Who for?"

"An old man named Jonah Stuckey."

Dan hesitated as if in deep thought. "Stuckey? Sorry, R.J. That name doesn't sound familiar."

"Well, I'm sure the proceedings must have occurred. Not more than a few weeks ago . . . maybe a month."

Dan's voice took on an uneasy edge. "I don't handle everything personally, you know, R.J. I can't keep up with every case."

One of R.J.'s brows shot up. "They must have come through you, Dan," he reasoned, "even if you don't handle all the groundwork. As clerk of county, you're bound to authorize incompetency and guardianship petitions."

"Sure . . . sure," Dan said hurriedly. "You're right, R.J. Just give me a chance to look into it, okay?"

"Fine, Dan. And then send me a copy of the transcripts, if you would. Here's the address. . . ."

Hanging up the phone, R.J. stared vacantly across his living room. His sixth sense was working overtime. He could have sworn that Dan had become uncooperative at the mention of Jonah Stuckey.

* * *

In the office of Clerk of County, Charleston County, Dan Shriver mopped a handkerchief across his broad, perspiring brow. He had gained weight, and his blood pressure was high, flooding his face with an unhealthy, red glow. Beneath the thick, carefully styled silver hair, his scalp prickled at the thought of what he must do.

Ah well, he thought. Putting it off will only make it worse. And reaching for the phone, he dialed the private number of the president of Ashley River Shipping.

Robert Morrisson stood at the wall of windows overlooking the river. The waterline was down. They needed rain. But it would come. At the end of summer, it would come like always, drenching the dried up peninsula and flooding the creeks and gulleys. The swirling waters of the Ashley would turn as red as Georgia clay.

He went back to his paper work. There was so much of it these days. His ancestors would be astounded! When Charles Morrisson, one of Charleston's original shipping magnates, founded Ashley River Shipping in the 1700s, he'd had no idea that over the centuries it would grow into one of the most substantial corporations in the city—indeed, in the Carolinas.

There was so much more to it now than just shipping. Robert permitted himself a satisfied smile. He himself was responsible for a great deal of that success.

Over the past two decades, during his reign as president of Ashley River Shipping, the Charleston area had experienced a commercial boom. And Robert had taken careful advantage of it. Corporation holdings had swelled to encompass packaging and trucking companies, printing and publishing houses, and of course, vast parcels of real estate.

Still, Robert wanted more. And though the opportunities in Charleston had multiplied, so had the competition. His distinguished face took on a disdainful mien.

Investors and entrepreneurs from all over the country were seeking fortunes in Charleston. In Robert's eye, they were no different from the crude, Yankee carpetbaggers who'd poured into the city after the War Between the States—greedy outsiders deserving no part of the Charleston treasures which had been guarded, fought for, and handed down through aristocratic families like the Morrissons.

Take Gossett, for example. Why, his granddaddy had been nothing more than a bootlegger, a 1920s carpetbagger who had taken advantage of a fine old family's hard times. Robert's grandfather had told him the story of how Lyle Gossett had snatched the Tarletons' home right out from under them, and then set up house there on Tradd Street.

And now, look at James Gossett. He'd become one of the city's wealthiest and most powerful men—the grandson of a bootlegger!

Robert's heated expression melted into one of cool satisfaction. At first, he'd been against Curt's going to work at Gossett Enterprises. But then he'd thought about it. Let Curt go. Let him infiltrate that infuriatingly successful man's organization. And then the daughter had come into the picture, and Curt had methodically worked his way up to the position of James Gossett's right-hand man.

Gradually, Robert had even come to approve Curt's talk of marrying Carole. She was a pretty little thing. And besides, how better to drain a little of the ill-earned Gossett fortune back to where it belonged?

Robert's thoughts lingered fondly on his younger son. Curt had surprised him. The once carefree boy had become a businessman with an instinctive, sharp eye for opportunity. *He* had come up with this idea; *he* had parlayed a bit of inside information into a land deal that would net them millions.

At first, Robert had been shocked by Curt's proposal. After all, it *did* hinge on a few "questionable" measures. But the more Robert listened to Curt's explanations, the more he rationalized away his own objections. Only one old, demented man stood in the way of a chance to skim an immense profit off Gossett Enterprises. It was an irresistible prize. And besides, it wasn't as if the old man were going to be left in the cold. He'd have everything he ever needed.

The ring of his private phone interrupted Robert's reverie. And a moment later, Dan Shriver's revelation had caused his thoughtful mood to tumble into one of grimness.

"So . . ." Shriver hesitantly ended, "what do you want me to do?"

The furrow deepened between Robert's darkly knitted brows. "You're a busy man, Dan. No one can blame you if you don't have time to get around to personal favors. And besides, records get lost, don't they? Secretaries misfile things?"

For the first time since R.J.'s call, Dan breathed a sigh of relief. "You're right, Robert. Poor old Loretta. She's been with me a long time, and she's a good old gal. But she's still looking for a paper I requested more than a month ago. These county files are notorious."

Robert let the words hang. "We understand each other, then?" he said finally.

"We understand each other," Shriver agreed.

Robert replaced the receiver, his eyes slipping closed at the thought. R.J. was nosing into the Stuckey matter. Upstanding, ramrod-straight, letter-of-the-law R.J. Suddenly, all of Robert's squelched reservations lurched into the stark daylight of his mind, where they loomed like dark, dirty clouds. He thought for a moment, then picked up the phone again and dialed.

"Hello, son. You free for supper tonight?"

"Sure, Dad," Curt replied. "What's up?"

"Just something I want to make you aware of. I

think we need to talk it through. I'd like to hear what you think.''

"Fine. Where do you want to meet?'' Curt sounded casual, but it still thrilled him, this new tone in his father's voice. There was an unmistakable timbre of respect in it.

"How about the Club?''

It was a carefully preserved, antebellum establishment, the age-old sanctuary of the Charleston gentleman. Robert's father, and his grandfather before him, had often retired to the Club on East Bay Street to talk business and politics, play a round of chess or billiards, or simply loll about the bar before supping in the lavish dining room. The hushed atmosphere and soothing, low tones of the black, uniformed waiters were just what Robert needed.

"Yes, Curt,'' he reiterated. "Go directly from your office to the Club. We'll have drinks and then supper.''

Thoughtfully, Robert hung up the phone and glanced at his watch. Nearly five o'clock. With a sigh, he shrugged into his jacket and prepared to leave the office—to meet his younger son, and inform him that his older brother had become a threat.

Kathleen lolled in the luxury of her bubble bath. A smile curved her lips as her gaze slid over the brass sand marble fixtures of the elegant master bath. Then, closing her eyes, she let her mind drift, floating on the memories of the past few days.

André had proven to be a more adept and caring lover than she could possibly have imagined. In her mind's eye, she recaptured the rippling muscles of his arms and back, the tapering waist and massive bulge of manhood. He'd brought her to climax the first time they made love on Saturday night—and every time since!

She chuckled in her solitude. She must be mad!

How deftly she had arranged her excursions from the house. After the first occasion—when she informed James that she was attending a dance seminar—it had been easy. So easy! And all this time she had hidden herself reclusively in the mansion, conjuring up nightmares of James's supernatural ability to ferret out even her smallest lie.

Now, she had lied to him about her whereabouts for three days in a row. And she felt no guilt, only a supreme satisfaction with her own ingenuity. Even if she *had* felt guilty, she would have somehow dealt with it for the chance to be with André again. He renewed her, resurrected her from a long, sad emotional death that Kathleen had not fully realized until she came to life once more.

Today, they'd gone to a secluded spot up the coast from Folly Beach. She'd worn a tiny, striped bikini that tied under her breasts and at each hip. André had worn a slight, beige racer's suit, and after he'd gotten wet and come strolling back from the surf, she'd been able to see straight through it.

They were the only ones on the beach, and they had spread a large, comfortable blanket. It started when André took some tanning oil out of his bag. Methodically, he rubbed his body down, and then— his warm, brown eyes on hers—removed the brief swimsuit to oil the impressive part of his body that seemed continually hard.

"This is great stuff," he said with a smile, holding up the container of oil. "I think you need some, too."

Kathleen surrendered to the sensual waves that were already sweeping through her.

"All right," she murmured and, lying back with closed eyes, felt his first touch on the backs of her hands. Slowly, he worked the oil up her arms and across her shoulders. By the time he encountered the brief barrier of her bikini top, her senses were crying for him to remove it.

He did, lavishing the oil on her breasts. Kneading

them, André filled his hands with them, capturing and tugging the nipples until they were as pebbles. Then he replenished the oil on his palms and began at her feet. She was breathless by the time his fingers moved to untie the remainder of her bikini and cast it aside.

"Let's do your back, too," he suggested. And when she'd rolled over, he moved to her calves, working ever so slowly up the thighs and hips. He spread the oil thick on her back and across the crest of shoulders. Then, it seemed, he was satisfied with her proper coating against the sun.

Now, the hands touched her again, this time merely for pleasure. Sneaking under her armpits, his fingers rubbed the swell of her breasts, then pressed and reached beneath her to cup them. A knee pressured the backs of her own, prodding the unresisting legs easily apart as he positioned himself there.

He bent over her, breathing and murmuring in her ear. One hand continued to fondle a breast while the other stole ever downward. As his fingers electrified her erotic nerve endings, he entered. Slow, but sure . . . more . . . more.

From his angle behind her, the penetration was encompassingly deep, and with each sleek thrust, she'd found herself gasping. The tremor began to build as she raised her hips rhythmically to meet him, welcoming him into her until he seemed to fill her body. The warm ache pounded harder, hotter, and then erupted so that she moaned and went rigid as her insides roiled and undulated. It was only then that she felt André reach his own orgasm deep within her. And that sensation renewed her own so that she mounted and exploded once more, falling weakly to the blanket as the waves subsided and her lover settled himself gently against her, resting his head on her back as he caressed an arm.

Just remembering it, Kathleen found herself newly aroused, newly warm and vibrant.

They'd spent another hour swimming and sunbathing in the nude, and were almost late getting André back to the city in time to depart Charleston with his dance company.

Now, he was on a bus bound for Atlanta, but Kathleen didn't despair. She knew he was thinking of her—just as she was of him. *And* he would be coming back in two weeks.

Eventually, she climbed out of the bathtub and donned a light caftan. There was no need to dress up. James had called and would not be home for supper. The sudden thought of food made her mouth water. She was famished! She didn't know when she'd been so hungry!

Still absently smiling in afterglow, Kathleen coiled her wet hair on the back of her head and, as she left the dresser, took a sidelong glance at the brandy decanter that was kept filled at her request.

With a lift of her chin, she turned to stroll buoyantly from the opulent bedroom. She didn't feel the need for a drink.

Charlotte Morrisson walked slowly through the house, dousing lights as she made her way to the great staircase.

The house is so quiet when they're away, she thought as she climbed the stairs to the spacious master suite. The girls were in their rooms, but neither of the Morrisson men was home. And Charlotte felt very alone.

It had become a familiar feeling. Margaret and Camille had their own lives, as did Curt and Randall. That was how it was supposed to be. Children grew up, carried on their own lives.

But, damn it, husbands and wives were meant to share! The way Charlotte and Robert had shared their first twenty-five years of marriage. But in the past few months, Robert had become a stranger—a cold, distant companion who, even when present in body, was absent in spirit.

He and Curt hadn't even thought to call until nearly eight o'clock that evening. By then, Charlotte had ruined supper by trying to wait for them and keep it warm. It had embarrassed her to finally tell Cecile to go on home, that she would do the serving herself. She and Margaret and Camille had made a dismally short meal of the elegant shrimp in wine sauce. It was one of Robert's favorite dishes, and Charlotte had asked Cecile to prepare it especially for him.

And then he hadn't even shown up, still wasn't home, though it was nearing eleven o'clock. If it weren't for the fact that she knew Curt was with him, Charlotte could almost suspect Robert of having an affair.

Donning an expensive, peach silk peignoir trimmed with Belgian lace, she sat down at her dressing table, running a brush through her shoulder-length chestnut hair. All of the sudden she paused, gazing assessingly into the mirror. She was still attractive; her classic features had aged well. With a wistful smile, she recalled a remark that Robert had made when she was pregnant with one of the children: "You were the best-looking young girl in all of Charleston. Now you're the best-looking mother-to-be. And one day," he declared, "you'll be the best-looking grandmother!"

With an empty feeling, she left the dresser and climbed into bed. How long had it been since her husband had said anything endearing to her? It used to be that they shared their hopes and worries and dreams—their lives! Now, Charlotte's days were filled with society and charity duties that had become increasingly unfulfilling. Robert's, she supposed, were filled with that ambiguous, possessive entity he called "business."

Reaching to the bedside table, she doused the

123

lamp. But long after the light went out, Charlotte stared into the darkness. And as she longed for the touch of Robert beside her, she feared that somehow she had lost her husband to a frightening, intangible mistress she could neither see nor fight.

It was almost dawn on Friday when Carole stepped back and tried to rescue an objective viewpoint from her obviously prejudiced mind. She had arranged the drawings like a patchwork quilt across the living-room floor. And now, as she studied them with the most objective eye she could muster, she judged them damned good.

She hadn't slept all night, and then she'd had to put in a full day at Carlotta's! But still, she felt radiant.

Carole's step was light when, a few hours later, she posted the carefully wrapped package, sending it first class to Mr. Jack Levy at Haut Nouveau. She had stretched the deadline he'd given her at the festival, but if he'd been impressed by the yellow frock she'd worn that day, he'd be doubly impressed with the safari line. It was head and shoulders above any work Carole Gossett had ever done.

Even the day at Carlotta's! went by pleasantly. Carlotta herself had always been pleasant and considerate. But since Spoleto, even Elsa and Cathy's attitude toward Carole had warmed. She liked to think it was because she'd sold the entire inventory of T-shirts in one day. But in truth, her own change in manner probably had something to do with it, too.

Like today. She hadn't taken the time to apply makeup or curl her hair. To her own way of thinking, she was unkempt. But that only seemed to endear her to Elsa and Cathy. For the first time in her employment at Carlotta's!, Carole felt that she had friends there.

124

It was toward the end of the day that she had a sudden inspiration and called April.

"Still got the graveyard shift?" Carole asked.

"No, mornings. I just got off an hour ago."

"Great! Then why don't you meet me at The Cotton Exchange for supper?"

"The Cotton Exchange? What's the occasion?"

"I mailed my designs to New York today."

"That's wonderful, Carole! Sure, let's go celebrate. Want to make the reservation for, say, seven o'clock?"

The Cotton Exchange was one of the finest restaurants on Market Street, indeed, in all of Charleston. Noted for its continental cuisine, impeccable service, and elegant atmosphere, it was often written up in the travel columns as *the* place to dine in the Historic District.

But the reason the restaurant was special to Carole and April went deeper than that. When they were much younger, James Gossett had often thrilled his daughters by taking them to the fancy establishment, where the waiters wore cutaway jackets and white gloves, and the maître d' insisted on serving the "beautiful, blond young ladies" a thimbleful of champagne.

Years ago, both Carole and April had decided on the favorite dishes they'd ordered without fail since then. Now, as Carole stood outside the white facade of the restaurant front—peering into the softly lit interior through one of the many bay windows and closing her eyes at the mouth-watering aromas that wafted out to the street—she knew she wouldn't be able to resist ordering her old favorite, duck with rice pilau. It would be interesting to see if April selected the squab.

She did, and as the sisters looked at each other across the familiar setting of fine linen and silver, they shared a laugh over the fact that some things never change.

April, for instance, looked just the same as always. She had the same thin figure, the same pale hair pulled back from the flawless complexion, and wide, serious eyes.

"You're the one who's changed," she said to Carole. "That flashy look is gone."

"Flashy?" Carole repeated with a pained look.

"Oh, you know what I mean. That fixed-up look that Daddy always pushed on you is gone. And I, for one, think you look great! A little tired maybe, but there's something different about you, kiddo . . . something genuine and very attractive."

Little did April know that those were the very qualities she herself possessed that Carole had always admired.

"Thanks, April," she said, her vivid sea-blue eyes glowing. "I guess for the first time in my life, I *feel* very attractive. Odd, isn't it? After all those years of dressing to kill, and having all those guys fawning on me, *now* . . . when there are no men in my life . . . *now* is the time I feel really attractive."

"No men?" April questioned in surprise. "What about Curt? I thought he was about to propose."

Carole slumped back in her chair. "He was."

"So, what happened?"

"Well, I just didn't have time to be with Curt . . . to even think of Curt! I mean, he has absolutely no understanding of what I'm trying to do. Honestly, he is the most unsupportive . . . narrow-minded . . . chauvinistic . . ."

April held up a palm. "I get the picture. So he didn't want you to submit your work to New York, right?"

"Right!"

"Sounds like he's afraid of losing you to a brilliant career."

"Exactly."

"Sounds a lot like Daddy," April offered with a solemn look.

126

Carole returned the look. "Funny you should say that, April. I've often drawn comparisons between the two."

A thought of R.J. dashed through Carole's mind, and her expression hardened. "But then, they're all pretty much the same. Anyway, at least the men I come across seem to be."

April regarded her curiously. "What are you talking about now? I thought you hadn't been seeing anyone but Curt."

"I haven't. Not really." Carole's voice dropped, along with her eyelids. "I met someone at Spoleto . . . just a chance meeting," she hastened to add. "He doesn't mean a thing."

April watched a colorful blush spread to her sister's cheeks. "Apparently, he means *some*thing."

Carole looked up sharply. "He means nothing! I'll admit there were a couple of times he had me going. I mean, he *is* devilishly good looking, suave, witty . . . But I found out soon enough that my first impression of R.J. Morrisson was on target. He's an arrogant, egotistical rogue, and personally, I find him even more infuriating than his brother!"

April blinked in astonishment. "Hold on a minute. Let me get this straight. This 'devilishly good-looking, suave, witty' guy is Curt's brother?" And as Carole nodded, April chuckled lightheartedly. "And *you* said there were no men in your life," she teased.

The evening carried on, and the sisters feasted. Beginning with she-crab soup—a traditional favorite in Charleston that was prepared like a bisque, the roe of the she-crab blended in just before serving, along with a liberal dash of sherry—moving on to duck and squab with an excellent side of rice pilau, the area's historically valuable grain crop prepared with minced onion and shrimp in tomato liqueur.

Just as Carole and April leaned back in their chairs—pleasantly full and moaning at the thought that the waiter had yet to arrive with their dessert of peach cobbler topped with cream—their father strolled into the restaurant with Kathleen. Carole, who was facing the door, saw them immediately. And not long after, James spotted their table and started over with his wife in tow.

"Hello, daughters," he announced, looking down from on high in his typically regal manner.

"Hello, Daddy," they responded in unison.

"April . . . Carole," Kathleen acknowledged quietly.

Carole glanced to Kathleen, searched quickly for the forlorn distress Miss Constance had mentioned, and found none. Indeed, Kathleen looked her best ever. Carole then caught the woman's dark eyes lingering on her with odd intensity. But almost as soon as their gaze met, Kathleen wiped the expression carefully away, turning back to her husband.

"Supper at The Cotton Exchange?" James went on. "What's the occasion?"

April fixed him with a cold look. To her, he seemed never to change or age. Always the same trim build, sharp features, and even sharper eyes.

"We're here to celebrate Carole's talent," she tossed insolently, then leaned forward in her seat to reach for the wine bottle and four glasses. "She's just sent her designs to New York, and with any luck, this could be her big break," April finished pouring the Bordeaux and looked up with a smile. "So I propose a toast to Carole's new career in fashion. Every success," she concluded, raising glass to her sister.

Across the table, Carole smiled timidly. Whenever April encountered her father, she always found it necessary to make some sort of rebellious gesture. Such as now, challenging him to toast something she knew he was against. Usually, April's antagonism made Carole uncomfortable. But tonight, strangely, she was vaguely amused, even though her father's face had gone a bit rosy, and she imagined he was raging inside.

Still, James Gossett was a picture of dignity as he selected one of the wine-glasses and turned to his younger daughter.

"I'm sure you're aware of my earlier reservations, Carole, about your . . . what should I call it? Free-lance work? But I want you to know that I was only thinking of your welfare. I found it difficult to understand your aspirations. But then, of course, you have the right to your own dreams."

As every woman at the table stared at him in disbelief, James raised his glass and looked down on his daughter with a wry smile. "So, here's to your new career, Carole . . . whatever it may be."

A hush fell on the group after the toast. After a moment, James set down his glass and bowed stiffly to his daughters, his eyes sliding briefly from Carole to April.

"If you'll excuse us, I believe our table is ready." And turning away from them he steered Kathleen efficiently away to the far side of the room.

"Did you get a load of that?" April huffed, as she looked over her shoulder at the receding figure of her father.

Carole remembered how upset he'd been after the Morrissons' dinner party. But in spite of that, he'd left her alone to do as she pleased. "I thought it was rather sweet," she said.

"What?" April laughed. "I haven't heard such a crock since he tried to dissuade me from becoming a doctor! He's up to something, Carole."

Remaining unflustered, Carole took a sip of wine. "What could he be up to? The work is done. The stuff is in the mail. Daddy couldn't do anything to stop me now, even if he wanted to."

April shook her head, smiling widely. "You sure have changed, little sister," she said.

James's expression soured visibly as he watched his daughters depart the restaurant a short while later.

Across the elegant table, Kathleen watched him like a hawk from beneath lowered lids. She hadn't had a drink in nearly a week, and she was still infused with the new, glowing confidence that André inspired. Perhaps it was *that*, more than the clear-headed sobriety, that made her bold.

"I knew it," she said, as she took in the hostile look he directed to his daughters. "All the things you said in that toast to Carole were meaningless. You don't wish her well with any career in fashion design. The only career you want her to pursue is that of wife to Curt Morrisson."

James dabbed at his mouth with a linen napkin. A look of amusement climbed to his face. "You surprise me, Kathleen. You really do. When your brain isn't pickled, you can actually be quite astute."

Kathleen folded her arms across her breasts. She wouldn't be shut up so easily.

"Carole has changed, James. Didn't you see the way she looked? She's not your little doll anymore. She has a mind of her own, and I don't think you'll find it so easy to marry her off to the man of *your* dreams."

The look of amusement faded. "She'll come around," James said, sweeping Kathleen with a mocking look. "They always do."

Chapter Six

R.J. ROLLED HIS eyes and shifted the phone receiver irritably to his other ear.

"And when do you expect him?" he asked curtly.

"I'm sorry, sir. I don't have that information. Would you care to leave a message?"

"I've already left two messages this week!" R.J. thundered.

The woman on the other end of the line became impatient. "There's no need to be rude, Mr. Morrison. It's my job to take messages. I can't be held responsible for when Mr. Shriver returns his calls. Would you like to leave a message?"

"No. I would not," R.J. returned succinctly, and immediately slammed down the phone.

Folding his arms on the desk, he looked beyond the stacks of law books and files that had collected there . . . glanced about the rather dated furnishings of his courthouse office.

Today was Thursday. It had been a week and a half since he'd asked Dan Shriver to send the transcripts. And now, the man was dodging his calls!

"Fine," R.J. muttered, leaping to his feet. He'd go down to Charleston, waltz into the county offices and go through the damned files himself if that's what it took.

Judge Harper, however, was not particularly agreeable about granting time off. "What's going on, R.J.? This is the third time in the past couple of months you've been down to Charleston, and this time you want to be excused from court. Is there something I should know? Is some firm down there romancing you?"

"No, your honor. It's nothing like that," R.J. explained. "A friend asked me to look into a case, that's all. It shouldn't take much time. I just need to check a few records."

Judge Harper looked at him sharply. "Let me give you a word of caution, R.J. Several of your colleagues have noticed a change in you. You've become impatient, almost abrupt, at proceedings. If something is bothering you, I wish you'd let me in on it."

R.J. flushed. He had, in fact, changed—ever since he'd seen Jonah Stuckey sitting on that damned floor. The judge was a perceptive man.

"There's nothing bothering me, Your Honor. Just something I need to get out of my system."

Judge Harper sent him on his way with a warning. "A lot of young attorneys would kill for your position, R.J. To keep it, you've got to pay your dues, do your homework, play the game, both inside and outside the courtroom. You're at a very important point in your career, R.J. Don't blow it."

It was dark by the time he drove into Charleston. Force of habit led him onto Meeting Street and toward Tradd and the Morrisson home. But the deeper he moved into the District, the more he thought of Carole. He'd tried to block her from his mind. And in Columbia, he'd been somewhat successful. But now that he was back in Charleston, and he knew that she was somewhere among these streets at this very minute, her blue-eyed face swam relentlessly before his eyes.

Suddenly, he dreaded seeing Curt at the Morrisson house . . . having to listen to his brother languishing over the girl while he, himself, gritted his teeth and felt guilty as hell. Without meaning to, Carole Gossett had driven a wedge between him and Curt.

Besides, this was the third time he'd been to Charleston in little more than a month. He wasn't up to explaining why he was here yet again, taking a day off from his clerkship no less. His family was sure to make a fuss. His mother would probably assume he was back for good.

Again, the image of Carole flitted before him. For the first time in his life, R.J. was loathe to go home. As he came upon the elegant Mills House Hotel at Meeting and Queen, he found himself wheeling in.

A soft-spoken valet in plush livery led him to the split staircase to a second-floor suite decorated in rich tones of forest green and tan. R.J. glanced about the room. He had often patronized the Mills House restaurant and bar, but had never seen the accommodations. It was easy to see why the inn had such an excellent reputation. This room was furnished with the solid grace of antique cherry. Fine, sporting prints were on the walls, an Oriental carpet on the floor. It had the comfortable feel of an old-fashioned, southern gentleman's study.

R.J. tipped the valet rather heavily, then went to a window overlooking Queen Street. His heart lifted at the sight of the well-known lanes and landmarks, illuminated now by the golden glow of streetlamps in the soft summer night. A horse-drawn carriage approached on the street below. R.J. watched undetected by the young couple in the rear of the carriage as it rolled slowly by.

It was great to be back in Charleston. But it was strange—looking out the window of the elegant hotel instead of lolling about the veranda of the Tradd

133

Street house, where the familiar voices of his family drifted from inside. Still—for now—R.J. liked the feeling that no one knew he was in town.

Stepping out of her shower, Carole wrapped her hair in a towel and donned a short, terrycloth robe. She was in a good mood. The next night, after work, she was going out with Elsa and Cathy for drinks. It was the first time she'd ever been included in the traditional, Friday-night tour of the singles bars. Of course, in the old days she'd usually had dates on all those Friday nights.

A pensive look came to Carole's face as she stepped into her slippers. How long had it been since she'd heard from Curt? Two weeks? The fact that he hadn't called or dropped by surprised her. She knew enough about men to recognize one who wanted her. And Curt did.

He must be really angry to stay away this long, she thought. She sometimes missed Curt's smiling face, but she was not willing to get in touch with him. First of all, she hadn't done anything wrong. Secondly, she didn't want to take the risk that he might again bring up the subject of marriage. Carole didn't want to think of marriage. Not yet. Not now, when for the first time in her life, she felt as though her future were her own.

Removing the towel, she began to comb through her wet hair. Unbidden and unwelcome, the image of R.J. came to mind—the perfect angular features, vivid eyes, and white smile. Just the thought of him brought fire to her cheeks and a hated, now-familiar longing to her body.

Yet . . . Carole had a feeling about R.J. Morrisson, and her woman's intuition had yet to be proven wrong. The cocky, blond stud was no more immune to *her* than she was to him. Two could play at his little game of touch and tease. And Carole was a master!

134

Huffily, she dropped the brush onto the dresser and stomped through the dark apartment to the kitchen. Feeling her way along the counter, she found a juice glass and filled it with tap water.

If ever again I run into him, she was fuming, we'll see who takes the upper hand! Draining the glass, she slammed it down and stared moodily out the window over the sink.

That was when she saw him, standing across the street near the alleyway—a man in a dark jacket and distinctive snap-brim hat. His head was tipped back, and Carole froze as it came to her that he was staring up at her apartment.

Suddenly, she felt the heat of unknown eyes searching through the night, spotlighting her in the blackness of her kitchen window. Instinctively, Carole dropped to her knees, ducking out of view. An icy shiver ran up her spine. For the first time in the two years she had lived on her own, she felt a stab of fear at being utterly alone.

There were three other apartments in the exclusive townhouse, and two of the tenants were gone for the summer. That left only ancient Mrs. Worthington in the adjacent downstairs rooms, and that frail old lady certainly couldn't be counted on for help against . . .

Against what? A peeping tom? A . . . burglar?

Really, Carole! she chastised herself. You're letting your imagination run away with you!

It was silly to be crouching by the sink. It was dark in the kitchen. The man couldn't see her—she was sure of it. Although a moment ago, she could have sworn he was peering directly into her eyes. Slowly, she raised herself until only her wide eyes peeked over the windowsill.

But the man was gone. Stretching over the sink, her face close to the window pane, Carole looked up and down the street. But all was as it should be—quiet and serene. Shadows swelled across the pavement, surrounding the yellow pools of light beneath the streetlamps. The dancing shadows of palms swaying in the breeze provided the only movement.

Shrugging, Carole mosied back to the bedroom, telling herself that she was turning paranoid. She determinedly ignored the fact that her heart had yet to calm to its normal pace.

R.J. dialed the number from memory, then pivoted inside the narrow phone booth, looking steadily across the busy street to the county office building Dan Shriver had entered no more than ten minutes before.

"Hello. This is R.J. Morrisson calling. May I speak with Dan?"

Annoying static clicked over the line as the woman put him on hold, and R.J. had a minute to berate himself for the cloak-and-dagger mentality he'd fallen into. Shriver would assume he was calling from Columbia, not from just across the street, where R.J. had been watching him.

At the moment R.J. felt more like an amateur detective than an attorney. But one thing was for damned sure: He felt more alive right now than he did sitting on a bench in the state supreme court. There was something mysterious, even ominous, about the Stuckey case. A whispering voice had haunted R.J. in his dreams, and now teased him with the idea that he was overlooking something important, something just out of his grasp. The whole matter had begun to captivate him, and though he sensed an air of danger, he was driven to get to the bottom of it.

"Mr. Morrisson?" The receptionist's voice came back on the line. "Sorry to keep you waiting. I'm sorry. Mr. Shriver is not expected in all day."

Thoughtfully, R.J. replaced the telephone receiver and stepped out into the morning sunshine.

That's it, then, he concluded. The man is purposely avoiding me. He's avoiding the subject of Jonah Stuckey.

R.J. toyed with the idea of marching straight into Dan Shriver's office and calling him a liar to his face. But reason got the better of him. At the moment, he had the element of surprise on his side. There was no sense in tipping his hand.

It was Friday. Ten minutes to one. Shriver would probably duck out early for the weekend. Banking on that, R.J. planned to return to the county office late in the afternoon. Between now and then, he'd come up with some ploy for the benefit of Shriver's secretary. And Dan himself would be nowhere around when R.J. made his move for the Stuckey files.

Now, the day stretched out before him, but R.J. already knew what he wanted to do. Within minutes, he was on his way to Belmont Pines. As he left the city behind, cruising into the countryside, he thought there was nothing so beautiful as the Charleston low country. Open fields, waving green and gold in the morning sun, were bordered by dark timberland. Stands of pine crowded up to the road, then receded from a swampy marsh where ghostly cypress trees stood gray and straight and tall.

It was a clear, hot day. In fact, R.J. suddenly remembered, tomorrow was the Fourth of July. A host of memories embraced him—happy boyhood times when the fourth of July was a holiday filled with picnics and games and a spectacular show of fireworks off the Battery. Hundreds gathered in the District, sharing in a flurry of festivities that had gone on every year for two centuries.

Charleston had been a Patriot hotbed during the Revolution. And there were still many families in town—including the Morrissons—whose ancestors had fought the Redcoats, endured British occupation, and emerged in victory. Even two hundred years later the city remembered and joined together, to celebrate Independence Day with particular fervor.

137

Sunbeams danced on the dashboard of the car, a warm breeze blew in through the open window, and R.J. was so enjoying his pleasant daydreams, that he cruised past the overgrown road that led eventually to the Ashley River and Belmont Pines. With a mild curse, he swung to the shoulder of the deserted highway, pulled a U-turn, and headed back.

As soon as he turned onto the dirt road, he felt as though the clock had turned back a hundred years. Brush crowded into the road while the twisted, black arms of live oaks reached overhead, trailing long skirts of Spanish Moss that lapped across R.J.'s windshield as he drove slowly along. There was a break in the trees on the right, and there rested a rusted-out, horse-drawn carriage—its day of glory obviously well past. And as R.J. pulled up before the dilapidated, two-story house, he imagined the carriage might be an apt symbol for the whole of Belmont Pines.

The once-circular drive had been encroached upon until it no longer had shape. R.J. left the car, walking across weed-ridden, patchy lawn that led to the house and climbing the steps to an extensive veranda surrounded by camellias and azaleas.

He tried the door and, finding it unlocked, stepped inside, shrugging off the knowledge that he was trespassing. He needed to look at Jonah's home, to see for himself if there were something here worth anyone's notice.

But as he toured the quiet, empty house, R.J. didn't see anything out of the ordinary. It was just a big, old, musty house. The upstairs hadn't been used in years. It seemed Louise and Jonah had shared the downstairs, and to all appearances, nothing had been changed since they'd left. The furnishings were cozy and neat. Clothes and linens still filled closets. In the kitchen sink a cereal bowl sat, as if waiting for someone to come along and wash it. And on a small table by the rocker in the parlor, an old pair of bifocals sat next to a lamp.

He looked around more closely. Cecile had insisted that Louise Stuckey had made a will providing Jonah a home for life at Belmont Pines. If only that missing document could be produced, R.J. mused, the man's troubles would be over.

He began by turning up the edge of the crocheted doily on the table and peeking nonchalantly underneath. But by the time he warmed to his task, R.J. had opened every drawer, peered behind every picture, removed and replaced every cushion in the parlor.

Having secured that room, he paused, passing the back of his hand across his perspiring forehead. It was relatively cool in the dim shelter of the house, but outside, the July day was turning into a scorcher. Glancing at his watch, he confirmed that it was nearly noon. With renewed determination, he stalked into Louise Stuckey's bedroom.

Several hours later, R.J. felt as though he knew Belmont Pines as intimately as the Stuckeys ever had. But he'd found nothing. A package of old letters discovered in Louise's chest of drawers had caused a brief thrill. But careful examination showed that the will was not among them.

Regretfully, he gave up his search and walked outside. If Louise Stuckey had *wanted* to hide her will, there were a hundred places she could have done it—in the chimney, in a wall, behind a loose brick in the foundation. R.J. knew it was useless to look any longer. And, it was time to return to Charleston.

Before climbing into the car, he took a last sweeping look at the place. The house and grounds bore sad testament to what the old place must have been in its heyday. But one thing hadn't changed. Surrounding the clearing, sweeping as far as the eye could see, were the cool, blue-green pines, in honor of which the place had obviously been named. Somewhere beyond the pines was the Ashley, and as R.J. surveyed the beautiful, rolling lands, he could easily imagine Jonah strolling along well-known paths, stopping to feed the animals of the forest, happy as a clam. Oh yes, this was where he belonged.

R.J. shook his head. Belmont Pines. It was just a broken-down, old house out in the middle of nowhere. And yet it was Jonah Stuckey's whole world.

The secretary ran her brightly polished nail down the page of her appointment book.

R.J. had waited until after four, then peeked carefully through the front office to confirm that the office behind the door marked Clerk of County was dark.

"Now, what did you say your name is?" the secretary asked.

"Why, it's Stuckey, ma'am," R.J. drawled in a slow, deep voice unlike his own. "Gerald Stuckey. Mr. Shriver was kind enough to draw up some papers 'bout my cousin, ma'am. He said I should come on by and get 'em today."

Loretta Hinson shook her head at her book. "Well, I'm sorry, Mr. Stuckey. There doesn't seem to be any mention of an appointment, and Mr. Shriver has left for the day."

"Aw, shoot!" R.J. exclaimed. "And here I am, just in town for the day."

R.J. gave the woman a once-over. She was perhaps fifty, with bright red hair that a stylist had obviously helped along. She had a somewhat flashy, bosomy look, and R.J. imagined that in her prime she'd drawn many a male eye.

"Course, I can't complain, ma'am." Slumping down on the corner of her desk, he offered his most

140

engaging smile. "I mean it was worth driving all this way just to get a look at you."

R.J. winked brazenly at the older woman, who launched into a flurry of smiles and fluttering lashes.

"Why, Mr. Stuckey," she said coyly. "I do believe your mama taught you some flirtatious ways."

"Yes, ma'am," he confirmed, grinning.

It was nearly five o'clock when R.J. left the office with copies of the documents under his arm. In courtly fashion, he had kissed the hand of Mrs. Hinson, thanked her for her help, and wished her well. With some guilt, he hurried away, thinking it was the least he could do, considering she was probably going to be in big trouble with her boss come Monday.

Loretta Hinson closed up the office, as she'd been closing up behind Dan Shriver for twenty years. But as she headed home to a drab night of TV with her husband, she dreamed of a world where she was young again, of a handsome man with hair the color of wheat and a deep southern accent that called to mind the grace of an age gone by.

Such a gentleman, he was! Maybe chivalry wasn't dead after all.

As the live band revved up at nine o'clock, pushing the noise level in the bar to a roar, Carole knew she had finally had enough. Coming to her feet, she looked down at Elsa and Cathy who were rocking in their seats to the music and gazing toward a group of guys at the bar.

"*Yoo-hoo!*" Carole called between cupped palms. On about her third try, Elsa and Cathy turned her way. Smiling, Carole had to yell above the din to be heard. "I'm going now! I had a great time!"

"What do you mean?" Elsa cried. "Nothing even starts happening around here until eleven!"

141

"Yeah, what's the matter?" Cathy teased. "Tired of all the action you've been stirring up?"

Carole shook her head with a look of mock forebearance. They'd been teasing her all night about the number of men who had approached her. Carole had to admit, it had been good for her ego, though she'd hadn't been interested.

"Want me to give you a ride home?" Cathy called.

"No! We're not that far from my place! I'll walk! And besides, I want to stop by the market!"

Cathy punched Elsa. "She'll walk! That must be how she keeps that figure that's been driving these guys crazy all night."

Rolling her eyes, Carole waved farewell and began to weave her way through the crowd. Stepping out onto the street, she took a welcome breath of fresh air. It was a beautiful summer night, and her blood was singing with a liberal amount of wine. But she was hungry, and she made her way quickly to the market that was just a few streets from home.

Coming out of the shop, she shifted the fairly hefty bag in her arms, deciding to take the shortcut through the alleyway that came out just across the street from her townhouse.

It was dark, the only light spilling from a single yellow bulb halfway along the alley. The only sound Carole heard was that of her comfortable sandals clicking along at a normal pace. But suddenly a crop of goosebumps rose on her bare arms. Had she heard something? Was there someone behind her?

Without warning, she whirled around. At first, her racing eyes didn't focus on anything. But then she saw it, clearly, contrasted against the light at the alleyway entrance—the silhouette of a man in a snapbrim hat.

* * *

Concealed in the moonshadows of a giant magnolia, R.J. stood near the base of the stairs, asking himself once more if he should forget the whole thing and get the hell out of there.

Try as he might to forget her, Carole had stayed powerfully on his mind. R.J. couldn't count the number of times he'd caught himself brooding about their furious parting the last time they'd met . . .

The whole thing was sticking in his craw—the attraction, the guilt about Curt. But more than anything, the fact that Carole Gossett thought R.J. Morrisson was a crude, lecherous oaf. He at least deserved the satisfaction of telling her the truth if he were going to end this hot-blooded thing once and for all—as indeed, he must.

So here he was standing in the fragrant summer darkness outside her door. And of course, she wasn't in. A long list of possibilities ran through his mind: What if she came home with a date? What if it was Curt?

The questions came to him in rapid-fire succession, and yet R.J. knew he'd stand there in the shadows and wait. He had to talk with her before he left Charleston the next morning.

After leaving the county offices that afternoon, he'd gone straight to his hotel room. Ordering a steak from room service, he'd settled down to pore over the copies of the documents he had so cagily obtained. At first, he'd been somewhat disappointed to find that everything seemed to be in order. Dan Shriver had dotted all his I's, crossed all his Ts. R.J. wondered why he'd been so reluctant to share the transcripts.

The only thing that came to mind was the Savannah address of the mysterious guardian, Geraldine Stuckey. Perhaps *that* was the information Shriver had been loath to divulge.

And then, the print had jumped off the page.

143

"Said guardian shall be entrusted with the parcel consisting of six thousand acres . . ."

R.J. blinked. That had to be it. The land! Six thousand acres of riverfront property. At present, it was rather off the beaten trail, but Charleston was growing in that direction. Hell, in a few years, with the proper development, the place could be worth millions. Why had he been so blind?

Within the confines of the alley, Carole's wide eyes scanned the tall, brick backs of the townhouses that had her hemmed in. She had allowed her pace to quicken only slightly—no small feat, considering the adrenaline that was pumping through her veins.

Carole didn't question the malicious intent of the man whose presence she felt behind her, trusting her instincts that there was something dark and sinister about him. When she reached a walkway off the alley, she darted rapidly out of the darkness, and into the light of Beaufain Street.

There was no going back. He knew she was running from him. As Carole hurried along, she tried to restrain herself from looking over her shoulder— but couldn't. And throwing a hasty look behind her, she glimpsed the man again, hovering at the edge of Beaufain.

Now racing, the bag of groceries forgotten as it bounced against her heaving breasts, Carole cursed the fact that the streets were deserted. She'd always loved the quiet peace of her neighborhood, but now she ran like a frightened hare, cutting around corners and through driveways. Breathlessly, she flew across Rutledge, through the courtyard, around the porch. Her feet were about to hit the brick steps leading up to her apartment when she froze. From the corner of her eye, she saw it—the tall shape of a man standing in the shadows.

Spinning toward the stranger, her survival instinct took over. Her wild, ringing shriek overrode the whoosh of air that left the man's body as the weight of the groceries she'd hurled full force caught him in the diaphragm, knocking him unsuspectingly against the brick courtyard wall. In the darkness, Carole heard a thump, as if a ripe melon had been thrown against the brick.

"What do you want?!" she screamed, as the shadowy figure slid down the wall to land with a plop on its backside.

"What do you want?" Carole screamed again.

"For God's sake, Carole," came a familiar voice.

"What?" She was unable, in her hysteria, to connect the voice.

"It's me, R.J.," he muttered, coming slowly to his feet.

"R.J.! What the hell do you think you're doing?"

He stepped out of the shadows, rubbing the temple that had smacked against the damnable brick wall. "I don't know. But whatever it is, I promise never to do it again."

"You idiot!" Carol gasped. "I could have killed you!"

"So I gathered."

She was speechless. She'd just been through the fright of her life. And now, this! With a quick, jerky movement, Carole whirled away from R.J. to peer into the darkness behind her. But she didn't see the dark shape of the stranger with the hat.

"What were you carrying in that bag?" R.J. asked. "A bowling ball?"

"Oh, just some sodas and . . . Oh, what difference does it make?" Turning decisively, she took R.J. by the arm. "Come on," she told him. "Let's get inside."

Once inside the lighted safety of her own home, Carole felt the gradual return of sanity. The fear of the chase faded as she took a good look at R.J. A rosy goose egg swelled just above his right temple, and realizing that *she* was responsible, she placed a

hand to her mouth and shook her head disbelievingly. The lump seemed to purple even as she
stared. Shock and remorse swamped through her,
blotting out her earlier anger and ambivalence for
the man.

"Oh, R.J.," she breathed. "I *am* so sorry. That
must hurt terribly. Come on over here and sit down.
Do you think you should see a doctor?"

"No, I don't think I should see a doctor," he
mimicked irritably as he followed her toward a red
lacquered table and chairs that formed the breakfast
nook. "Bigger guys than you have decked me, and
I've come through all right."

R.J. sat stoically as she examined him, then gathered antiseptic and Band-aids. As she bent over to
clean the injury her breasts swelled invitingly at the
neckline of her scoop-necked dress. R.J. found his
eyes glued there as the mounds swayed enticingly
with her gentle movements, making him go hot inside and long to forget the reason he'd come here.
The feeling irritated him. After all, he'd come here
to put an end to this foolishness.

But there he was, R.J. thought after she'd applied
a large, square Band-Aid, and stepped back to survey her handiwork. R.J. Morrisson, distinguished
attorney. The white, square bandage failed to completely cover the coloring bruise. And below the
swelling lump, his handsome face was the image of
sullenness.

Suddenly Carole dissolved into laughter. Turning
away from R.J.'s pained expression, she tried to stifle her hilarity, but at each memory of the outrageous incident in the courtyard, she howled all the
louder.

"I'm glad you find this so amusing," came R.J.'s
irritated voice from behind her.

When Carole glanced over her shoulder, she
found that he'd begun to smile. "I never knew a bag
of groceries was such an effective weapon!" she

managed before succumbing to another gay chorus of laughter.

R.J. began to smile despite himself. "A weapon is only as good as the person who wields it," he said at last. "From what I've seen, you deserve a black belt in grocery bags."

Gradually, Carole's chuckling subsided, and she slumped into the chair opposite R.J., wiping away the tears of laughter that had rolled down her cheeks.

"Good heavens, R.J.! Whatever were you doing, skulking around in the dark like that?"

"I wasn't skulking," he said seriously, reminded of the purpose of this visit. "I was waiting for you."

Carole met the blue-gray eyes and, for the first time since the bizarre encounter began, experienced the familiar, electric stirrings the man always managed to evoke. But then the memory of their last meeting came hurtling back—of the hot kiss followed by his cold, accursed boasting. He had hurt her that day. He had wrenched a passionate response from her and then made her feel cheap for it. Carole's absent smile faded.

"Wouldn't it have been a bit more traditional to have waited up on the stoop?" she asked, raising a supercilious brow. "Instead of secreting yourself in the garden like some sort of cat burglar?"

R.J. folded his arms on the tabletop, leaned slightly toward her. "I intended to have a chance to make my presence known. I didn't expect you to come hightailing through the courtyard like the devil himself was on your trail!"

"It might have been the devil, for all I know. Someone was following me."

"Who?"

"I don't have any idea." Carole's thoughts dashed back to the chase, some of her earlier fear returning. "But last night, he was looking up at my apartment. And tonight, he followed me from the market."

R.J. took on a slight look of worry.

"Look, Carole, I don't want to frighten you," he told her, "but maybe you should report this to the police. They could patrol the street, at least. Maybe scare off any ardent admirers. You're a single woman living alone, Carole, and you really can't be . . ." R.J.'s voice dropped off as he took in her sarcastic smile.

"Why, R.J. Morrisson," she began with a flutter of lashes that immediately reminded him of the Scarlett O'Hara he'd met during the Spoleto Festival. "Could it be you're worried 'bout little old me?"

R.J. felt a wave of heat rush to his face. She was so damned beautiful, especially with that fresh, natural look she had lately. The simple dress she was wearing was the color of her eyes, and with the blond hair hanging past her shoulders, she was a vision of blue and gold.

"I'd like to get something straight between us, Carole," he began huskily. "That's why I'm here."

Only a moment ago, she had armed herself with sour memories. But now, as Carole saw the heated look in his eyes, she could feel her resolve begin to slip. What was it about his eyes that could make her want to stop fighting when he looked into them? She warned herself that R.J. was once again casting his spell, and yet she merely sat there, helplessly waiting, like the hypnotized prey of a snake, for him to strike.

"I didn't mean what I said to you last week," he blurted in his deep, ringing voice. "That line about stealing Curt's woman . . . I don't even know why I said it—" R.J. caught his words, then jumped ahead. "No, I *do* know why I said it. Because of Curt. Because suddenly, I found Curt's woman in my arms."

A cold feeling crept to Carole's breast. "I see," she said knowingly. "So you've come here to intercede for your brother!"

148

R.J. shook his head. "No. Maybe that's what I *should* be doing, but I'm not."

"But you said—"

"I said I found Curt's woman in my arms!" he broke in. "What I failed to add was that she felt damned good there!"

His eyes flashed at her, and Carole's blood warmed in rebellious response.

"Look, Carole. It should come as no great surprise that I've been attracted to you from the first—from the very beginning at Spoleto, when I didn't even know who you were. I came on to you like a buck in heat. When I found out you belonged to Curt, that should have been the end of it. But it wasn't . . ."

Carole's pulse pounded away as R.J. was staring at her intently. What was he leading up to?

"Curt spends a night telling me he wants to marry you," R.J. continued slowly. "And the next afternoon I find myself kissing you . . . with Curt waiting for me just outside!"

He paused, holding her spellbound with the wonder of what was coming next.

"I'm leaving Charleston in the morning, Carole, but before I go, I want you to know two things. One. I'm not some jackass who goes around hitting on his brother's women. Two. From now on, it's hands off. My only excuse for being carried away on a couple of occasions is that you're a very attractive woman. But I'm through with feeling guilty. I want you to know that I'll never again intrude. I may find you desirable, but Curt's my brother and he's in love with you!"

As Carole pushed away from the table, removing herself from those blazing blue-gray eyes, she realized she was disappointed by R.J.'s last remarks. At the same time he'd stated Curt's feelings. R.J. relegated his *own* to an inferior, base level. Strolling to

149

the sink, Carole refused to look at him, settling her gaze on the window.

So, what would you expect, she asked herself, from a man who once said he saw you as a courtesan? Somewhere deep inside, she was hurt by R.J.'s honorable declaration.

"You know it's true, Carole," R.J. said. "Curt is crazy in love with you. He's planning to ask you to marry him."

"Curt isn't in love with me," she returned quietly. "He's in love with a dream he *thinks* is me. An entertaining, empty-headed little hostess . . . just what Daddy always raised me to be."

She turned swiftly, her eyes sparkling as they confronted R.J. "But that's not all that I am anymore! In the past few weeks, this fashion-design thing has turned me completely around. I have the chance to be *somebody* . . . not just an ornament on the arm of the appropriate man. Now, I know how it feels to try and accomplish something on my own. Now, I know there's more to life than just clothes and parties and country clubs."

R.J. was gazing at her, entranced. This was a side of her he had guessed at. But she hadn't revealed it to him until now. "Got something against country clubs?" he asked with a lazy smile.

Carole turned away, embarrassed to have run on so. "Let's just say I've had my fill of them," she mumbled.

R.J. was thoughtful for a moment. "And how does Curt fit into this life you want?"

"I don't even know how *I* fit into it!" she exclaimed. She was shocked at the way her innermost thoughts were tumbling out on the ears of R.J. Morrisson, of all people, but she was incapable of stilling the flow of words.

"This is so new for me!" she went on. "But of course, you must find it difficult to understand, you've been making your own decisions all your life.

150

It hasn't been like that for me, R.J. All my life, one man has been calling the shots. And now, he's ready to pass me on to another one who'll do the same thing!"

Carole began pacing back and forth before the kitchen sink and the red lacquered table where R.J. sat, rubbing at the back of her neck. "That's not enough for me anymore. I've gotten my hopes up so high, even though I promised myself I wouldn't. If this thing with New York doesn't come through . . . After all the work . . ."

R.J. rose to his feet as her voice trailed off. Placing himself directly in her path, he forced her to stop the pacing.

Carole stiffened as he enfolded her in his arms. But this was a different R.J. This one held her like a brother. She found herself longing with shame for the old, fiery overture that would leave her breathless.

After only a moment of feeling her warm body against him, R.J. realized his folly. He'd thought he would just comfort her. But it mattered little what he told himself, his body still responded to this woman. And as he picked up her rich scent of gardenia, his heart rocked into a gallop. Swallowing hard, R.J. stepped back to put an arm's length between them. He found a place for his hands in his trouser pockets.

Carole, too, looked uncomfortable. In the past quarter of an hour, they'd shared their innermost feelings, related on a level that surprised them both with its intimacy. Now, the atmosphere of closeness evaporated.

"Seems we've learned a great deal about each other tonight," R.J. ventured.

"Yes. . . . I've learned you have no tolerance for tincture of iodine," Carole joked nervously.

R.J. grinned, raising a quick hand to the tender bump on his forehead. But then as he focused on

151

Carole's pretty, dimpled face, he remembered her worrisome tale of having been followed. His expression turned solemn.

"I'm serious about your calling the police, Carole. I'm sure that guy is harmless, but you're better safe than sorry."

She looked down at the floor. "I'll do that."

R.J. shrugged. "Well . . . I guess I'd better be going. I said what I came to say."

Sure, Carole thought with a sinking feeling. That your brother is in love with me, and that you'll keep out of his way.

She followed him to the doorway, where he turned to look at her. "I'll tell you something, Carole. If it weren't for Curt, I'd be hot on your trail."

What could she say? He spoke of his brother's feelings in reverent tones. What of your own? She wanted to ask him. Are they no more than the hunger of a wild beast? Her pride kicked in, twisting her feelings of hurt into anger.

"Like 'a buck in heat'? " she challenged boldly.

He stared down at her. "At least."

"Then I suppose I'm lucky to be left with the honorable intentions of your brother," she sniffed, her ire swelling. "I'm not a wild doe to be trailed and snared, R.J."

He shifted his weight to one hip, regarded her quizzically. Now, where was *that* coming from? "You can't blame me for finding you attractive, Carole, but I told you I'm stepping out of the picture. I thought we'd come to a truce. What went wrong?"

You stupid brute! she fumed silently. Nothing went wrong. I'm happy you won't be pawing me, anymore. I'm glad I won't have to worry about the way I feel when you do.

The unbidden feelings were welling up, choking her into silence. He stood there waiting for a reply, but all she could do was glare.

You walk away so easily. You act as though I'm

152

nothing but a cheap little tart to be passed around. Certainly nothing worth jeopardizing your precious relationship with your brother! Even as the thoughts were born, Carole knew they were unfair. But the knowledge didn't keep them from coming.

R.J. watched a hard set come to her mouth. He cocked his head to one side, looked at her curiously. "Carole? What's going on in that pretty head of yours?"

"Don't patronize me!" she flashed.

"Patronize you?" Now, he was completely bewildered. "Who's trying to patronize you?"

"You are! You and every other man in my life!"

"Don't group me with the other men in your life, Carole! I'm the one who came here with my tail between my legs to try and make amends. And *this* is what I get for my trouble!"

Her words came cool and aloof, belying the inner rage that had her trembling. "Well, I'm sorry you went to so much trouble on my account, Mr. Morrisson. And all over a silly, meaningless little encounter."

R.J.'s eyes were blazing now. "Bullshit!" he muttered. "I've been straight with you, Carole. And I think I deserve for you to be straight with me. This triangle we've gotten ourselves into with Curt is not silly or meaningless. All night, I've been taking the whole thing on myself, but we both know you joined in our . . . 'encounters,' as you so quaintly put it, with nothing short of abandon!"

"You flatter yourself, R.J.!"

"And you delude yourself, Carole!"

They were glaring at each other, faced off like two warriors. Carole hated him for seeing through her. But even in anger, she remembered how his firm, ruddy lips had closed over hers and realized with horror that even now, she burned for R.J.'s kiss.

Tearing her eyes away, she gazed at the door. "I think you'd better go," she said icily.

"I think you're right!"

But he continued to stand there, willing her to return her eyes to his. She looked back in a huff. "I said—"

"I heard you," he broke in stonily. "I assure you, Carole. I came here with the best of intentions. I suppose . . . I suppose I just wanted to say goodbye."

He said nothing more—only looked and looked. Carole's breath stopped in her chest. She feared that if he didn't soon go, she'd drown in the sparkling, dark blue of his eyes. He could wrench her heart so easily. All it took was a look. She glanced away disconcertedly.

And then, R.J. was gone, and she was alone with the quivering feelings he had provoked. Quickly, Carole bolted the door behind him and turned to lean against its solidity.

Her eyes closed, but she couldn't shut out the image of his face. Her fury at being cast off slowly ebbed, replacing itself with a confused sense of loss. Was this her destiny then—to be shunned by the one man who fired her blood?

Considering the anger and confusion she had spent on R.J. Morrisson, she ought to derive satisfaction at being free of him. But it wasn't so. The knowledge that he'd found it so easy to dismiss her from his life left a vacant feeling in Carole's breast.

And now, her willful feelings for the man were even more worrisome. Her best defense had been to think of him as a cad, but she could do so no longer. He had laid his cards on the table, made no denial of the attraction they both knew was there. He would not betray his brother, and Carole had to respect that. A man of honor, she thought with wonder. And in her mind's eye, the stature of R.J. Morrisson swelled.

The irony was that he had just walked out of her life.

She bustled about the apartment. Turning on the television, she tried to put her thoughts to something else. But try as she might, they always returned to R.J.

It wasn't until she began to get ready for bed that the memory came racing back to her: The man who had been following her! Who was he? What did he want?

Suddenly, the night had eyes. Methodically, she checked all the doors and windows of the apartment before turning out the lights. Still, when Carole climbed into bed she lay rigidly, listening to every unusual sound that pricked the darkness.

Across the District, the phone rang at the Gossetts' Tradd Street house.

"What is it?" came Gossett's alert voice after he reached for the receiver.

"Just checking in," Horton answered. "It's one A.M., and she's tucked in for the night. However . . . I do have a small piece of information. I didn't see the Corvette, but the same guy came by her place. He stayed for the better part of an hour."

Horton didn't report that Carole had spotted him tailing her. He'd be more careful in the future. And besides, Gossett didn't have to know everything.

Chapter Seven

R.J. DROVE ALONG the sunny coastal highway, which afforded him the luxury of seaside scenery. A hot Fourth of July sun burned down, bleaching the sea oats that waved atop the dunes, failing to daunt the clusters of sea gulls that darted occasionally overhead and then swung back to the water's edge to join scurrying sandpipers. Their cries called to mind the carefree days of his boyhood, vacation times when the primary responsibility of the day had been to build the best sand castle on the beach.

R.J. looked away from the coastal panorama, concentrating his gaze on the road. But as if his thoughts had a life of their own, they returned to Carole. For the life of him, he couldn't figure out what had happened. R.J.'s hand climbed to his head, and once again he tenderly felt around the bruised lump above his right temple.

No matter how he approached Carole, he couldn't seem to do it right. When he was passionately forceful, she pushed him away. When he was logical and honorable, she got mad. When he reached out to say a tender good-bye, she dismissed him with a haughty glance. Caustically R.J. wondered just what the magic formula was. How the hell was he supposed to reach Carole Gossett?

The voice of conscience whispered that he wasn't supposed to reach her at all. And yet she stayed unnervingly on R.J.'s mind.

Crossing into Georgia, he approached the Savannah city limits. Charleston, established in the 1670s by the British, was older than Savannah, which was founded by General James Edward Oglethorpe in 1773. Still, the two cities had much in common. Both were busy eastern-seaboard ports; both were surrounded by elite, seaside resort communities; both were infused with the rich antebellum spirit of the Southland. As R.J. drove through historic areas, he was reminded of Charleston not only by the graceful Georgian architecture, but also by the palmettoes, magnolias, and great live oaks that lined his route.

It had been a long time since R.J. had been to Savannah. Perhaps ten years had passed since the family had spent a month at Hilton Head, just across the South Carolina line. The family had gone swimming and boating at the resort, but mostly they had gravitated toward the world-famous Hilton Head tennis courts. During that month, they drove often into Savannah to dine at the fine seafood restaurants along the Savannah River front or to take those damned historic tours his father always arranged.

R.J. grinned, remembering the four of them—Camille and Margaret still little girls, and he and Curt barely in their teens—being dragged through one of their father's intellectual afternoons of museums and historic sites. Every vacation, they knew it was coming. The land in which they lived, where Morrissons had made their fortune, was rich in history. And few southerners were more knowledgeable or proud of their heritage than Robert Morrisson.

R.J. stopped to pick up a city map. Then, leaving the historic area behind, he drove around the perimeter of the city and approached a black section of town. It took a while to find the street listed on the guardianship petition. Once he did, R.J. was glad the sun shone so brightly overhead. In the dark, this neighborhood would have been threatening.

Basically, it was a slum. The buildings were ramshackle, joined by the tentative, sloping arms of clotheslines. On broken-down porches sat swings, bicycles, televisions—and people, who without exception stared at the silver car that purred along their narrow street.

With relief, R.J. finally spotted the street number he sought. The dingy frame house had once been green but had faded to chartreuse. Against this background, patches of new, raw wood contrasted at several spots on the front porch and walls. Parked in front of the tattered dwelling was a brand new, white Cadillac sedan.

Pulling up behind the Caddy, R.J. leaned forward for a moment and studied the house. The first thing he noticed were several black children of varying ages. They must have hidden as he first came into view, but now that he'd stopped, they popped up from behind an old refrigerator and a couple of chairs and scampered off the porch in opposite directions.

R.J. got out of the car and took a sweeping look up and down the street. The people he noticed as he drove up had retreated out of sight, but he could still feel their eyes on him. He'd worn no jacket—it was too damned hot—but as he made his way across the meager yard, R.J. found himself fidgeting with his tie, drawing it taut under his chin as if for support.

The simple planks creaked noisily as he climbed to the porch and crossed to the screen door that yawned back against the raw wood frame surrounding it. The door was open to admit whatever cool the outside would deliver, and R.J. reached out to rap smartly by the screen. But before he could com-

158

plete the movement, a giant black woman stepped up to the other side.

"Whachoo want?" The words boomed.

"Miss Stuckey?" R.J. asked, but she made no reply. "I'm looking for Geraldine Stuckey." It was dark inside the house, and the most he could see of the woman was the voluminous, pink floral muumuu she was wearing. But then a white smile lit her face.

"I bet I know who you is, honey," she told him. "Come on in. It's hotter 'n blue blazes out yonder."

R.J. thought the stench inside would overpower him. Gradually, as his eyes adjusted to the dim light, he saw the incongruous trappings of poverty: bare wood floors, a velvet couch with springs popping out of the cushions, a rusted-out patio table covered with dirty plates and cups. But in the corner, going full blast, stood a luxurious, nineteen-inch color television.

The mammoth woman had waddled over to the TV, and was watching, entranced. "Hold on jest a second, honey. This is goin' off, and I gots to keep up with my soap!"

R.J. stood behind her at a discreet distance, his eyes roaming the massive bulk of her. About five feet five, as wide as she was tall, she wore slippers, the pink dress, and a black wig, done up in curls high on the crown of her head. She was older than he'd first thought—maybe close to Jonah's age, though she'd obviously led the kind of life that left its aging mark with bloodshot eyes and wrinkles.

She turned suddenly, catching him in the midst of his perusal. Helplessly, R.J. could feel the color flooding his face as she strolled up to him.

"Well?" she then asked. "Where is it?"

R.J. blinked. "Where is what?"

"My check, honey. That's what you done come over here for, ain't it?"

For a perplexed instant, R.J. only looked at her.

159

She was smiling widely, affording him the view of several gold teeth.

"Are you Geraldine Stuckey?" he asked firmly.

She rolled her eyes in exasperation. "Course I'm Geraldine Stuckey. Who'd ya think I was? Princess Di?"

"You're the cousin of Jonah Stuckey . . . from Charleston?"

"Damn right, I am! Who wants to know?"

"I'm sorry, Miss Stuckey. I just wanted to be sure."

A pacified, knowing look came to her round face. "Well, that's all right, honey. We wouldn't want ya givin' that money to the wrong Stuckey, now, would we?"

She thought he was someone else, R.J. realized, someone who was supposed to be paying her off.

"One more question, Miss Stuckey. How much money are you expecting?"

A stunned look. "Two thousand, just like the last two months. Ain't that what they sent?"

"Who?"

"Why, that fancy comp'ny that done bought my land! Ain't that who you're here for? The Land Grant Comp'ny?"

Land Grant . . . The name echoed in R.J.'s head.

"Land Grant? That's the name of the company that bought the property you got from Jonah Stuckey?"

A suspicious look sprang to the woman's leathery face. "Jest who the hell are you, boy?"

"I should have introduced myself. My name is R.J. Morrisson. I'm an attorney."

"And whadya want with me?"

New, unimagined pieces were beginning to fall into place, and this woman could be the key to the puzzle. R.J. smiled in what he hoped was a beguiling fashion.

"I'm just following up on the Jonah Stuckey matter . . . you know, all the legalities involved. If you don't mind, I'd like to take a look at the bill of sale for that land."

"I ain't gots to show you nothin', boy!" the woman proclaimed in a hard voice. "I know my rights. And them spit-shined boys from Charleston done told me all I needs to know 'bout Jonah. If you ain't brought me no check, I ain't got no business with you."

R.J. backed toward the door. "Your 'check,' " he repeated. "Is that where your new Cadillac came from? Your check?"

"You leave my car out of it, and git on outta here 'fore my Clarence gits home and throws you out!"

"That won't be necessary, Miss Stuckey," R.J. said coldly. He stepped outside the rickety screen door. "But tell me. . . . Are you really Jonah's cousin? Or did you just happen to be born with the last name of Stuckey?"

The screen mesh helped the harsh look on her face, but it did nothing to soften her voice.

"My granddaddy came from up Charleston way," she said, deftly latching the screen door. "And even if he didn't, you wouldn't have no way to prove it!"

And with that, she turned and waddled into the dark interior, a satisfied cackle shaking her girth.

That night, R.J. lay across the foot of his hotel bed, making odd and disjointed doodles on a Sheraton note pad: *Belmont Pines . . . Savannah . . . Geraldine Stuckey . . . six thousand acres . . . Land Grant* . . . And as he gazed down at the paper, the words finally came together and the pen in his hand moved to draw a line that connected them all.

Land Grant . . . The pen fashioned a question mark. Just what, or who, was Land Grant?

After a while, he rolled off the bed and went to stand by the sliding glass door that opened onto a patio. There was nothing more he could do this weekend. Tomorrow, he had to go back to Columbia. There were briefs to be gone over before court convened on Monday, and R.J. had the feeling that Judge Harper would be keeping an eye on him, making sure he had done the necessary homework to function properly in the prestigious capacity of state clerk.

It was stealing over him again—that dread of returning to his life in Columbia. And as R.J. stared moodily into the Savannah night, he watched Fourth of July fireworks light up the rooftops across town . . . and dreamed of the Battery in Charleston.

Curt was humming to himself as he stepped out of the brilliant summer daylight into the dark, cool interior of the Club. His father had again sought him out, this time for lunch, and Curt had been pleasantly surprised.

Everything was going along even better than he had hoped, Curt reflected. His father was treating him with dignity and respect, his boss had promoted him and had taken him into his closest confidence. He felt quite the success this hot Monday—except for the nagging thorn of his breach with Carole. Still, if James were right about his daughter—and James was *always* right— it wouldn't be long before she'd be back to her old self and romance would bloom anew.

Curt spotted his father, already seated in one of the anterooms, and strolled up with a smile. But one look at Robert Morrisson wiped the pleasure from his face.

"Sit down, Curt."

He sank onto the plush, upholstered chair. "What is it, Dad? What's the matter?"

Robert's face looked as though it were carved from stone. "I don't know why . . . I don't know how . . . but your brother is on the trail of this Stuckey thing."

162

For a moment Curt's heart sank. But just as quickly, it was buoyed by a surge of fierce protectiveness. "What's happened?" he demanded.

The grimness of his mood etched unusually deep lines across Robert's distinguished face. "On Friday, R.J. went to the county clerk's office. Dan was out, and he hoodwinked the secretary out of copies of the Stuckey files."

"I didn't even know he was in town."

"Neither did I!" Robert thundered. "Doesn't that tell us something right there?"

"Don't get paranoid, Dad."

Robert's dark blue eyes shot a look of indignation across the table. "I'm not the kind to get paranoid, Curt, and I think you know it. But I want to know exactly where we stand. You pulled this thing together. Tell me . . . how much can R.J. learn from those documents? How well are we screened? I don't want to end up having to confront my own son on this deal!"

A familiar pain burst inside Curt. Your own son! he wanted to cry. Am I not your own son? You don't have any trouble confronting *me* on this deal!

But when his words came, they showed none of the hurt he felt. "We're completely screened," he told his father. "There's nothing of any import that R.J. can learn from the guardianship petition. Hell, even if he got hold of Geraldine's bill of sale, he still couldn't trace us!"

Curt was warming to his subject now. He'd never been able to compete with R.J. in terms of sports or academics. But in the world of business, where ingenuity and craftiness reigned supreme, Curt put his older brother in the shade.

"Land Grant is a corporation of three men," Curt went on. "And if R.J. looked in every phone book in the world, he wouldn't find their names. Even if he tracked the sale to Gossett Enterprises, he could never prove our involvement."

A black-uniformed waiter stepped over to take their order. Robert and Curt proceeded through the meal in relative quiet, a pall having fallen over their table. After lunch, they stepped onto busy East Bay Street. Before heading to his car, Robert looked once more to his younger son.

"Don't get the wrong idea, Curt. I'm not faulting you in any way. This scheme of yours is going to make us millions, and I'm not one to throw stones."

Robert's expression turned dark. He didn't like the way he was feeling, the way he'd felt ever since Dan Shriver called. R.J. was perhaps the one person in the world who could make Robert question the ethics of some of his latest business dealings. The eyes he trained on his younger son were midnight blue.

"Why did this have to happen?" he asked. "Why did R.J. have to get involved?"

Curt squinted through the sunlight, eyeing his father steadily. "He's not involved, Dad. Not really. He'll get tired of this soon enough and return his attentions to his life in Columbia."

But as Curt climbed into the BMW and raced back to G.E. headquarters, an undeniably cold feeling settled in his breast. He stalked blindly into his office, turning with a start when he realized that James sat nearly hidden in one of the high-backed chairs at the desk.

"Hello, Curt. Have a nice lunch?"

Curt's mood was raw, and being startled by James didn't help any. "It was nice enough," he answered brusquely. "What can I do for you?"

James looked him over ambiguously. "More likely, I can do something for *you*."

"What do you mean?"

"How close an eye have you been keeping on Carole?"

"Why, I haven't been keeping an eye on her at all, James."

A slight feeling of guilt crept up under Curt's col-

164

lar. Ever since his blowup with Carole, he had been finding his ease with Laura Murphy. James, of course, knew nothing of his clandestine activities; so far Curt had been able to keep things confined to the discretion of Laura's apartment. But lately she'd begun to complain that he never took her anywhere.

The affair had started the night of the dinner party, when Carole had first seemed so distant. Then, Laura had been a warm, willing presence that soothed away his feelings of rejection. But now, Curt was beginning to regret his actions. Things were going to get sticky when Carole finally came back to her senses and realized that her future lay with Curt Morrisson.

The expression he turned on James was a picture of innocence. "I haven't felt the need to keep an eye on Carole. Ever since you and I talked last week, I've been under the impression that working things out with her is just a matter of time. In the meantime, I've thought it best to simply give her a little space."

"Careful you don't give her too *much* space," James cautioned.

Curt suddenly lost patience. His words were abrupt, though a grin softened them somewhat. "Okay, James. Why don't we cut through all the crap? Is there something I should know about?"

James smiled faintly. "I'd say that's a fair question. For instance, did you know that your brother was over at her place again this past Friday evening?"

Uncomfortably familiar heat rushed to Curt's cheeks. "How do you know that? How do you know he ever went to see her at all?"

"I've had her followed."

Curt's eyes went wide. "You've had her followed?" he asked, although it struck him immediately that he really shouldn't be surprised. "You mean you hired a detective?"

165

James nodded. "I knew that something was brewing with Carole. I thought it in our best interests . . . *yours*, as well as mine . . . to find out what she was up to. And it paid off. My man tracked down Haut Nouveau for me . . . got rid of that interfering little fashion scout. And he made note of any men Carole might spend time with. There hasn't been anyone, Curt." James paused, raising a suspicious brow. "Except your brother . . . twice."

He watched Curt spin on his heel and cross the room to stare unseeingly out the picture window. James liked the young man, wanted him for a son-in-law, but he couldn't deny the pleasure he felt at setting a fire underneath him.

"R.J. was there for nearly an hour, Curt. Now, what do you think he and Carole could have been discussing for that period of time?"

Curt turned at the window, the blinding light behind him turning him into a silhouette whose expression James couldn't read.

"There could be any number of things, James. We Morrissons are a close-knit family, maybe more so than you understand. It wouldn't surprise me to learn that R.J. had gone over there to try and smooth things out for me. He knows Carole and I have been having problems, and he knows how much she means to me."

James rose to his feet, meandering toward the door. "I might concede you Morrisson men have something in common. One thing's for sure . . . you seem to share a weak spot for my little girl!" A rare chuckle punctuated James's exit.

Whirling back to the window, Curt banged his fists against the heavy glass. First, the interference with the Stuckey matter and now, Carole! What the hell are you doing, R.J.? he wanted to scream. Trying to ruin my life?

Wall Street may have coined the phrase, "Black Monday," but at that moment, Curt felt it had been designed just for him. Never in his life had a Monday been so black!

But then, slowly, a transformation came over Curt. The feeling of trepidation was obliterated, leaving behind the spirit of an enraged lion prepared to defend its hard-won trophies.

"Hit me with your best shot, big brother," he finally muttered to the unhearing windowpane. "We'll just see who wins this time. . . . We'll just see."

Friday marked the fourth morning in a row Constance Trippley had spotted Kathleen taking a stroll along Tradd Street. Today, she waved the younger woman over.

"Good morning to you, Kathleen. I've missed seeing you these past months. Glad to see you've started taking your daily constitution again."

Kathleen smiled at the friendly old lady in her floppy straw hat. "It's nice to *feel* like taking it again, Miss Constance."

The sharp eyes of Constance Trippley flew over the younger woman. She looked wonderful. Her dark hair was pulled sleekly back from her face, showing the shining, clear dark eyes to advantage. She was wearing a pretty pink jogging suit that mirrored the flush in her cheeks.

"I must say you look fit as a fiddle, Kathleen. Had you been ailing before?"

Kathleen's expression turned briefly thoughtful. But then the cheerful radiance returned as if it would not be held at bay. "You might say I was ailing, Miss Constance. But who could feel poorly on such a beautiful day as this? Just breathe that Charleston air. There's nothing like it, don't you agree?"

Constance smiled at the girl's ebullience. "Well, seeing as how you feel so all-fired good, would you have time to help an old lady move a stone marker to the other end of this flower bed?''

Pleased at being asked inside the exclusive Trippley property, Kathleen hurried through the wrought-iron gate to join Constance among her glorious rose gardens. Together, they transported the stone marker to its new spot, and then—after a quick tour of the prize-winning roses—Kathleen went on her way.

Constance looked after her with pleasant surprise. The pretty young woman looked as happy as could be. Perhaps James Gossett wasn't such a brute after all.

Leaning on her garden hoe, Constance thought of the concerns that would occupy her day. She and Aurora planned to drive up the coast later on. Constance wanted more crushed shell for the garden paths, and Mr. Benton, from up close to Folly Beach, always gave her the best portion for her money. After that, she and her sister would dine at The Breakers, a favorite seaside establishment of theirs. It would be almost like a holiday, a break from their ordinary routine.

It was late afternoon when Mr. Benton finished loading the car trunk with as much as it would hold. Thanking him, Constance turned the ancient, black Rolls Royce back onto the coastal highway. She'd often suggested they sell the old gas guzzler, but Aurora always insisted that if it was ''good enough for Daddy,'' it was good enough for them. And so the sisters puttered slowly along, the traffic building up behind them, until they pulled into The Breakers, a once-popular playground of the elite which—though now rather old and deserted—was still maintained in the grand tradition. The sun was just beginning to set as they were seated at a window table overlooking the elegant grounds of the adjacent hotel.

Constance was looking over the menu and had

just decided on red snapper, when Aurora kicked her under the table.

"*Ow!*" Constance scowled. "For heaven's sake, Aurora! What are you doing?"

Aurora's silver-blue hair danced as she nodded emphatically toward the window. "Look at that. It's that Gossett woman! Why, she's going in that hotel room with a man. And he surely doesn't look like James Gossett to me!"

Constance peered curiously out the window. Sure enough, it was Kathleen. She was still wearing that pink jogging suit from earlier in the day. Constance eyed the muscular-looking young man who accompanied her. There was no doubt about it, he was not her husband. Just before they disappeared swiftly inside their hotel room, which was almost directly below the overlooking restaurant window, Constance saw Kathleen look up at the man with a wide, happy smile.

Constance nodded. "Good for you, Kathleen," she said softly.

Across the table, Aurora gasped. "I'm sure I didn't hear you correctly, sister," she huffed. "You know very well what's going on in that room. Why, it's an outrage against every principle a southern lady stands for. Surely you can't condone such lurid behavior!"

Constance looked over at her sister, unconcerned. "I certainly can. Life is too short to miss out on something . . . or some*one* . . . that brings happiness. That's a lesson I wish we'd learned long ago, sister."

"Constance Trippley! Are you suggesting that either of us should behave in such a fashion? To meet a man in a hotel?" Aurora began to fan herself furiously with the linen napkin. "Why, I'm simply appalled! Honestly, sister! Sometimes I just don't know what to make of you!"

Constance rolled her eyes and looked back to the

menu. "Simmer down, Aurora. I'll be sure to warn you before I plan my next rendezvous."

"You are incorrigible!" Aurora sputtered.

Constance extended the menu to her sister.

"Crab?" she asked innocently, though a sparkling look of mirth danced in her eyes.

The package came with the swift, deadly impact of a bullet.

Ironically, the whole way home from Carlotta's!, Carole had strolled along wondering if she should call Jack Levy. She'd been trying to be patient, thinking that it would appear more professional not to seem too eager. And then, she'd climbed the stairs and seen the package on her stoop—and her breath had stopped.

Now, she sat in the dull quiet of her living room as the soft, gray light of dusk gradually faded away. Unmoving, Carole stared straight ahead, unable to see anything but a replay of her earlier actions. Over and over again, she tore at the wrapping of the package, recognized that the entirety of the work had been returned, opened the accompanying letter with trembling fingers.

Now, in the quiet dark, the crisp words burned with merciless accuracy at the backs of her eyes:

Dear Miss Gossett:

We appreciate your sending samples for our consideration, but in the future, we ask you to keep in mind that we have no interest in reviewing unsolicited work.

Mr. Levy, who invited you to submit, is no longer with this company. However, out of courtesy, a panel of our most respected people took time to look through your book. The consensus is unanimous. Unfortunately, Miss Gossett, we cannot consider inclusion of your designs in our line, either now or in the future. Quite simply, they do not meet our standards. . . .

Carole's eyes slipped shut as she sank back against the sofa, feeling as if someone had just knocked the wind out of her.

Down the street, Joey Horton stepped into the phone booth outside Woodgreen's Drug Store. Dialing the number from memory, he then waited, a crooked smile curving his lips.

"Hello," came a gruff voice. James was not in a particularly good mood. The house was too quiet for his taste. The servants had already retired, and yet Kathleen was still not home from her exercise class.

"The pigeon has come home to roost," Joey remarked.

"What the hell are you saying, man?" James barked. "Don't talk in riddles. Just tell me straight if you've got something to report."

"Carole got the package this afternoon. She hasn't budged from the apartment since. Hasn't even turned on a light."

James paused for a moment, imagining his daughter's reaction to the bomb that had just decimated her foolish, selfish dream. He'd dictated the rejection letter, himself, much to the surprise and ill-concealed dismay of the Haut Nouveau staff. They'd actually wanted to buy Carole's damned collection! Thank God his instincts had been working; otherwise, his daughter might be on a plane to New York right now!

The corners of his mouth dipped in a slight grin. The rejection letter was short and to the point. Unless he'd lost his touch, it would destroy Carole's desire to hear the words *New York* ever again.

A vague thought of pity crossed his mind, but James quickly crushed it. The destiny of his daughter was to bear him grandchildren by the name of

Morrisson, *not* to fly off to New York on some half-baked ambition that she'd tire of in six months' time anyway.

"Anything else?" he asked Horton.

"That's it. You want me to continue watching her?"

"For the time being, yes," Gossett confirmed. "But it shouldn't be much longer."

James hung up the phone, sat back in his chair, and considered his next plan of action. It shouldn't be much longer, indeed, before Carole put her mind back on what she knew best—spending money, having a good time, and entertaining the most eligible bachelor in all of Charleston.

How much time should I give her? James wondered for an idle moment. But then he vaulted out of his chair, left the house, and drove the short distance to the corner of Broad and Rutledge.

It seemed to Carole that she was in a dark, safe tunnel. But then somewhere in the distance, a noise materialized—a nagging, insistent rapping that grew louder and louder, until it broke through the protective, subconscious barrier and pummeled her conscious ear. She pivoted as if in a daze, peering through the dark in the direction of the doorway.

"Carole!" came her father's voice. "Carole! Open the door this instant. Do you hear me?"

"Daddy?" The whisper was a dry sound, like wind rustling through the palms.

"Carole! I know you're in there! Open this damned door!"

She moved at the command, floated unfeeling toward the door. Magically, it seemed, the door opened. And there was her father. Rushing past her, he flipped a switch on the wall, and the chandelier in the living room flooded her sanctum with shattering light. Carole winced and, squinting against this new intrusion, closed the door, then strolled wordlessly into the room.

172

For an instant, a whisper of worry flitted through James's mind. Carole looked nothing like herself. Her fair hair hung straight and limp, her bare, unadorned face wore a vacant look. But she'd come through it in time, he reasoned. This was for her own good. One day she'd be grateful he'd intervened—one day when she embraced the destiny she was born to fulfill.

"Carole, my dear," he said in a voice of concern. "You don't look well. Are you ill?"

She said nothing, only pointed to a package lying on the nearby drawing table. James stepped over, looked down curiously, picked up the letter that was typed on a Haut Nouveau letterhead.

"This?" he questioned. "Is this the reason you're acting so strangely?"

Gradually, Carole's presence of mind was returning. "Read it," she murmured.

James's dark eyes raced over the short epistle, then darted to Carole. She was dressed in casual slacks and shirt, both white, and it occurred to him that she had an unearthly look.

In a quick, uncharacteristic gesture, James stepped to his daughter and took her in his arms. It caught Carole by surprise, this unwarranted embrace from her father. And suddenly, the eyes that had been dry with shock, filled with tears. James held her as she cried, offering the comforting strength of his chest as tears streamed off her face and onto his shirt.

Get it out of your system, he was thinking. Get it all out.

Eventually, the sobs subsided, but Carole continued to hold onto her father tightly, as though she would cram the deprived affection of a lifetime into this moment.

Leaning back so he could look down into her tear-streaked face, James asked softly, "Feel better?"

When she nodded, he stepped back, still gripping

173

her shoulders, and said, "I'll tell you what you need. You need to come along with me, have a good night's rest, and wake up in the morning to Mrs. Denning's homemade biscuits!"

Carole managed a tearful smile.

"Yes!" James said matter-of-factly. "That's just the ticket for you . . . a change of scene. Come along now. Gather your things."

And in a matter of minutes, Carole found herself bundled up and transported to the familiar, soothing opulence of her father's house. As they climbed the stairs, the clock struck eleven. James noted that Kathleen caught sight of their reflection in her dressing-table mirror when they filed quietly past the master suite. His wife turned with surprise and James threw her a silencing look, continuing along the hallway with his quiet ward to the frilly, pink-and-white chamber that had been her own.

Carole looked about the familiar furnishings, drew comfort from the setting of an earlier, more carefree life, when the only thought of failure had to do with displeasing her father.

"You'll be comfortable here, Carole," he told her. "You always were. Everything's pretty much the same as you left it. There are even some of your clothes in the drawers and closet. You could take a nice, hot bath. There are some bath oils . . ."

"Thank you, Daddy," she said with a wan smile. "I know where everything is."

"Why don't you get some rest?" he suggested, coming to stand before her. "Things will look much better in the morning."

"I'm not so sure of that," she replied dispiritedly. "But I'm looking forward to at least forgetting about it for a while."

"You'll see, Carole. Everything will work out just fine."

As she studied his well-meaning face, the sense of failure swept over her anew. Suddenly, she spun away from the sight of her father, away from the fact that he had every right in the world to scream, I told you so!

"Oh, Daddy!" she managed, burying her face in her hands. "I've been such a fool! I actually thought I had talent . . . that I was gifted!"

James took her again by the shoulders and made her face him. "Don't you know by now, Carole, that you *are* gifted?"

"That's not what the letter said!"

"I'm not talking about any letter, I'm talking about *you*, Carole. Do you know how many women would kill for what you have? You have the greatest gift of all . . . the beauty and sparkle of an irresistible woman."

A bitter taste lurched to Carole's mouth. "Like a courtesan?" she asked woodenly.

James's black eyes gleamed with fervor. "Some of the most powerful women in all of history were courtesans. Do you deny the gift of someone like Josephine . . . or even Cleopatra? Those women ruled the whole damned world! And you, Carole . . . some day, you could virtually rule the whole of Charleston, if you put your mind to it. So, don't decry your gift, daughter. Not to me."

Carole sniffled, her gaze falling to the carpet's rich pattern of twining roses. "All right, Daddy." Even as she spoke, Carole wondered how many thousands of times in her life she had uttered those very words.

Bidding his daughter good night, James closed the bedroom door. With an immense feeling of satisfaction, he sauntered along the hallway to the master suite, unbuttoning the shirt still damp from Carole's tears. And as he entered the suite, he was unaware of the pleased look firmly entrenched on his face.

Kathleen, who had donned her dressing gown and finished brushing her hair into long, dark waves, now rose from the dressing table. Her eyes

175

were focused intently on James as he stripped down to his boxer shorts and tossed his rumpled clothing on the chaise.

"Cleopatra?" she taunted. "That's laying it on a bit thick, don't you think?"

James turned and strolled to the side of the bed. "Eavesdropping doesn't become you, Kathleen."

"It was hardly eavesdropping, James. The door was open, and your voice carried quite distinctly down the hall. What's the matter with Carole?"

His expression remained calm, betraying no emotion. "That New York fashion house rejected her. I've brought her here for the night." Saying nothing more, he turned down the covers, climbed into bed, and doused the light on his bedside table.

Kathleen shrugged out of the dressing gown and slid under the covers. "So, you've got the chickadee back under your wing again. Tell me, James. How ever *did* you manage it?"

"You know, Kathleen," he said without turning to look at her. "I think I like you better when you're drinking. You've become irritatingly nosy of late." Deftly, he turned the subject away from Carole. "How was your exercise class? That *is* what kept you out so long tonight, isn't it?"

Kathleen kept her face carefully bland. It was just the sort of question which would have set her fears aflurry in the old days.

"Yes," she answered steadily. "That was what kept me away so long."

"So, did you work out any of the frustrations you women complain of all the time?" he asked drily.

Kathleen stretched an arm toward her bedside lamp, switched off the light.

"You could say that," she replied. Rolling to the far edge of her side of the king-sized bed, Kathleen went to sleep in the quiet peace of darkness, with a smile on her face and the memory of André's touch in her heart.

The next morning Carole awoke slowly, her eyes aching. She went into the bathroom and splashed water on her face. But when she looked into the mirror that had been hers as a little girl, she felt as though she wasn't all there. Part of Carole Gossett was dead. The independent woman who had lived and hoped so exultantly the past month and a half had been murdered yesterday afternoon.

With a rather numb feeling of acceptance, she got dressed and went downstairs to breakfast. Her father and Kathleen were already seated at the dining table. Mrs. Denning fussed about the silver serving dishes, but when she saw Carole, a smile broke across her withered features.

"Welcome home, Miss Carole," she offered with a bob of her head.

Carole smiled in return, wishing the innocent words didn't seem to carry such a ring of doom. "Thank you, Mrs. Denning. It's good to see you. Good morning, Daddy . . . Kathleen."

Once again as she looked at Kathleen, Carole found herself remembering Constance Trippley's misguided appraisal. Kathleen didn't look sad or fearful. Indeed, she had a vibrant, healthy glow. Sourly, Carole wished *she* herself looked half that good.

"Hello, Carole," Kathleen was saying. "Please, sit down. Would you like some coffee?"

James set aside the newspaper. "How did you sleep, daughter?" he asked as Kathleen graciously filled Carole's cup.

"Fine, Daddy." Carole helped herself to one of Mrs. Denning's legendary biscuits and began applying peach preserves.

"That's my girl," he commended.

Kathleen rolled her eyes at her plate. It was high time, she decided, to broach the long-standing barrier between herself and this step-daughter who was very nearly her own age.

"Your father told me what happened with the de-

177

signs, Carole," she began hesitantly. "I just want you to know that I'm awfully sorry."

Carole looked in wary surprise across the table. Several cutting remarks sprang to her tongue, but she held them at bay. The concern on Kathleen's face seemed to be sincere, and at the moment, Carole had little energy or care to fight her father's wife. She accepted the peace offering with a slight smile.

James broke the tense air with a loud harumph. "Well, the time has come for Carole to put all that behind her now. Look to the future. Have some fun. Smell the roses. You've been cooped up in that apartment of yours too long, Carole. How about some fresh air and exercise? I'm going to the Isle of Palms to watch a tennis tournament tomorrow afternoon at Wild Dunes. I wish you'd join me."

He paused a moment, fixed his daughter with a penetrating look. "Curt will be there."

And suddenly, Kathleen knew. Somehow, some way, James had caused this. From the boundaries of Charleston, his powerful arm had spanned the miles to New York, reached into the fashion world, and crushed Carole's opportunity. Just so he could match her up with the high-and-mighty Morrissons!

Her dark eyes flashed to where Carole sat so quietly across the table. I know that look, Kathleen thought with pity. It's the look of defeat . . . of ultimate surrender to the will of James Gossett. She wasn't surprised when Carole agreed—with a seeming lack of care—to accompany him to the Isle of Palms.

Kathleen wished she could think of something to say, some warning to give. But then, Carole was excusing herself, announcing that she was going to walk home. And Kathleen found herself simply sitting there, watching the young woman walk out the door under James's satisfied, watchful gaze.

Carole spent a great deal of the afternoon and evening just walking the District. Loath to be locked up in the same space with her drawing table and rejected designs, she strolled aimlessly in the out of doors. She was mindless of the eyes she had so fearfully felt watching her, unburdened by the fear of being approached by the man in the snap-brim hat. She had no cares, no worries, no feelings. It was as if she were empty.

She slept little that night, plagued with dreams of falling from the high towers in New York City over and over again. And the next morning, when she confronted her mirror, she saw the purple smudges beneath her eyes that testified to a restless night.

"You really *do* look quite the dreadful, old thing," she said to her reflection.

Glancing down, her eyes rested on the endless assortment of preparations and beauty aids arranged next to the sink. She had all the accoutrements she needed—and more—to mask the ravages of the past two nights.

An hour later, the face in the mirror was the one everyone remembered as Carole Gossett. Blue-green eyes looked out from between a dark fringe of heavily mascaraed lashes. She had carefully applied blusher, highlighter, and lip-gloss, so that the entire, dimpled face seemed to shine rosily. Looking over her makeup with her old eye for perfection, Carole decided she was "fixed."

With a sigh, she plugged in the electric hair-curling rod that hadn't been touched in more than a month.

Chapter Eight

THE ISLE OF Palms, one of the most beautiful of Charleston's barrier islands, offered resort living at its finest. At the chic Wild Dunes Club, exquisite condominiums overlooked the ocean and the two renowned, eighteen-hole golf courses. Here, the fashionably athletic dawdled over lunch at poolside, danced under the stars, or more frequently, populated the competition-ready tennis courts that were often reserved four weekends in advance.

But not during the July Bake Off. The annual three-week competition drew tennis buffs of amateur standing from all over Charleston, dominating the Wild Dunes courts during the last weekends of July.

Eliminations began during the first round robin of play, and on the last Sunday of competition, all finals matches—men's and women's singles and doubles—were played. It was rumored that in the past, courtside seats for the July Bake Off finals had been scalped to the tune of as much as a thousand dollars. Silver trophies were awarded the winners, but it was the prestige of winning a Bake Off that tantalized the local competitors.

The afternoon was clear and hot, typical for

Charleston in mid-July. In deference to the heat Carole knew would be amplified by the tennis crowds, she wore a red, halter-top sundress that belted at the waist but left arms and back open to the air. Now, as she walked with her father along the palmlined path leading to the courts, she was glad of her choice. Even the ocean breeze that flitted through surrounding palmettoes and roses did little to relieve the heat of the sun. And at the courts, which were recessed and screened against interfering, seaside wind, she knew the temperature would be sweltering.

She took a sidelong glance at her father. He'd been pleasant and conversational on the drive out to the isle. Carole could tell he was immensely pleased to have his daughter once again on his arm. His ebony hair gleamed in the sunlight, and although he was nearing fifty, his lithe build and springy step made him appear ten years younger. He could almost be a male model, Carole mused, strolling along in the lightweight slacks, Lacoste shirt, and Avia running shoes. The look was sporting, and every accessory bespoke the wealth of James Gossett.

As they approached the courts and caught the rhythmic sounds of the batted tennis ball, Carole returned her attention to her surroundings. The roar of the crowd told her a point had been won.

"Forty, love," confirmed the booming voice of the announcer. "Game point, Misters Parker and Gottfried."

Carole and her father hovered at the crest of the bleachers, watching quietly across the swaying field of hundreds of heads as another point began in the men's doubles match. Her eyes swept the panorama. In the distance, the surf rolled onto a creamy beach before the green and white awning of the beach cabana. Moving closer, she glimpsed the sprawling wood exterior of the restaurant. Then, a dozen green courts with red and white trim stretched up to the championship court, where four men in tennis whites were dashing furiously about. And finally, immediately below Carole, the horde of colorful spectators who turned their heads in unison as the ball was swatted back and forth across the net.

The crowd applauded once more as the game was won, and the players prepared to change sides.

"This is the first round robin of play," James said. "The match we came to see won't start for a half hour yet."

Carole looked at him curiously. "I didn't know we were coming to view a particular match. Who's playing?"

James tossed her a casual look. "Curt and Robert," he said nonchalantly, and then began to stroll down the steps toward courtside.

Carole said nothing as she fell in behind him. It didn't take him long to jump right back into the driver's seat of her life, she thought. In the past month, she'd forgotten much about her father's heavy-handed style. Now, it all come back. It was just like him to deliver her to Curt like some gladiator's prize.

Without being told, Carole knew what was expected of her: She was to sit up there in the stands, cheer Curt on and put an end to the cold silence that had built up between them this past month. A feeling of rebellion welled up within her, but it quickly ebbed. At the moment she simply didn't have the heart to fight her father—or Curt.

She was, as they had known all along, nothing more than a man's woman. The delusion that she could ever be anything else was over—like a dream one loses upon waking.

Taking a deep breath, Carole pushed aside the annoyance her father's strategies had aroused in her, slipping back into the role she knew best. And if there were an aching emptiness within her, no one would be able to detect it behind the dimpling guise of the old Carole Gossett. Sauntering down the steps, she waved gaily to occasional acquaintances as she followed her father to a pair of reserved seats at center courtside. Making her way to the exclusive spectators' box, she found that she was seated next to none other than Charlotte Morrisson. It wasn't until then that Carole realized the extent of his manipulation.

"Why, Carole!" Charlotte exclaimed pleasantly. "I'm so glad to see you. It's been a long time."

"Hello, Mrs. Morrisson," she murmured.

"And this," Charlotte added, sweeping her hand toward a pleasant-looking couple seated on her left, "Is Dr. and Mrs. Gottfried. Henry and Gwen, Carole Gossett. Of course you know her father, James."

James leaned over to shake the man's hand. "Hello, Henry. Good to see you. I gather that's your boy out there."

"That's Jeffrey, all right. He's doing well, too," the man returned proudly.

Carole immediately recognized his nasal accent as being from New York; he used the same intonation Jack Levy had. Pushing that thought quickly from her mind, Carole concentrated once again on the match.

Jeffrey Gottfried and his partner made a quick kill of their less-aggressive opponents, and a moment later the announcer boomed, "Game. Set. Match, Misters Gottfried and Parker." The crowd applauded as the men shook hands over the net.

"Oh, look!" Charlotte said excitedly, as the players filed off the court and were replaced by a new group, "There they are . . . Curt and Robert!"

Following Charlotte's gaze, Carole picked out the figure of Curt, looking so blond and handsome in his white tennis finery—the very picture of an all-American guy. He was laughing at something his father had said, then moving onto the court to begin warming up with their opponents—"only vacationers," according to her father's snide comment.

Just before the match began, Curt scanned the bleachers. He waved upon spotting his mother. Then as his gaze landed on Carole, he seemed to freeze. From their depths, a burning question leapt across the court and up into the stands. *Are you back?* his blue eyes demanded. *Have you come back to me?*

Carole's heart fluttered once, and then she answered with an affirming smile and quick, coquettish wink.

Curt felt as though his world had just tipped upright. A white smile broke across his face. Turning, he trotted into position, casting another look in Carole's direction just before the first serve sailed over the net.

He played brilliantly. Even his father, who was a smooth, experienced player, was overshadowed by his son's quick, masterful strokes.

"It seems that Curt is inspired today," Charlotte commented at one point, turning a knowing smile on Carole.

As the afternoon wore on, Carole gradually surrendered herself to the sunny day, to the soothing camaraderie of the club set and the flattering attention of the handsome tennis player who gave her a smile every time the crowd cheered one of his shots.

Beside her, James kept a discreet, watchful eye. And his spirits rose each time he caught one of the quick, distant exchanges between the two.

Curt and Robert won in straight sets. And after the thunderous applause marking the end of the match, the small group that had cheered them on left the bleachers and meandered toward the nearby club restaurant, The Island House. A goodly portion of the tennis crowd was milling about the patio where drinks were being served under a series of green-and-white striped cabanas.

The afternoon drifted toward sunset as Carole and

James sipped cocktails and socialized with Charlotte Morrisson and the Gottfrieds.

"And where is that attractive wife of yours, James?" Charlotte asked. "I've seen her from afar, but I've yet to meet her."

A dark look passed swiftly over James's face before he fixed Charlotte Morrisson with a pleasant smile. "Kathleen? Well, she's a dancer of sorts, you know. Lately, she's been spending quite a bit of time at the studio. It's as if she's become newly enamored of the ballet."

Carole didn't miss the abrupt light that flashed in her father's dark eyes.

"Yes, that's it," James concluded thoughtfully. "I believe Kathleen has, in fact, become newly enamored."

Carole had been a student of her father far too long not to recognize the alert look of a bloodhound. And apparently, Kathleen was the quarry.

"The ballet?" Gwen Gottfried questioned eagerly. "Oh, I absolutely adore the ballet! I so hope that Henry and I can soon move into the city so we can start taking advantage of these things . . . the ballet, the symphony, the theater . . . Charleston has an excellent reputation as a cultural center, you know."

Fortyish, Henry and Gwen seemed very friendly. And when Carole heard it mentioned that Henry was a teaching physician at Medical University, Carole remembered that April had once told her about the man. If she remembered correctly, Dr. Gottfried had an impressive reputation and had moved recently to Charleston from New York.

"Yes, we've only been here about seven months," Gwen was saying in her clipped, northern voice. "At the moment, we're leasing one of the duplexes on the windward side of the isle. I must admit it's lovely here, but it's like being on vacation all the time. We'd like to find a real home. And last week we spotted the most beautiful house on Tradd Street.''

"It's just a couple of blocks from your place, James," Henry added. "A big, red brick place with Georgian columns out front,"

"Ah, yes!" Charlotte smiled. "The Devereux house. How absolutely marvelous it would be if you could manage to snap it up. It's a beautiful house, and it's a shame to see it sitting empty, now that the family spends so much time abroad."

"I certainly hope we can come to terms," Gwen said thoughtfully. "I'd like to sink some roots, get the boys settled. Simon is doing fine, but Jeffrey . . ." She sighed. "To be frank, tennis seems to be the only thing he takes pleasure in anymore. He hasn't been very happy since we left New York."

Just then, Robert Morrisson broached the group. An easy smile played about his lips as he was applauded on the doubles win, and he slid his arm protectively around his wife's shoulders.

Carole looked in admiration at the well-bred couple. How right they seemed together. Within the circle of her husband's arm, Charlotte Morrisson looked as though she hadn't a care in the world.

"Thank you, thank you," Robert began. "Although I must admit, the lion's share of the credit goes to my son."

Carole spun in the direction Robert had indicated, and suddenly found herself face to face with Curt, who had come up unnoticed behind her.

He was looking at her expectantly, but for some reason she couldn't find her voice. For one horrible awkward moment she just stood there. But then her father stepped over, slapping Curt on the back. "Great match," she heard him say, proudly.

Carole watched quietly as the group drew Curt away from her side and into its midst. Freshly show-ered and dressed, rosy-cheeked and smiling, Curt accepted their accolades with his typical suave good manners. But every few seconds, Carole felt his pale blue eyes turning in her direction, searching beyond the people crowded around him until he could meet her gaze.

She still has that quiet way about her, Curt thought. But at least she looks like her old self. . . . At least she's here.

He endured the jovial, well-wishing comments of his friends and relatives, but what he really wanted was Carole—to talk to her, kiss her, reassure himself that she was really back. As soon as he could escape the center of attention, he weaved his way through the swelling crowd and sought her out.

That red dress set her off to perfection—like fireworks—accenting the tiny waist and round bosom, leaving bare the shoulders and arms that even during the short span of the match had taken on a rosy hue. For a moment he could do no more than look at her. It had been so long since he'd touched that smooth skin, looked into those vivid aquamarine eyes, kissed that heart-shaped mouth.

"Hello, doll," he said finally.

"Hello, Curt."

"You look beautiful."

"Thanks," she replied. "So do you. You played beautifully, also."

He shrugged. "What are you doing here?"

"I came to watch the tournament, of course."

"Is that the only reason you came?"

His eyes darted between hers, and for a fleeting moment Carole wondered, why had she come? But it seemed too late to be asking that question now. Taking refuge in the old, teasing ways, she asked him, "Why . . . whatever could you mean, Curt?"

A slow smile spread across Curt's face. This was the Carole he knew and loved. Her sultry voice rang with invitation. Reaching down, he took her hand, then looked over his shoulder, searching the crowd until he spotted James.

"I'm taking your daughter!" he called as he caught his boss's eye.

James grinned, cupped his hands and called back, "To the victor belong the spoils!"

Carefully, he watched his daughter disappear beyond the cabanas with Curt, then turned back to Robert and Charlotte Morrisson, smiling at them intimately and with great satisfaction. His dream would soon be coming true.

Curt twined his fingers around Carole's, enjoying the feel of her hand as they walked through the carefully groomed club grounds toward the parking lot.

"Where are we going?" Carole asked.

He looked down at her with warm eyes. "How about supper downtown? I feel like celebrating."

As they crossed the lofty bridge back to the mainland, a brilliant sunset painted the ocean red and gold. But Curt was immune to the view, his every nerve alive with the awareness of Carole alone. They barely spoke a word during the drive and the dinner that followed at the Restaurant Phillipe Million. He was content simply to be with her for now. He ached with the desire to be alone with her, but he couldn't. Not yet. It was too soon.

There were things he needed to know first. Had James's plan really paid off? Was she back for good? And what of R.J. ? Why the hell had he been to see her . . . twice? But that was something he dared not ask, for to do so meant having to divulge that her father was having her followed.

When they pulled up in front of her townhouse, it was after ten o'clock. Switching off the engine, Curt turned to look at her through the darkness.

"What happened, Carole?" he asked in a serious tone.

"What do you mean?" She'd known this was coming. Was she really going to give up, to give in to him?

"Why have you come back?"

Carole's gaze dropped to her lap. "Well, I suppose you'll find out soon enough anyway. I failed, Curt."

"Failed at what?"

"My designs were rejected by that company in New York."

"I see," Curt said quietly. He reached over and took her hand. "Look at me, Carole. I want to know the truth. Have you gotten it out of your system?"

"Yes," she answered woodenly. "It's out." And she knew it was true. It *was* out—the excitement, the hope, the confidence, it was gone.

Curt stifled his exhilaration the best he could. "Listen to me, Carole. It's good that you tried. I can respect that. But now that it's over, why don't we put it all behind us? The reason you decided to come back is of no consequence to me, just as long as you're back. Now . . ." he added, a grin curving his lips. "You're not about to send me away without inviting me up for a nightcap, are you?"

He took her in his arms as soon as they walked through the door. Plastering her against the wall, his body held hers as his mouth descended on hers with hungry familiarity. His hands traveled up her arms to grip her shoulders as his tongue filled her mouth over and over again. Passion racing through his blood like a fever, he moved a hand to fill it with her breast.

Carole willed herself to feel something. This was the man she would marry. He brushed her nipple through the taut fabric of the red dress, then dropped to his knees, burying his face in her midrift. But as his hands climbed up her thighs under the dress, Carole quickly detached herself, halting his advance.

189

"Curt," she said softly, her hand reaching to smooth his hair.

But he paid no heed, his hand caressing, searching, up to the pantyline.

"Curt!"

He leaped to his feet, an intense, burning look in his eyes.

"For God's sake, Carole!" he exploded in frustration. "Just how long do you propose to say no to me?!"

Carole bristled at his pushiness. Her body was *one* thing that was hers alone to give. "Until it feels right to say yes!" she flashed.

Curt stared at her, his chest heaving, until gradually, his exasperation wilted. He was too damned glad to have her back. He could wait for the sex—although it wouldn't be easy.

"All right . . . all right," he mumbled sheepishly.

Carole watched from the kitchen window a few hours later as the BMW drove out of sight. Then, coursing thoughtfully through the apartment, she doused the lights, marveling at the ease with which she had slipped right back into her old niche. They'd had a couple of drinks, watched some TV, reestablished themselves as a couple. And when Curt left the townhouse late that night, his kiss told her he was happier than he had been in weeks.

It was as if there'd been no deviation in the past month, no chance of an independent life, no liaison with Curt's brother . . .

She squelched the thought—as she had been doing ever since Curt's kiss triggered an immediate, comparison with the memory of his brother's. Turning her mind firmly to other things, Carole prepared for bed.

On Tradd Street, Curt and Robert Morrisson shared a quiet nightcap in the study. Lately, when the two of them were alone, the conversation always turned to the Stuckey matter and R.J.'s unexpected involvement. Earlier in the week they'd received word that "a fancy lawyer named Morrisson" had paid a visit to Geraldine Stuckey. Now, in quiet tones, they assured each other that all they could do was wait and see what R.J. would do next.

Upstairs, Charlotte Morrisson lay alone in bed, a tear sliding off her cheek to wet the silken pillow slip.

A few blocks south, James Gossett paced angrily through the deserted master suite, shooting a damning look at the Swiss clock that began chiming midnight. Damn, but the wench had grown bold. And he'd been so caught up in Carole he'd barely noticed! Grabbing the phone, he dialed the number decisively. He'd be blind no longer.

"Yeah?" came Horton's voice.

"It's Gossett."

"Just got back from the other side of town. The little girl is all tucked in after being seen home by Curt Morrisson."

"Good. I think it's time to change your assignment. I want you off Carole and on Kathleen."

"Who?"

"My wife." The words gritted from between James's teeth.

And in the townhouse at Broad and Rutledge, the subconscious brought forth what consciousness had held at bay. And once again, though in her dreams, Carole was stirred to passion by the touch of R.J. Morrisson.

In a far corner of the fashionable drawing room, the formally attired chamber musicians finished tuning up. R.J. selected a fresh scotch from a passing waiter, then settled in his seat as the group began playing Schubert's Trout Quintet.

It was a black-tie affair, and as R.J. scanned the well-dressed audience of perhaps forty, he recognized some of the most prominent members of Columbia's law circle. Seated in the first row were Judge Harper and his wife, host and hostess to this little social fete he'd been commanded to attend. Oh well, he supposed he had nothing better to do on a Wednesday night anyway.

Ever since his return to Columbia earlier in July, the judge had kept him busy day and night. If not being pressed for briefs or research, he was pressed to attend some after-hours gathering which Judge Harper always assured him was "imperative" to his career.

That was the way it had been for the past two and a half weeks. The judge had been instrumental in procuring R.J.'s appointment to a state clerkship, and now it was as if he were intent on protecting his investment—making sure R.J. had no opportunity to pursue the mysterious matters which seemed to be luring him away from the prestigious post. In brighter moments, R.J. was almost flattered by the attentiveness. But mostly he was annoyed.

The judge had left him little time to pursue even a thought about the Stuckey case. About a week earlier, however, he'd finally managed to take a long lunch. Going over to the secretary of state's office, where corporations were required by law to list a registered address, R.J. had been sure he'd be able to learn something about the company that had purchased Jonah's land from Geraldine Stuckey. But there was nothing in the files under the name Land Grant. No company, no partnership, no corporation—nothing.

Maybe he'd misunderstood Geraldine Stuckey. Maybe the woman had pulled the name out of a hat. Maybe there was no Land Grant at all! Dismally, R.J. had begun to think he'd reached a dead end.

R.J. heard a faint stirring behind him in the drawing room. And when he glanced over his shoulder at the late arrivals, he beheld Vicki Monroe. Chic as always, the redhead was dressed in a floor-length white gown, its simplicity setting off the flaming color of her hair. She was on the arm of a rising young prosecutor from the district attorney's office. He was shorter than Vicki, and not particularly attractive. R.J. knew from having met the man a few times that he was dull. He turned back to the musicians, smiling to himself at the thought of Vicki with such a man. She was sure to be bored. Yet, apparently, she was willing to put up with it, considering his position. Nothing but a man of promise would do for Vicki Monroe.

At the end of the musical selection, she and her date took seats a few rows in front of him, and through the remainder of the concert, R.J. found his gaze drifting to the back of her bright head. She must have met the prosecutor on the job. That's how he himself had met her all those months ago. Vicki was a wiz with computers, and she worked in records. It was a position that gave her easy access to the parade of attorneys, judges, and politicians who consulted the files.

Some day, R.J. mused, the right one would walk through her door, and Vicki Monroe would become the wife of a state-capital man—with all the wealth and power and social position she apparently longed for.

When the concert ended and the crowd began to mill, R.J. chatted with various groups, but his eyes continued to search out the sleek figure of Vicki. They'd had some hot times together, but it now seemed like part of another life. And R.J. had no difficulty putting his finger on what had put an end to the old life. It was Carole. Even now he couldn't keep her off his mind. Next to her, Vicki was a shallow attraction.

But then it hit him. Vicki had access to state records! If there were, in fact, a Land Grant Company, she'd be able to access the computer network and find it.

R.J. began to watch her more closely. And when the prosecutor was drawn away by Judge Harper, he made his move. Stepping around the circle of guests, he drew ever closer to the redhead in the white gown.

"Why, R.J. Morrisson!" she declared in a sugary voice when he came face to face with her. "Long time, no see."

"Hi, Vicki," he smiled. "It *has* been a long time. How have you been?"

Vicki's eyes raced over the tailored white dinner jacket and black tie, then climbed to R.J.'s face. He was even more handsome than she had remembered. For a fleeting instant, Vicki recalled the feel of that pale hair beneath her fingers, the long, hard body pressing her into the sheets. It was a damn shame. A man like R.J.—with both power *and* a pair of blue eyes that could melt you with a look—didn't come along every day. She put on one of her best smiles.

"I've been just fine, honey," she said. "And how are you?"

"Well enough." The blue eyes gazed at her intently. Taking her by the elbow, R.J. steered her to a more private spot by the window. "But I need a favor."

Vicki's brows went up. *"You* need a favor? Mister 'I'll-do-everything-myself' Morrisson?"

R.J. grinned. "Is that the way I am?" he asked disarmingly.

She was still perturbed with him. She'd never really known what had gone wrong between them, and R.J. most certainly hadn't gone out of his way to make any explanations. But Vicki knew she'd grant the damned favor, whatever it was. When he told her, however, she looked up at him in a rather hard way.

"Do you know what you're asking, R.J.? My area is restricted. Computer research is to be done only with proper authorization, confined to official matters. If they find out I'm accessing the network on personal business, they could have my job."

R.J.'s eyes darted between hers solemnly. "I know. I realize I'm asking a lot. If you don't feel comfortable doing it, I'll understand."

She looked up at the irresistible man, placed a hand huffily on her hip. "Land Grant, huh?"

He nodded.

"Call me tomorrow afternoon," she said finally. Then she stepped around him to go in search of her date, turning to look at him one last time.

"R.J. Morrisson," Vicki said with glib finality. "You really are a bastard, you know that?"

And then she swept away, leaving R.J. to smile at her disappearing, shapely behind.

The next day, armed with the chance of making progress on the Stuckey case, he went to work with more enthusiasm than he'd felt in weeks. There was no denying it, the case that sprang out of Charleston had become far more important than the daily routine of the state supreme court. R.J. knew he was crazy. He knew he was messing up a great opportunity. He also knew he was moving closer and closer to getting out of Columbia for good.

As son as court recessed, he hurried to his office and called Vicki.

"It isn't just Land Grant," she informed him. "It's Ashley Land Grant Corporation, filed just this year."

Ashley, R.J. thought quickly. Yes, that fits.

"Filed just this year, huh?" he asked.

"That's what it said. Some time back in April."

"Got an address?"

"What, Mr. Langley?" Vicki said suddenly.

Langley was her boss.

"Oh yes, I'll be sure to have that information for you tomorrow. . . . Yes, sir. In the morning."

When she spoke back into the phone, her voice was a hurried whisper. "Damn it, R.J.! I'm going to get in trouble. Now write this down, and hurry."

R.J. grabbed a pen from the holder, whipped the note pad to a clean sheet. "Okay," he said. "Go ahead."

"Registered address . . . one one two, Mimosa Lane, Charleston. Mailing address . . . post office box two one three eight, Charleston."

R.J. was writing fast and furiously. "Great, Vicki! That's just great. Did you get the names of the principals?"

"You don't miss a trick," she accused hurriedly. "Three men . . . John Carrolton, Cornelius Blakely, James Hargrove."

"Hargrove," R.J. repeated as he scrawled the name. "Anything else?"

"Like what?" Vicki exclaimed quietly.

"Like who these guys are? Where they live?"

There was a moment of quiet on the other end of the line.

"This one's going to cost you a drink," Vicki snapped. "Tomorrow after work. The Gamecock Inn."

R.J. and Vicki had often met at The Gamecock Inn when they were dating. He got there early, securing a table against the onslaught of the Friday-night crowds. The Gamecock Inn was a popular place—the drinks were good, and there was always the convenience of the adjacent, cozy hotel rooms. He and Vicki had availed themselves of the accommodations on a number of occasions. And as he waited, R.J. idly wondered if it were purely by chance that Vicki had suggested the place sure to turn both their thoughts to the steamy nights they'd spent together.

When she arrived, R.J. rose courteously to his feet. It would be very easy to let things take their natural course with Vicki, he realized. She looked great in the black, tailored business dress. It had always been one of his favorites.

R.J. bided his time. They ordered drinks, made a little small talk about things at the capital. He didn't want to seem crass by jumping immediately to the issue that was burning in his mind. Eventually, he became aware that the look in Vicki's eyes had turned warm and sultry.

"Seems like old times, doesn't it?" she asked invitingly.

"Yeah," R.J. grinned. "In a lot of ways, it does."

"Makes me want to forget that the only reason I'm here is to give you some damned information."

R.J.'s grin faded, and he regarded her seriously. "I don't mean to use you, Vicki. Whatever you've been able to find out will be a big help, and I want to return the favor whenever I can. I'm well aware I owe you one."

"One?" she questioned with an arched brow. "I should think you owe me two . . . considering the way you dropped me without so much as a warning."

R.J. colored. As far as he was concerned, the end of their affair had been painless. But it *had* happened damned quickly . . . and without warning. Vicki had always seemed so strong and unflappable. For the first time it occurred to him that perhaps he had actually hurt her.

"I . . . I'm sorry," he stammered, embarrassed. "I've been going through kind of a confusing time. I guess you got caught in the middle of it."

Vicki studied him for a moment, watched him squirm. "Forget it, R.J. It's over, right? And don't worry, I managed to get the information you were

197

looking for . . . although I doubt it's exactly what you were expecting."

He looked at her curiously. "What do you mean?"

"John Carrolton, Cornelius Blakely, and James Hargrove . . . the three principals in Ashley Land Grant Corporation? Interesting group. Ingenious, really, since the corporation was formed three months after the unfortunate Mr. Hargrove died and went to join his associates."

"What?"

"I said they're all three dead, R.J. Besides which, they share a common address at Ashley Grove Memorial Cemetery in Charleston County."

R.J.'s eyes widened. "You're sure about this?"

"Of course I'm sure! I cross-referenced every available source of data: birth certificates, social security numbers, death certificates, everything. Your Ashley Land Grant Corporation is a dummy run by dead men!"

"Well, I'll be damned," R.J. murmured.

"Most probably," Vicki sniffed.

R.J. snapped his head up to look at her. Breaking into a grin, he told her, "You're a sweetheart, Vicki."

"Am I?" she asked with a glowing look. "Then why did you have the poor sense to let me slip through your fingers?"

R.J. turned serious once more. "It wasn't you, Vicki. It's me. Something's happening with me right now . . . a change in attitude, priorities. Hell, I've even been thinking of taking a leave of absence from the clerkship."

"You don't want to do that, R.J.," she returned immediately.

"Why not?"

"Because the position might not be waiting for you when you get back. It's all over town that Harper is displeased with what he's calling your lack

198

of dedication. Lately, he's been seen lunching with Congressman Lawford's son . . . fresh out of Harvard and eager to please.''

R.J. slumped in his chair and frowned. ''Well, if that's what happens, maybe it's meant to be. I can't deny that I've lost interest in the court scene. Hell, I've been more turned on by this Charleston case than *anything* I've ever come across in the capital.''

''Even me?'' Vicki asked softly.

R.J. leaned across the table, took her slim hands in his own. ''We had a great time, Vicki. I'll never forget it, and I hope you won't.''

''Right,'' she said in a clipped voice, her hazel eyes assessing the attractive man across the table. ''I don't know what it is about you, R.J. Somehow, you manage to put a girl down and still have her eating out of your hand. Here I am sneaking around on clandestine business, doing favors that are liable to get me fired.''

''I'm sorry,'' he told her sincerely.

Vicki chuckled wryly, withdrew her hands. ''Hell, that's all right, honey. Hey, I pulled it off, didn't I? No one will ever be the wiser, and all's well that ends well. Incidentally, can I at least take satisfaction in the knowledge that you're going to be tracking down some bad guys?''

''It looks that way.''

''Good. Then it was worth the risk. And as for that other matter . . . Between you and me, I always knew our little fling would come to an end anyway.''

''You did?'' R.J. asked in surprise.

''Hell, yes!'' Vicki drawled as she came to her feet and collected her purse, motioning for him to keep his seat. ''Any fool could see you're smitten by another mistress.''

An immediate thought of Carole popped into R.J.'s mind. ''What other mistress?''

Vicki smiled. ''Why, Charleston, R.J.! Your first

love. I knew all along I could never take you away from her."

As Vicki Monroe swaggered out of the bar, drawing many a male eye, R.J. settled back in his seat. There was a lot more to her than he'd ever suspected. She was a damned attractive woman, and, on top of that, she was right. But before she'd even disappeared from view, his mind had turned to the information she'd given him. By the time he paid the check and left The Gamecock Inn, he was making plans for his departure to Charleston.

R.J. stood on the veranda of the impressive home of Judge Earl Harper. Mrs. Harper admitted him with a smile and showed him into the study, where the judge was having a cup of coffee and perusing the *Wall Street Journal*.

"Good morning, R.J." The judge greeted him with a hooded look. "What brings you here so early on a Saturday?"

"Good morning, Your Honor." R.J. took the chair the judge proferred. "As to why I'm here, well . . . I suppose I've been needing to talk to you for a while."

"You do seem to have acquired a strange attitude." Judge Harper looked at R.J. closely as he spoke. "I hope that's what you've come to discuss."

The judge looked so serious and sage. This wasn't going to be easy. "I'll try," R.J. began. "But the truth is I'm not sure I understand it myself. All through Vanderbilt, and when I first arrived here at the capital, I dreamed of the supreme court, of working with someone like you. I realize it's one of the best training grounds in the world . . . that the potential is endless for a state clerk who has ambition and drive."

The judge nodded.

"But lately," R.J. went on hesitantly, "I've found myself . . . losing interest." Registering the look of shock on the older man's face, he hastened to add, "One of the reasons I came here today is to apologize to you. Because you're right, the past month or so, I *haven't* been giving a hundred percent."

Pride and pleasure marked the judge's heavily jowled face. "See here, R.J. Your performance up to the past couple of months has been exemplary. No real harm is done. Not as long as you've come to your senses."

R.J. smiled somewhat sheepishly. "I'm not certain you'll think I've come to my senses when you hear what I'm about to propose. . . ." He paused. There was no way to soften the impact. "A leave of absence."

"What?" The hawkish look returned to the judge's eyes.

R.J. rubbed absently at his forehead, eyeing Judge Harper from beneath his fingers.

"Is someone in your family ill?"

R.J. shook his head.

"Are *you* ill, then?" the judge demanded.

"Please try to understand, Your Honor. I've simply gotten caught up in a case down in Charleston. I need some time to work it out. That's all."

"That's all? You want a leave of absence from a supreme-court post so you can work on a personal case in Charleston? That's *all*?"

"That's right," R.J. snapped. He had respect for Judge Harper, but he was losing patience. It wasn't fair that he was being put on the defensive in such a fashion. It was almost as if *he* were on trial.

"It's really not very difficult to understand, Your Honor. Consider my relationship to the supreme court. When court convenes, I could be sitting right there in one of the pews, or I could be a thousand miles away, and it wouldn't make any difference. The court would carry on, just the way it always has, just the way it always will—with brilliant rhetoric and wise, sweeping decisions.

"But in Charleston, there's a man whose land may have been stolen, a man who has been wrongly confined in an institution. And no one but me is doing anything about it. Don't you see?" R.J. pointed emphatically to his chest. "*I* can make the difference! And that's the reason I became interested in law in the first place."

"You sound like a damned public defender!" the judge accused.

R.J. took in Judge Harper's look of horror. Suddenly he was very tired of trying to explain his reasoning. "Maybe so," he muttered. "All I know is that I need some time. I'm not going to be able to function properly as your clerk until I can get this case off my mind."

Judge Harper drew up his round, short frame. "I must tell you, R.J., I find this grave news, indeed. I like you. You have a fine legal mind, and you come from a fine family. But I want someone sure and certain working by my side, someone who will pursue his duties with fervor, be there whenever I have a need, day or night happily. I offer a tremendous future to my state clerk, and I demand loyalty in return.

"So, there will be no halfway, R.J.," the judge continued, "no leave of absence. Make your decision now. Either put this foolishness behind you and come back to work . . . or pursue the foolishness and kiss the capital and your future here good-bye. It's up to you, son. But I'll have your answer now."

R.J. rose to his feet, looked down at the judge, then offered his hand.

"Good-bye, Your Honor," he said firmly.

R.J. stepped soberly out of the house and onto the veranda, where pots of red geraniums were in vibrant bloom beneath the hot, Columbia sun. He took a long, deep breath of freedom, but the inland

202

summer air seemed hot and stifling to someone who longed for the coast.

Whistling to himself, R.J. jogged down the steps and hopped into the Corvette. There would be a cooling breeze in Charleston.

Chapter Nine

"**Y**OU INTEND TO do what?"

Robert's voice boomed so that Charlotte raised a hand protectively to her ear.

"I'm going to set up my own practice here in Charleston," R.J. replied matter-of-factly.

Charlotte clasped her hands together as tears of joy started to her eyes. "Your own practice? Here?" she breathed. "How wonderful, Randall!"

"Now, Mother," R.J. returned with a smile. "Don't you remember we made a deal? You said that if I moved back to Charleston, you'd start calling me R.J."

"Certainly . . . R.J." she laughed.

"When did this come about?" Robert asked sternly.

"This morning. I went to Judge Harper to ask for a leave of absence, but he gave me an ultimatum. Either stay . . . or leave. Period. End of conversation."

"And you chose to leave?" Robert questioned. The gray-blue eyes so like those of his son had gone dark and opaque. "I thought you were happy at the capital. Your position was certainly one of great

204

promise. What happened? Why did you want a leave of absence anyway?''

R.J. shrugged. After his ordeal with Judge Harper and the long drive to Charleston, he didn't have the energy to hash over the Stuckey case and why it was so important to him. Besides, Dan Shriver was a good friend of his father's. R.J. wanted to get some more information, find out for certain why the county clerk had been withholding that file, before he discussed the case with him. ''Lately, I've just become interested in other things. It's time for a change.''

''You'll be living here at the house?'' Charlotte asked eagerly. ''In your old room?''

R.J. put up a cautioning hand. ''Just for a short while, Mother. Until I can find an apartment and get my things moved from Columbia.''

''That's just fine, dear. At least you'll be back here in Charleston where you belong.'' Still beaming, Charlotte turned to her husband. ''Isn't that so, Robert?''

Her dark luminous eyes sought his, detected the puzzling, cold look within them. Yet his reply seemed warm enough as he put an arm round his eldest son, patted him on the back and welcomed him home.

''Where is everybody?'' he asked his mother a half-hour later, returning to the living room after unpacking. ''Every time I come home, this place is practically deserted.''

''If you can believe it, right after lunch, Margaret and Camille decided to go shopping . . . together.'' Charlotte's eyes were sparkling. ''Can you imagine the selection of stores the two of *them* would agree to go into? And Curt has already left for the Isle of Palms. He and your father are playing doubles in the July Bake Off this afternoon. They've reached the semifinals.''

"The semis!" R.J. exclaimed. "I'm impressed. Dad and I never made it past the third round."

Charlotte smiled comfortingly. "He says the competition isn't as stiff as it has been in years past. The best team in the tournament is Jim Parker and the Gottfried boy. Oh, I don't suppose you know the Gottfrieds, do you?" she added. "They're lovely people, really. Henry is a doctor, and Gwen does some sort of counseling, I believe. At any rate, they moved down from New York not long ago, and haven't had a chance to make many friends. In the past couple of months, your father and I have sort of taken them under our wing."

"New York?" R.J. repeated curiously. "That's interesting. I can't really picture Dad taking New Yorkers under his wing."

"Careful," his mother put in with a scolding look. "You're beginning to sound like Margaret."

R.J. laughed in surprise. "God forbid! I didn't say *I* was a Charleston snob. I just implied that Dad is."

"Randall! Your father is *not* a snob!"

R.J. raised a doubtful brow.

Eventually, Charlotte surrendered to his lighthearted teasing. "Ah well," she admitted with a chuckle. "Perhaps a bit of a snob. But tennis is a universal language, I suppose. The Gottfried boy is quite good. He and Jim Parker play today, just prior to your father's match, and he fully expects them to make it to tomorrow's finals. Of course, if Robert and Curt win this afternoon, they'll go on to the finals as well.

"Your father and I are going to be leaving for the isle in about half an hour. And after the match, there's a small supper party at the club. Why don't you join us, dear? It would be so nice for me to have all my men together for a change."

* * *

"You're sure you won't change your mind and come with me?" James queried.

Kathleen's hairbrush halted midway in its stroke through her thick raven tresses. She glanced at her husband's reflection in the mirror, took note of the taunting, self-assured look he wore, and was immediately suspicious.

"Why the sudden interest in my accompanying you to a tennis tournament? You never cared before about taking me to mix with your Isle of Palms buddies."

James gave her a short, mocking bow. "An error on my part."

Kathleen calmly resumed her brushing. "Right," she muttered and began twisting the mass of hair into a coil at the nape of her neck.

James's dark eyes traveled slowly down the upraised arms, trailing down and along the lines of her back. She was wearing black dance tights and a clinging, plum-colored top that etched her figure clearly against the creamy backdrop of the French provincial dresser. At that moment, Kathleen was very desirable; James experienced a tightening in his loins. But then, that's the way he always felt when he was tracking. It was a thrill, a turn-on, to watch and wait as the unsuspecting prey danced ever closer to his lair.

Having completed her coiffure, Kathleen glanced once again at the man in the mirror, and discovered that his intense eyes were still upon her. A shiver raced up her spine. She recognized that look. Surely he wasn't going to announce suddenly that he'd forego the tennis match in favor of more intimate athletics. They hadn't had sex in more than three weeks. It would be just like James to choose *now*, and spoil everything!

"Aren't you going to be late?" she asked casually. She rose to her feet, escaping the heated line of his vision as she crossed to the dresser and began putting a few things in her bag.

"I've got time," he replied lazily. "Where did you say you were going?"

"To the studio, of course. I'm to be included in a performance this fall. It's going to take consistent work for me to stay in shape." The lies rolled off her tongue so easily these days.

"You look in fine shape to me," James offered obliquely.

Again, the shiver. "Ah, but you have the eye of a civilian," she parried. "Anyone in a dance troupe could see I still have a long way to go. And Gay Templeton will accept nothing but a dancer's best."

James folded his arms across his chest, continued watching her from across the room. He was enjoying this.

"For months, you hardly went to the studio," he commented. "And now you go there nearly every day. Certainly every weekend. What's the new attraction?"

He was baiting her, and Kathleen knew it.

"No new attraction, just the same old one. Not long ago, you yourself told me you were glad I'd renewed my interest in dance. You were the one who suggested I start getting your money's worth out of the studio. Remember?"

"Yes. I do." James warmed to the game. She was more of a challenge than before. He liked that. "I'm simply surprised at the change in you. The spring in your step . . . the roses in your cheeks. Are they due simply to a revived interest in ballet?" A dark brow shot up. "Or could it be a dancer, *hmm*? Perhaps there's a new, virile, decidedly masculine performer in the troupe?"

Kathleen's heart skipped a beat, but she didn't allow the tremor to show. He was fishing, that was all. In the past he would have reduced her to a quivering mass of nerves that would take refuge in a bottle. But not now. Now, she was cold sober.

"Yes, of course, James," she said without looking at him. "But actually I haven't narrowed to just one. You see, I take on the entire troupe . . . one at a time."

He grimaced. It was not the reaction he would have liked. He'd have preferred to see her cower. Then he could leave with the satisfaction that Kathleen's afternoon would be spoiled in fearful wondering of what her powerful husband might know . . . or do.

"What time will you be home?" he pressed.

"About sixish," she tossed. Kathleen continued to dawdle across the room, picking up keys and sunglasses, putting as much distance between them as she could diplomatically manage.

"See that you are," he growled. And turning on his heel, James walked out.

Kathleen closed her eyes in relief as she listened to the receding sound of his footsteps. A moment later she heard the slam of the kitchen door, then the distant rattle as the automatic garage door raised to release his Seville.

She decided it would be best to wait a discreet few minutes. Then, racing down to the Mercedes, she gunned out of the garage and into the hot sunshine. It had been a narrow escape. True . . . she was going to the studio for a short workout, but it was primarily for appearance's sake. There, she would meet André, and they'd drive to the coast. They'd already made plans to spend the afternoon at The Breakers. After today, she wouldn't see André for about a month. A month. It sounded like forever. But considering James's unexpected, suspicious questioning, perhaps it was for the best.

She would miss André, but she could wait. Her fondness for him was genuine, and his ardent lovemaking was thrilling. The time they spent together

209

was like a beautiful gift. Yet the most important gift André had given her, Kathleen often thought, was herself. She liked herself once more. It was with a glorious, smiling sense of freedom that she drove away from the Gossett mansion.

Constance Trippley looked up from her gardening as the red Mercedes rolled past. Catching sight of Kathleen's dark head, she leaned closer to the courtyard wall and watched the retreating convertible make its way up the palm-lined street. Only a few minutes earlier James's Cadillac had gone up three intersections and turned right. Now, Kathleen proceeded to the same crossing and turned in the opposite direction.

A knowing smile on her lips, Constance went back to watering her roses.

The hot summer sun beat down on her back like a molten shower, and Carole felt as though she were baking. At the opposite end of the pool from where she lay on her lounge chair, a small group of club-goers clustered under an umbrella. But most of the summer crowd was out on the wide, sweeping Isle of Palms beaches or over at the courts, watching the tennis tournament.

Only the most seasoned of sunbathers should lie out on a day like this, Carole mused. It was the end of July, and the strong, Carolina sun would blister defenselessly pale skin in a matter of minutes. Yet, she knew she was in no danger; she'd built up a substantial tan base in the past few weeks, and now her skin was the rich, bronze color that vacationers envied. It was with a nagging feeling of self-recrimination that Carole realized she had little else to show for her time.

She'd hardly been to Carolotta's! at all, begging off with the excuse of needing a vacation. Elsa and Cathy had immediately noticed the change in her.

210

They'd even questioned her about what was wrong. But Carole had merely said she had a lot on her mind. How could she tell them or Carlotta that she felt like a hypocrite every time she walked in the salon door? That each time she remembered the letter from Haut Nouveau she felt like a fool who had no right to connect herself with the identity of a designer in any way?

The rejection had sliced Carole to the core. Every time she went to Carlotta's!, the wound opened anew.

It had been amazingly easy to drop back into the numbing life-style she'd left behind. Every day she sunbathed and swam at Wild Dunes; every night she dined and danced with Curt. The past two weeks had gone by in a whirl of luncheons, tennis matches, cocktail parties, and late-night suppers. It was the social world Carole had so recently spurned as meaningless. But it was comfortable and familiar. And she had come to accept the fact that it was where she belonged.

Shifting out of the sweltering, prone position, Carole sat on the edge of the cot and slipped her feet into waiting sandals. After a moment she stood, and then meandered to the intricately designed brick wall surrounding the pool deck. A clean ocean breeze blew in from the east, lifting the damp strands that had escaped her ponytail to curl against her hot neck. Propping her elbows on the brick wall, Carole looked to the west, across the manicured, palmetto-studded lawns to the tall chain-link fence bordering the tennis courts.

A crowd swelled about the bleachers at courtside. Curt was over there somewhere, watching the women's semifinals. It would be time for the men's competition soon. In a few minutes she'd have to clean up and change so she'd be ready to watch Curt's match.

It had become something of a tradition these past

few weekends. Carole mentally rattled off the pattern. Curt picked her up and drove them to the Isle of Palms, where he watched the tournament while she sunned by the pool. Then, when the time drew near for Curt's match, she changed in the clubhouse lounge, watched him play from the prestigious box seats. And afterward, they inevitably went out to celebrate. She'd been wined and dined and pursued ever more amorously by Curt than ever. It must seem the ideal way to spend a summer, Carole mused— most women would kill to trade places with her.

With a deep sigh, Carole turned away from the courts. Leaning back against the rough brick, she looked out across the distant dunes to the open freedom of the blue-gray sea. She'd seen quite a bit of her father these past weeks, too. Like Curt, he'd been unusually attentive and warm lately. She hadn't been blind to the steady precision, if not ardor of his actions. He was throwing a small dinner party for the Morrissons that very night, in fact, in the tropically opulent dining room of The Island House here at Wild Dunes. It was almost as if the two families were already joined.

Carole closed her eyes, lifted her face to the heat of the sun. A marriage proposal was coming, she could feel it. And this time, she wouldn't be able to say no.

R.J. meandered across the carefully tended grounds of Wild Dunes. His parents had gone on to the courts, but he'd wanted a chance to look around. It had been a long time since he'd been to the Isle of Palms, not since the summer he'd spent here as a tennis pro, the last summer he'd come home from Vanderbilt. That had been three—no, four years ago.

Approaching the clubhouse, he paused by the pro shop, and glanced inside remembering. Then R.J.

shook his head and walked on. How quickly the years had flown.

Rounding the corner of the pro shop, he stepped onto the walkway to the pool. He'd spent a fair amount of time there, too, that summer—in the pleasurable company of a good-looking brunette who had lifeguarded there, if he recalled correctly.

A smile was on his face when he stepped toward the gate to survey the crystal-blue pool, surrounded by clusters of palms and bright yellow umbrellas. It was nearly deserted, R.J. noticed. Most of the usual pool-goers were probably over at the courts watching the semifinals.

And then he saw her. Her skin had darkened to the color of caramel, her hair was sunbleached to pale gold. But it was Carole. R.J.'s heart slammed up to his throat.

She was only a half-dozen yards away, by the brick wall, oblivious to his presence. R.J.'s eyes started at the ankles, burning a path up the shapely legs, along the outrageous curves confined by the meager white bikini to the fine lines of a face turned up to the sun as if in worship. The analogy fit. At that moment, he could easily imagine her as some kind of golden sun goddess.

It was time to go, Carole reminded herself. Turning, she moved back to the cot, gathered her suntan oil and towel, and strolled toward the gate.

"Hello, Carole."

Before she could help herself, Carole had thrown her hands up in a gasp, the slippery container of oil flying from her fingers.

Looking over with wide eyes to the shadowed walkway the voice had come from, she recognized R.J. He was chuckling now—a deep, thrilling sound, and like a rocket, her pulse was off again.

"R.J. ! For heaven's sake," she sputtered. "Must

you be forever frightening the life out of me from the shadows?''

He laughed pleasantly, bent down to pick up her tanning oil. ''I believe this belongs to you,'' he said, offering the bottle to her. ''Looks like you've used it to good advantage. You've got quite a tan there.'' Against his will, R.J.'s gaze swept boldly over her body.

''What are you doing here?'' Carole asked. She looked up at him as if in simple curiosity, but secretly, her eyes devoured the tall, blond sight of him. In white deck pants and a navy shirt, he looked his usual, casually aristocratic self; yet it seemed to her that R.J. grew decidedly more handsome each time she saw him.

''What are you doing here in Charleston?'' She asked once again, as much to herself as to R.J. ''Curt didn't mention anything about your coming to town.''

R.J. regarded her steadily, taking in the startling effect of her blue eyes against the bronze suntan. ''Curt doesn't know everything I do, Carole. He didn't know I was coming to town. No one did. I just decided this morning. I'm moving back.''

''To Charleston?'' she asked, trying too late to quell the rebellious note of hope that suddenly rang in her voice.

R.J. smiled. Whether Carole chose to admit to it or not—and despite Curt's involvement—there was still something between them.

''Yes, to Charleston.''

Carole looked away. Without a word, she proceeded through the gate and along the path to the clubhouse, and R.J. fell in step with her, looking down on the top of her fair head as they walked.

''How have you been?'' R.J. finally asked, breaking their silence.

''Fine. And you?''

214

"Fine. Have you heard anything yet from New York?"

He wasn't prepared for the pain that flared in her face at his question. But then it was gone, carefully stifled, and once again she was looking straight ahead.

"Yes, I've heard."

"Well," he pressed, "what's the word?"

She peered up at him defiantly. "The word is . . . according to Haut Nouveau, I've got no business trying to be a designer."

R.J. came to an abrupt halt. So *that* was it. No wonder she'd looked so hurt. And he hadn't had the brains to figure it out. Taking her by the shoulders, he looked down on her intently.

"Carole, I'm sorry. Really I am. But that's just one fashion house, right? Who else are you planning to contact?"

Carole shot him a look of disbelief. "No one!" she returned. With an angry shrug she stepped out of his grasp and began to swing her way up the clubhouse stairs.

"You mean you're just going to let it go?" he called after her.

Trying to keep his eyes off her swaying hips, R.J. bounded up the stairs to confront her. "I thought you had more spirit than that."

Carole raised her chin, her eyes flashing. "You didn't see that rejection letter! So don't try and give me a pep talk, okay?"

"I'm not giving you a pep talk. I'm just surprised you're giving up so easily."

"Easily!" she blurted. "What do *you* know about it?"

R.J.'s voice was quiet and firm and—dared she hope?—caring. "All I know is that not long ago you were all fired up about this design thing. All I know is that you said country clubs weren't enough. And

215

yet here you are, three weeks later . . . at the country club, claiming that you're not giving up easily."

He touched a chord in her no one else could reach. He always had, Carole realized. The painful sense of worthlessness swelled anew.

"Why should *you* be surprised?" she lashed out. "*You're* the one who said I never looked like a designer anyway . . . that I looked more like a . . . a floozy!"

R.J. frowned. "I never said you look like a floozy."

"It meant the same thing!" she accused. "I should think you'd be *expecting* me to fail and give up, just like all the other men in my life. You've let me know *exactly* what you think I'm good for, R.J.!"

Now, he was completely bewildered. "What the hell are you talking about, Carole?"

Her eyes were sparkling now with tears of frustration. "I'm talking about your coming over to my apartment—informing me that your intentions were those of a 'buck in heat.' You made your opinion of me perfectly clear, R.J. And you were right, okay? All of you were right!"

Carole spun away in the direction of the ladies' lounge, leaving R.J. to stare after her ravishing, fast-retreating figure, wondering how the hell she could have gotten such a wrong idea.

Robert diplomatically steered Curt from the midst of a group of tennis players who'd been eliminated from the July Bake Off in earlier rounds and were waiting to play a consolation match.

"I want you to be prepared," he told his younger son quietly. "Your brother is here today."

Curt's pale eyes snapped to his father's. "R.J.?"

Robert nodded. "He's moving back to Charleston."

A rosy flush raced to Curt's face. "For good?"

216

"It sounds that way."

"Why?"

"Your guess is as good as mine. He said he's become interested in other things." He paused, fixing Curt with a significant gaze. "Let's just hope it's not the Stuckey matter. If so, it looks as though your fancy footwork is about to be put to the test."

Curt thought for a moment. He'd taken care of everything, but there was a danger in being too smug. Once again he reviewed each step that had been taken, looking for possible weaknesses. But it was all smooth as silk, no ugly seams, he was more sure than ever. "I have no worries."

But when he and his father sidled up to the court to watch the end of the Parker-Gottfried match, his eyes took on a feral glint as they searched across the court and into the stands, looking for the light blond hair that would identify his brother. Curt had a second reason for being wary of R.J., and she had not yet appeared in the box seat from which she always cheered him on.

But there was R.J., he noted, making his way toward their mother, then taking a seat behind her. Curt's scalp prickled; the mere sight of his brother revived all the accusatory questions he longed to scream. Why are you moving back? Why are you investigating old Jonah Stuckey? Why have you been to see Carole behind my back—twice?

As he stood in the late-afternoon sunshine, Curt kept a watchful eye trained across center court. But it was too late. His day had already turned sour.

Carole put the final touch to her crown of curls, then stepped back to assess herself in the mirror of the lounge. The royal-blue dress had a rather Oriental look, with its high collar and simple sleeveless lines. The shimmering silk picked up the color of her eyes, conformed flatteringly to her figure. Carole knew she

217

looked her best. She lingered, putting her suit and towel in the woven shoulder bag, checking her reflection one last time. But she'd put off going to the courts as long as she could. It would soon be time for Curt's match, and she had to be there when it began. The dread of having to face R.J. again couldn't keep her in the ladies' lounge forever.

A few minutes later, Carole arrived at the court just in time to watch Jeffrey Gottfried make the final, winning shot of the doubles match.

"Game. Set. Match, Misters Parker and Gottfried," the announcer boomed.

Making her way toward the box seats amidst the ensuing applause and cheering, she watched disinterestedly as Jim Parker, in apparent high spirits from the win, attempted to leap over the net to shake the hands of his opponents. But his foot caught. Carole stood frozen as he twisted in the air, landing with a howl of pain on his back.

A collective gasp arose from the bleachers, and she was vaguely aware of someone rushing past her and pushing through the crowd gathering about the injured man. Dr. Gottfried, she realized. And a moment later the doctor and his son broke through the circle, helping Jim Parker hobble off the court.

As the three moved away in the direction of the clubhouse, Carole took the seat that had been saved for her between her father and Mrs. Morrisson. R.J. sat behind his mother, giving Carole a dark once-over before she could turn her back on him and sit down.

"Carole! Did you see what happened?" Charlotte exclaimed.

"Yes. I hope he isn't badly hurt."

"Henry will know," Gwen said hurriedly. "I'm sure he'll come and tell us as soon as he can."

"Damn rotten luck," James muttered. "After they just made it to the finals."

"Oh, that's right!" Gwen commented worriedly,

218

and turned to look again in the direction in which her son had disappeared. "Of course the most important thing is that Mr. Parker is all right. But Jeffrey will be so disappointed if he can't play."

"Well, let's cross that bridge when we come to it," Charlotte suggested comfortingly. Turning to Carole, she asked, "Carole, you remember my son, Randall?"

Carole nodded briefly over her shoulder. "Yes, we've met."

"It's R.J., Mother," he corrected. He leaned forward to put a hand on Carole's shoulder. "Always a pleasure to see you, Miss Gossett."

"Thank you," she sniffed. *Miss Gossett.* Really, wasn't he carrying this a bit far? Carole looked blatantly ahead as Curt and Robert Morrisson strolled onto the court.

James Gossett turned nonchalantly sideways in his seat, but his gaze was anything but casual. He hadn't missed the way R.J.'s eyes had lingered on his daughter. Carole seemed happy to be back with Curt, but perhaps the danger wasn't past yet. Only when he saw R.J. sit back in his chair did James allow himself to relax and turn his attention to the upcoming match.

Normally, Curt came over to wave up into the stands before the match began. But today, he simply stepped into position and waited for the serve. Curious, Carole began to watch his uncharacteristic behavior, taking note of the unfathomable, hard looks he occasionally tossed in the direction of the box seats. Yet his odd mood didn't seem to affect his performance. Possibly, he was playing more aggressively than ever.

When the players changed sides at five-two, Curt turned a particularly cold stare in their direction before continuing past the stands.

"What in the world is the matter with Curt?" Charlotte voiced the question that had been running through Carole's mind for the past seven games. "He's practically won the first set single-handedly, and he looks as sour as if he's just eaten a lemon."

Seated beside Carole, James kept a smug silence. He could feel the heat of the battle, and he loved it. *She's too close to that brother of yours, isn't she, boy? All that talk about you Morrisson men standing together doesn't amount to a hill of beans right now, does it?*

"The ambulance just left," Henry Gottfried told them, regaining his seat just after Curt and Robert had won the first set. "I don't think his ankle is broken, but it's a pretty bad sprain. I'll wager Jim Parker will be on crutches for at least a few weeks."

"Oh no. How awful," Charlotte exclaimed.

"Just one of those things," Henry went on. "Of course, Jeffrey is pretty despondent. To make it all the way to the finals and have something like this happen is pretty hard for the boy to take."

"Where is he?" Gwen asked, sweeping the area with a concerned look.

"Oh, he's all right," Henry assured her. "He's getting cleaned up at the clubhouse. He's just a little down."

"I suppose this means he has to forfeit tomorrow's match?" Charlotte asked.

"It does . . . unless he can find a substitute for Parker overnight," James put in. "Someone who hasn't been otherwise registered in the tournament."

"I could play."

Collectively, Carole, Charlotte, James, Henry, and Gwen turned to look at R.J.

"Why yes, that would be perfect!" Charlotte beamed. "R.J. was pro here on the isle a few years ago."

Carole continued to gaze at him. She hadn't considered he was a tennis player. R.J. was full of surprises, it seemed.

"If your son wants to take me on as a partner, that is," R.J. continued. "I've been watching him and he's a fine player. I'll admit I haven't been playing too regularly the past couple of years, but—"

"Pooh!" Charlotte broke in. "My son is an excellent player."

James leaned back in his seat, looking over his shoulder at R.J. with an amused expression. This was getting better all the time. "Are you sure you want to play in the finals, R.J.? After all, you could be pitting yourself against your own brother and father."

R.J. returned the look with an arched brow. He didn't like James Gossett. The man was too damned pushy. He could swear Gossett was egging him on, although for the life of him R.J. couldn't imagine to what end. "*If* Dad and Curt make it to the finals, Mr. Gossett," he replied. "I'm sure they'll prefer to play a fair match rather than accept the championship on a bye." He smiled in a rather forced manner. "After all, it's only a game . . . isn't it?"

Oblivious to the tension of their exchange, Gwen laid a hand on R.J.'s arm. "Would you talk to my son, R.J.?" she asked. "Jeffrey has enjoyed this tournament so much. It would mean a great deal to him, I'm sure, if he didn't have to forfeit."

"I'll go find him right now," R.J. said, rising to his feet. "And if he's agreeable to the idea, we'll go ahead and register with the officials."

Carole watched his tall, attractive form ramble to the aisle, admiring the fine figure he cut as he moved. But then he caught her. Turning unexpectedly, his eyes carved a path straight to her, trapping her in the midst of her perusal. His smile taunted Carole, and she could feel the color rising promptly to her cheeks. Irritably, she turned back to the tennis match, unaware of James's hawklike eye upon her.

As the match wore on, Curt seemed to relax and

221

take a little more pleasure in the game. His playing remained sharp, as did his father's. They played masterfully, and, although their opponents were a strong team, the Morrissons eventually won out.

It was nearly six o'clock when Curt and Robert approached the net with wide smiles to shake hands with their opponents. But their smiles quickly faded when the announcer's voice informed them that Jeffrey Gottfried would play the finals match with a newly registered teammate, Mr. R.J. Morrisson of Charleston.

As the fans responded with a round of applause, Curt and Robert looked at each other in surprise, each silently wondering at the way R.J. seemed to be popping up in their lives—and always on the other team. But after a moment, Robert merely shrugged, draping his arm across his son's shoulders. And Curt smiled in return. They left the court together, maintaining the facade as they headed for the club locker room.

But once he was alone in the showers of the clubhouse, Curt allowed his festering thoughts full range. And the more he thought—and doubted . . . and suspicioned—the blacker his mood became.

Brother against brother. How was it going to end?

Carole dawdled on the deserted patio outside the slowly filling dining room of The Island House. Feeling a need to escape her father's party of guests—a group of about a dozen, who were having cocktails in the adjoining lounge as they awaited the arrival of Curt and Robert Morrisson—Carole had escaped to the open solitude of the outdoors.

Thoughtfully, she strolled along the edge of the patio, her eyes searching beyond the pampas grass and palmettoes to the brilliant sunset. The orange sun was huge and tropical, melting slowly toward the dark blue water of the horizon, leaving behind a sky streaked with rose and purple. It was breathtaking. Carole soaked up the peaceful beauty of the scene as a sea breeze caressed her face.

It had been so easy to feel nothing these past weeks, to simply float along like a cork in a stream, being carried to a destiny over which she had no control—and for which she no longer had any concern. She should have known R.J. would come back into the picture and get her all stirred up. In a few short hours his mere electrifying presence had made her forget that nothing really mattered anymore. Suddenly, the anxious sense of discontent had returned. Not that it could make any difference now, or change the inevitable.

Standing on the fringe of the crowd in the lounge, R.J. tossed down the last of his scotch. He appeared to be listening with great interest to Henry Gottfried, laughed at the appropriate moment when Gwen made a joke. Had he been less preoccupied, he might even have enjoyed the conversation. But he couldn't keep his dark blue eyes from sweeping the crowd; every few minutes they launched on a new search for the blond topknot of curls that would pinpoint Carole. And each time his search proved fruitless. He hadn't seen her since he and Jeffrey had arrived at the restaurant from the tennis officials' tent to join the party.

How the girl managed to misunderstand him so completely amazed R.J. He'd never before had trouble communicating with any woman. But then, he'd always known what he was after and gone confidently about the business of getting it. Maybe that was it. With Carole, he didn't know *what* he was after.

It had started as a purely physical attraction, but now it was something altogether different. How exactly, R.J. wasn't sure. And it made him feel uncomfortable, almost disloyal, to even think about. He was backing off for Curt's sake, he'd told himself, but whenever he ran into Carole, he found himself seeking, trying once again, however fruitlessly, to establish some link between them.

Forbidden fruit, R.J.'s conscience warned. But he knew the epithet didn't come close to explaining the deepening feelings he had for Carole Gossett.

On the pretext of getting another drink, R.J. excused himself and rambled away from the crowd in the direction of the bar. Then, passing the glass wall overlooking the patio, he stopped short.

Carole stared out to sea, her thoughts lingering on R.J. and what he had told her earlier that afternoon. Other than R.J., April had been the only person who had ever supported her designing; both had urged her to try another design house following Haut Nouveau's rejection. But then, they were just alike, April and R.J.—independent and successful. They were not the sort of people who could understand failure.

As if summoned by her thoughts, the sound of his steady, approaching footsteps reached her ears. She wasn't surprised when she turned to find R.J. there.

"I'd like to talk to you, Carole."

His voice was deep and commanding. The blue eyes were dark and intense as they darted between her own.

"What is it?"

"About that 'buck in heat' nonsense . . ." R.J. paused, briefly considering his words, then rushed on. "Yes, Carole, I find you attractive. And yes, I'd even like to take you to bed, although that's hardly possible under the circumstances. But I don't think that's the extent of your worth, damn it. I'm not like 'all the other men in your life,' as you put it. And I certainly wasn't hoping you'd fail. If you remember

224

correctly, you'll recall that I wished you luck with your career. And I meant it!''

Carole was surprised by his outburst. For an instant she watched his impassioned features closely. But then she merely sighed and turned back to the sunset.

''It doesn't matter,'' she said quietly. ''It's out of my hands now anyway.''

R.J. hesitated. Her changes of mood were driving him to distraction. ''What's out of your hands?''

''Oh, nothing important. Just my future.''

''Your future is what you make it, Carole.''

''For you, maybe,'' she countered.

''For you, too.''

She looked up at the handsome face next to her, her eyes blank. ''That's easy for you to say, R.J. But I'm not like you. Don't you understand? My one dream for a future of my own is dead.''

''One dream? You're willing to give up after just one dream?''

''Don't start that again.''

R.J. studied her look of resignation with new acuteness. He hadn't realized the great depths to which Carole's spirit had fallen. It was as if she'd lost touch with the will to live.

''So, what do you do now?'' he pressed, an uncomfortable feeling of worry overtaking him. ''If you give up on your dreams, just what kind of a future can you expect?''

Carole regarded him calmly. Her voice was steady and bland as she replied. ''That of a Morrisson.''

A sinking feeling rocked R.J.'s stomach. He'd have rathered not hear the words—some part of him still refused to recognize the truth behind them. ''What?''

''Hadn't you heard? I'm practically one of the family.''

God, she was so beautiful standing there in the

225

light of the setting sun. The picture of this woman marrying his brother made R.J. feel suddenly sick.

"You don't seem very happy about it. What happened to the Carole of three weeks ago?" he asked quietly. "The one who didn't want to be handed down from one man to another, the one who wanted to be able to run her own life?"

"She's gone," Carole looked again toward the horizon. "This one is wiser. She knows she has no more control over what's going to happen than that piece of driftwood over there."

R.J. drank in the fine lines of her profile, resisted the urge to reach out and shake some sense into her. "Don't talk like some damned Victorian who has no freedom of choice! Is that what you want, Carole? To be Curt's wife?"

"It doesn't matter what I want," she said quietly. "Two of the most powerful houses in Charleston will be joined. It's expected."

R.J. couldn't help himself any longer. He'd fought his attraction to her, stepped out of Curt's way. But now, everything went out of his head but the need to touch her, to know if she felt for him what he had grown to feel for her. And if she did, R.J. thought, Curt could be damned!

Stepping in front of her, he took a firm hold on her bare arms and made her look up at him. "If you talk like that, you have no one to blame but yourself for ending up unhappily. If you want Curt, that's one thing." R.J.'s eyes burned into her like blue flames. "But if you don't, that's something else again. I, for one, would like to know how you feel. Do you love him?"

Carole hung suspended in the sheer magnetism of his gaze. Caught in his grasp, the old spark flickered into life. With a dull sense of surprise, she realized that despite the way everything else in her life had changed, R.J.'s dynamic impact was as constant and sure as the tides.

226

* * *

Curt stopped before the patio door as if he'd slammed into a wall. It was R.J. and Carole! Something exploded in Curt's skull. He was barely aware of what he was doing as he stomped across the patio to where his brother was holding her. Grabbing a startled R.J. by the arm, Curt jerked him away from Carole and thundered, "Get your hands off her!"

"Curt! What are you doing?" Carole cried as he took a threatening step toward R.J.

But Curt barely heard her. His eyes were riveted dangerously on his older brother—the older brother he had idolized, the older brother who had always bested him at everything. "Just what the hell do you think you're doing, R.J.?"

R.J. stood his ground. "I need to talk to you, Curt," he replied solemnly.

"Shut up! I know what you've been up to. And I know you want to snake Carole. I just didn't think you'd have the nerve to try it right here in front of everybody!"

"Curt!" Carole protested, reaching out to grab his arm.

He swatted her hand away and snapped, "This is not your business, Carole."

"There's no need to talk to her like—"

Carole gasped as Curt's fist came flying from the right to connect with R.J.'s jaw, cutting his words short.

Some of the guests within the dining room had witnessed the punch, and now all eyes seemed to be peering through the expansive glass wall overlooking the patio.

R.J. stumbled back a few steps, then regained his footing. He focused on his brother with a dangerous, piercing look.

"I'll give you that one, brother," he stated grimly. Raising a hand to the corner of his mouth, where a

227

small trickle of blood was beginning to show, R.J. added, "Maybe you deserved a shot. But let me give you fair warning. From now on, it's every man for himself."

From beneath hard-knitted brows, R.J. threw a smoldering look at Carole, then stalked away, ignoring the stares from the dining room as he exited the patio and disappeared across the grounds.

"Curt!" Carole was staring at him horrified. "What in the world has gotten into you?"

Curt turned his pale eyes to her, and gradually, his vision cleared. "You have," he returned, looking at her with a strange, fixed gaze that made Carole's heart begin to thud. "You've gotten into me." Taking her by the hand, he proceeded to draw her swiftly across the patio. "Come with me."

"Where are we going? Curt! You're going too fast!" she objected as her legs moved rapidly within the tight skirt of the royal blue dress.

Down the steps, around the clubhouse, out to the parking lot, and all the way to the BMW, Curt hurried her on.

Unlocking the car door, he retrieved something from the glove compartment, stuffed it in his pocket, and slammed the car door shut again. Then he grabbed Carole's hand, and they were off again.

"Why are we in such a hurry?" Carole asked, breathless, as he put his arm around her to give her more support, accelerating their pace.

Curt glanced at her soberly. "I can't wait any longer," he said, and then looked ahead to the fast-approaching clubhouse. "Not now."

Skirting through the foyer and along the hallway, Carole caught sight of their flight in the occasional mirrors. The few passersby who were in the corridor stepped aside as Curt smilingly cleared their path, and Carole followed along in breathless embarrassment.

She was thankful when he finally slowed somewhat as they reached the dining room. But still, he held tightly to Carole's hand, winding her through the dinner crowd and toward the Gossett party. Conversation at the banquet-sized table fell to a hush as Curt brought them to a halt near the table's head.

"Hello, everyone. Sorry we're late," Curt said.

Carole could feel the curious eyes boring into them. The Morrissons, the Gottfrieds, and of course, her father were all looking at them expectantly.

"Here now," Robert Morrisson said in his distinguished, authoritative voice. "What was that business out on the patio between you and R.J. ?"

"A private matter, Father. Its significance pales beside that which I now would like to bring everyone's attention. I have an announcement to make."

You could have heard a pin drop in the dining hall.

"What is it, Curt?" Charlotte Morrisson asked. She was troubled by this unexpected flare-up between her boys. "Has it got something to do with your brother?"

A hard edge came to Curt's voice. "It has nothing whatever to do with R.J. No," he added, turning to Carole and softening his tone, "it has to do with this lovely lady right here."

He fished in his pocket, looked in her eyes, and Carole's knees went weak.

He took her left hand.

"Here and now, I'm inviting you to join in my happiness as I have the honor . . ."

He was slipping the ring on her finger. Carole sank into a daze.

". . . of asking her to become my wife." Curt smiled confidently into her eyes, closed his warm hand around the fingers that had turned to ice beneath the new weight of the diamond ring.

The expectant silence erupted into a resounding round of o-o-hs and a-a-hs. Then someone began to applaud—in her shocked state of mind, Carole had the dim impression it was her father—and it was immediately taken up by everyone in the fashionable dining hall.

With such encouragement, Curt leaned down, taking advantage of Carole's speechlessness, and kissed her thoroughly. The distinguished crowd hooted its approval.

R.J. stormed up the stairs to his old room and began collecting his hastily unpacked garments. Never, he thought. Never—through all the competitive, growing-up years—had there been such a breach between him and Curt. They both wanted the same woman. It was impossible for them to abide under the same roof.

Stepping into the bath to get his shaving gear, he glanced into the mirror over the sink. At the sight of his swollen, bloodied mouth, R.J.'s temper flared anew. With angry speed, he gathered the rest of his belongings, and cleared out of the Morrisson mansion.

And as he drove the short distance to the Mills House Hotel, R.J. was completely unaware that his brother and Carole Gossett were engaged to be married.

Chapter Ten

THE CLOUDS HUNG over the Isle of Palms, turning the mirrorlike ocean a dank gray and sealing in the humid heat like a thick blanket. It was almost August, summer storm time in the low country. Late in the afternoon, there would probably be a downpour, complete with jagged lightning, crackling thunder, and high winds that would whip the palms and the tides into a frenzy. But for now, it was forbodingly still, as if the forces of nature were tensing up for a later show.

The tennis fans crowded around the center court shifted in their seats and fanned themselves. But it did little good. Even that brief stir of air was hot and heavy.

Below the bleachers, the four women playing in the July Bake Off championships, were beginning to show the effects of the heat. Now, as they changed sides after an odd game, they stopped at courtside and mopped at their perspiring red faces, taking a brief break before play continued.

Carole sat in her usual seat between her father and Charlotte Morrisson; the Gottfrieds were in their places to her left. The five of them had become an institution in the past few weekends, Carole mused,

231

gathering in the same spot every Saturday and Sunday to cheer on the men's doubles teams. Today the finals between Gottfried/Morrisson and Morrisson/Morrisson would mark the climax and the end of the competition.

She let her eyes drift across the court. Somewhere over there, Curt and his father were milling about the players' tent, waiting for their time of combat. As she scanned the distant figures across the way, many of whom were dressed in tennis whites, she found herself wondering if R.J. had yet arrived.

A sudden motion next to her prompted Carole to look at Charlotte Morrisson, who was fanning herself distractedly. She had been somewhat unlike herself today. As soon as she arrived, Charlotte had begun questioning her about what was wrong between her sons.

"You were there, dear," Charlotte had said quite anxiously. "I can't get a thing out of Curt, and when Robert and I returned home, R.J. was gone. Can't you tell me anything, Carole? What were they fighting about?"

Carole had regarded her pensively, realized how much she liked this woman who was going to become her mother-in-law. She couldn't very well say that she herself was the cause of the blowup between the Morrisson brothers. In fact, Carole couldn't quite believe it herself. How could she explain it to their mother?

"I really have no idea," Carole told her, coloring slightly.

"More than likely, just high spirits about today's match," her father commented in casual dismissal.

But when Carole had glanced his way, she'd caught a smirking look on his face that left her wondering just what, indeed, her father knew of the true circumstances surrounding the brothers' fight.

As the women's doubles resumed play, Carole reached for the program that lay in her lap. She'd worn a white halter sundress—one of the coolest things she owned—and she'd put her hair up, leaving her neck bare to catch any hint of cool air. Still, she was sweltering. She began to fan herself with the program.

Carole stopped in midstroke as the jewel flashed out at her, catching her once again off guard. She looked at her left hand another countless time. The immense, square-cut diamond sparkled back at her, winking in the overcast light as if at some monstrous joke. Its mere presence on her finger amazed her.

"Curt has exquisite taste," her father observed.

Carole glanced at him, discovered that his dark eyes were on the ring.

"Yes. It is exquisite," she admitted.

"Have the two of you set a date yet?"

"There's hardly been time, Daddy."

Yet *he* had certainly found the time to make a few arrangements, Carole thought to herself wryly. Before the dinner party had adjourned the evening before, James Gossett had announced with typical flair that he would be throwing an engagement soirée within the month. He'd added that the affair would be held on his yacht, *The Instigator,* at Mariner's Cay. Carole had been only too aware of his pleasure. He'd been planning this little social coup for quite some time.

Charlotte reached over, patted Carole's bejeweled hand encouragingly. "You'll be a beautiful bride, Carole," she said, "whatever the wedding date. But at Christmastime, with the candles and poinsettias, and you in winter white . . . Ah, couldn't you just see it?" Charlotte's dark eyes sparkled at Carole with fond teasing. "Just an idea now, mind you. I don't intend to be a meddlesome mother-in-law."

Carole gave her a smile that hid the sense of impending doom that struck her at the mere mention of a wedding date. What was the matter with her?

233

Curt was handsome, wealthy, mad about her. She was going to marry him, and that was that.

She looked back to the court. The women's finals were nearly over. Soon it would be time for Curt . . . and R.J.

R.J. rambled up to the players' tent, greeted Jeffrey Gottfried, then selected an out-of-the-way spot to do a few stretches. It wasn't long before his father and Curt mosied over to join him.

R.J. eyed his brother guardedly, though it was his father who spoke.

"And just where the hell did you disappear to last night?"

R.J.'s blue-gray eyes swept back toward Curt, eyeing the fashionable tennis duds and the sun-burnished face. He answered his father without so much as a glance. "I decided I'd be more comfortable at the Mills House."

"You might have left a note explaining your absence."

Still, R.J.'s unsmiling gaze was locked on his brother. "Didn't think of it."

"Look at me," Robert demanded. "I'm your father. I think you owe me the courtesy of looking at me when I speak to you."

R.J.'s eyes snapped moodily to his father.

"I've already talked to Curt," Robert went on with a grave look. "He won't tell me what's going on between the two of you. I don't suppose *you'd* like to explain the little spectacle of misconduct the two of you put on last night?"

R.J. nearly lashed out that he was no longer a kid, that his father could keep his misplaced scolding to himself. But when his words came, they were courteous, if a little short.

"With all due respect, Father, I think that what

happened last night is strictly between Curt and me.''

"Fine!" Robert boomed. "As long as you keep it confined to the two of you. Your name is Morrisson, and you have an image to uphold—one of dignity and honor. Certainly not one of common vulgarity, such as your behavior last night suggested. I don't intend to witness another such gross display. Is that clear?'' He looked back and forth between his sons.

A sly smile slid over Curt's visage. "I'm willing to let bygones be bygones.''

R.J.'s hand climbed to the slight swelling at the corner of his mouth. "Yeah, I'll bet you are.''

"I'd like to see the two of you shake hands,'' Robert stated.

"For God's sake!" R.J. blurted with an irritated look.

Curt extended his hand, the smile fading to a cagey grin. "Again . . . I'm willing.''

R.J. looked back to his brother, slouched to one hip. Eventually, he grasped Curt's hand and shook it once, hard.

"Sure. Why not?'' he muttered grimly, then stepped to retrieve his tennis gear as the tournament announcer called for the men's finals.

Robert walked between his silent sons as they made their way toward center court, pondering the rift between the two boys who had always been so close. But they're boys no longer, he reminded himself. Briefly, he might have wondered if the breach had anything to do with the Stuckey matter, but dismissed the possibility. Surely not, for Curt would have told him. No . . . it was something else.

They had reached the center court fence, and seeking to instigate a little friendly conversation between his sons, Robert unknowingly brought up the one subject that was inescapably volatile.

"Curt, aren't you going to tell your brother the good news?''

Curt looked round his father to R.J., an odd light in his eyes. "That's okay, Dad. Why don't you tell him?"

Robert looked up at his tall, firstborn son. "Your younger brother is about to become an old married man, Randall. Last night, he and Carole Gossett became engaged."

"What?" R.J. sputtered, his mouth gaping open.

And then he spun to his brother, stared at the smiling, well-known face. A lifetime of memories flashed through his mind: teaching Curt to play ball, defending him against the school bully, sneaking smokes together, chasing girls. . . . There were a dozen happy images. And suddenly, a cloud of jealousy billowed up to swallow them all.

Curt was fairly glowing. "That's right, brother," he said. "Carole is going to become Mrs. Curt Morrisson. I'm a lucky man. Wouldn't you agree?"

The announcer bellowed something across the loudspeaker, but R.J. could make no sense of the words. Jeffrey Gottfried had joined them, and the crowd began to applaud as the four of them walked out onto the court.

R.J. was stunned. They began warming up, and he found himself performing as was expected—his limbs seeming to move on their own recognizance—hitting the ball rhythmically back and forth, opposite his father.

By the time they finished warming up, however, R.J.'s fuzzy head had cleared, though a bitter taste lingered in his mouth. He looked across the net at Curt, took note of his happy smile as he conferred with his father before they parted to take up their doubles positions. And then just before the first service, R.J. surrendered to the nagging urge. He searched through the stands until he found her, sitting above him like some unattainable, fair-haired angel in white.

R.J. knew he had no right to feel that she had

betrayed him. He, if anyone, had betrayed everyone with his clandestine yearnings. But the acknowledgment did nothing to relieve the dark animosity within the look he turned on Carole.

Feeling conspicuously on display in the box seat, Carole had found she could do nothing to prevent her eyes from returning to R.J. again and again. All through the warm-ups she had discovered her gaze lingering on the tall, muscular body, admiring his excellent form as he stroked the ball evenly from the baseline.

Curt's fiancée or no, Carole had been unable to keep her eyes off R.J. She was instantly aware of the cold look he shot her way. The dark brows were knitted, the mouth grim—wordlessly accusing her from across the distance between them. A sick feeling lurched to the pit of her stomach, and Carole dropped her gaze to her lap—only to find herself staring at Curt's diamond.

The men began to play, and it was immediately obvious that the match was going to be a killer. All four of the players were strong, and the tennis fans cheered regularly at an outstanding shot made by one or the other of them. The steamy afternoon wore on, the massive clouds gathering more closely over the little island where the tennis match raged. The men were now so drenched with perspiration they looked as though they'd just climbed out of a swimming pool.

It began to happen gradually. A point to Curt . . . one to R.J. . . . then Curt . . . R.J. Eventually, it became obvious that the match was developing into a battle between the Morrisson brothers. Curt was perhaps a bit quicker. But R.J. had the reach, and his net game was deadly.

Each team had won a set, and now, as R.J. took the serve, the score was six-five. This could be the championship game. His wristband was sopping, but through force of habit, R.J. swiped it across his forehead, then bounced the ball once . . . twice . . . before the toss. The ball rose from his fingertips, the racquet went back, and he slammed a hard-driving serve to his father. It was returned to center court. R.J. took it with a backhand to Curt's sideline. But his brother was ready and shot a sizzling forehand up the undefended alley.

The crowd roared, and Curt smiled blatantly—tauntingly—across the net at his brother.

R.J. remained unflustered, caught the bounce from the ballboy, then lined up to serve Curt. With a deadly look of earnest, he made the toss, brought the racquet around, and sliced into the ball with a masterful spin.

The ball dusted the far corner of the serving court, then soared in a spinning arc to the sideline. Curt never had the chance to get a racquet on it. Again the crowd roared.

"Ace!" the announcer boomed, and R.J. raised a brow in his brother's direction.

Thunder rolled across the isle as R.J. and Curt battled out the next two points, with R.J. running both times up to the net and firing a winning volley at Curt's feet.

Curt's flushed face looked to be on fire as he lined up to receive what could be the final serve of the match. He crouched in position, straining his pale blue eyes to focus closely on his brother's face. But the familiar features were like a stone mask. R.J. made the toss and brought his racquet around with awesome force.

The ball cleared the net by an inch, hit the court, and spun wildly. Curt made a lunge, but it was gone without having been touched. R.J. had claimed the finals victory with a service ace.

The crowd leaped to its feet, cheering and applauding as the announcement was made: "Game.

Set. Match, Misters Morrisson and Gottfried," followed by, "Join us now for awards and cocktails in the clubhouse."

The four tired and sweaty men approached the net. R.J. shook his father's hand, then reached across for Curt's with a humorless, victorious smile.

Curt met his look, shook hands, and shrugged.

"I'll give you this one, brother," he said, echoing R.J.'s comment from the previous day. "After all, we both know I've already won the most important match."

Curt gave his brother a last smug look, then turned and followed his father off the court as R.J. watched with a raging feeling of frustration.

A bolt of lightning flashed against the darkening clouds. Thunder rolled threateningly on the stagnant air. The storm was on its way.

The sizable crowd that filled the Wild Dunes ballroom applauded as R.J. and Jeffrey were presented a silver bowl engraved with July Bake Off Doubles Champions, and wound their way to the front of the room to take their place with the other tournament winners. Shaking hands all around, they smiled as a number of camera bugs snapped pictures. But the flare of the bulbs seemed lost in the larger, blinding siege of lightning that flashed suddenly outside the ballroom windows. And the subsequent crash of thunder drew a gasp from the crowd. A few large splats hit the windows, and then the rain came down with a vengeance.

Safe and sound within the opulent arms of the building, the tanned crowd began to split up, gravitating in clusters to the fully stocked bars that had been set up throughout the ballroom. Liquor and talk flowed freely as the storm howled outside.

R.J. gave Jeffrey Gottfried custody of the silver bowl, drawing a grateful look from the boy before he turned away from the stage and began making slow, solitary progress through the crowd of guests. Many of them he'd known since he was a boy, and he paused often to accept congratulations on the doubles win or catch up with an old acquaintance.

Every now and then, however, R.J. cast a glance toward the far end of the ballroom, where his family's party had gathered. Carole was with them, standing with her back to him, and whenever he ran his eyes down the shapely lines of her figure, he began to get riled all over again. He was in the midst of one such covert perusal, having maneuvered close to the group, when Curt and his father stepped up to him, blocking his view.

"You're empty-handed, son," Robert observed, offering R.J. his glass of champagne. "Here. Have mine."

R.J. took the glass, noting that all three of them had donned traditional tennis sweaters over their still-damp playing clothes and now looked somewhat ridiculously like the three musketeers. Shooting his brother a glum look, he tossed off the contents of the glass in a long gulp.

His father grimaced. "That is an insult to a superior vintage."

"Sorry." R.J. smiled glibly. "I forgot I was in the presence of a connoisseur."

An impatient look came to Robert's face. "What's the matter with you, R.J.? You won the match . . . played brilliantly. And yet you're behaving as if you're mad at the world."

"Maybe I am, Dad," he said with a sidelong glance at Curt.

"Does it have anything to do with your leaving Columbia?" his father probed.

Curt gave him a piercing look. "Yeah. Why are you moving back to Charleston anyway?"

You mean, why besides Carole? R.J. thought sourly. The caustic reply was out of his mouth before he could stop it. "Why, I've missed your smiling face, brother. And I was sure you missed mine, too."

Curt merely stared, gave a derisive snort, and turned away.

"What the hell is going on between you two?" Robert demanded of R.J. as Curt moved out of earshot.

"I told you once before, Dad. It's private."

Robert shifted his weight irritably to one hip and looked into the dark blue eyes so like his own. "Well, just what *can* you tell me, son? I get the impression your life is in an uproar. And I must say your mother is worried, though of course she won't say anything for fear that you'll think she's interfering. But I'd at least like to know why you left your post with the supreme court."

R.J. shrugged. "I was bored."

"*Bored?*" Robert boomed the word, then carefully lowered his voice as he swept his son with a look of disbelief. "Well, well . . . I've never heard tell of an attorney fresh out of school growing *bored* with the supreme court!"

R.J. regarded his father solemnly. He supposed he *did* owe him an explanation. "It happened, Dad. They're a very professional, responsible group. But they're so far removed from the people. Anyway . . . I've been wanting to come home for a long time. I just didn't realize how much until recently, when I got caught up with a case here in the Charleston area. I guess it's just gotten under my skin. I thought it best not to discuss the case at first, a man's welfare is at stake. But maybe . . ." R.J.'s brows lifted. "You're a man about town," he asked. "Do you happen to know anything about a company called Ashley Land Grant?"

Robert's eyes widened, then quickly narrowed as a tongue-tied instant of silence fell. For that instant, father and son were marooned on a quiet island,

241

suspended in time and space amongst the shifting sea of loud, talkative people. After a moment, Robert cleared his throat and broke the silence.

"Ashley Land Grant? No. Can't say the name rings a bell."

R.J. studied his father's rigid expression. He stared a few more seconds, then shook his head as if to clear it of the bothersome notion that had come to him. What the hell was wrong with him? Suspecting his own father? This case must really be getting to him! And yet, the rationalization did nothing to quell the haunting voice in the back of his mind, the dream voice he could never quite put a finger on. Every so often its presence was overpowering.

"What's the problem, R.J.?" Robert asked with a hooded look. "You seem to have gone pale all of a sudden."

James Gossett's commanding voice sliced through the awkward tension.

"I'm proposing a toast, gentlemen," he informed them. He stepped away long enough to retrieve Curt from a nearby group, then turned to the crowd and began tapping a spoon against his glass until he had the attention of everyone in the room.

"A toast!" he announced, glancing pleasantly to the three blond men who stood at his elbow. "I propose a toast to the Morrissons, the finest family of tennis players ever to grace a July Bake Off. To Robert." He turned and raised his glass to the man with a suave smile. "For an excellent show against these young whippersnappers."

The crowd chuckled appreciatively.

"To R.J.," James went on, "for an outstanding doubles win . . . And to Curt. For those of you who don't already know, he's won the sweetest prize of all . . . the hand of my daughter, Carole, in marriage. Here's to Curt and Carole."

The voices resounded through the hall like a swell of trumpets as glasses clinked in toast.

Carole felt her cheeks go red with embarrassment. She was cringing, yet the practiced smile that climbed to her face convinced everyone that the sudden high color was only that of a blushing bride. She felt as though a hundred well-wishing eyes were upon her: her father's, gleaming with dark brilliance; Curt's, sparkling pale and bright against his suntan; Charlotte Morrisson's, glowing with warm welcome.

Yet when an irresistible pull drew Carole to look beyond the smiling faces of Charlotte Morrisson and the Gottfrieds, the dark blue eyes that met and held her were flashing with accusal. A sense of breathlessness swept though her. Helplessly, she stared at R.J., watched him raise an empty glass in mocking parody of the toast. And then he turned brusquely away as the crowd surged in her direction, hemming her in with hugs and congratulations.

Carole lost sight of R.J. And Curt, too. Swept into the midst of the curious throng of well-wishers, she felt overwhelmed by the barrage of questions and comments that seemed to come at her from all sides.

"When did you two meet?" "That ring is absolutely gorgeous!" "Have you set a date?" "You'll be such a beautiful bride!" "Carole Morrisson . . . The name has such a lovely ring, doesn't it?"

After what seemed an eternity, the circle around her thinned somewhat. She could see her father and Charlotte Morrisson standing nearby. And in between embraces with two society matrons who had never before given her so much as a hello, Carole caught a snatch of their conversation.

"I believe we'll plan the engagement party for the last Saturday of August. *The Instigator* will easily accommodate a crowd of up to seventy or so. I was wondering, Charlotte . . . do you think you could give me some help with the guest list?"

"Of course, James," Carole heard Charlotte reply in her gracious, refined way. "You know I'll be happy to help."

"Fine . . . fine. Since Carole is going to be joining your family, I think it would be a great help if she could start meeting some of the Morrisson crowd."

Carole couldn't see her father's face, but she could imagine its look—the look of ultimate satisfaction. He was finally getting what he had always wanted.

The crush became stifling, and the forced smile on Carole's face began to tremble as perspiration broke out across her upper lip. It was really happening. . . . She was about to become Mrs. Curt Morrisson. A gorge seemed to lodge in her throat, the many faces crowding round her beginning to swim as she went suddenly dizzy.

"Are you all right, Carole?" someone asked. "You're white as a sheet."

"Excuse me," she managed to murmur. "I think I need some air."

Excusing herself, Carole began winding through the crowd, carving her way aimlessly, driven by the urge to escape. Gradually, she made her way to one of the windows, peered out at the storm that continued to rage. Against the dusky backdrop of twilight, the rain was coming down in dark sheets, battering the palms and reducing the meager light from the heavens to nonexistence. Everything—the storm, the crowd, Curt's smiles, R.J.'s frowns—*everything* was closing in on her!

Carole could only smile rather wildly when yet another well-meaning, elderly couple approached her and wished her well in her upcoming marriage. Her heart was pounding erratically, and as soon as she could disengage herself from them, she fled across the room and skirted out one of the doors into the quiet hallway. Once there, she flattened herself against the solid wall, and closing her eyes, she took several deep breaths.

244

From this safe distance, the laughter and chatter of the crowd drifted to her, a humming lull. And after a few moments, Carole felt her pulse begin to slow. Her eyelids drifted open, and gradually she straightened up and stepped away from the wall. Putting a hand to her forehead, she took a few steps in the direction of the foyer.

R.J. stood to the left of the double doors of the entrance, propping one elbow against the wall as he stared moodily out the window at the storm. All he wanted to do was get the hell out of there, yet the storm held him captive. Well, he'd be damned if he'd spend his captivity smiling and toasting to Curt and Carole's future.

Once again he shook his head in frustration. Despite all the warning signs, something within R.J. had refused to believe that they would end up married. Now, he realized it was really happening, and he was swamped with rolling waves of jealousy and disappointment—*and*, unreasonable though he knew it was, the painful feeling that he'd been betrayed. And so, here he was in the clubhouse foyer, waiting out the storm, his mood as black as the rainy night.

R.J. had been standing there for perhaps a quarter of an hour when he had the sudden feeling that he was no longer alone. Glancing over his shoulder, he spotted Carole, quietly watching him. How long she'd been there, he had no way of knowing; nor could he allow himself to care any longer. Gradually, the lines of R.J.'s mouth took on a hard set. And then his feet were moving, taking him to the door where he made a hasty, angry exit.

Carole's high-heeled sandals moved quickly as she clicked her way behind him across the parquet floor of the now-deserted foyer. She didn't stop to question her motives, it was so basic an instinct. Heaving open the double doors, she ignored the sudden gust of wind that whipped at her blond curls and sent the skirt of her white dress swirling about her.

R.J. had halted at the edge of the sheltered veranda, peering angrily into the raging winds and torrents of rain which seemed determined to thwart his escape. He turned at the sound of the door. There she was, outlined against the spilling light of the foyer where she had left the doors heedlessly open behind her. The howling, rainy winds were deafening; yet the sudden thunder of R.J.'s heart overrode even the din of the storm.

She stood there, poised like a white dove unsure of where to alight. A lump swelled to R.J.'s throat, leaving it dry and aching. Damn the storm! he thought. Spinning away, he flew down the veranda stairs and into the furious tempest.

"R.J.! Wait!"

He halted, squinted unseeingly ahead as the torrential rain plastered his clothes against his body and his hair into his eyes. Finally he turned, beheld her standing at the edge of the veranda, peering anxiously through the heavy rains.

"What?" he yelled. "What do you want?"

Carole hesitated, then called, "Come back!"

He eyed her warily, but as if of their own accord, his tennis shoes began to squish back across the sodden ground in her direction. He climbed the stairs to the shelter of the portico, looked down on the angelic face as water streamed unheeded down his own.

"Well?"

Carole jumped at his curt tone. Her eyes darted between his. "I only wanted to ask one thing of you," she said tremulously. "Don't hate me, R.J."

He laughed once, derisively. "Don't hate you? What is this nonsense, Carole? You couldn't care *less* how I feel about you!"

"I *do* care," she said more firmly. "That's why I'm here."

"Well, hooray for you," he returned in a flash of sarcasm. "You come out here for a stolen moment with me, and meanwhile, you're wearing Curt's diamond on your left hand. What is that supposed to prove? Oh yes, Carole! I can certainly see a great deal of care in that!"

"This whole thing with Curt started long ago," she said quietly. "Everyone knew engagement was just a matter of time. Everyone . . . your family . . . my father—"

"Ah, yes," R.J. interrupted. "And that's the telling factor, isn't it? Your father. Tell me, Carole. If he wanted to marry you off to some Arabian shiek who already had a dozen wives, would you go along with that, too?"

"That's not fair, R.J."

"Oh, really? I don't see why. You've given up total control of your life, so why should it matter *what* your father tells you to do? Even when he passes you along—as you once put it—to another man who's going to run your life the same way *he* always has!"

Carole lowered her blue-green eyes. "Please, R.J. You don't understand—"

"You're damned right, I don't understand! I won't understand any of this . . . unless you tell me you're marrying Curt because you want to!"

"I care a great deal for Curt."

"That's pretty weak testimony, Carole. You seem to forget I'm an attorney. If you're trying to make a case for the fact that you're in love with him, you're doing a poor job. Why don't you just come right out and say it?"

He paused, but Carole only peered up at him mutely.

"Go ahead!" he fired. "I'm in love with Curt. That's all you have to say."

Carole looked at him wordlessly, unable to force the lie from her throat.

"I thought so. You're not in love with him, but you're going to marry him anyway . . ." He paused for a second, then raged on.

"And what about you and me, Carole? Are you going to deny there's something between us? What are we supposed to do? Tuck it away in a closet somewhere and pretend it doesn't exist? I can see it now. Birthdays, Christmas . . . the whole family together, and me sending you hot looks behind Curt's back!"

Her eyes were luminous with the look of resignment he had come to hate.

"We'll be brother and sister, R.J.," she said. "And knowing you, I'm sure you'll handle the situation with honor."

"Don't be so sure of that, Carole." His look turned hard, his eyes like two blue jewels. "I'm not."

He reached out swiftly, secured his palms on each side of the heart-shaped face.

"Like right now. I don't give a damn whether you're engaged to my brother or not!"

His lips came down hard on hers, and as her mouth opened to receive his tongue, Carole knew she'd been longing for it all along, that this was why she'd flown through the clubhouse determined not to let him go.

The storm crashed about them as they held each other more closely, taking each other's breath away with the passion that arced between them. The wet warmth of his body covered her, seeping through her dress and firing her blood.

Finally, R.J. drew away from her, kissing her a few gentle parting times. Slowly, he raised his face to look at her with hungry eyes. "Can you deny that you want me as much as I want you? That if we

248

were in some private place, we'd be making love right now?''

His husky question broke the spell, grating at the sense of worthlessness Carole carried around inside her like a raw wound. She stiffened in his arms.

"That's all it boils down to, isn't it, R.J. ?'' she asked in a sudden cool tone. "A roll in the hay. A toss in the sack. How would you put it?''

The fire in his eyes died as quickly as it had flared. This was crazy. *She* was crazy. Once again, he balked at the unfairness of it.

Stepping back, R.J. removed his hands from her waist as if he suddenly couldn't bear the touch of her. "That's right, I forgot,'' he snapped. "I'm just like all the other men in your life, right? The only thing I see in you is a pretty pair of thighs to ride between.''

He looked her over with an ambiguous expression. "You know, maybe you're right, Carole. I knew a woman a few weeks ago who had a lot to offer—humor, spirit, ambition. She never would have submitted to someone else controlling her life, to someone else making the biggest choice of her life. She might not have fixed her hair as carefully as you, or worn the same sophisticated makeup. But you know . . . I liked her the way she was. Fresh, natural . . .''

"I told you yesterday,'' Carole stated in a low voice. "That woman is gone.''

"That's a shame,'' he replied bitterly. "Because I fell in love with that woman. I just never had the chance to tell her.''

R.J.'s eyes held hers, read in the empty, blue-green depths that his declaration made no difference. A defeated, heavy feeling mushroomed within his chest, and he whirled away, running once more into the cover of the storm.

Carole stared after him. "R.J.!'' she called miserably. Suddenly she realized that he was not like the others. Not at all!

This time he didn't look back as he trotted dog-gedly in the direction of the parking lot.

She had thought her heart dead. She'd convinced herself she was immune to further pain. But now, as Carole buried her face in her hands, she felt her heart shatter.

James watched until he was sure R.J. wasn't going to return. Then he hurried to Carole's side.

"What's the matter with you, daughter?" he demanded.

Carole looked up at the dark features of her father through tearful eyes. He took note of the damp spots along the front of her dress—the disheveled hair and running mascara.

"You're a mess," he scolded in low tones. "Now get inside, and get yourself fixed up. Curt has been looking for you everywhere!"

Numb and uncaring, Carole allowed him to steer her to the ladies' lounge. He pushed her inside, mumbling, "I'll wait out here. See that you don't take any longer than ten minutes."

James leaned against the wall outside the lounge, recalling the heated little encounter he'd just witnessed. That R.J. was a wild card. At first James had thought it amusing—he'd never imagined that *both* the Morrisson brothers would be hot for his little girl. But now, R.J. had gone too far. Now, he'd become a threat. Curt Morrisson had put a ring on Carole's finger, and James was not about to let anyone jeopardize the upcoming marriage—not even the brother of the groom.

Curt was a known quantity, James knew. Curt was dependable. But R.J. was a maverick.

Carole emerged from the lounge a short while later, looking much repaired. Wordlessly, James steered her back to the ballroom, looking at her only once to assure himself that the familiar smile came to her face as she broached the crowds.

James took her directly to Curt and couldn't pass up the opportunity to plant a seed of warning.

"You'd better watch out for that brother of yours," he whispered to Curt as he delivered his daughter's hand into the younger man's possession. James raised an accenting, dark brow as his protégée met his eyes with a startled look that turned quickly to one of fierce hostility.

By the time the postmatch party broke up at The Island House, the storm had receded, dissolving into a steamy drizzle that enveloped the whole of Charleston in a mist that seemed decidedly tropical. Curt sped through the misty night, saying little to Carole as they left the Isle of Palms behind and returned to the city. But when they reached her apartment, he insisted on coming inside.

Carole felt that she had no choice but to acquiesce.

"All right," he said firmly as soon as they'd walked into the living room. "Let's have it. What's going on between you and R.J. ?"

Carole glanced at him with lifeless eyes. "Nothing, Curt. Absolutely nothing."

"Bullshit!" he returned. "Ever since last night, I've been thinking about it. And slowly, it came to me. R.J. has *always* acted strangely around you, ever since the first time he met you at my parents' house. And I know for a fact that he's been here to see you behind my back at least twice, and neither of you has bothered to mention it!"

Her look turned suddenly sharp and alert. "How do you know that?"

A flush of red leaped to Curt's face. "Never mind."

"No! I'd like to hear about this. How would you know R.J. came here, Curt?" she demanded. "Have you been following me?"

"No!" he thundered. "It wasn't me!"

"Well, who was it, then? I knew someone was watching . . ." Carole's eyes strained to read his, and suddenly it dawned on her. "A man in a snap-brim hat?" she asked slowly.

The wind seemed to leave Curt's body. The cat was out of the bag, now, he realized. Worse than that, it was James Gossett's cat. He could only stare at Carole, wondering what to say, as a knowing look of accusation climbed to her beautiful face.

"You *hired* someone to follow me?" she asked disbelievingly. "Curt . . . that man nearly frightened the life out of me! And you're telling me you *hired* him?!"

Curt's shoulders slumped. "I didn't hire anyone, Carole," he said in a low voice. "You know better than that. I would never deceive you in such a way."

Carole blinked. "Then who . . ."

And suddenly, she knew. "My father," she muttered, beginning to nod in slow understanding. "Ah yes, the old story. Just looking out for my own good. Never mind that his deceitful measures might invade *my* privacy . . . *or* scare the wits out of me. Yes, that's my father's style, all right. But I must admit I'm surprised at you, Curt. To have been in on his plan and accepted it! I didn't realize you and my father had quite so much in common!"

Her scathing look reminded Curt of the Carole who had become the fiery woman he'd had no idea of how to reach several weeks before, of the Carole James had assured him was gone forever.

"I wasn't in on it all along, Carole. He simply told me about it one day at the office."

"And did it never occur to you to enlighten me?" she challenged.

Curt sighed. "Your father took me into his confidence. After all, he *is* my boss."

"And *I'm* only your fiancée!" she returned sarcastically.

Curt reached out to her and managed to capture her hands before she could jerk away. His pale blue eyes pleaded with hers. "Carole, please . . . let's not fight. We've had three beautiful weeks together, the happiest weeks of my life."

He moved closer, locking her gaze with his own. "You know I would never hurt or deceive you . . . I love you," he whispered in conclusion, bending down to her.

Carole submitted to his kiss rather than try to force the reciprocal three words from her mouth. Curt moved gently against her at first, but then quite suddenly his arms went round her, one hand sliding to secure her buttocks as the other grasped her bare shoulder. His mouth slanted passionately across hers as his tongue plunged within.

On and on he went. This was the kind of romance which *should* leave her head reeling, Carole found herself thinking. Obviously, Curt's was. Yet here she was, almost completely detached. And then it struck her: Though Curt and her father, and even the fates might demand that she be mated to this man, even *they* could not dictate a response that simply wasn't there.

Carole's breath came in quick gasps as his mouth continued to move bruisingly over hers. He held her so closely, imprisoning her arms beneath his, that she couldn't have moved if she tried.

One of Curt's hands moved to her breasts and began to fondle them intimately. Moving lower, his hand began to fill itself with bunches of skirt, and then reached boldly beneath and inside her panties. As the shock of his warm hand connected with her bare behind, Carole tore her mouth from his.

"Stop it!" she demanded, her lips still trembling and glistening from his kiss.

Curt's grasp relaxed somewhat, but he continued to hold her. "Stop it?" he repeated with burning eyes. "Is that all you can say to me? Damn it, Car-

253

ole! Haven't I played the fool for you long enough? I've taken you everywhere . . . put a ring on your finger, and still . . . night after night you turn me away. I don't know of any self-respecting man who'd be put off so long!''

Curt's eyes darted feverishly between her chest and her face. When his voice came, it was low and husky and tormented. "I've had enough of stopping, Carole,'' he told her, his arms pulling her hips tight against his hardness. "I intend to have what's mine . . . now!''

He was squeezing her so tightly she thought her ribs would crack. And then his mouth came toward her once more. Quickly, summoning a hidden strength, Carole broke free, stumbling back a few steps. Her breasts rose and fell with heaving breaths. A loosened strand of hair fell across her face.

"I think you'd better go now,'' she managed to say, her chest still pounding.

Curt stood only a yard away, his face red and passionate, his fists clenched at his sides.

"You think I'd better go?'' he mimicked.

Briefly he considered another attack. But somehow, as he looked at her—standing there with her back up like an enraged feline—the notion died. This wasn't right. Women came to him willingly . . . wantonly. Carole would, too.

"Fine,'' he said ultimately. "I'll go. But let me tell you something, Carole. I intend to be a most loving husband—both outside *and inside* the bedroom. Once you become my wife, these coy theatrics of yours are going to end. I intend to have the warm, seductive woman I used to know, and there will be no telling me to stop or go!''

The tone and words struck Carole with a slap of recognition. They were so like the domineering ones her father always used. And they prompted the same automatic response. A feeling of limp acceptance coursed through her.

"Do I make myself clear?" Curt pressed, his pale eyes bright.

She could only stare at him then. All the strength of anger had fled. Now that she knew he was leaving, she had no intention of prolonging a battle that might provoke him to stay any longer. Silently, she nodded.

Curt stormed out without a backward glance. Locking the door behind him, Carole sagged against the strength of the barrier as her eyes slid closed. So this was what it's going to be like, she thought. I'm going to end up married to my father.

Down below, Curt leaped into the BMW and raced away. The smooth perfection of the past few weeks with Carole was spoiled. In angry frustration, he made the familiar turns to Tradd Street. But then, on a sudden urge sped past the Morrisson mansion and proceeded to Meeting Street.

He reminded himself that he was engaged, that what he was about to do was underhanded. But the thought was fleeting. After all, this sort of thing had been going on among Charleston gentlemen for generations. The lady of the house or heart had nothing to do with the willing woman from the wrong side of town.

Curt drove north on Meeting Street. The chauvanism of his thoughts escaped him altogether, for he was thinking only of the frustrated throbbing between his legs, and that Laura Murphy would make short work of it.

R.J. peered out the window of his suite at the Mills House hotel, his thoughts cloudy as the Charleston night. It was late, but he had the sudden impulse to call Cecile Laroche. Crossing to the phone, he found the number in the book and dialed it. The voice that finally answered was sleepy, but it became quickly alert when R.J. stated that he was moving back to

Charleston and intended to pursue the Stuckey case full time.

"You think there is a case, then?" Cecile asked.

"It looks that way. Apparently, Geraldine Stuckey sold the land to a company that seems a little shady."

"Geraldine Stuckey!" Cecile huffed. "That woman isn't any more kin to Jonah than I am!"

"I got the same impression."

"R.J. . . . I can't tell you what a fine thing I think it is you're doing. I'm gonna be driving up to that hospital next week, and I can't wait to tell Jonah you're gonna help him get out of that place and back to where he belongs!"

"Now, wait a minute," R.J. cautioned. "Let's not get ahead of ourselves. We don't know enough yet to be making hasty promises. I just wanted you to know that I'm in town. Let me give you the phone number here at the Mills House."

"The Mills House? How come you're not staying with your folks?"

R.J. hesitated. "Curt and I have had a difference of opinion. . . . I'd rather not go into it if you don't mind, Cecile. It's just better that I'm here for the time being. Anyway, it will only be until I can find an apartment." Giving her the number, he hung up the phone and wandered aimlessly to the center of the living room. Looking around at the expensive furnishings—taking in the legal papers that littered the antique writing table—he felt unbearably hemmed in. With a muttered oath, he grabbed a light jacket and stalked out, letting the heavy door slam behind him.

He nodded in acknowledgment to the bell captain as he passed through the hotel lobby, proceeding out the door and down the steps to the sidewalk. The night air was heavy with the humid aftermath of the storm. The lights of the streetlamps were like hazy, golden pools glowing in the mist along Meeting Street. With no particular destination in mind, R.J. turned up his collar against the dampness, and began to wander aimlessly toward Broad Street, where he turned in the direction of the distant Ashley River.

From somewhere out in the harbor, a foghorn sounded, calling long and low like a lonely voice. No one was about, and in the dense, muggy fog it was easy for R.J. to imagine that, but for him, the whole of the District had been deserted. It was an appropriate setting for his mood. He'd never felt so alone in his life.

The creeping feeling of alienation intensified as he strolled along the palmetto-lined streets overlooked by silent courtyard walls and deserted wrought-iron balconies. Nowhere else could he feel as at home as in Charleston. Yet Charleston seemed different now. The breach with Curt had somehow set him apart from all he knew and loved.

R.J. shook his head thoughtfully. Turning, he unconsciously allowed his feet to follow a path to the intersection of Rutledge and Broad. With little surprise, he looked up to find that he had stopped in front of Carole's townhouse. His eyes climbed the stairs to the top level, darted about the dark windows. And a sense of loss swept over him—not just for the woman he'd never have, but for the one Carole had lost, as well.

All the way back from the Isle of Palms he'd been thinking of her, through his shower and supper and most of the night. He recalled the empty eyes, the mournful sound of the voice that had called to him through the rain. And eventually, R.J. thought, he'd grasped the situation.

Carole truly couldn't help herself. The rejection from New York had devastated her. Even if there could have been something between them once, there never would be now. For that to happen, Carole would have to stand up not only to Curt, but

257

also to her father. And R.J. could see she hadn't the strength to do that—not anymore.

She'd been right when she'd told him the woman he'd fallen in love with was gone. There was nothing he could do to bring her back. Carole would marry Curt and become a member of the family. And perhaps R.J. would be the one Morrisson in all the years to come who would miss the fiery, free-spirited blonde who had once pursued a dream . . . one that turned into a nightmare that sucked the very life out of her.

R.J. hung his head and walked slowly away from the townhouse.

On the other side of town, Curt lay beside a quietly sleeping Laura Murphy and peered into the darkness as the realization hit him. He hadn't learned a damn thing about what was going on between Carole and his brother.

PART III

Chapter Eleven

A S THE CLASS ended, Kathleen watched Gay
Templeton and the other dancers exit the studio.
She wanted to stay behind to polish the last se-
quence of the routine, a series of pirouette turns that
stretched clear across the room.

Setting her eye on a spot in the far corner, she
raised her arms, pointed her toe, and began the
spins. Pointe, pirouette, snap the head round to
spot. Pointe, pirouette, snap the head round to spot.
On and on she went, until she arrived at the corner,
went up on toe in a pique, then sank to the floor
with head bowed.

A series of appreciative, staccato claps came from
near the door. With a start, Kathleen turned and
searched the doorway—finding him leaning against
the wall, smiling broadly.

"André! What are you doing here?" she asked,
happily coming to her feet. "I thought you weren't
coming to town for another two weeks!" she added.
Her toe shoes thudded on the floor like webbed feet
as she flew across the deserted studio.

He chuckled, gathered her in his arms in a long
hug. "There's no law that says the only time I can

visit Charleston is when I dance, is there?" He leaned back to look her in the face, took in the sparkling, dark eyes and rosy cheeks. "I missed you," he murmured, lowering his head for a kiss.

Kathleen stepped back abruptly. "Not here, André. Another class is going to be arriving in fifteen minutes."

He let her go, a solemn look climbing to his face. "So? You know, Kathleen, there's something I want to tell you. That's why I came. I'm tired of all this sneaking around. I'm tired of missing you all the time I'm in Atlanta and you're here. This thing has turned into a lot more than just an affair for me."

Her heart began to pound. "What are you saying, André?"

He glanced away before meeting her eyes again. "I think you know what I'm saying. . . . I've fallen in love with you."

Kathleen stared up at him. This beautiful, talented man made her blood sing. "Are you sure?"

"I've never been more sure of anything." He smiled, then touched her cheek softly. "But how do you feel?"

Her gaze fell to the floor. "I . . . I don't know," she stammered.

A few young dance pupils came strolling into the studio, causing Kathleen's head to snap up. "All I know is that we shouldn't be discussing this here," she whispered.

"I have my car outside. Why don't we take a drive to the coast? Perhaps I could press my case a little more persuasively in private," he concluded, a twinkle lighting his brown eyes.

A slow smile came to Kathleen's lips. *You certainly could.*

Joey Horton sat in his nondescript black sedan and surveyed the entrance of the posh dance studio just across the way. The hot August afternoon air was stifling inside the cab of the car, and Joey shifted once again in his seat. He was bored. The Gossett bitch hadn't done anything of interest in the entire two weeks he'd been watching her.

But then, as if his derisive thoughts had triggered the woman into action, he saw her emerge from the studio with an attractive, muscular young man who looked to be about her own age. Joey perked up, then started his engine as she climbed into her red Mercedes convertible with the guy.

Discreetly, professionally, he tailed them all the way to the coast, where they pulled into an old, out-of-the-way resort Joey immediately recognized. He pulled around to the side of the main building as Kathleen's companion went into the lobby. Quickly, Joey flipped open his notebook and wrote, *"Saturday, August 15, 2:30 P.M. The Breakers.* Then he found a parking place behind a camouflaging group of palms, from whence he could view the entrances to the long stretch of hotel rooms.

This is going to be good, he thought with a smirk. Retrieving the camera with the telephoto lens from the seat beside him, he lined up and began to focus.

Minutes later, the Gossett woman and her escort strolled into view—holding hands. Click, click. She turned toward the camera and smiled up at the guy. Click. He extended his arm to encircle her hips in an intimate fashion. Click. They paused at the entrance to a room on the first floor. Click. They disappeared inside, and Joey watched the drapes close across the front window.

He waited a suitable ten or fifteen minutes before climbing out of the sedan. Then, nonchalantly, with only a cursory look across the deserted grounds, Joey made his way to the back of the building and counted the appropriate number of patios until he came to the one he sought.

The drapes had been pulled across the sliding

263

doors, also, but someone had been hasty, and there was a slight parting where the two panels should have met. Again, Joey smirked to himself as he climbed smoothly over the wrought iron-border of the patio and noiselessly approached the glass.

He peered through the breach in the drapes. The lighting was poor, the line of vision limited. Still, it was obvious that the man and woman inside were engaged in the oldest, most intimate act in the world.

Raising his camera, Joey adjusted the aperture, focused and fired a quick succession of a dozen shots, several of which caught a good, recognizable angle of Kathleen Gossett's face.

Kathleen drove slowly along Tradd. She was late, but she wasn't yet ready to give up her privacy. Confusing thoughts tumbled through her mind. André was wonderful. André was in love with her. She couldn't honestly say whether she returned the feeling. However, she knew it was entirely possible that she might, if only she had the freedom to spend more time with him.

But that would mean . . . God forbid, could she even think it? That would mean leaving James, leaving all the wealth and power and position that had drawn her into the marriage in the first place. Granted, her husband no longer made her happy. In fact, he had made her outright miserable for the better part of two years. But he offered the opulent life-style for which Kathleen had hungered all of her middle-class life. After having lived as Cinderella, could she really give it all up to run off with a penniless Prince Charming?

It was nearly six o'clock when she pulled up the drive and into the garage. She had hoped that James would be out, but his Seville was there, and she knew she was in for an interrogation. With a heavy sigh, she climbed out of the car, left the garage door up, and stole quietly into the house. If she could manage to sneak up to their chambers unnoticed, perhaps she could dodge the confrontation for a while, anyway.

Her soft-soled exercise shoes made no noise as she glided through the kitchen and the dining room to the foyer. She was nearly to the base of the staircase when James's voice exploded from the direction of his study.

"Why the hell didn't you call me sooner?" he yelled. "What? . . . *Pictures?*"

Kathleen heard the word clearly; a chill of paranoia raced up her spine.

"All right," her husband went on. "Yeah. Just get them over here as soon as they're developed."

Kathleen heard the phone slam down hard, and took off like a silent shot up the stairs.

She had bathed at the hotel and now began to dress for supper in hurried, frantic movements, half-expecting James to storm into the bedroom at any moment. But he remained conspicuously absent, and gradually the fact began to grate on her nerves. Her apprehension mounted when her husband met her at the supper table with a smile—and absolutely no questions about where she'd been all afternoon.

That night, James never came to join her in bed, and Kathleen slept fitfully. The next morning, she was up earlier than usual. James seemed startled to see her entering the dining room at a little past seven on a Sunday morning.

"What in the world are you doing up?" He scowled over the top of his newspaper.

Kathleen looked back at him, unperturbed. "Couldn't sleep. Is the coffee ready?"

He nodded in the direction of the silver service, and she helped herself to a cup, then selected the

Entertainment section from the part of the paper he'd set aside. Less than ten minutes later, there was a quiet knock on the front door. James bolted out of his seat as Kathleen looked on curiously. Then her blood turned cold as she saw Joey Horton come into the adjacent foyer, a manila folder in his hands.

"Kathleen, I believe you've met Mr. Horton?" James asked smoothly.

She nodded, forced an inane acknowledgment from her throat as the detective attempted a smile that came off as a leer. They retired to James's study. Kathleen was still sitting steadfastly at the dining table when the man left a quarter of an hour later. This time he carried no manila folder.

Her thoughts raced. She had heard James give Joey Horton the assignment of watching Carole only weeks ago. But now—somehow—Kathleen was certain the slimy man had been on her own trail. As for the "pictures" she had heard James mention . . . the memory of her afternoon with André blazed through her mind. Kathleen leapt out of her chair.

Using the feeble excuse of asking what he would like for supper, she sauntered into the private domain of her husband's study. He looked up in surprise as she entered, then hurriedly slammed the center drawer of his desk.

"What did you say?" he fired, rising from the tufted leather chair.

"I asked you what you'd like to have for supper tonight."

His expression was dark and thunderous—much more like the old James than the smiling countenance he'd been wearing since last night.

"I don't care what *you* have," he snapped. "I doubt I'll be here."

Rising from his chair, he swept by her, heading in the direction of the kitchen. A moment later, Kathleen heard the garage door go up and a car engine turn over. Quickly, she stepped over to the one window in the study, watching covertly as the black Seville raced down the drive.

Her dark eyes turned back to the room, settled on the massive desk. Seconds later she was pulling open the center drawer. With disappointment, she saw that it was empty. And when her fingers tried the side drawers, she found them locked.

"Damn it!" she whispered to herself, and once more drew open the center drawer. And that was when she found the key, tucked in a hidden slot. A look of satisfaction lighting her face, Kathleen withdrew it and quickly went about unlocking the side drawer of her husband's desk.

There, on top of several other files, was the manila folder Joey Horton had delivered. With trembling fingers, she opened it, withdrew the pictures, then gasped as she saw herself and André in a dozen compromising shots taken the day before.

Kathleen's eyes slid closed as the black-and-white halftones slipped from her hands. She leaned forward, grasped the desk for support as the breadth of James's sly machinations crushed her, once again, like a steamroller. She could only guess at what he planned to do now. Divorce her? Or possibly, use the pictures to intimidate and control her? Yes, that was more his style.

Eventually, she began collecting the photographs where they had fallen on the floor and desktop. As she reached for one that lay in the side drawer, her dark eyes fell on a folder beneath the photographs marked Haut Nouveau. The name rang a bell, though she couldn't quite put her finger on it. With the license of someone who has nothing left to lose, Kathleen withdrew the folder and opened it curiously.

There didn't seem to be anything much in it. An annual report. A bunch of papers that apparently testified to the fact that Gossett Enterprises had purchased controlling interest in the firm. And then, at the bottom, a few papers on letterhead. One was a copy of a termination notice for someone named Jack Levy. The next, a letter to the stockholders from Curt Morrisson, describing Haut Nouveau as an up-and-coming fashion-design house he was proud to announce as Gossett Enterprises' newest investment.

Again, a bell rang in Kathleen's mind. *Design house,* she was thinking as she glanced to the third sheet of paper—a sickeningly respectful note to James from the company's president:

I've enclosed copies of the correspondence you requested, and I trust the measures we've taken will meet with your approval . . . Kathleen didn't bother to finish reading it. She thumbed to the last paper in the file—a copy of a letter to . . .

Quickly, Kathleen snatched the document into the light, her eyes racing over its contents. They certainly hadn't spared Carole's feelings. The rejection was harsh—the rejection of the very design work on which Carole had pinned such hopes!

It all fell together. James had purchased control of the company and masterminded the rejection of his daughter's efforts. All so that Carole would be easily led into marrying Curt Morrisson.

Kathleen looked across the room, her eyes wide with unbelieving sympathy. Her thoughts raced back to that night nearly a month ago, when Carole had been so distraught that James had brought her to the house to spend the night. For a moment, Kathleen gave in to a deep and heartfelt pity for her estranged stepdaughter.

But then her gaze fell to the desktop, caught sight of a picture of herself and André entwined in the throes of lovemaking. A sneer contorted her features.

"Bastard!" she hissed.

268

* * *

R.J. climbed into his Corvette with disgust. He'd wasted a week finding the old building on Mimosa Lane and confirming that there was, indeed, a door on the second floor marked Ashley Land Grant Corporation. For a couple of days, he'd observed it from a distance; then he'd ventured up the fire escape at the back of the building. The blinds of the one window were partially open disclosing a deserted room with nothing inside but a desk and phone.

Now, he'd wasted a second week making sure no one would, in fact, show up at the dummy company. Certainly, none of the corporate officers were about to! A quick check with the coroner's office had produced death certificates listing no next of kin for either John Carrolton, Cornelius Blakely or James Hargrove. The three men were, quite literally, dead ends.

Someone had gone to quite a bit of trouble, R.J. reflected thoughtfully—a bogus company, a phony relative—all to get hold of Jonah Stuckey's land. R.J. was determined to find out who that someone was. He now felt sure that keeping watch on this building would get him nowhere. The only other possible avenue was to stake out the post-office box mailing address that Vicki Monroe had managed to uncover.

He started the engine and roared away from Mimosa Lane. He was already a good half hour late for an appointment with a realtor who had called that morning. But the gray-haired woman who met him, a Mrs. Thorndyke, shooed his apologies pleasantly away.

"It might not be *everything* you had in mind," she drawled as they drove along Broad Street. "But it *is* in the District, and it *is* a lovely apartment. The tenants have decided to remain abroad indefinitely, and would like to sublet."

269

She pulled to a stop near the corner of Broad and Rutledge. "This is it," she said. "As I told you, it's quite a lovely townhouse."

R.J. looked up with disbelief at the familiar building surrounded by the bricked-in courtyard. A sly smile came to his face. "Which apartment is available?"

"The upstairs on the left. See the brick steps leading up this side of the building? They go to a second-floor landing and apartment entrance. As you can probably tell by the Georgian architecture and the gardens, this townhouse was originally a private residence. Now, it's been split into four apartments. There's only one other unit on the upstairs level. A single girl lives there . . . a mighty pretty one, too," the older woman added with a teasing smile.

"I'll take it," R.J. stated, his eyes searching the upper floor for any sign of movement.

"There *is* one catch," Mrs. Thorndyke admitted. "You asked for an unfurnished apartment. This one is fully furnished. The tenants don't want anything moved."

The stuff from Columbia was already in storage, R.J. thought. It could stay there. "That's all right," he reaffirmed. "I'll take it."

"Don't you even want to tour the inside?" the woman asked curiously.

"That isn't necessary." R.J.'s eyes finally left the attractive building and turned to Mrs. Thorndyke. "How soon can I move in?"

"How soon do you want to sign the lease?"

He grinned, feeling more lighthearted than he had since his return to Charleston. "How about today?"

It was evening by the time R.J. packed his things, checked out of the hotel, and returned to the townhouse. Parking the Corvette in the appropriate spot in the garage, he began pulling suitcases out of the back and the trunk. Then, having gathered an armful, he made his way to the side of the building and climbed to the second level.

Like Carole's, the apartment entrance was recessed under a small private porch, but the two sets of quarters shared the upper landing. R.J. shifted his burden and searched his pocket for the key as his eyes peered round the corner and across the short common way that was somewhat like a widow's walk.

It was not yet dark enough for people to be turning on their lights, and as he eyed Carole's front window, he couldn't tell if she was home or not.

A smile came to his lips. There was time.

He let himself into the apartment and took a tour of the attractive rooms, noting the arched doorways and exquisite furnishings. No wonder the tenants want someone living here, he thought as he looked around. There must be a fortune in antiques here. The look of the place reminded him somewhat of his own family's house.

He'd made a very wise decision indeed, R.J. thought. He began to whistle absently as he trotted back down the stairs and out to the garage. On his third trip from the car, he noticed that the lamp in Carole's front room had been turned on. His pulse quickened.

And then, when he was bringing up the last bundle, he saw that the familiar white BMW had been parked out front. R.J. climbed the stairs to the landing warily, reaching the common walk just as Carole stepped out to join Curt. Wearing a pale blue sheath, and with her hair hanging in golden curls to her shoulders, she looked beautiful. She locked her door, then glanced casually across the way.

"R.J. ?" she questioned hesitantly, peering round Curt's shoulder.

Curt turned with a start, stared through the gathering darkness.

"Hello, Carole," R.J. rumbled.

"What are you doing here?" Curt demanded, taking a few steps in his direction.

R.J. matched the maneuver. "What does it look like?" he remarked with a shrug toward the pillowcase full of linens. "I'm moving in."

"The hell you say!" Curt exclaimed. "That apartment is already leased."

"*Sub*leased," R.J. corrected with a grin.

"You are *not* going to live here!" Curt thundered.

The grin drained from R.J.'s face, leaving behind a hard mask of determination. "I beg to differ with you . . . brother. It's a free country. I can live wherever I choose."

The stony look softened somewhat as R.J.'s eyes slid to Carole, who had moved up beside Curt. "Anyone can," he added.

Carole caught his innuendo. She recognized the subtle dare. And despite the fact that she stood only a hand's breadth from her fiancé, her heart was pounding erratically at the presence of his brother. She hadn't seen R.J. since that stormy night on the Isle of Palms two weeks earlier. Common sense reminded her that her feelings for him could amount to nothing. Yet now, just the sight of him made her throat go dry, while the rest of her body turned dewy. As always, he stirred in her a willful response.

"All right!" Curt spat. "Why don't you just come out with it? What does your moving here have to do with Carole?"

"Nothing. Unless she wants it to," R.J. returned brazenly.

Carole's brow shot up at their comments. "I'll thank you two not to talk around me as if I weren't here," she broke in.

"Sorry, ma'am," R.J. returned with a lazy smile.

Curt just glanced over his shoulder, impaling her with a steely look.

"Why don't you relax, brother?" R.J. went on with taunting calm. "Someone with half an eye might think you're not too confident about your hold on the lady, there."

Curt adopted the tone, though he drilled his brother with a hostile look. "Oh, I have every confidence in her," he assured R.J. "It's *you* I'm having a problem with!"

And with that, Curt took a firm hold on Carole's arm and turned away. "Come on," he snapped.

Carole had the opportunity only to throw a last questioning look at R.J. before she was hauled down the stairs to the BMW.

That night, she went through the excellent dinner at The Cotton Exchange with unusual, witty flair. And as the night wore on, Curt gradually began to respond to her gaiety. Carole drew him out, charmed him as she hadn't done in a long time, and Curt— lost pleasantly in the sparkling, blue-green eyes— had no idea that it was the influence of his brother that had brought about the change in her.

His spirits sagged momentarily when he took Carole home and looked up to see the glowing lights in the apartment that was now occupied by R.J. But he didn't lose heart completely. For although she denied his request to come inside, she kissed him at the doorway with such warmth that it left his head reeling. And as he drove away that night, Curt thought with a false sense of security that it didn't matter what his brother did—Carole was his.

He had no way of knowing that after his fiancé crawled into bed, she ended up staying awake most of the night. Her eyes kept popping open as she remembered, with a futile thrill, that R.J. was just on the other side of the wall.

273

* * *

R.J. stood before the ornate gilt mirror and adjusted his black tie. The look on his face was somber. He was not particularly pleased about where he was going tonight . . . had put off getting ready until he was already running an hour late.

Sure, he'd have the chance to see Carole—who had been altogether elusive the past two weeks—but only to celebrate her upcoming marriage to his brother.

Smoothing his hair a final time, R.J. stared at his reflection, toying with the idea of taking off for the waterfront clubs, of escaping amongst the rowdy Saturday-night crowds. Yet the recollection of his mother stopped him.

She had come to the apartment that very morning and pressed him to attend the engagement party. "Now, Randall," she had said, her dark eyes taking on an imploring look. "I've stayed out of your business. I've allowed you and your brother to carry on this mysterious feud of yours. But please, son, don't miss the party tonight. It means a great deal for me to have my entire family gathered about me on such an important occasion. Besides, dear . . . come what may, Curt is still your brother."

And so, shrugging dutifully into his white dinner jacket, R.J. left the sanctity of his rooms. Hell, he'd never been able to say no to Charlotte Morrisson and probably never would be.

The summer night was clear and warm, perfect for an outdoor gala aboard a yacht. R.J. drove toward Mariner's Cay, his car windows open to the sea air, and his thoughts drifting over the past couple of weeks. Except for the fact that he had settled comfortably into the townhouse at Broad and Rutledge, his time had been spent absolutely fruitlessly.

There had been no break whatsoever in the

Stuckey case. R.J. had tracked down the post-office box in an out-of-the-way station. He'd found a good vantage point and watched the damn thing for ten days straight. But no one came near it. He was no closer to making any sense of the matter than he had been when he'd first returned to Charleston.

As for Carole, he'd only seen her coming and going. One afternoon, he'd just returned from casing the post office when she pulled into the garage in her red Mercedes. His eyes had widened when she climbed out, clad only in a swimsuit with a towel wrapped around her hips. Waiting outside the garage for her, he'd fallen in step as she started toward the townhouse.

"Where do you go every day?" he asked with an appreciative look over her scantily clad body. "That doesn't exactly look like the sort of thing you'd wear to work at Carlotta's!."

Carole had replied somewhat hesitantly. She'd quit working at Carlotta's!, it seemed, and spent most of her days on the Isle of Palms. And then she skirted quickly into her apartment, using the excuse that she had to shower and get ready for a supper date.

Curt had taken her out every night during the past two weeks, leading R.J. to wonder if such regularity was their typical pace—or if his brother simply wanted to remove Carole from his reach.

Days at the club . . . supper dates . . . yacht-board parties. Sourly, R.J. considered the way Carole had become completely immersed in the society whirl she'd once scorned. His mouth settled into a caustic line as he drove across the Wappoo Creek Bridge to James Island and headed out on Folly Road.

James stood at the head of the receiving line and suavely greeted the latest group of Charleston blue bloods who sauntered aboard *The Instigator*. A great many of the names on the guest list had been supplied by Charlotte Morrisson, and James's spirits had soared as the evening had gotten under way. The arrivals included some of the foremost names in the city, people who prior to this linking with the Morrissons would never have given James Gossett the time of day.

He glanced to his right, where Kathleen stood beside him looking darkly beautiful in basic black. The sight of her adulterous face made his blood boil anew. But James quelled the feeling. This was not the night for a confrontation. His eyes turned beyond his wife to Charlotte and Robert Morrisson, and then to Curt and Carole. James smiled. His daughter was a ray of sunlight in her shimmering golden gown.

Once the initial rush of arrivals had passed, James took a sweeping look about, taking in the lush spectacle. He'd reserved the entire floating dock for tonight's festivities, and from the deck of his yacht the place had a tropical look of splendor. Fashionable guests milled among decorative palms and flowers, lighting now and then at one of the linen-covered tables to be served by the white-jacketed waiters who offered the finest liquors and a sumptuous spread of delicacies.

Torchlight lined the way to *The Instigator*, the largest yacht ever to be docked at Mariner's Cay. Below deck, the berths, captain's quarters, and formal dining room offered guests a place to relax and chat, while on the expansive foredeck, a dance floor had been set up. Just now, the nine-piece orchestra was breaking into a classic forties tune that swelled above the party chatter and drew several couples out onto the floor.

James scanned the aristocratic crowd. It seemed as though nearly every person on the list had arrived—officials and dignitaries, as well as the old, established families of Tradd, such as General Regis and his group and even the matriarchal Trippley sisters.

Torchlight illuminated the soft, summer night. Music floated on the air. And Charleston's crème de la crème was out in full force. James's chest swelled. The evening was on its way to becoming an even bigger success than he'd hoped. It would be a long time before Charleston's upper crust forgot *this* party!

The receiving line broke up, and as the orchestra began a slow, romantic tune, Carole found herself drawn out on the dance floor by Curt. He looked quite handsome tonight, and Carole smiled into his light blue eyes before he drew her closer, putting both arms possessively around her.

As they swayed to the music, Carole looked over his shoulder and scanned the crowd. Her gaze fell on April, who looked cool and lovely in a stark white gown that accented her classic beauty. She had shown up with Charlie Regis, an architect she'd just started dating. Their families were neighbors on Tradd Street, yet Carole barely knew the Regises. But their entire clan was in attendance tonight—even the legendary "General," who'd provided military expertise to more than one U.S. president.

Curt turned her slowly in the center of the dance floor. Carole's gaze shifted to the Morrisson sisters, who were standing with their backs to each other near their parents. Carole didn't much care for Margaret, who seemed to be continually looking down her nose. Camille was more approachable, and Carole smiled as she watched Jeffrey Gottfried, who was obviously besotted, approach the redhead once again.

Just before the melody came to an end, Carole's eyes met the sharp, gray ones of Constance Trippley. When Carole raised a hand in acknowledgment, she received a wide, well-wishing smile in return before she looked to Miss Aurora. Sitting next to Constance, the blue-haired spinster was eyeing her with disapproval. Carole could only guess, with a sense of amusement, that Curt was holding her far too close for the old lady's prim and proper taste.

She and Curt parted as the music ended, clapped politely, then left the dance floor and began to circulate among the guests. It seemed to Carole that everyone who had been invited had shown up to wish her and Curt well. Everyone but R.J.

The evening waxed on. Liquor and music flowed. The crowd grew noisier. Carole found herself passed from one group to another, answering the same questions over and over. When Curt stepped away to discuss something with his father, she took the opportunity to leave the party behind for a moment and escape to the quieter darkness of the side deck.

Standing at the railing, she looked toward the shore. A full moon hung above the silhouettes of shoreline villas and palms, shedding a silver path across the dark water to the yacht. A warm breeze stirred her hair, and Carole drew her first peaceful breath of the night.

"Good evening, Carole."

The deep, male voice came from just over her shoulder, causing Carole to whirl with a start. Her heart thundered to a gallop as she spotted R.J. But just as quickly, Carole recovered her wits.

"Still sneaking about in the dark, I see," she commented wryly.

He smiled, mosied closer. Carole couldn't help noticing how wonderful he looked in the formal jacket and tie.

R.J. took another step. She looked all gold and silver, standing there in the moonlight. "I was wondering if I'd get the chance to tell you how beautiful you are tonight."

278

Flustered, as she always was when he caught her unaware, Carole ignored the compliment. "When did you get here?" she asked casually.

"About an hour ago."

Her eyes jumped to his face. "An hour? I've been all over this yacht, and I haven't seen you anywhere."

R.J. regarded her curiously, a faint smile curving his lips. "I've been on the sidelines, while *you've* been the center of attention. But you almost sound as if you've been scouring the crowd . . . like you missed me," he suggested in his old cocky way.

"I didn't say that," Carole replied. She turned back to the shoreline. "I was simply beginning to think you weren't coming."

He had watched her from the crowd, waited impatiently for the opportunity to get her alone. Yet now that she was near, he only felt the bitter frustration well up anew.

"What?" he asked the back of her head in a rather cutting tone. "Miss my own brother's engagement party? Surely, you jest."

Carole turned, propped against the waist-high railing to look him in the face. "Come now, R.J. We both know things haven't been particularly amicable between you and your brother."

"True. But then family ties are strong . . . particularly among the fine old families of Charleston." His look turned uncontrollably harsh. "You'll learn that as Mrs. Curt Morrisson, if you don't know it already."

"Mrs. Curt Morrisson," she repeated in a dull voice. "I guess it's really going to happen."

"Of course it is," R.J. returned with mounting irritation. "It's what you want, isn't it?"

Carole glanced away. "We've already been over that."

"Yes, we've been over it," R.J. said in a low tone.

279

"Well then, why must you continually bring it up? You only make things harder, R.J."

"Harder for whom?"

She looked up with shining eyes. "For me!"

R.J. gazed down at the beautiful face. Suddenly an unselfish feeling of care overrode the bitter jealousy that had been eating away at him. He reached out to caress her cheek, locking his eyes with hers.

"If that's true," he said ultimately, "then I'm sorry. . . . I want to tell you something, Carole. I understand now, I really do. Ever since that night on the Isle of Palms, I think I've understood what happened . . . how hurt you must have been just to give up on everything. For a long time, I guess I thought I could say or do something to make it change. But I was wrong. You're the only one who could change things, and I've finally realized you can't."

She was staring up at him unblinkingly, seemingly surprised into silence by his insightful comments.

"I don't want to make things any harder for you," R.J. added softly. He hesitated, then forced himself to ignore the sick feeling rocking his insides. "So, if this is the way it's going to be . . . Welcome to the family."

His free hand moved to cup the other side of her face as he bent to press a brotherly kiss on her forehead. His lips lingered against her skin, his nostrils picking up the scent of gardenia. R.J.'s eyes slipped closed, his body going rigid as he managed to steel himself momentarily against the sensual onslaught.

But then, of their own accord, his lips began trailing between her brows, along the bridge of her nose to the very tip, where they hovered in midair just above her.

Their breaths mingled in hot anticipation. And

when R.J. gave in to the irresistible urge, Carole's mouth was open and waiting.

James had spotted his daughter's exit and had followed to a discreet spot in the shadows some way along the railing. Now, his entire body went tense as he saw Carole raise her face to receive R.J.'s kiss. He had already taken a purposeful step in their direction, unaware that his wife had crept up behind him.

Kathleen whipped out her hand, closing her fingers around his arm. "Leave them alone, James," she ordered.

James glanced back at the feminine hand clutching his jacket, then to Kathleen's sparkling dark eyes.

"What?" he laughed in disbelief. "Since when do you think you can give *me* orders . . . Mrs. Gossett?"

He tried to pull away, but she only held on all the tighter.

"Since I found out *you* were behind that Haut Nouveau deal! *You* were the one who sent Carole that rejection, just so you could marry her off to Curt Morrisson. And if you don't back off, I'll go over there right now and tell her all about it."

The melodic sounds of the orchestra swelled across the deck as James regarded his wife in silent astonishment. But it didn't take long for him to overcome his surprise, his black eyes abruptly narrowing.

"Blackmail? How very enterprising of you, Kathleen." He snatched his arm from her grip, began to jerk his cuffs back into place. "But you see, the success of blackmail rests on the premise that you have someone backed into a corner. The plot rather loses its effectiveness when the 'blackmail-ee' has something rather more sordid to hold over the head of the 'blackmail-er'!''

His eyes swept haughtily over his wife. ''If you'll excuse me.'' Shooting her a dismissing look, James took a few steps in the direction of his daughter.

Kathleen followed, caught up to him at the gate break in the railing. ''If you're referring to those pictures of André and me, you can forget it. They're not going to do you any good, James. I've already decided. After I get packed tomorrow, I'm leaving you!''

James whirled toward her, grabbing her by the arms as he took a quick, precautionary glance in the direction of the nearby crowd of guests.

''You listen to me, you little slut,'' he hissed. ''You're not going to do anything unless I tell you to. Understand? I bought you two years ago, and I'll get rid of you when I'm damned good and ready!''

Kathleen laughed in his face. ''How silly I was to be afraid of you. You're pathetic, James! You actually think you're God. . . . But I've got news for you. You're *not* God. You're just a man with too much money, who gets his kicks out of ruining women's lives. Well, you won't have mine to ruin any longer!''

With great effort, James managed to keep his voice low and innocuous.

''This is neither the time nor the place to discuss this, Kathleen.'' Again, he turned toward the secluded spot where R.J. and his daughter continued to embrace.

''Shall I announce it here and now?'' Kathleen challenged, lunging once again after his trailing sleeve. ''To all your fancy guests? James Gossett's wife is having an affair with a male dancer, and is about to run off with him? That ought to make for some interesting party chatter!''

Rage swept through James like a wildfire. Without thinking, he whirled, jerking one limb out of the women's grasp as he violently pushed her away with the other. There was a startled instant as Kathleen stumbled back, lost her balance, and then toppled over the gate and out of sight.

Curt had been looking everywhere for Carole. And now, as he returned from the aft of the yacht along the promenade, he suddenly saw her up ahead in the shadows. Her head was thrown back in abandon—and R.J. was kissing her passionately. Everything went red. Before he knew it, Curt was rushing up to them, whipping his brother away from Carole, and drawing back his right.

R.J. turned quickly, pushed Carole aside, then ducked as his brother's fist whirred by, without connecting.

"I told you weeks ago you deserved a shot, brother," R.J. threatened. "But if you push it, don't expect me to stand here and be your punching bag!"

Like an enraged bull, Curt charged, butting his head into R.J.'s midsection so that the two of them stumbled, then crashed to the deck.

Carole's hand flew to her mouth, her eyes wide as she watched the two scrambling men. But then, a woman's scream pierced the air, followed by a loud splash. Carole spun to the railing, saw the roiling water below, and then a dark head popping out of it.

"Curt! R.J.!" she screamed. "Someone's gone overboard!"

But the brothers seemed not to hear. They couldn't quell the violent eruption that had been brewing for months. Carole ran past them toward the gateway break in the railing, biting her knuckles in distress. And as she reached the break, she saw

283

her father's white dinner jacket disappear as he dived over the side.

She rushed to the border of the crowd of people drinking and dancing in merry oblivion. But when Carole screamed that someone had gone overboard, a wave of guests rushed to the ship railing. Peering down, they watched wide-eyed as two people splashed in the dark water below. The music stumbled discordantly into silence. Several men ran along the side deck to break up the fight between the Morrisson brothers, while someone else threw life preservers over the side for Kathleen and James.

The crowd at the railing swelled. Necks craned. Whispers flew.

"What happened?"

"I don't know!"

"I think Carole screamed!"

"Who is it?"

"James Gossett and his wife!"

Speculation flashed among the formally attired guests as a number of people ran down to the dock to retrieve the host and hostess.

Robert Morrisson made his way along the deck, accosting his two sons with a forceful, low-toned interrogation.

Carole backed away from the spectacle of Curt and R.J., who continued to glare at each other around their father as they adjusted their disheveled clothing. In mortification, she turned and hurried across the deck, waiting as her father and Kathleen—dripping wet in their evening finery—were helped aboard by a group of guests.

Carole was close enough to hear the explanatory accusation her father hurled at his wife. "That will teach you to drink!" he snapped harshly, his black eyes shining as water streamed down his face.

Kathleen, looking pitifully like a drowned rat,

only stared at the man in amazement. And for some reason, Carole found herself stepping forward.

"Come along, Kathleen," she said as the hushed crowd looked on. "Let's go below and get you changed."

Putting an arm around the taller woman's waist, Carole led her to the spacious berth she usually claimed as her own, then closed the door against the curious stares and whispers.

Kathleen looked round the comfortable berth in a seeming daze.

"Perhaps you'd like to take a quick shower," Carole suggested.

"Yes. . . . Yes, that would be nice," Kathleen mumbled. She disappeared into the bath.

A moment later, Carole heard the water, and shaking her head in disbelief, she began to look through the drawers of the dresser until she found a selection of clothes she'd left aboard. The shorts and T-shirt ought to fit Kathleen well enough. It was certain that she wouldn't be putting on the ruined Jean-Paul Gaultier gown again.

A few minutes after the shower had stopped running, a brief knock sounded at the door. April slipped in, quickly closing the door behind her.

"What the hell is going on?" she asked.

"I don't know," Carole replied. "Kathleen fell overboard, and Daddy went in after her. That's all I know, except that Daddy made some remark about her drinking."

"I wasn't drinking," Kathleen announced from the doorway to the bath. She strolled into the berth, wrapped in nothing but a towel, and eyed the Gossett sisters steadily. "And I didn't fall in. Your father pushed me."

"What!" Carole and April sang out in unison.

"Oh, I don't think he meant to. He simply lost his temper. Believe me, he wouldn't have done anything to mess up this little fête of his. It's all he's been talking about for weeks.''

''Well, I hate to be the bearer of bad news,'' April put in. ''But the party is royally messed up. A number of the guests are leaving, and the rest are milling around, having a field day with gossip.''

A look of satisfaction climbed to Kathleen's face. ''I guess that's *another* way I've managed to spoil his plans.''

''Are you all right, Kathleen?'' Carole asked. ''I mean, falling off a yacht is hardly an everyday occurrence.''

Kathleen smiled. Now that she was over the initial shock, she felt free and exhilarated.

''I'm fine. I'm more fine than I've been in years.'' Kathleen's eyes darted between the two sisters, a whimsical smile coming to her lips. ''You know, the whole time I've been married to your father, I never felt as though I knew what to say to either of you. It's ironic that it took my leaving to bring all three of us together.''

''You're leaving him?'' April asked in surprise.

''Yes. I told him so tonight. Your father didn't realize I'd found out he was having me followed, that he'd discovered I was having an affair. He also didn't realize that I was past caring what he would do *if*, in fact, he did find out. I don't think I realized it myself until tonight.''

Kathleen's chin came up, and she regarded the fair-haired women before her. ''You see, the two of you were right about me. I married your father for his money. It's true, I admit it. But I'll also tell you that he made me pay the price every day for two years!''

A look of understanding climbed to April's face. ''I can believe that!''

''So can I,'' Carole agreed.

''You don't know the half of it,'' Kathleen said.

She turned to Carole, looked earnestly at the gold-clad young woman. "Prepare yourself for an awakening, Carole. It was your father who ruined all your dreams. That design company up in New York, Haut Nouveau? James bought controlling interest, had that talent scout fired, and then had them send you a rejection letter."

Carole's ears began to ring. Keeping her eyes fixed on her stepmother's pretty, dark-eyed face, she breathed, "What?"

"He did it so he could marry you off to Curt Morrisson," Kathleen went on. "Who, by the way, knew exactly what James was doing all along."

"Well, I'll be damned!" April exclaimed, her wide eyes turning to her sister. "I knew your work was too good to be turned down. I knew it!"

Carole's brain was whirling in a state of shock. "You mean . . . it was all a farce? They didn't really turn me down?"

"I saw the papers in your father's desk, Carole. He masterminded the whole thing from start to finish."

"I can't believe it."

"Well, I can!" April exploded, her serene face a picture of outrage. "I told you when we went out to supper that night that he was up to something!"

"One thing I've come to know, girls," Kathleen said wearily. "Is that your father is *always* up to something. He's like a giant puppeteer, pulling the strings and watching with satisfaction while we jump. . . . All except you, April. I don't know that he ever got control of you, to his everlasting frustration."

Carole was barely listening, as the stifled spark of spirit within her flared once again into a beautiful, glowing flame.

"What are you going to do now?" April asked.

Kathleen had wandered over to the dresser to look

287

at the clothes that had been laid out for her. With no sense of modesty, and the glorious feeling that she was stripping clean for the first time in two years, Kathleen now discarded the towel and began to pull on the casual clothes.

"Eventually?" she said with a smile at April's reflection in the mirror. "I'm going to Atlanta to live with a wonderful man. And right now . . . As soon as I can get my hands on a car, I'm getting the hell out of here!"

"I'll go with you," Carole said suddenly, drawing the other women's eyes with her forceful tone. "*If* you don't mind waiting a few minutes while I settle a couple of scores."

Chapter Twelve

CAROLE'S THOUGHTS WERE burning, hot coals. Her scalded blue-green eyes were blind to the stares of the lingering guests who whispered curiously as she pushed her way along the hall below deck to the captain's quarters.

Politely, she knocked at the oak door, heard her father answer, and stepped inside to close the door behind her.

"Carole?" James looked up from the dressing table as he calmly combed his wet, dark hair into place. He was barefoot and bare chested, but had already donned the trousers of the spare tux he kept on board. "I'm glad you're here. We must get back to our guests before this whole thing turns into a fiasco."

"It's already a fiasco, Daddy," Carole said.

"Nonsense," James muttered. He had covered Kathleen's ignoble plunge with a seemingly heroic rescue. He could salvage the rest of the evening as well. "Pour a few more drinks. Get the music started up. Everyone will forget."

"I won't," Carole challenged in a hard voice.

James paused, turned to look his daughter in the face. She was curiously pale and wide-eyed. A wave

289

of suspicion washed over him. She had taken Kathleen away to her berth. What had the bitch said?

"What's the matter with you, Carole? You look as though you'd seen a ghost."

"Why did you do it, Daddy?" she gritted between her teeth. "Why?"

"Do what?"

"You know what. Why did you have my work rejected when you knew it meant the world to me?"

So, the dark-haired traitoress had spilled the beans. James stepped over to an overstuffed chair and retrieved the pleated white shirt resting on the chair arm.

"I was just trying to save you some embarrassment," he tossed, shrugging into the formal garment. "It was obvious you'd lost your head over that design thing . . . thinking you could make it in the big leagues. Really, Carole. And all the while, you were throwing away a chance for a perfect life here in Charleston . . . and the chance to marry a Morrisson!"

He turned to her with his most condescending glare. "Haven't you learned what that means yet, to be the wife of a Morrisson?"

Carole regarded him scathingly. A host of memories played through her mind—the enthusiastic, all-night efforts toward a career of her own, the heartbreak when she thought all hope was lost, and the way her father had been right there, ready to scoop her up and settle her once again, so easily, in the niche he had selected. Just as Kathleen had said . . . he was a cruel, manipulating puppeteer.

Carole stepped up to her father and met his black eyes with a look of ice. "We'll just see who can make it in the big leagues," she stated evenly.

"You know, Daddy, all these years, you've been larger than life to me, like some god I could never quite appease. But now I see you as you really are. You're just a cold, unfeeling man. There's only one thing in this world you care about, and that's being part of the high-and-mighty blue-blood society of this town! What's so wonderful about them, Daddy? What makes them so much more important than your own daughter?''

James's face turned to stone. ''Haven't I given you everything you ever wanted? Haven't I footed the bills for every silly notion you ever had?''

''Oh yes, you footed the bills . . . as long as I did exactly as you told me!'' Carole cried. The angry tears were welling up, though her gaze remained steady. ''But you *never* gave me what I really wanted. *Love,* Daddy! Your heart is so filled with your obsession for acceptance that there's no room for love. Not for any daughter . . . not for any wife . . .''

Tears spilled down her cheeks. ''Now I understand why Mother ran away. Because if she hadn't, you'd have destroyed her . . . just the way you've tried to destroy all of us.''

''You don't know what you're talking about,'' James accused, eyeing his daughter with a deadly look as he began to button the shirt.

''No, *you* don't know what *I'm* talking about! You don't have any grasp of the idea of love!'' She flashed a look of pure scorn over her dashing, powerful father.

''I pity you,'' she sneered finally.

Before he knew what he was doing, James lashed out an arm and slapped Carole smartly across the cheek. For an instant, he almost wished he could take it back. But then, his daughter turned back to face him with an expression of loathing defiance, and any feeling of regret was displaced by anger.

She was his daughter, damn it! Yet, as James returned her hard stare with one of his own, he had the feeling he was looking into the eyes of a stranger.

''Good-bye, Father.'' Carole turned on her heel.

''Where are you going?'' he demanded.

She opened the door, then paused, sending a mocking look over her shoulder. "To tell Curt Morrisson *exactly* where he can put his diamond!"

As she slammed the door behind her, Carole heard her father yell something, probably about making her regret what she was doing. But then she was moving along the hallway and climbing the stairs to the still-crowded deck of the yacht, her head held high.

She felt as though she'd grown a foot as she wound her way through the gaping crowd. Several people tried to flag her down to get news about the condition of James and Kathleen. But Carole passed them by like an unhearing machine, an engine chugging with gathering steam toward the Morrisson family, which had grouped near the boarding ramp.

R.J. stood apart from the rest, his back turned. But they were all there—all the members of the honorable Charleston family her father had schemed so cleverly to buy his way into. A number of elegant guests stood with them, among them the Gottfrieds and the Trippley sisters. Undaunted, Carole strolled directly up to Curt, fixed him with a cold look of accusation. Conversation dribbled to a halt—aboard the entire vessel, it seemed—as Curt stepped forward. All eyes settled on the engaged couple.

"Hello, doll," he said hesitantly.

He and R.J. had already received a hurried tongue-lashing from their father. Now, as he took in the frigid look on Carole's face, a new pang of fear lurched through Curt's body. He watched, frozen, as his fiancée twisted the ring off her finger, reached out to take his hand, then dropped the diamond in his palm.

Behind her son, Charlotte Morrisson gasped. Beside him, his sisters looked on with wide eyes while their father grimaced. R.J. began to push through the crowd to find out what exactly was going on.

"I knew you and my father had a lot in common," Carole said in a cutting tone. "I just never realized how much. A few weeks ago you vowed you'd *never* hurt me . . . *never* deceive me. And yet, you knew about Haut Nouveau all along. You knew, and you didn't say a word. I'll never forgive you for that, Curt."

His pale blue eyes were sparkling painfully. "Now, wait a minute . . . ," he began.

"No waiting," Carole broke in with a warning glare. "No talking. Nothing. It's over."

The crowd dissolved into noisy whispering as Curt stared wordlessly at the woman who was to have been his bride. And then Kathleen Gossett—clad in shorts and with her dark, wet hair streaming down her back—strolled up to Carole, breaking the tense moment with the casual announcement that they needed a getaway car.

"Here, my dears," Constance Trippley said hurriedly, and began searching through her evening bag. "If you can drive that old Rolls Royce down there, you're welcome to it."

"Constance!" Aurora exclaimed with horror. "What are you doing?"

"Oh, hush up, sister." Constance reprimanded, her smiling eyes darting from Kathleen to Carole. Handing over the keys, she grasped both their hands. "You know . . . I always had a feeling the two of you were destined to become friends. Now, get along with you . . . and good luck!"

As she and Kathleen turned from the friendly old lady, Carole found herself confronting the gawking crowd. Glancing over their heads and across deck, she spotted her father as he dashed into view at the head of the stairs.

Her chin came up another notch. "If you'll excuse us, everyone?" she said smoothly."I believe, as they say, the party is over."

And with that the two women strolled regally off the yacht. James stared helplessly after them with an expression of murderous rage that was lost on the backs of the heads of the society folk he had held in his palm only twenty minutes before.

Standing behind his newly jilted brother, R.J. couldn't prevent a feeling of relief from soaring within him. Across the deck, April gave Charlie Regis a proud smile. And as for the rest of the dignified guests, a wave of horrified chatter spread through them like wildfire.

James Gossett had been right. It would be a long time, indeed, before "anyone who was anyone" forgot the engagement party thrown aboard *The Instigator* at Mariner's Cay.

Carole and Kathleen puttered over to the Gossett mansion, where they flew through the master suite, packing a multitude of Kathleen's belongings and racing to load them in the ancient Rolls Royce. Then they went on to Carole's townhouse.

"If your father decides to track us down, he won't find it very difficult," Kathleen commented. "For all I know, he's still having me followed anyway."

Carole regarded her stepmother with bright eyes. "Let him come," she said boldly.

And so the two women put on comfortably shabby robes, brewed a pot of tea, and settled in the breakfast nook to compare notes. Carole learned all about André, the way she'd turned him away when he had approached Kathleen the year before, and how she'd become so intimidated by James's heavy-handed control that she'd sought refuge in the numbing depths of the bottle.

"There's just something he can do to you," Kathleen explained. "He can make you feel like you're nothing. And then, a couple of months ago, I saw André again. And this time . . . out of desperation, I guess . . . I became involved. Each time I saw him, I came back to life a little more . . ."

"I thought I saw a change in you a couple of months ago," Carole mused.

"Yes. . . . And there was one in you, too," Kathleen said, a sympathetic glow lighting her dark eyes. "As soon as that design thing went down the drain, you became putty in your father's hands . . . just as he expected. What do you plan to do now?"

Carole got up from her chair and skirted to the back bedroom to retrieve the package of drawings. She returned to the kitchen and held them up before Kathleen.

"I intend to sell these," she said fervently. "I intend to sell them if it's the last thing I do!"

As if in accent to her declaration, a thundering knock came at the door. The women's eyes snapped to each other for a pregnant moment. Then the knock came again, and Carole moved hesitantly into the living room, followed by Kathleen. Both of them eyed the door as if the devil himself were waiting on the other side.

"Who is it?" Carole called

"R.J."

Carole glanced at Kathleen, who heaved an obvious sigh of relief. But Carole, herself, was not so relieved. Her emotions and thoughts were whirling like a cyclone—as they had been ever since the man who now stood outside her door had kissed her on the deck of the yacht. She had realized then, once and for all, that when it came to R.J., she had absolutely no control over herself. That realization had been the beginning of the earthquake and its series of aftershocks—the fight between R.J. and Curt, Kathleen's being pushed overboard, the revelation of her father's and Curt's deceit, and the termination of the engagement.

"Could I come in for a minute?" the muffled voice inquired.

Moving to the door, Carole placed her hand upon the barrier. "Not now, R.J. I'm not dressed."

There was a brief instant of silence before his voice came through to her again. "That's all right. I don't mind."

She could picture the white, teasing smile that was probably curling the seductive lips. "It's been a long night, R.J."

"You're telling me? The party broke up not long after your grand exit. Curt has taken off to who knows where, and the rest of the family is up in arms. I just wanted to make sure you're all right."

Carole's eyes closed. "I'm fine."

"Okay . . . so you need a little time to yourself. I can understand that. We can talk tomorrow. But let me tell you something, Carole. . . . I'm so damned proud of you, I feel as if I could bust wide open."

She said nothing, and for a moment silence reverberated between them. "Just one more thing before I go, Carole . . . I love you."

Carole's eyes popped open, and she turned with wonder to Kathleen, who arched her brows and smiled knowingly.

Another half minute of silence ticked by.

"Good night," came the soft male voice from the other side of the door. And then she heard the sounds of receding footsteps.

Carole wandered away from the portal, her ears ringing with R.J.'s declaration, her heart thumping madly.

"He was the one you were kissing on the yacht deck tonight, wasn't he?" Kathleen asked.

Carole nodded mutely, her wits slowly gathering.

"It's obvious there's something between you two," Kathleen added. "Why didn't you let him in? I could have made myself scarce."

Slowly, Carole's vision cleared, focused on the woman before her—the last person in the world she would have envisioned as a confidante.

"I can't deal with him right now, Kathleen. Don't

you see? For so long, my life has centered on . . . no, has been *controlled* by . . . men. I'm through with being Daddy's little girl. I'm not going to be anybody's little girl! All I want to do now is concentrate on the fact that I have a second chance to make it on my own. If I can sell my designs, I can be my own woman for the first time in my life. I'm determined to make it happen. So, for the time being, I don't want anyone . . . not even R.J. . . . getting in my way."

Kathleen nodded slowly. "Very admirable. But of course you realize you're taking a chance on losing him."

"It's a chance I have to take. If it takes losing R.J. to find myself, then that's simply the price I have to pay."

Kathleen smiled. Her liking and admiration for this unknown stepdaughter was growing by the minute. "So, how are you going to proceed with this great plan of yours? How do you propose to sell your designs? And to whom? Someone here in Charleston?"

Carole shook her head. "No, not here. My father is too powerful here. He would interfere all over again."

"Where, then?" A look of dawning switched on in Kathleen's dark eyes. "I've got it!" she exclaimed. "That guy your father fired from Haut Nouveau! What was his name? Levy? Why don't you see if you can get in touch with him? He liked your style. If he's still in the business, maybe he can make a contact for you!"

Carole raised her brows at the suggestion. Reaching immediately for the phone she dialed long-distance information and secured Jack Levy's number. And at break of day the following morning, Carole made the call.

After a somewhat groggy greeting at six-thirty on a Sunday morn, the man's nasal voice perked up.

Yes, he remembered her. Yes, he was still in the rag trade, working on his own now as an independent representative. And yes, he'd be happy to take a look at her work.

Carole then called April. Asking her sister to thank Miss Constance for the loan of the Rolls, which was parked out in front of the townhouse, Carole then informed her sister that both she and Kathleen were leaving town.

"Are you okay?" April had demanded.

Carole's face was alight with optimism, though her eyes hadn't closed all night. "I've never been better!" she assured her sister. With the promise that she'd return to Charleston within a couple of weeks, Carole clicked off.

It was still bright and early when Carole and Kathleen took a cab to the airport. But once there, their newly joined paths split: After a long hug and quick wishes of good luck, Kathleen Gossett boarded a flight to Atlanta, while Carole Gossett flew north to New York.

On Monday morning, Curt showed up at the office with purple circles underscoring his pale eyes. He'd been up all of Saturday night after the party, as well as most of Sunday, consoling himself in the arms of Laura Murphy while at the same time removing himself from anyone who could remind him of the horrendous incidents that had taken place aboard *The Instigator*. Yet he couldn't erase the vision. Carole in the arms of R.J., Carole breaking off the engagement.

Now, as he sat behind his desk in the quiet privacy of his office, Curt buried his face in his hands, rubbing his eyes as the scene played through his mind. Once again, Carole was standing before him with a despising look, dropping the diamond in his hand. *I'll never forgive you, Curt*, her words echoed.

Then he saw once more the distraught face of his mother, the scolding expression of his father, and the eyes of fifty people—targeting him, questioning him, condemning him.

Curt's reverie was interrupted by the sound of the door opening. Looking up with bleary eyes, he beheld James Gossett, looking dapper as always, though his expression was tense and unsmiling.

"Good morning, Curt. Thought maybe you might decide to take the day off. Glad you didn't."

"What good would it do?" Curt mumbled. "Carole is gone. It's over and done with. I suppose I could rake myself over the coals, but I went along with you on that Haut Nouveau deal with my eyes wide open."

He paused for a moment, trying to gauge the look in James Gossett's opaque eyes, then hurried to mollify the faintly accusing comment. "Don't get me wrong. Even after what happened, I still think it was a good idea. After all, it brought her back to me for a while. The unfortunate part is that we both got caught."

"Caught? You make it sound as though we did something wrong. Remember, Curt, that whole business was for Carole's own good. We weren't 'caught,' we were betrayed!"

"By whom?"

"By that black-haired witch I used to call a wife!" James hissed.

Curt regarded his boss with mounting surprise. He'd seen him angry before but never quite like this. "Kathleen? How?"

"She went through my desk at home . . . found some papers."

Curt expelled a long breath as he considered the woman's foolhardiness at crossing a man like James Gossett. "Whew! So, where is she now?"

"Kathleen is gone," James muttered in a voice of steel. "My man tailed her to Carole's the night of

299

the party, then lost her. Hell, he lost them both! They've disappeared! I don't have to tell you that Joey Horton is no longer on *my* payroll!''

Curt nodded, a little in awe at the man's vengefulness. "Oh, well," he said ultimately. "I've accepted the fact that Carole is gone. Wherever she is, she won't be coming back to *me*. There's nothing I can do to change that. I simply have to get on with my life.''

"My sentiments exactly," James boomed with a determined look. "Let's get down to business, shall we? The New York boys called. They're just about ready to transfer the necessary funds to proceed with the land acquisition for the theme park. It's time we went ahead and sealed the deal.''

Curt's business mentality kicked into gear. "Now, you're talking. The survey has been done, and the papers are all lined up. The only thing we've been waiting for is the money.''

"Good." James nodded his approval. "As soon as the funds arrive, I'll have the order drawn up. It should only take a couple of weeks for everything to clear. Do you want to set up an appointment with the principals of Ashley Land Grant?''

"That won't be necessary," Curt answered with the first invigorating breath of confidence he'd drawn in two days. "They've agreed to all the terms and conditions. They simply want us to drop a check in the mail.''

James's dark brows raised in surprise. "Drop it in the mail? That's a bit casual, isn't it?''

Curt smiled reassuringly. "The principals are getting on in years. I'll admit they're a bit eccentric. But then, that's why we're getting the land at a relative steal.''

"I've got to hand it to you, Curt. *You* found the property. *And* you negotiated the sale. You must really be on the inside with these guys.''

"They're just old-fashioned, upper crust,

Charleston folks," Curt explained lightly. "Perfectly willing to pursue a life of leisure while they leave business matters to someone they trust."

Once again, James felt the sting of being on the outside of the special aristocratic world his young vice-president seemed to take entirely for granted. Fine! Let Curt handle the "old-fashioned, upper crust" with the comradely bond of breeding that stretched back over the centuries. But he'd be damned if he'd stand around in the office of an employee where—despite all his wealth, all his power— he felt the infuriatingly familiar ache of inferiority.

"Handle it, then," he ordered. And giving the young blue blood a glare from beneath hooded lids, James turned and stalked to the door. Once there, he paused, directed his gleaming, black eyes across the room. "As for the matter of Carole, it's not over and done with as you seem to think. Not for me! I tolerate no failure . . . no deception . . . no disloyalty. You'd do well to remember that, Curt . . . if not as a son-in-law, then as my right-hand man!"

With that, James swept out of sight. And for the first time since he concocted the rather daring scheme to use Gossett Enterprises for personal gain, Curt was swept with a wave of reservation.

R.J. was standing on his private second-story patio, looking into the sunset. A mild sea breeze rustled the palmettos that reached up to the balcony. The sky was streaked with brilliant color. It was a beautiful, clear evening.

Yet R.J.'s thoughts were murky. Why the hell had he come back to Charleston anyway? He hadn't accomplished a damn thing since he'd left the supreme court. Oh yes, he'd staked out Mimosa Lane . . . *and* the mailing address of Ashley Land Grant Corporation. But he was no closer now to figuring

301

out what was going on than he had been in Columbia.

It made no sense! The only way the Stuckey matter would hold any water as a case of fraud was if someone could be shown to be making a sizable profit on Jonah's land. So far, all R.J. had was a questionable cousin who had relinquished the property to a dummy company. It wasn't enough. Someone was behind the deal, someone was risking an indictment of fraud in order to take possession of the river acreage at Belmont Pines. But the phantom was smart and elusive, and R.J. had no more idea of how to go about finding out who it was, than he had of how to find Carole.

Once again, his thoughts turned to the haunting blonde. Where could she be? Was she all right? When was she coming back? The wondering had tormented him for five long days now.

He'd waited until the afternoon on Sunday, holding off as long as he could before walking across the landing to Carole's door. Utter silence had greeted his knock. But he hadn't thought much about it until that night, when her apartment remained dark and obviously unoccupied. Finally, at about ten o'clock, he'd tacked a note to Carole's door, asking that she simply let him know when she returned home. Monday morning, he'd gone over to discover that the note was untouched, and there was still no sign of any presence within the adjacent townhouse apartment.

All through that Monday, when he had stood futilely outside the post office watching box number 2138, he'd thought about her. But that evening, he'd rushed home to discover that Carole had not yet returned.

In desperation, he'd dialed up the Gossett mansion. After all, Carole had left the yacht with Gossett's wife. But the housekeeper who answered, a Mrs. Denning, only added to the mystery when she informed him that Kathleen Gossett had disappeared, also.

Finally, on Tuesday morning, R.J. had a brainstorm. He called up the Medical University, and after hounding a succession of nurses, he'd been able to reach April Gossett, who assured him that she was certain her sister was fine, but was sorry she couldn't give him any information concerning her whereabouts. That same day, just as he was leaving the apartment to continue his stake-out at the post office, he spotted Mrs. Thorndyke on Carole's porch.

Mosying over, he'd greeted the silver-haired woman, then noticed she was affixing a realtor's lock on the door.

"What are you doing?!" he'd demanded."

Mrs. Thorndyke turned, looked at him in a self-deprecating manner. "I have no say-so over this action," she explained. "James Gossett holds the lease on this apartment. He pays the rent. So, if he suddenly decides he wants it padlocked, all I can do is follow his instructions."

The older woman had shrugged rather balefully, bade him good day and departed, leaving R.J. to think, with mounting realization, that James Gossett would stoop to anything to bully his daughter.

Those thoughts lingered in his mind on this early September evening, as he stared out over the rooftops of Charleston morosely, watching the orange sun sink toward the distant horizon where sky met sea. The approaching sounds of a truck interrupted the quiet, and R.J. tossed his gaze disinterestly below. He watched a white tow truck pull up to the garage, then saw a black man in work uniform step over to Carole's Mercedes. When the man checked something on a piece of paper and then began hooking up the red car to the tow truck, R.J. raced down the stairs.

"What the hell do you think you're doing?" he yelled, striding forward to confront the man.

"Be cool, brother!" the man cautioned, looking up with a start from the hook he was preparing to lodge under the fender of the Mercedes. "I came to get the car on orders from the owner. You got something to say about it?"

"The owner is away!" R.J. barked. "I don't see how you could have any orders from *her*."

The man fished in his pocket and withdrew a work order. "Ain't no *her* a'tall. This here car is registered to a James Gossett, and I got orders from him to pick it up and take it over to Tradd Street. Now, you got anything else to say?"

R.J. could only stare at him helplessly. After a moment, the man went back to his work, and a few minutes later, he drove the tow truck away, pulling the Mercedes behind. R.J. watched the auto disappear up Broad Street. She had broken away from her father, and now he was pulling every bit of support he'd ever given her. With new understanding, R.J. began to imagine the terroristic tactics that Carole had probably put up with all of her life.

R.J. turned on the coffee maker and went down to retrieve the daily newspaper. Glancing up at the sky, he took note of the heavy clouds that were gathering over the peninsula. Charleston was in for a day of rain, he thought as he climbed the brick stairs, cast a quick look of longing at Carole's vacant apartment, and went back inside his own.

Settling at the formal dining table, he began to sip his first cup of the day while he thumbed through the front pages and then selected the business section. When he caught sight of the black-and-white photograph on page two, he nearly sprayed a hot mouthful of coffee across the mahogany table surface.

Gossett Enterprises, Inc., is in the process of acquiring acreage along the Ashley River for the development of a multimillion-dollar theme park, the caption read. *Construction is due to begin after the first of the year. James Gossett, corporate chairman, predicts that the park will draw visitors and tourism dollars from across the nation.*

But the caption was not the illuminating part of the photo. There in the background, nearly hidden behind a wall of pine trees by the angle of the camera, was the unmistakable, sagging front porch of Belmont Pines.

R.J. looked unseeingly across his dining room. Jonah's land was being purchased by the giant conglomerate, Gossett Enterprises. . . . The development of a theme park would net millions. . . . That was it! The final connection, the reason behind Jonah's removal to a distant institution, the buying of his land by a dummy company. *This* was the method in the madness!

R.J.s mind raced. Who was the mastermind behind it all? Gossett? He certainly qualified when it came to the kind of underhanded savvy that had been employed in the scheme. But if it *were* Gossett, then why the need for the ruse of Ashley Land Grant Corporation? Why not just buy the property directly from Geraldine Stuckey?

No, it wasn't Gossett. . . . R.J.'s fingers tapped absently on the photo as he mulled over the question. It was someone on the inside, someone who had known about the need for extensive, developmental acreage—and could skim a discreet fortune right off the top of a guaranteed sale to Gossett Enterprises. The whole thing would go through the carefully constructed screen of Ashley Land Grant, and no one would be the wiser.

A look of dread came over R.J.'s face as the finger of suspicion pointed ever more directly toward one person. Suddenly his subconscious reared back and pitched forth a stinging, nearly forgotten memory. *Nobody's going to care about an old geezer like Stuckey,* the voice in his dreams had said.

And the voice belonged to Curt.

And suddenly R.J. knew it hadn't been a dream at all! Some time, in the dark recesses of time past, he had actually *heard* his brother make that remark. *No one will bother to look into the affairs of a daft old geezer like Stuckey.* . . . It all came rushing back to R.J.

Curt! The name rang in R.J.'s head. *Curt!*

R.J. shivered in his chair. Was Curt really capable of such a plot? A scheme that was beginning to look like criminal fraud?

Granted, Curt would have known about Gossett Enterprises' development plans. But how would he have known about Belmont Pines, or that Louise Stuckey had died without a will to safeguard the land for her defenseless son?

R.J. glanced back at the caption to the picture. *Gossett Enterprises, Inc., is in the process of acquiring acreage* . . . So, the land—and the money—had not yet changed hands. But soon . . . it would be soon.

R.J. shot out of his seat and over to the phone. But when old Olivia Laroche answered, she informed him that Cecile had already left for the Morrisson house. R.J. paced the floor until he was sure Curt would have left for the office, then drove the short distance to Tradd Street and vaulted up the steps of the house.

His mother and Cecile were in the kitchen, chatting over a cup of coffee as Cecile tidied up after breakfast. Charlotte Morrisson rushed to her elder son, throwing her arms around him and welcoming him home. It was the first time he'd set foot inside his homeplace since the blowup with Curt back in July, over a month earlier.

"I'm just here for a short visit, Mother," he cautioned teasingly. "Don't go running up to my old room and change the sheets."

"Oh, Randall!" she exclaimed, and then corrected herself when he raised a warning brow. "I mean, R.J., of course," she added with a smile.

He meandered over to Cecile. "And how are you?"

"Fine, R.J. A lot better than poor old Jonah. How are things going? Any news yet?"

"Possibly," R.J. hedged. "That's the reason I came by. I wanted to ask you a question."

Cecile turned from the sink, wiping her hands on a dish towel as her dark eyes began to sparkle hopefully. "What is it?"

"Who exactly knew about Louise Stuckey's will? About the fact that it was missing?"

Cecile shrugged. "Well, lots of folks, I guess. Most everybody from the church. Why?"

"Anyone else?" R.J. pressed.

Cecile frowned thoughtfully. "Not that I can think of. Not too many folks outside the church knew Louise."

"Wait a moment, Cecile," Charlotte put in. "You know . . . you came here and told me all about it. About the fact that you had searched high and low and couldn't find the poor woman's will. I remember specifically that you told me the reason you were so sure she had one. You said you'd witnessed it, yourself. Remember?"

"Lord have mercy, that's right!" Cecile admitted.

"Who else heard?" R.J. demanded grimly.

"Well, no one, really," Charlotte answered. "Perhaps your father and Curt were at the table. That's all."

R.J.'s expression turned dark as the final piece of the puzzle fell into place. Curt had overheard Cecil's story, checked out Belmont Pines, and discovered it was perfect for the needs of Gossett Enterprises. The rest was history.

"What is it, R.J.?" Cecil asked worriedly. "Did I do something wrong?"

"No," he returned glumly. "Something wrong

307

has been done, all right. But it wasn't you who did it.''

A short while later, R.J. left the mansion with a heavy step. At least he could forego the boring stake-out at the post-office station across town. But a sick feeling gripped his gut as he realized the only sensible course of action left to him was to spy on his brother. Perhaps Curt would prove him wrong. But deep inside, R.J. suspected the hope was a foolish one. Thunder rumbled across the peninsula, and as he climbed into the silver Corvette, the first hesitant drops of rain began to fall.

Meanwhile, in the business district across town, Curt opened his interoffice mail and nearly gagged. For there, in an envelope from the publicity department, was a clipping of a news story that had run that morning. The text of the story centered on major theme parks in the Southeast; there was nothing revealing about Gossett Enterprises or the purchase of the development site. Still, anyone who had ever been to the property was sure to recognize the old, dilapidated house in the photograph as Belmont Pines.

Curt strolled down the hall to get a cup of coffee. It was too late to do anything about the overly zealous department that had pounced on the publicity item James Gossett had more than likely thrown their way. They were only doing their job, and besides, the press release would probably do no harm, anyway.

But as Curt meandered back to his office, it was with a sense of forboding. His partner, Robert ''keep-everything-confidential'' Morrisson, wasn't going to like it. Not a bit.

The flight from New York had run late due to the weather, and as Carole rode along in the back of the cab, the rain beat on the roof with steady precision.

The streets were slick; the city, wet and gray. Looking out into the darkness at the dreary sight, she suspected it had been falling all day. But the endless, towering skyscrapers of New York had been left far behind, and it was wonderful to look out on the familiar sights of Charleston, however rain soaked they might be.

Carole settled back in the seat of the cab and closed her eyes. It was nearly eleven o'clock, and she was tired. Now that she was home, she realized that she'd spent her entire trip on edge, wondering with ragged nerves if all her efforts—as well as those of Jack Levy—were for naught.

The thin, hyperactive little Yankee seemed truly to believe in her, and after they'd signed an agreement making him legally Carole's agent, Jack had managed to set up appointments with three topnotch fashion houses. But all they'd been able to accomplish in a week and a half was the introduction of herself and a few tantalizing samples of her work. Now, Jack had said, they would simply have to play the waiting game.

"Don't lose hope," he had warned her that evening as he packed her in a cab for LaGuardia Airport. "Any sale will have to be approved by committee, and who knows how long that could take. It could be weeks, or even months."

So now, she was back in Charleston, uncertain if she'd made any legitimate progress but determined to try again if she hadn't.

The cab pulled to a stop at Broad and Rutledge, and though the driver carted her bags up to the dark landing, Carole—minus an umbrella—was soaked by the time she made it to the shelter of the doorway. She fished in her bag and found the key as the taxi departed on the quiet street below. It wasn't until she reached for the lock that she withdrew her hand with a sense of shock.

It was padlocked! She stood for a moment staring

309

stupidly through the darkness at the faintly gleaming silver of the massive lock. And then it suddenly came to her: this was her father's handiwork.

"Damn it!" she muttered. Pulling her light jacket over her head, Carole darted back out into the rain and down to the garage. She would have to spend the night with April. But when she saw that the Mercedes was gone, she gasped anew.

She was tired, wet, hungry. It was eleven o'clock at night, and she had two dollars in her purse. A sense of cruel injury swept over her as frustrated tears started to her eyes.

"Didn't miss a trick, did you, Daddy?" she whispered. Standing alone in the deserted garage, she looked instinctively about her for some avenue of aid.

Her eyes fell on the silver Corvette, then turned to search through the rainy darkness, up to the second floor of the townhouse. His lights were on.

R.J. was pacing the floor of his living room. Outside, the rain came down as it had all day; it was the perfect companion to his dreary mood.

He had kept an eye on Curt all day, but it wasn't until the evening that his brother had done anything that would suggest he had anything up his sleeve besides continuing to perform as Gossett's fair-haired boy. Then, after Curt had supped with the Morrisson family, he'd driven to the Isle of Palms.

Maintaining a safe distance, R.J. had discovered that his brother met a realtor at the site of an immense residence that was under construction. It was then that R.J. remembered Curt had once mentioned the possibility of buying a house on the isle. R.J. had wondered then how his brother planned to lay his hands on that kind of money. Now, he thought with grim suspicion, he knew.

Crossing to the patio doors, R.J. looked blindly

out into the darkness. He hoped the charade would soon come to an end. Regardless of the huge rift that existed between them, this crafty business of tailing his own brother was making him sick.

Carole . . . The thought of her jumped into his mind as it had every day since he'd met her. With masochistic thoroughness, R.J. found himself going over everything once again, from their meeting at Spoleto to her engagement to Curt, to R.J.'s own discovery that he wanted her beyond all reason—despite his brother, or his own dedication to a free-wheeling bachelor state, or the fact that she had continually turned him down every time he'd tried to break through to her.

None of that mattered. R.J. was surprisingly, consumingly in love with her. And as he stared out into the darkness, he could almost feel his heart reach outside his body, searching the night for the woman who had disappeared from his life as suddenly as she'd dropped into it.

A knock sounded on the door. R.J. looked over his shoulder in surprise. It was after eleven. Who the hell? . . .

Crossing the room with quick, long strides, he opened the door—and his heart seemed to stop. There she was, looking rather like a drowned urchin, but it was her.

"Carole?" he whispered. "Carole?"

And then he was stepping outside, throwing his arms around her as the rain drummed steadily just beyond the meager shelter of the porch.

Unbidden, uncontrolled, Carole's arms went around the man's waist, holding him to her with an urgency that seemed to swell out of nowhere.

R.J. backed away enough to stare down into her blue-green eyes. They were devoid of makeup. The fair hair was wet and stringy. And she was the most beautiful thing he'd ever seen. He'd missed her so

311

much . . . been so worried. Suddenly, he pulled her inside, slamming the door shut behind her.

"Where the hell have you *been*?" he demanded angrily.

She laughed rather shakily, and for a moment he thought there were tears mixed in with the rain that ran down her cheeks.

"For heaven's sake, R.J.," she said. "Give me a minute. I just got back."

"Back from where?"

"New York. I went up there to see if I could make any contacts in order to sell my designs."

"Well, you might have told me, instead of letting me wander around here for the past weeks worried to death about what had happened to you!"

She stared at the flashing deep blue eyes that managed to warm her through the soaking garments that clung to her body. "I . . . I'm sorry," she managed.

"Sorry? You're *sorry*? Do you have any idea what you've put me through?"

R.J.'s angry vision suddenly cleared, and he saw her—standing there in his foyer, making a puddle, looking at him forlornly as if he had been her last hope. And now *even he* was condemning her.

"I . . . I'm sorry to bother you, R.J.," she stumbled. "I know it's late. But my car's gone . . . and I can't get into my apartment."

"I know. Your father has been swinging his weight. They closed up the apartment a couple of days after you left, and then some guy showed up and drove off with the Mercedes. . . ."

He halted abruptly as he noticed her teeth beginning to chatter.

"Come on," he then said. "You need to take a hot shower. Don't you have some bags or something?"

"They're outside," she mumbled. "I was hoping,

maybe, I could stay here . . . just for the night, mind you. I don't want to put you out."

R.J. stepped back, slouched to one hip as he regarded her disbelievingly. "Put me out?"

A slow smile came to his face. He couldn't resist the urge to tease. "After all the time I've been trying to get you in the privacy of my bedroom?"

"I didn't mean that!" Carole said quickly. "A spare room . . . a couch . . . anything until I can get my bearings . . ."

Her voice trailed off as she took in his expression. There it was again, that old look of amusement.

"Still playing hard to get, eh?" he asked with a raised brow, but then put teasing aside as he saw her begin to shiver. "It's fine," he assured her. "You stay here. I'll get your bags."

In the alleyway across the street, Joey Horton watched as R.J. darted out of his apartment and through the rain to retrieve the bags Carole Gossett had deposited in front of her door.

Rain streamed off the brim of Joey's hat as he looked down to make the notation: *11:30 P.M., R.J. Morrisson.*

Snapping off his flashlight, Joey stared up at the second story of the townhouse with a satisfied grin. He'd been standing futilely in the alleyway for ten days, but now it looked as though his efforts might pay off.

James Gossett was too good a meal ticket to lose. Joey intended to get back in his good graces. And keeping tabs on the daughter who had defied "old moneybags" was as good a place to start as any.

Chapter Thirteen

CAROLE PEERED INTO the cabinet above the bathroom sink. It was filled with all sorts of masculine cosmetics: shaving cream, razor, after shave, and of course, the familiar, clean-scented cologne which assaulted her nostrils immediately, driving home the fact that R.J. waited just outside.

She took a last glance in the mirror. Her face had little color, the glorious tan acquired on the Isle of Palms having faded to a pale beige during the sojourn in the cloistered climes of New York. A white towel was wrapped turbanlike round her wet head. A terrycloth robe of the same plain color muffled her figure. The reflection almost made her cringe. And as Carole regarded herself disparagingly, she thought she looked rather like a dull housewife—certainly nothing like the charming southern belle who had made a career of bedazzling men, young and old, for most of her life.

But the days of primping and fussing were past, left behind as surely as the miserable months she'd spent playing the role of "doll" for Curt and her father. This was the real Carole Gossett, and if R.J. didn't like it, that was just too bad.

Shrugging, Carole turned away from the mirror

and walked hesitantly out of the bath. She halted in the center of the living room. R.J. was standing by a Queen Anne coffee table, a white linen napkin draped over his left arm and a bottle of champagne in his right hand. Behind him, a Duncan Phyfe loveseat, covered in burgundy velvet, sat sedately beneath an oil pastoral in a gilded frame. When R.J. looked over at her and smiled, his classic looks seemed to complete the scene, conjuring up the impression of an aristocratic lord at home in his castle.

His eyes swept over her. "You look rather sexy, all clean and shined up like that."

"Sexy?" Carole questioned disbelievingly. She turned a quick, derogatory glance down the front of her robe, than returned her gaze to him, only to be met by an intense look that made her pulse race.

"Yeah. I always preferred you this way. You don't need makeup, Carole. You're pretty just the way you are."

Disconcertedly, she changed the subject, nodded toward the champagne. "What have you got there?"

R.J. proceeded to open the bottle, the loud pop of the cork preceding a gush of the bubbling liquid which he caught with the linen napkin.

"I've been saving this for a special occasion," he said. "And I think this is it."

He poured two glasses, strolled over, and handed one to her. "After all, it's not often that I open my door at midnight to find a beautiful blonde on my doorstep."

"Really, R.J.!" she said, with a self-mocking flourish of her hand to her bathrobe. "At the moment I'm hardly a beautiful blonde!"

His eyes took on a warm glow. "On the contrary, you look exactly like a woman I knew in the early summer . . . a beautiful woman I'm awfully happy to see again.

"I'd like to propose a toast" R.J. said, raising his glass. "To the return of Carole Gossett."

An uncomfortable thrill raced through her as she looked up the tall length of him. Taking a quick sip of the champagne, Carole turned away and began to ramble about the elegant room, taking note of the luxurious furnishings of the apartment.

"Nice place," she commented.

"Thanks."

"It makes me think of your parents' house."

"Funny . . . I thought the same thing."

Carole turned at the arched doorway to the dining room, leaned against the wall and looked piercingly across the distance of the room's breadth.

"Is *that* why you moved here?" she asked. "Because it reminded you of home?"

R.J. moved smoothly, like a great cat making its noiseless way across the floor, until he cornered her against the wall. Placing a palm near her head, he slouched to one hip and looked down. "I think you know better than that," he commented.

His very nearness promptly sent Carole's heart up to her throat. She glanced away and, rolling her shoulders along the wall, made a graceful escape into the dining room. Meandering toward the dining room, she tossed a quick look over her shoulder.

"It's generous of you to take me in like this, R.J. It really is. The spare room is lovely."

She sensed, rather than heard, him moving into the room behind her.

"The spare room wasn't my idea," he said.

Carole came to a stop at the far end of the table, having put its length safely between the two of them.

R.J. looked curiously across the mahogany surface. "What's got you acting so jittery?"

Carole took a gulp of champagne, then smiled nervously. "A lot of things, I guess. After all, it's past one o'clock in the morning, and I've just flown in from New York to find my apartment padlocked

316

and my car confiscated. You might say I'm a little disoriented."

"Maybe I can make it better," R.J. suggested huskily. Leaning down, his eyes on her all the while, he deposited the champagne glass on the nearby sideboard.

"Come here, Carole."

Willfully, her eyes locked with his across the span of the table. Her feet turned to lead.

"No," she whispered.

He watched her silently for a moment.

"All right then," he pronounced and stalked purposely around the dining table.

Cupping his palms on each side of her face, he bent to kiss her. And when his mouth found hers, the electric shock happened all over again. Her eyes drifted shut, her mouth opened. Her body was melting; in another instant, she would be gone.

Gently, but firmly, she pushed away from him. "Please, R.J.," she said, turning away from his searching, deep blue gaze.

"What is it, Carole?" he asked. "What's stopping you from letting it happen? For the first time since we've known each other, everything is perfect. We're here, we're alone, and I've wanted you for a long time."

She took a few paces, turned to face him in a somewhat defensive manner. "That doesn't mean we're going to jump into bed together."

"Don't make it sound like something cheap. I've told you how I feel about you. And I think you feel something for me." R.J.'s expression transformed into one of heated determination. "One thing I know for certain is the way you respond when I touch you. As far as bed is concerned, you and I both know that if I pressed my case, I'd probably win it."

Carole's chin came up. "That's why I'm going to rely on the fact that you're a gentleman who won't press. I need some time."

R.J. suddenly lost all patience, his temper erupting. "Time? Do you have any idea how much *time* I've already spent on you?"

At his outburst, Carole promptly turned her back on him and walked out of the room. "I'm sorry you feel it's been wasted," she tossed over her shoulder. "If you'll excuse me, I'm going to bed."

R.J. stared angrily after her retreating figure. "By all means, go to bed, Carole," he called angrily. "And be sure to let me know when you've had enough *time*. I'm certain I'll just be hanging around, waiting to hear the good news!"

R.J. whirled into the master bedroom, slamming the door shut. He was halfway to the bed when it struck him: He'd heard his brother yell nearly identical words to Carole. R.J. threw a sudden punch at the wall, allowing the frustrations that had been building for months some release. But all he got for his trouble was a set of bruised knuckles.

The next morning, he overslept. After throwing on some clothes, he ventured sheepishly out of his bedroom, determined to make amends. But he was too late. Although her bags remained neatly packed in the spare room, Carole herself was gone.

Carole took the familiar stroll through the District and walked purposefully into the Gossett mansion.

"Why, Miss Carole!" Mrs. Denning exclaimed. "How lovely to see you."

"Thank you, Mrs. Denning. Where is my father?"

"Why, he just went out to his car," the old woman quickly informed her. "If you hurry, you can catch him."

Carole strode boldly through the garage, took a firm stance in front of the black Seville.

James looked up with a start. Carole! His gaze swept over the straight hair and took in the casually

318

unkempt look about his daughter. And then his black eyes narrowed as all the rage returned, washing over him like a tidal wave. Quietly, slowly, he shut off the engine and climbed out of the car.

"So, the prodigal returns," he commented. "And where, may I ask, have you been?"

"New York," Carole replied succinctly. "Believe it or not, I'm taking a shot at 'making it in the big leagues,' as you so quaintly put it."

She walked around the automobile, meeting her father's dark look with one of her own. "I'd like to ask a favor."

"Favor?" James repeated with an infuriatingly faded smile. "I thought you wanted to be entirely free of me. I'm surprised to hear you asking for a favor." His pleasant expression turned abruptly into one of viciousness. "Especially after what you've done. . . ."

Carole regarded him defiantly. "I can see this was a mistake. I only came to ask if you'd have that lock removed long enough for me to get my things out of the apartment."

His eyes were like two dark serpents, snaking their way over her. "I see. . . . Well, perhaps we can work something out after all."

Carole raised her chin haughtily. "You've taken the apartment . . . and the car. I don't suppose you have alternative plans for my clothes, do you? Or would a hefty donation to the Salvation Army be in order?"

"No," James replied firmly. "I'll tell you what *would* be in order . . . would be for you to take back what you've done. Come back, Carole. Let bygones be bygones, and everything is yours again. . . . The apartment, clothes, car . . . everything!"

Carole looked at him in disbelief. "You can't be serious, Daddy."

"I'm serious."

She laughed harshly. "Don't you understand

319

what's happened? Don't you know that I'll never go back to being your little girl?''

An evil grin tugged at the corner of James's mouth. ''You're here, aren't you?''

Anger spilled from Carole's eyes like water. ''Not for long,'' she declared, and stalked away, leaving her father chuckling behind her.

''You'll be back!'' he called. ''You'll be back for all the things you've become accustomed to!''

Carole turned briefly at the doorway to the kitchen. ''Don't hold your breath!'' she spat, and was gone.

When R.J. returned that evening after uneventfully trailing his brother from the office to the Morrisson mansion, Carole was sitting out front on the steps.

''Well, well,'' he commented lightly, ''You do show up at the oddest times.''

''Hi,'' she said, coming to her feet and moving out of his way rather skittishly. ''I . . . uh . . . I need to collect my bags. Sorry I left so abruptly this morning. But you seemed to be sleeping late, and I had a lot to do.''

R.J. flickered a look in her direction. He noted the beautiful, natural look of her face and hair, the casual dress of her jeans and shirt. ''Like what?'' he asked carelessly as he unlocked the door and led the way inside.

''Like finding a job . . . a place to live.''

He didn't look at her, just waltzed into the foyer and began emptying his pockets onto the receiving table. ''Any luck?''

''I'd say so . . . after a rather poor beginning, that is. My father won't let me into the apartment to get my things. Carlotta won't take me back at the shop. After all, James Gossett set her up in business, and she can't very well go against his wishes. But I found a job cocktail-waitressing at Myskyn's, and I'm going to sublet a studio apartment from a friend of April's who just moved in with her boyfriend."

"When can you move in?"

"Tonight."

"Quick work," R.J. delivered cuttingly. "So, what happens now?"

"Now, I wait to see if Jack Levy can sell my designs to one of the three houses we called on. If he doesn't, we'll start all over again with other houses. If he *does*," she added, venturing a slight smile, "maybe I'll make enough to take over my old apartment and pay the rent myself!"

R.J. finally turned to look at her. And when Carole's eyes lit on the handsome face, she turned all warm inside. Why was she doing this? Why was she walking out on him? But the answer was clear: She was simply too reluctant to give up her newfound independence—even to R.J.

"You know," R.J. said, breaking into her thoughts. "For months, I've thought the main thing standing between the two of us was Curt. But I was wrong." His serious expression hardened. "It's you, Carole. You've been acting for so long; I don't think you're up to a relationship that makes you *really* feel . . . *really* care."

His words stung, causing her defenses to spring to the surface. "I'm awfully tired, R.J., and I have to be on my way. Can we forego the psychoanalysis?"

She strode past him, retrieved her bags from the guest room, and returned to the living room to find him staring at her morosely.

"Have I been wrong about you?" he asked in a low voice. "Don't you feel anything for me?"

"Yes," she answered sincerely, "I *do* feel something. But right now, my head is so muddled, I don't know what it is. I haven't enough presence of mind, or energy, to deal with anything but my own life."

R.J. nodded, folding his arms across his chest, and

eyed her coolly. "There we have it, don't we? Carole's life. Carole's head. Carole's feelings. Sounds a little self-centered, doesn't it? Maybe one day you'll grow up enough to realize there are other people in the world besides yourself!"

Her eyes darted to his. She was more hurt than he knew by his cutting words.

"Good-bye," she muttered, and lugged her baggage out the door.

For R.J., the succeeding week passed in oblivion. She was gone—again.

One night he went over to Myskyn's, but when he peered over the saloon doors and saw Carole—dressed in a scanty uniform and smiling coquettishly as she served a tableful of guys—he turned and left. At least she was back in Charleston and not gallivanting about the streets of New York. But somehow, ironically, R.J. felt that Carole Gossett had moved farther out of his reach than ever.

Besides thinking of her, he had only the duty of trailing his brother to fill the days. R.J. was beginning to think the whole distasteful business was to no avail. All he'd learned from watching Curt was his brother's routine, which he now felt he knew as well as his own. Gossett Enterprises in the morning, lunch in town, and at the end of the day, either the Morrisson house or Laura Murphy's. Once Curt went to Laura's, R.J. knew he was in for the night.

One afternoon, R.J. was parked in his usual spot down the street from Gossett Enterprises. As he waited for the end of the business day, he scanned the newspaper, paying particular attention to offices for lease and opportunities in the legal field. But there were no new developments. The Stuckey case was beginning to look like a wild goose chase. And to make matters worse, the whole time he'd been pursuing it, he'd let his life go to hell in a handbasket. He still had some of the funds he'd been stock-piling since appointment to the supreme-court post, but sooner or later, he was going to have to go back to work.

As his thoughts continued on their rather depressing vein, he happened to glanced up. Further up the street, Curt's BMW was just pulling out of the Gossett Enterprises lot. He was early today. It was only half past four, and Curt never left the office before five. R.J. turned the ignition, allowing several cars to pass before pulling the Corvette out into traffic.

Up ahead, the BMW turned left, veering away from the typical path to the Morrisson house. Maybe he's on his way to Laura's again, R.J. thought rather resignedly. But then, Curt turned once more. And as the two vehicles continued across town, R.J.'s mind went suddenly alert. This was not the route to any of his brother's usual haunts. As they drew even closer to the out-of-the-way neighborhood R.J. remembered so well, his heart began to pound.

And then, just when he was certain Curt would pull into one of the spaces across from the postal station, the white BMW purred on past. There was only one car between them now. R.J. dropped back discreetly, put a block between them. But he still saw quite clearly when Curt turned up ahead.

Keeping his distance, R.J. turned in suit, and then glimpsed the white car turning once again. Then he caught on. Curt was circling the block. R.J. gunned around the second corner, then slammed on the brakes and pulled over as he saw the BMW pull into a parking space a short distance up the narrow lane.

R.J. killed the engine, watching with sweaty palms as his brother got out of the car and glanced at his watch before starting along the walk opposite the post office. R.J., too, checked the time, discovering that it was nearly five o'clock. The post office would close in only a few minutes.

Good timing, brother, he thought. Quickly he climbed out of his car. He hurried along the palm-shaded lane, watching as his brother entered the post office and turned toward the wall of numbered boxes. R.J. darted across the busy street and took shelter in the old vantage point that afforded him an excellent view of box number 2138.

Sure enough, Curt produced the key, swiftly opened the box, and withdrew an envelope. Tearing it open, he glanced quickly at the contents before slipping it into a second envelope, which he withdrew from his pocket.

He couldn't be certain, but from where R.J. stood, the mysterious document had looked like a money order. His heart was thundering now as he watched Curt cross to the postmaster, hand over the newly sealed parcel, and begin a discussion.

The postman affixed some sort of label to the envelope, then produced a record sheet and made a notation. Curt turned, and R.J. darted into the shadows of a group of palms as his brother exited the post office with a wide smile, and then trotted across the street in the direction of his car.

He waited under cover until he saw the BMW turn onto the busy street and move away. Then, R.J. leaped toward the entrance of the post office, just in time to see the postmaster approaching the door with a heavy set of keys.

R.J. burst through the swinging doors. ''Wait a minute!''

The plump, gray-haired man jumped, looking up with wide eyes.

R.J. smiled in a quick, friendly fashion. ''I'm sorry. I didn't mean to startle you. But I wanted to make sure I got in before you closed up. If I hadn't, my brother would have had my hide.''

''Your brother?''

''Yes. He was just here. You know, the one who sent the registered letter.''

324

"Oh, yes. He just left."

"I know. He sent me back to double-check something. He's afraid he wrote the address incorrectly."

"Well, now, I'm sorry, son," the older man said condescendingly. "But that letter is now the property of the United States Post Office. There ain't no getting it back once it's been sent."

"I'm sure you're right. No, I don't need it back. Just need to check the address." R.J. smiled engagingly. "Hell, if my brother put it down wrong, he can always send another letter. Right?"

The man surrendered to a comradely grin. "Well, all right. It's lying right on top of the registered-mail basket yonder. Guess it won't hurt nothing for you to have a look."

R.J.'s blood was racing through his veins as he followed the kindly, old man to the counter.

"Now, you just wait right here, son," the man instructed. "Can't have you coming behind here. In fact, can't have you touching the letter a'tall!"

The postmaster reached for the letter lying on top of the silver basket and turned to R.J., peering at the address through heavy bifocals.

"Here we go. Sent from Ashley Land Grant Corporation to a post-office box in Switzerland." He leaned forward, held up the envelope for R.J.'s perusal. "There, now. Is that the right number?"

R.J.'s eyes fixed on the envelope clearly imprinted with Curt's handwriting. Switzerland! "What?" he mumbled. "Oh, yes. That's correct after all."

The man retrieved the epistle, and redeposited it amongst the registered mail as R.J. turned away.

"Thank you." he said courteously.

"My pleasure, son."

R.J. wandered through the doors, coming to a dazed stop outside the building as the postmaster locked up behind him.

Switzerland. It was a land known for many things:

towering mountains, exquisite clocks, legendary chocolates—and untraceable, numbered bank accounts.

The silver Corvette careened around the corner, speeding across town. Curt had a fifteen-minute head start on him, but if R.J.'s guess was right, his brother was not on the way to Laura Murphy's, but to the Morrisson home.

All through the drive to Tradd Street, R.J.'s head was hammering with the question: *Why?* Smiling images of his brother flashed through his mind, images that spanned a lifetime. With a sense of painful bitterness, R.J. wondered once again at how quickly—how irrevocably—they had become enemies.

He screeched up the drive to the house, switching off the engine as he spotted Curt's white BMW in the garage. R.J. stalked into the house like an avenging angel, banging his way through the double doors to his father's private study. As he'd expected, Curt and Robert Morrisson were comfortably ensconced in a couple of leather chairs, sharing a before-dinner cocktail.

"What the hell are you doing, R.J.?" his father exploded as the oak doors slammed noisily against the walls.

R.J. came to stand before them, glared down at Curt. "Better yet, what the hell are *you* doing?"

"What are you talking about?" Curt asked with a casual sneer.

"You know damned well what I'm talking about. I'm talking about Belmont Pines and Ashley Land Grant and Gossett Enterprises. I'm talking about fraud!"

Curt leapt to his feet, his face going abruptly red. "Watch you tongue, R.J.," he warned.

"Settle down, both of you." Robert broke in,

vaulting out of his chair. "I'll not have your voices raised in this house. Now, calm down!"

R.J. ignored his father. "I know everything, Curt," he said, his eyes glinting. "You had Dan Shriver line up the phony guardian so she could hand over the property to Ashley Land Grant. And then, how convenient it must have been to locate the perfect lands for the theme park Gossett Enterprises is going to develop. How much did you make off the deal, Curt? A couple of million? On its way right now to a comfortable, little Swiss bank account?"

Curt was caught off balance by his brother's surprisingly accurate accusations. The nagging reservations, the qualms of conscience Curt had methodically dismissed over the past months seemed suddenly important. Suddenly he saw his scheme not as a brilliant ploy, but as a tawdry swindle. The thought made the muscles in his jaw twitch guiltily. But then the resentment he felt for his self-righteous brother mushroomed, clouding his brain, blotting out any care that R.J. had figured out his plan.

"So what?" Curt hissed. "Where's your proof . . . brother?"

"I don't need proof . . . brother," R.J. returned sarcastically. "A mere trip to court with such allegations would be enough to ruin you and Dan Shriver and anyone else who's involved."

"Now, wait just a minute!" Robert interrupted firmly.

But his effort was in vain. R.J. ranted on, his eyes locked on his brother. "How about Louise Stuckey's will, Curt? Did you manage to abscond with that, too?"

"Didn't have to," Curt replied valiantly. "Fate took care of that for me. That's what made the whole thing so easy!"

"Both of you. Be quiet this instant!" their father

327

commanded. "You forget to whom you're speaking, R.J. This is your brother, not some dismal little perpetrator you're out to convict. We're family here, and nobody's taking anybody to court."

R.J. turned to his father in surprise, well aware that Curt had settled back on his heels with a look of relief.

"Let's just talk this thing out," Robert thundered.

R.J. regarded his distinguished father with mounting, shocking suspicion. "There's nothing to talk out, Dad . . . unless you're in on this, too."

Robert hesitated a moment, then squared his shoulders and gazed steadily into the blue-gray eyes that were a mirror of his own. "Curt had a good plan, R.J.. He needed some up-front money, and I invested in a very sound business opportunity. That's all there is to it."

Curt stepped back out of the way. For once in his life, Robert Morrisson, III, was on *his* side.

"That's *all*?" R.J. repeated disbelievingly. "The whole business was a swindle!"

Robert took a step toward his son. "That's a harsh word, son. It was a business transaction."

"Dad, you *bribed* an official."

"We didn't bribe anyone," Robert thundered. "Dan and I have been friends since early on in his political career. He came in on this deal as a partner, willing to take a percentage of the profits."

R.J. folded his arms across his chest. "Yeah, and all he had to do to earn that percentage was sabotage an old man named Jonah Stuckey."

Robert gave his son an authoritative look. "Listen to me, Randall," he said, reverting to the formal use of his name. "It makes no sense for that old man to squat unproductively on property that has earned us millions. Stuckey will be well taken care of. He'll have everything he ever needs."

328

"How kind of you to make that decision for him, Father," R.J. returned bitingly.

Robert's eyes turned dark and stormy. "It seems to me, Randall, that you've forgotten where your loyalties lie. You . . . me . . . Curt . . . We're family. The Morrissons helped found this city. Morrisson stock fought in the Revolution, carried on through occupation by the British, helped to rebuild after the War Between the States. Morrisson dollars helped to see Charleston safely through the Great Depression, and every recession since.

"Now, tell me, Randall. Who has the right to profit from Charleston's resources? Not those Yankee bastards Gossett has fallen in with. And not some illiterate black who lucked into property because his old man bedded down with his mama one night. It's up to us, the fine old families, to carve Charleston's destiny. Always has been, always will be. You know that, Randall. You're one of us."

R.J. gazed at his father with newborn scorn. "The privileged, Charleston aristocracy, eh?"

"That's right!"

"Just who do you think we are, Dad, some sort of superior race? Above everyone else? Above the law?"

Robert ground his teeth against an uncomfortable jab of guilt. "In some cases," he confirmed.

R.J. shook his head in disbelief. "Well, if that's what being a Morrisson means, then I claim no part of the name."

R.J.'s eyes darted from his father to Curt, who was standing only a few feet away, a bright look on his face that hovered somewhere between rebellion and embarrassment.

"I don't think I know you two," R.J. said. "Perhaps you'd feel differently if you could see what I saw, a helpless, harmless old man sitting on the floor of a hospital ward. When you were pulling the strings that stuck him in that institution, did either of you stop to think that Jonah Stuckey might *die* in there?''

''Is that what all this yelling is about? Jonah Stuckey?''

Charlotte voiced the question from the doorway, surprising all three of the men as she strolled calmly into the private chamber she'd entered but twice in her life.

''This doesn't concern you, Charlotte,'' Robert said with a scolding look. ''This is just between us. And I'd appreciate a little privacy. Please, close the study doors on your way out.''

''This is my home just as much as it's yours, Robert,'' she returned with shocking defiance. ''Our sons are just as much mine, as well. I'll have an answer to everything that's been going on around here the past few months, and I'll have it now.''

Curt stepped forward, his eyes flying to R.J. with ill-concealed terror. ''Well, Mother, it seems your favorite son here isn't content with trying to steal my fiancée. Now, it seems, he's bound to take Father and me to court!''

''What!'' Charlotte exclaimed. Her dark eyes turned to R.J. ''What is he talking about, Randall? What's all this about Carole . . . and Jonah Stuckey?''

''It has nothing to do with Carole.'' R.J. hesitated, then went on with daring honesty. ''It has to do with the fact that Curt and Dad swindled Stuckey out of his land to make a huge profit by selling it to Gossett enterprises.''

Charlotte's luminous eyes turned to Robert. ''Is this true?''

He met her look, refused to flinch. But in truth, Robert's misgivings about the whole matter were mounting by the minute. ''That's a very unflattering recitation of the matter,'' he said.

Charlotte stared at the man she loved, realizing that this intrigue, this plot, was the mysterious mis-

330

tress that had stolen her husband's thoughts and time.

"I'd like you to go now, Randall," she said, without taking her eyes off Robert.

"Something needs to be decided," R.J. insisted, his angry eyes shifting from his father to his brother. "Fraud has been committed here, *and* criminal misconduct by Dan Shriver, an elected official. Something has to be done!"

Charlotte looked at her son with dignified calm. "Perhaps there's nothing to be done," she said quietly.

"What?" R.J. exploded.

"You know as well as I that you can't turn on your own father and brother," Charlotte countered. "We're the Morrissons. Whatever goes on within our walls is for us alone . . . not the public eye."

"So!" R.J. exclaimed. "Because we've got money! Because this is the way things have been done in Charleston for generations! This whole thing is going to be swept under the rug? Is that it?"

"None of this can be decided haphazardly while tempers are running high," his mother returned. "Please leave, Randall. We'll discuss it another time."

"Mother! You can't just . . ."

"*Randall!*" Charlotte gave her son a look that would brook no rebellion.

R.J. expelled a long, shaky breath. Then, turning, he stormed out of the Morrisson home.

Ever regal in an ivory dress of silk, Charlotte inclined her head in the direction of her husband and younger son.

"Dinner will be on the table in five minutes," she said quietly and exited the study, drawing respectful stares from both men.

The rest of the evening in the Morrisson household went as usual. Cecile served an excellent supper. Margaret complained about her new beau

331

leaving for the University of South Carolina. Camille teased her about all the alluring women who lived in the capital city.

After supper Robert had donned a smoking jacket and gone down to his study for a nightcap. Soon returning to the master suite, however, he found the doorway blocked by the attractive figure of his wife. His dark blue eyes studied hers as he tried to decipher her mood. She was definitely solemn, had been so ever since that business in the study. He decided a firm approach was best.

"What is it, Charlotte?" he asked. "I'm tired."

"In a way I'm relieved it isn't another woman. . . . But in another way, I'm extremely disappointed in you."

"Another woman? What are you talking about?"

"I'm talking about your preoccupation and distance these past months. Now, I know where they were coming from. It isn't like you, Robert, to exploit someone like Jonah Stuckey. You don't need the money. What is it?"

Robert's eyes widened. After all these years, his wife's astuteness could still surprise him.

"Gossett," he ground from between his teeth. "The jackass has paid us millions, and he doesn't even know it."

Charlotte looked at him with mounting sadness. "I think you'll be more comfortable in the guest room," she said. Quietly, she closed the bedroom door in her husband's face.

September turned into October, and the warmth of Indian summer lingered in the Charleston air as the trees turned red and gold.

It was late afternoon. Golden shafts of sunlight danced along the streets between the palmettos glinting off the silver Corvette as R.J. drove toward his apartment.

He hadn't seen his family in three weeks. They had done nothing. He had done nothing. And Jonah Stuckey still sat in an institution, growing "more and more poorly," Cecile had reported.

Cecile knew nothing of the conspiracy, or of the fact that her own lips had indirectly sealed Jonah's fate. Only the Morrissons knew. Only they. What was the old saying, *the rich get richer?* The sentiment dawned on R.J., dimming his appreciation of the graceful, scenic beauty of Charleston. Charleston, where such division of power had existed for centuries.

He pulled up to the townhouse, saw with surprise that his mother's car was parked out front. She was waiting on the stoop.

"Where have you been?" she asked.

R.J. glanced at her, thought how tirelessly appropriate Charlotte Morrisson was in her light tweed and snowy-stocked blouse. "Looking at office space," he answered. "I still have a practice to set up, you know."

Charlotte looked up into the eyes of her tall firstborn. "I'd like to talk to you, Randall."

He closed the door behind them, watched her stroll into the center of the living room, and then turn dramatically to face him. She still cut a dashing figure, his mother.

"Randall, this situation has been troubling me greatly. Every day, Cecile comes to the house, often mentioning this poor man, Jonah Stuckey. And all I can do is think. 'If only you knew!' Oh, Randall, I'm so weary of it all. Isn't there anything you can do to put things right without dragging our name through the mud?"

R.J. looked at his mother gravely. "There's nothing I can do, even if I *did* drag our name through the mud. Curt was right. I have no proof. I know every single thing he did to set up this little fraud,

333

but I haven't a shred of evidence that would stand up in a court of law. He was very clever."

Charlotte sank onto the Duncan Phyfe sofa. "I can't believe it. I just can't! Why would Curt *do* such a thing?"

"How about a beachfront resort home on the Isle of Palms?" R.J. asked snidely.

"What?" she said, her eyes flying wide.

"Nothing," R.J. replied tiredly. "It doesn't matter. At this point, the only thing that could remedy the situation is the discovery of Louise Stuckey's will. A document, I might add, which I'm beginning to suspect never existed!"

"But Cecile said—"

"I know what she said!" R.J. interrupted irritably. He began to rub at his forehead. "I know," he muttered again.

He took a few steps forward, his eyes coming to rest on his mother with a look of defeat. "There's nothing I can do."

A spark lit in Charlotte's dark eyes. "Perhaps there's something I can do."

"What do you mean?"

"I'm not altogether without influence on your father, you know. He's been sleeping in the guest room ever since this mess came to light. Perhaps he's ready to move back into the master suite."

A lighthearted look came to R.J.'s face. "Mother!" he exclaimed in a tone of mock shock. "Are you saying you plan to *seduce* him? And then what?"

"Then," Charlotte explained with a shrug of her shoulders. "I can persuade him that this whole business is beneath him. He can simply give the money back, and that will be that."

R.J.'s look of levity faded. "I'm afraid it isn't that simple, Mother. All that money showing up out of nowhere? Father and Curt would never agree to that. At this point, it would be an out-and-out confession to fraud."

"What are we to do, then?" his mother asked quietly.

"There's nothing *to* do . . . unless you want me to expose them and take them to court, when I know damned well I don't have a snowball's chance of winning!"

Charlotte considered the dreadful thought—envisioned pictures of her son and her husband splashed across the newspapers. She shuddered.

"No . . . no," she said, looking at her son with sad eyes. "You can't do it, Randall. In the end, we Morrissons must stick together. It's our way. It's our blood. In time, this will pass. Things will go back to the way they were."

R.J. shook his head doubtfully. "In a way, I guess you're right. I've come to realize that the families like ours are an institution in Charleston, just as much a part of it as the Ashley or the Cooper or the southern heritage Dad always made so much of. And just as surely as the Ashley flows to the sea, the great families bind together and carry on. I know that."

His face took on a grim look. "But in another way, you're wrong, Mother. Because things will never again be quite the same . . . not for me."

Chapter Fourteen

HALLOWEEN FELL ON a Saturday night. At half past seven, Carole stood before the rather old, dingy mirror above the rather old, dingy dresser. The appointments of the sublet apartment were meager in comparison to the luxury she was used to; the location near the Medical University was unfashionable compared to the address near Tradd Street. But Carole had no complaints. She, herself, was footing the bills. And to her, the shabby apartment was a castle.

As she regarded the reflection in the cloudy looking glass she was in high spirts. Myskyn's was throwing a Halloween bash that night, complete with decorations, special drinks, and an award for the best costume that showed up at the place. It would be a night of big tips; for a huge crowd was sure to turn out.

The entire Myskyn's staff had been ordered to get in the spirit of the thing. And now, Carole grinned at the spectacle she made as a black cat. The costume fit as closely as a leotard, complete with black tights, a long, arching tail, and a cap with pointed ears, under which all of her golden hair was hidden.

Carole applied the final touch of carefully drawn whiskers, then walked out front to wait for April.

The October night was clear and nippy. Rubbing her hands together, she glanced up at the stars, then watched smilingly as a crowd of small trick-or-treaters made their way from house to house across the narrow street.

April looked entirely ethereal as an angel with a glowing halo when she arrived to pick Carole up. By the time they got to Myskyn's, the place was already filling up with goblins and devils and witches.

The music was loud; the growing crowd even louder. Laughingly, Carole moved toward the waitresses' station and called farewell to April, who went off to the bar to join Charlie Regis, a pirate for the night.

The night wore on, and the place was rocking. Carole had her hands full keeping up with orders—*and* with preventing too familiar hands from yanking on her tail. Still, she was having a good time. At eleven, when she took a quick break and went to join April at the bar, Carole was still glowing. Charlie moved off to get another drink, and Carole took his seat for a moment, pivoting on the swivel stool. A smile lit her face as she took a sweeping look about the rollicking crowd.

That was when she saw R.J. He would have been hard to miss—sitting glum and alone at a table, the only person in the entire bar who was not decked out in Halloween glory. He hadn't been there a few minutes ago, Carole knew, for she'd been waiting that table all night. The smile drained from her face as she sat there, unobserved by R.J., and studied him.

"He just got here," April said, following her sister's gaze. "I saw him come in."

Carole turned with a start. "It's a free country," she said after a moment. "R.J. can have a drink wherever he likes."

April grimaced. "You know damn well the reason he's here. You."

"April! I told you what he said to me. And I haven't heard from him in over a month. What makes you think he came here to see me?"

"What makes me think it? The way you two feel about each other. For heaven's sake, Carole, it's been going on ever since you met. Whether you admit it or not, this man is an important part of your life."

A determined gleam came to Carole's eye. "The most important thing in my life is my career. Jack Levy wants me to come up to New York next week. He says a good house is very interested in the collection. I've saved my money, and I'm going! That's all I have time to think about right now."

April regarded her sister with concern. "I'm proud of the way you've come into you own, Carole. But there *is* such a thing as going too far, you know. There are other important things in our lives besides careers . . . other people besides ourselves."

Carole's eyes snapped defensively. "You're beginning to sound just like R.J.," she returned. Sliding off the stool, she went to the waitresses' station to pick up her tray and pad.

By the time she made her way to R.J.'s table, an auburn-haired beauty dressed as a Gypsy had already approached him.

"You remember me, don't you, R.J.? Bunny Alexander? I was in Curt's class," the woman was saying as Carole strolled up to the table.

"Oh yeah . . . Bunny," R.J. shot the woman a dazzling smile. "How are you? You're looking great."

Carole felt the color race to her cheeks. "Evening, folks," she said briskly. "What can I get for you?"

R.J.'s head snapped around at the sound of her voice. He'd *thought* the shape of the black cat looked mighty familiar. "Is that you, Carole?" he asked with a faint smile.

"It's me."

338

"I'll have a margarita, honey," the gypsy said with a sidelong glance as she slid smoothly into the vacant chair beside R.J.

An outraged sense of jealousy flashed through Carole, and at that moment, she wished the cat costume had come with a set of claws! Silently, furiously, she made the note about the margarita, then glanced to R.J. with a cold look that vented her anger.

"And for you, sir?" she whipped.

R.J. hadn't been in good spirits anyway. Now Carole's frustrating coolness triggered him into a dangerous mood. "I'll have a gin and tonic," he replied with an arched brow. "Heavy on the gin . . . honey."

As he turned abruptly back to the auburn-haired woman, Carole raced away from the table with her cheeks burning. By the time she returned with their drinks, R.J. had his arm draped round the back of her chair. And shortly thereafter, he left a ridiculously large tip and strolled out of Myskyn's with the Gypsy on his arm. Carole watched them go, feeling her insides suddenly tilt in a dizzying, sickening fashion.

R.J. tried to keep his mind on what he was doing, but his thoughts kept wandering back to Myskyn's. He had gone there just to see Carole. Everything in his life seemed to have turned sour; the Jonah Stuckey thing was eating him alive. He'd somehow thought that just seeing her would help.

Cecile had asked him several times to go with her to visit Stuckey, who was, she said, losing weight and looked peaked. R.J. knew she was surprised each time he vehemently refused the invitation. But he couldn't tell Cecile that he couldn't bear the sight of Jonah Stuckey. Hell, he couldn't even bear the sight of her, nor of the hopeful, trusting eyes she turned on him every time they met.

And so, he had gone to Myskyn's. But once he saw Carole and felt the old frustrations well up like festering wounds, he was stricken with the urge to lash out. Now, he realized he'd wanted to hurt her as deeply as he himself was hurting.

That was why he'd brazenly picked up Bunny Alexander. That was why he was lying here in bed, kissing the woman—pretending that the eyes behind the closed lids were blue-green, and that the hair beneath his fingers was a silky, golden blond.

The good news came eight weeks after her return from New York. Carole was puttering around the apartment, doing a little cleaning, when the phone rang.

"Carole! We did it!" Jack Levy announced with a tone of triumph that rang all the way down the line from New York.

For the next few days, she wandered around in a dazed state. Besides the money, which was more than enough to keep her comfortable until she could work up some new designs, the fashion house wanted an option on her future work. She'd made it! Carole Gossett was a success!

But gradually, Carole's chattering, euphoric high seemed to tumble into a mood of quiet, grave solemnity. And the closer the Christmas season drew, the more morose she became. April was the first to notice the change. One night, a couple of weeks before the holiday, she showed up unannounced at Carole's apartment holding a Christmas tree. They spent the evening stringing lights and hanging ornaments.

"So, how's everything going?" April asked casually as they sat down with a glass of wine after they'd finished the decorating.

"Fine," Carole replied. "I got a letter from Kathleen today."

"Really?"

"She and André plan to be married when the divorce is final."

April shook her head thoughtfully. "Isn't it funny? All the time she was married to Daddy, we never really knew her."

"I don't think she knew herself," Carole replied in the same serious-minded tone that had prompted April's visit.

"Carole, what is going on?" April blurted. "You should be on top of the world, and yet you're dragging around like you've lost your best friend."

Carole turned misty eyes to her sister. "That's pretty much it," she said in soft admission. "I miss him. I did everything wrong, and now I've lost him."

"Who?" April fired. "R.J.? You couldn't have done *everything* wrong, Carole, or you never would have gotten him to fall in love with you in the first place!"

Carole shook her head doubtfully. "A lot of time . . . a lot of trouble has passed since he said that. You were right. . . . *He* was right. Both of you warned me that I was too wrapped up in my own dreams. And now that I've made it, I know you were right. I was so concerned with myself, I didn't stop to think about anyone else."

"Give yourself a break," April scolded. "You were entitled, Carole. All those years, you were crushed under Daddy's thumb. It doesn't take a genius to understand that you needed a chance to make it on your own."

"Maybe. But now . . . the success . . . The whole thing, seems kind of . . . hollow."

"Because you don't have R.J." April concluded mater-of-factly.

Carole nodded miserably.

"All right," April commented briskly. "Let's get down to business, then. I don't have to tell *you*, of

341

all people, how to go about getting a man. Go over to his place. Talk to him."

"You think so?" Carole asked tremulously.

"You love him, don't you?"

Another nod.

"Then go after him!"

Carole got out of the cab at the familiar corner of Broad and Rutledge. Looking up to make sure R.J.'s lights were on, she waved the cabby on. The December air was crisp and clean; and the streetlamps were festive in their greenery and red ribbon. Carole buried her hands in the pockets of her white cashmere coat and walked hesitantly across the street and up the brick steps.

As she stood before his door, her mind filled with memories of the dazzling smile at Spoleto, and the blazing kiss as they embraced just outside the reaches of a furious, tropical storm. She hadn't before been ready for R.J.'s love. Then she hadn't been able to look beyond her own shallow, manipulated life to answer the need in someone else's. But now she was ready, she vowed firmly as she raised a hand to the door. Now, she was ready to give R.J. Morrisson all the love and care he deserved . . . if only it wasn't too late.

She was unprepared for the R.J. who answered her knock. He hadn't shaved, and a jacket hung haphazardly off one shoulder, as if once half-done with putting it on, he'd forgotten all about it.

"Carole? I was just on my way out."

He reeked of alcohol, and the booming words were slurred. Carole advanced, firmly pushing him back into the apartment and closing the door behind them.

"I don't think you need to be going anywhere just now, R.J." she said, taking a quick glance about the disheveled apartment. "Are you alone?"

342

"How else?" he asked snidely, unable to prevent himself from rocking on his feet. He ambled over to the coffee table, lit up a cigarette.

Carole was further surprised. She'd never seen him smoke. "What's the matter with you?" she demanded.

"Me?" he asked with a sloppy motion to himself. "Why, nothing, ma'am. Nothing a good old court order couldn't fix."

"What are you talking about?"

"Don't you read the papers, Carole? There was a write-up this morning about Belmont Pines. Your old man is going to raze the place just after the turn of the year. . . ." His head snapped up in sudden awareness, as though he'd just remembered something. "That's where I'm going!" he exclaimed. "Belmont Pines!"

He swept the room with a frantic look. "Where's my jacket?" he muttered.

Carole leaned back on her heels, crossed her arms across her breast. "You're wearing it."

R.J. looked down in surprise. "Oh . . ." He glanced back up to Carole, a look of fury returning to the bloodshot eyes.

"Well, I'm going out there, damn it!" he cursed sloppily. "I'll tear the place apart if I have to!"

Carole lashed out a hand, grabbed him by the arm. "R.J., you're in no condition to go anywhere. Certainly, you're in no condition to drive!"

He raised his eyes from Carole's hand to her face, tried to look her steadily in the eye. "I'm going," he announced.

She rolled her eyes in frustration. "All right, all right. But you're not going alone . . . and *I'm* driving!"

Carole loaded R.J. into the passenger's side of the Corvette and then climbed into the driver's seat. Immediately she was assaulted with a barrage of

343

slurred instructions on how to drive. Gently, she removed R.J.'s hand from the steering wheel.

"I can handle it," she assured him, and proceeded to back neatly out of the garage. "Now . . . where are we going?"

He glanced at her from the corner of his eye. "Head out toward the old Ashley River Road," he said and sank back into the seat.

All the way out into the countryside, R.J. intermittently raged and mumbled about Belmont Pines. Gradually, Carole pieced together a basic story from his jumbled remarks. Apparently, Gossett Enterprises was about to develop some land that had been virtually stolen from a poor old black man. The more Carole understood, the more respect she felt for the drunken man sitting beside her.

Outside the silver car, the winter countryside flashed by; the December night grew blacker and more frigid. Inside, Carole had never been more warm.

"So, that's what we're going to try and find?" she asked. "Louise Stuckey's will?"

"That's right," R.J. mumbled. "Hell . . . why am I telling you all this? What are you doing here, anyway?!"

She glanced over. His bleary-eyed face was illumined by the soft dashboard lights. For a moment there was only the hum of the Corvette's engine.

Carole looked back to the road and took a deep breath. "I'm here because you were right about me. Because for a very long time, I thought only of myself. I've sold my designs, R.J. My dream has come true. And now I realize how empty everything is unless you can share it with someone."

She paused, chewed at her bottom lip. "I'd like to share it with you if . . . if it's not too late."

R.J. felt as though a skyrocket had just gone off in his alcohol-dulled brain. He stared at her profile, momentarily speechless.

344

"You know, this is just like you, Carole," he then said. "To decide you want me when I'm too damned drunk to do anything about it."

When Carole glanced over, she caught the grin on the rugged, unshaven face. A moment later, he reached out to cover her hand on the gear shift. She smiled wordlessly ahead as she twined her fingers within his.

Fifty yards behind, Joey Horton trailed at a discreet distance, keeping the taillights of the Corvette clearly in sight.

By the time they arrived at Belmont Pines, some of R.J.'s lucidity had returned.

"First things first," he told Carole as they stepped inside the dark, chilly house. Carting in some wood from the stockpile outside, he built a healthy fire in the old stone fireplace, then retrieved his flashlight from the car.

Carole glanced around the parlor. The fire helped. Now, the furnishings of the old house seemed less foreboding, a little more cozy. Still, the old house creaked noisily as the wind moaned outside. There was a definite air of spookiness about the place.

"Where are you going?" she asked as R.J. headed toward another room. Hurriedly, she caught up to him.

He smiled over his shoulder, reached out to take her hand. "Come on. There's nothing to be afraid of. It's just an old house."

Carole looked fearfully over her shoulder. "Yeah. . . . Except I'm half-expecting to meet the ghost of Louise Stuckey everywhere I look."

"Just stay with me," R.J. suggested soothingly.

They moved through the old house room by room. There were very few places she thought of looking that R.J. hadn't already checked, and they all revealed the same thing—nothing.

When they returned to the parlor, the fire had died down to a few coals, and R.J. looked at her, disappointment creasing his brow. "I don't know what I was trying to prove," he mumbled. "Come on. Let's go."

They wandered out onto the veranda, into the night air. Their breath clouded around their faces in the clear and invigorating cold.

Stuffing his hands into the pockets of his leather jacket, R.J. broke their silence. "I was drunk and crazy when I decided to come out here," he said, his breath clouding about his face. "But I'm sober now, and I'd like to tell you part of the reason I've been so hot about this Belmont Pines thing. It's Curt . . . him and my father."

"Curt?" Carole repeated in surprise. "What does he have to do with it?"

R.J. looked at her grimly. "He planned the whole thing. Dad put up the money. They hoodwinked Jonah Stuckey out of his property, and . . . to make a long story short, it's fraud. They've made millions by selling this land to Gossett Enterprises. And your father doesn't know a damn thing about it."

Carole reached out, placed a consoling hand on R.J.'s arm. "What are you going to do?" she asked.

"I can't prove anything. And even if I could, how could I take my own family to court? The only thing that would straighten everything out is Louise Stuckey's will."

An idea flickered in R.J.'s head. "Hold on!" he exclaimed. "Let me just check something around the side of the house. There was a recess in the wall." He started backing away. "Wait right here, Carole. I'll just be a minute."

She started to reach out to him, but he was already vaulting off the veranda in hot pursuit of his latest brainstorm. She took a few paces across the creaking planks, then paused and looked out into the scraggly yard. She could see the Corvette parked just beyond the sagging fence, gleaming an eerie silver in the light of the near-full moon.

Just then, Carole heard something in the camellias surrounding the veranda.

"R.J.?" she called, turning in the direction from which the noise had come.

Suddenly a man popped out of the bushes. Carole screamed, stumbling back toward the door as he hesitated at the base of the porch steps, a tense, black silhouette in the moonlight. As she saw the outline of the snap-brim hat and recognized the fearful presence who had terrorized her months before, Carole shrieked again.

"R.J.!" she screamed as the man took off and began running across the yard.

And then, from out of nowhere, a second shape was running, too.

R.J. slowly gained ground and tackled the man. But Joey Horton was quick and agile, while R.J. was still suffering the effects of a drunken binge. Horton wriggled out of his grasp, rolled over, and kicked R.J. squarely in the stomach. Then, leaping to his feet, he continued running for the road. R.J. stumbled after him, gathering speed as he regained his balance.

R.J. caught the man just before he reached a sedan parked secretively by a stretch of pines. Grabbing his coat, R.J. hauled him up short, whirled him around, and then hit him with such force that the man stumbled back and sprawled onto the hood of the sedan.

But like a bulldog, he jumped up and came at R.J. again, catching him off guard with a shoulder in the diaphragm. By the time R.J. recovered, Horton was starting his engine. R.J. ran to the sedan, yanked open the driver's door.

But then the driver floored the gas pedal, and the car shot forward. R.J. lurched back as the door wrenched out of his grasp. Helplessly, he watched

347

as the sedan careened into the ragged yard and crashed into the rear end of the Corvette, pushing it forward and crunching its nose into a fence post.

"What the hell!" R.J. exploded and vaulted into a gallop toward his car. Meanwhile, Horton backed up, made a hard turn, and screeched off across the yard, stirring up a trail of dust as he hit the dirt road.

Carole had plastered herself against the door of the house, her eyes straining wildly through the night as she watched the spectacle unfold. It had all happened in less than a minute. And now, as R.J. ran up to survey the damage done to his car, she stumbled across the yard to meet him.

"Damn it!" he yelled. "Damn it! Damn it! Damn it!"

Suddenly, R.J. seemed to regain his senses, looked frantically to where Carole stood motionless on the other side of the car. "Are you all right?" he demanded.

She nodded. "I'm sorry I screamed like that. I know who it was . . . a detective my father hired to follow me."

"A detective?"

"Yes. Joey Horton. I gather he's a sneaky little man . . . but not dangerous."

"*Not* dangerous?" R.J. exclaimed incredulously. "Look at my car!"

When he tried to start it, the engine made a sick, lurching noise. R.J. climbed out of the Corvette and kicked at the ground with disgust.

"It will have to be towed," he announced. "And we'll have to hitch a ride on the highway tomorrow. We're stuck here for the night, Carole. Come on," he added with a heavy sigh. "Let's go inside."

He rebuilt the fire while Carole pulled an old sofa close to the stone hearth. Within minutes, the orangey flames leaped and crackled cheerily, warming the room so that Carole removed the cashmere coat.

She wandered over to join R.J. where he stood rather broodingly by the fire.

"This whole thing is ridiculous," he muttered. "And all because I was drunk. You could have gotten hurt, Carole. I'm sorry I dragged you into this."

She took his arm, turned him round to face her, and stared up into the deep blue eyes. "Are you?" she asked, going up on tiptoe and putting her arms round his neck. "I'm not."

R.J.'s worries, self-recriminations, everything but the woman before him went out of his mind. His arms circled her waist as he gazed down at her.

"You're incredible, you know that?"

"I was hoping you'd notice," she said with an alluring smile.

His eyes darted between hers. "I love you, Carole," he said softly. "I have for a long time."

"I love you, too."

R.J.'s eyes flashed. "You do?"

Her smile widened. "A little while ago, you said you were sober," she murmured. "Care to prove it?"

R.J. stared into the blue-green eyes and thought he'd drown in the feelings that closed over him in scintillating waves. He bent to kiss her, promised himself he'd go slowly. Yet as he filled his arms with Carole, he lost all sense of restraint.

His hands roved her body, down the hips and along the rounded buttocks, then back up to slip under the white sweater and close round the bare breasts. Carole's breath came in quick gusts through her nostrils as his tongue lunged deep within her mouth.

Her palms roamed down his muscular back to the firm backside. Brazenly, she pulled his hips against her, felt the hardness of him. Her fingers moved round between them, began to unsnap his jeans. And in the fleeting moment before she gave herself over completely to the feeling of uncaring abandon, Carole thought that she'd lost all sense of decency.

There before the ancient hearth they undressed each other. The firelight danced across their bare limbs as they embraced, drawing each other ever more closely as though they would climb inside each other's skin. R.J.'s blood was on fire. In a sort of daze, he swept Carole up in his arms, stalked to the sofa, and climbed carefully onto it with her beneath him.

Carole pulled his head down for another kiss. Gradually, R.J. lowered his body onto her, his legs prodding between hers. Carole was on a plane of ecstasy, her body turning liquid and running into one hot pool. She felt him probing, taking her ever higher, until when he finally entered, she arched up to meet him—gasping beneath his kiss as he drove home.

As the December night grew ever colder in the low country, within the firelit parlor of Belmont Pines, two lovers created a powerful heat of their own, building it with intense, long-denied passion, until it flared and consumed them both. . . .

It was past midnight when Joey Horton's black sedan careened onto Tradd Street and screeched to a halt. He leaped out of the car, taking the steps two at a time as he raced to Gossett's door and rang the bell frenziedly.

James was reading in the study. It was a late-night habit he'd fallen into lately, now that the house was forever quiet and empty. And inevitably his sour thoughts seemed to dwell tortuously on Carole and Kathleen and all the other people in his life who had ever betrayed him.

At the urgent sound of the bell, he stalked quickly to the front of the house. His expression turned dark

350

when he threw open the doors to find a smiling Joey Horton.

"I thought I told you our business relationship had come to an end," James growled.

Undaunted, Joey brushed past the man and sashayed into the foyer. "I think you'll change your mind when you hear what I have to tell you."

A quarter of an hour later, Horton stepped out of the mansion and took a deep breath of the cold, winter air.

He grinned, the movement drawing a wince of pain. The jaw was sore where that Morrisson jerk had nailed him with an uppercut. But hell, it was worth it. Joey was back on James Gossett's payroll. And as for R.J. Morrisson . . . he lived in Charleston now and was easily within the reach of an enterprising detective with a grudge.

There will be other days, Horton thought, gingerly massaging his aching jaw as he drove away from Tradd Street.

James returned to his study—a murderous gleam in his eye. So, the little upstart had pulled a fast one, had he?

"Curt Morrisson!" he sneered aloud.

The arrogant little blue blood couldn't manage to get Carole to marry him, but he could sure as hell use privileged Gossett Enterprises information to make himself a tidy little profit! All the time James had been taking the boy under his wing, Curt had been scheming behind his back—using him, betraying him!

"You're history, boy," James muttered to the quiet, deserted room.

"You look beautiful," R.J. said with a silly grin.

Carole and R.J. had caught a ride early that morning with a passing tractor trailer. After showering and getting cleaned up, they had decided to go out for breakfast. As they chowed down on healthy portions of bacon and eggs, grits and biscuits, they gave each other occasional glowing glances across the table.

Carole wore no makeup, and her hair was straight as a stick. "Sure I'm beautiful, R.J.," Carole replied saucily. "You just go right on believing that."

Carole looked at R.J. over her cup of coffee, a sudden thoughtfulness on her face. "You know something? I've had this little thought nagging at the back of my mind ever since you told me about Jonah and the missing will."

R.J. glanced up from his coffee. "What?"

"Well," Carole began slowly. "You've searched the house at Belmont Pines. You've searched all the records. But have you ever asked Jonah, himself, about his mother's will? I know you said he was retarded, but he's the one person in the world who lived with Louise Stuckey. Maybe he knows where she put it."

A glowing light flickered in R.J.'s eyes. Suddenly, he leaned across the table, planting a quick kiss on the waiting lips.

"You're brilliant!" he exclaimed. "I'm going to call Cecile right now. If she never asked him about the will, I'm sure no one has!"

Carole watched with a wide smile as R.J. leapt out of the booth and hurried toward the public phone at the front of the coffee shop. With a sigh of happy satisfaction, she took a sip of coffee and thought how wonderful life was when you could share it.

"No," Cecile replied thoughtfully. "Now that you mention it, I don't think I ever asked Jonah about the will. Oh, R.J.!" she added with a quick flush of hope. "Do you think he might know something?"

"It's worth a try," R.J. told her. "Listen, Cecile.

352

Can you drive us up to the hospital today? I'm afraid I don't have access to a car."

"Today?" She hesitated, but only for a moment. "Let me call your mama and tell her I need the day off. Where can I pick you up?"

An hour later, Cecile, R.J. and Carole were on their way to the institution. But when they got there, they were informed by a rather hefty nurse that visiting hours had not yet begun.

R.J. stepped forward, whipped his wallet out of his back pocket, and produced a supreme-court identification card. "I'm R.J. Morrisson, Nurse . . . Barnett, is it? If you'd be so kind as to show us to Mr. Stuckey's room? I'm on state business, and I'm afraid I have no time to lose."

The woman's mouth had gaped open. Without further protest, she snapped it shut and proceeded to lead the way down a long corridor. R.J. tossed a silent, victorious grin at Carole, who returned it with one of her own. Their levity floundered, however, when they ventured into Jonah Stuckey's room. They found him lying on the cot, his face turned to the wall.

Carole and R.J. hung back near the entrance as Cecile walked over to the narrow bed, reached out and touched his shoulder.

"Jonah? It's me. Miss Cecile."

The man turned, and R.J. was horrified by what he saw. Jonah Stuckey must have lost twenty pounds. He was a shell of what he had been only a few months before. Once again R.J.'s eyes drifted to the floor as he was seized with the familiar pangs of pity and guilt.

Sensing R.J.'s distress, Carole reached beside her to take his hand. And then both turned their attention to Cecile as they heard her begin to croon questions to Jonah, gently rocking him back and forth.

"Jonah, honey? I want you to think about your mama for a minute."

"Mama?"

"Yes, honey. She had a very important paper. Do you know where she kept it?"

Jonah continued to rock silently in the woman's arms.

"Her favorite thing," he said after a moment.

Cecile wrenched her neck around to peer at R.J. with a sudden ray of hope lighting her eyes.

"And where is her favorite thing, Jonah?"

He leaned back and looked at Cecile with baleful hazel eyes. "I know. I have it safe and sound. Like Mama. At home. Home," he repeated and then began to cry.

R.J. stepped forward. "Jonah? Could you show us where it is?"

"Take Jonah home!" the man ordered tearfully.

"Yes," R.J. assured him. "If we take you home, can you show us where it is?"

"With Miss Cecile?" Jonah asked suspiciously.

Cecile broke in with a smile. "Yes, honey! We'll all go home together."

By the time Cecile's old Chevy chugged up to Belmont Pines, the afternoon was late. It had taken some time to wangle an emergency leave of absence for Jonah, even with R.J.'s ruse about the supreme court. Jonah bolted out of the car and ran sloppily, but with great apparent joy up to the house, then circled to the side.

"Come on!" he called.

He knew the forest well. Jonah trotted eagerly ahead while Cecile, Carole, and R.J. followed. They marveled at the way the man took the intricate, forest paths, and at the way he'd seemed to come back to life once he set foot on Belmont Pines. In short order Jonah led them to a clearing at the edge of a creek. Then, plopping down on the ground, he began digging in the dirt.

A moment later, he looked up at his three companions—his rheumy eyes alight with pride. "I kep'

354

it safe and sound," he said, pulling the old, black book out of the ground. "Just like Mama."

Cecile stepped over, reached out for the book with an attitude of reverence. "It's Louise's Bible," she said softly. Opening the cover, she withdrew a piece of paper and turned to Carole and R.J. with a look of shock. "And her will!" she announced triumphantly.

"Did I do good?" Jonah asked with a one-sided grin.

Cecile leaned over, took the boy-man in her arms and hugged him tightly as the tears ran down her cheeks.

"Yes, honey, you did good. You did real good!"

Curt was preparing to pack up for the day when the pink slip arrived. It was short, impersonal and to the point. "Your services are no longer required," it read.

Curt lunged for the phone and dialed James Gossett's private number.

"I told you once that I tolerate no disloyalty," James stated in a cold tone. "I've been informed of your—shall we say, clandestine?—activities, Curt. At this point I consider it in everyone's best interest to keep the whole thing quiet. I'll maintain that policy as long as you're out of here today. And that, Mr. Morrisson, concludes our association."

The phone clicked dead in his ear. Curt raised his pale eyes—wide with shock—to stare unseeingly across the plush office.

As the group of four drove along the highway toward Charleston, they decided that Jonah would stay at Cecile's until the will could be probated.

"He's been put in my custody for this leave of absence," R.J. rumbled. "And it's my decision that

355

he won't go back to that damned institution. Hell, it will only take a couple of days before the guardian's order can be revoked anyway."

Jonah was ecstatic. Cecile was thrilled. R.J. was swept with relief. And Carole glowed with warm, loving pride for the man who sat beside her in the backseat of the Chevy.

Now, as they drove past the Charleston city limits, R.J. asked Cecile to drop him and Carole at the Morrisson house.

"Your parents' place?" Carole asked with a quick look of dread. She hadn't seen any of them—Charlotte, Robert, or Curt—since the disastrous engagement party.

"I want to get this fraud thing undone as quickly as possible," R.J. whispered. "And besides, we need to tell them we're getting married anyway."

"Married!" Carole whirled in her seat, her wide eyes flying across R.J.'s handsome features.

His face broke into a smile. "Don't you want to?"

"Don't I . . ." The rest of Carole's words were lost as she lunged for him. And when the Chevy pulled up before the Morrisson mansion, they were still locked in an embrace.

Charlotte Morrisson was in the foyer alone, decorating the mammoth Christmas tree that reached up to almost touch the chandelier. The girls were out socializing, and Robert and Curt were in the private study—as usual.

She'd put on some Christmas music, but somehow the nostalgic carols only further dampened her spirits. Christmas was a time of joy and sharing, of families drawing close. Yet Charlotte had never felt more distant from her loved ones. Curt, involved in a seamy plot, R.J., estranged and resentful, and Robert, so cold and angrily silent each night as he

356

plodded into the guest room and closed the door behind him.

Tears started to Charlotte's brown eyes as she prayed for the day when Robert would once again reach out for her. She was grateful for the interruption when a knock sounded at the door. Her eyes widened considerably when she beheld R.J. and Carole waiting outside . . . holding hands.

"May we come in, Mother?" R.J. asked formally.

"Certainly. Hello, you two," she greeted, giving each of them a peck on the cheek as they stepped inside.

"Where are Father and Curt?" R.J. asked.

"Where do you think?" his mother replied with a nod toward the study.

R.J. squeezed Carole's hand in parting, then moved off to his father's private domain, walking in without so much as a knock. Left behind with Charlotte, Carole met the woman's questioning, dark eyes.

"He found Louise Stuckey's will," she explained.

Behind the oak doors, male voices rose heatedly. And then Curt came busting out of the room.

"There's nothing you can do about it now, Curt," Robert thundered, hurrying after his younger son. "Just accept it. I have. The will invalidates everything that's happened. The money will be returned, and the whole matter will drop. It's not so bad. And as for a job, you can always come to Ashley Shipping. You know that."

Curt was backing away, glaring at his father. "You're offering a position at Ashley Shipping when I could have been set for life?" The vision of his beachfront house on the Isle of Palms went up in smoke; Curt's dream had crashed in flames. And all because of R.J. !

R.J. meandered out of the study behind his father, caught the raging look of hatred Curt threw his way before whirling in the direction of the staircase.

"You're already set for life, Curt," his mother said quietly. "Haven't you always gotten everything you've ever wanted?"

Curt pivoted to glare across the foyer. For the first time he noticed Carole standing there with his mother. His fury swelled.

"No . . . I haven't always gotten everything I've wanted," he hissed with a vicious look at Carole. "What the hell *you* doing here?"

R.J. took long strides to Carole's side. "She's here because I'm here, Curt," he said with a dark look. "You might as well know now as later . . ."

R.J. hesitated, his gaze darting from his brother to his father to his mother. "Carole and I are going to be married as soon as we can arrange it."

Charlotte's hands flew to her cheeks. Then she responded instinctively, taking Carole into a hug.

Curt's mouth slacked open; the wind seemed to leave his body. It was the final defeat, the final indignity. Even his rage dissolved as the wave of failure swept over him. Turning, a dead look in his eyes, Curt walked up the stairs with the stiff movements of a zombie.

Robert's concerned gaze followed his younger son's retreat. But then, Curt was young. He'd get over it. As for himself, Robert was going to be surprisingly glad to put the Stuckey matter behind. What had begun as a clever plot had turned into something ugly, something beneath a Morrisson.

Robert took slow, unsure steps to join the three people in the foyer.

"Congratulations, son," he said and hesitantly extended his hand to R.J. "On everything," he added with a meaningful glance. "Sometimes, it seems, it takes a son to remind a father of his own teachings."

R.J. reached for his father's hand, shook it hard.

358

"Thanks, Dad," he replied with a welcome feeling of returning closeness.

Robert leaned over to kiss Carole on the cheek, looked at her with a light, teasing smile. "Welcome to the family, Carole," he said. "I always had a feeling you were destined to join us one way or another."

A short while later, R.J. asked to borrow one of the family cars. And when the two young people left, Robert followed his wife's swaying gait up the stairs and into the master suite.

Charlotte turned to look at him questioningly, saw the "Morrisson-blue" eyes filled with the light she had thought forever extinguished.

"Thank God the whole mess is over," Robert rumbled. After an agonizing moment of hesitation, he stalked to his wife and took her into his arms.

"I need you, Charlotte," he murmured against her hair. "Please . . . take me back."

And Charlotte Morrisson's eyes slipped peacefully closed as she knew her Christmas prayer had been answered. Her husband was home.

The announcement of the marriage ran in *The Post and Courier* the first Sunday after the New Year, stirring a ripple of astonishment throughout the upper crust of Charleston.

"Carole Gossett married to R.J. Morrisson?" "Why, she was engaged to his brother, you know!" "Will wonders never cease?

Behind the ornate wrought iron that screened their dining hall windows, the Trippley sisters sat at breakfast. A glowing smile came to Constance's face.

"My, my, isn't that wonderful?" she asked her sister. "Pretty little Carole married to R.J.!"

"*Hmph!*" Aurora snorted. "Always was a hussy. Always will be a hussy, whether she changes her name to Morrisson or not!"

Farther along Tradd, James Gossett saw the notice and arched a dark brow. Slowly, an evil, self-satisfied smile spread over his features. Whether the little brat knew it or not, Carole had fulfilled his fondest dream. In time, things would be patched up between them. In time, his blood would run in the veins of grandchildren named Morrisson.

And in the Morrisson home, Curt stormed into R.J.'s boyhood room and sent a row of tennis trophies smashing to the floor. If he had any nerve, Curt thought angrily, he'd go out and kill the bastard!

Unaware, uncaring of the furor their actions had elicited, Carole and R.J. Morrisson settled themselves on the patio of their townhouse apartment at Broad and Rutledge. The January morning was chilly; and they had laughingly tucked a blanket around themselves and snuggled together on the couch.

"I enjoyed the ballet last night," she said.

"So did I. But I liked the performance that took place later a lot better."

"R.J.!" Carole scolded, but her eyes were alight with happiness and humor. "Seriously! Kathleen and André dance beautifully together, don't they?"

"Yeah," he admitted. "They do."

"They're a great couple on and off the stage. And how about April and Charlie Regis? They're getting to be a pretty hot item!"

"We're a pretty hot item!"

"Yeah," Carole replied dreamily. "We are. I'm very proud of you, by the way."

"For what?"

"For becoming a public defender."

R.J. looked at her with tolerant amusement. "Legal Aid, honey," he corrected. "I'll be working for a branch of legal services that's funded through Congress."

Carole squinted up at him. "Don't you go to bat for the little guys against the big guys?"

R.J. grinned down at her. "Something like that."

"Well, that sounds like a public defender to me," she insisted.

"Whatever you say," R.J. chuckled, pulling her close. "But you know, I won't be making nearly as much money as I would be in private practice. You sure you don't mind?"

"Don't worry, Mr. Public Defender. We can live on *my* income if we have to." Carole chuckled lightheartedly. "Never thought I'd be saying *that* to any man . . . much less a Morrisson!"

R.J. looked down at his new bride. "Now, you're a Morrisson, too," he reminded her.

"Yes, I am. And proud of the name for just one reason . . . because it's yours."

He peered into the fathomless blue-green eyes. And as always, they swallowed him whole. "I love you," he said thickly.

"I love you, too," she returned, raising her lips for a kiss.

With a feeling of warm radiance, Carole settled against her husband's shoulder. R.J.'s cheek came to rest on the top of her head. Quietly, peacefully, they watched the morning sunlight sparkling on the sea beyond the rooftops.

The city they looked out across was one of great beauty, great tradition, great wealth. And within it, the struggles of power and heart, love and money, would continue as they had for centuries.

But for two of the mere mortals who snuggled in the ancient, wisteria-laced arms of Charleston, it was a bright new day.

In the continuing saga of CHARLESTON,
Tradd Street becomes a hotbed of
highly classified *and* passionate secrets. . . .

Fearing her husband's covert operations
have replaced her in their marriage, Stephanie
Regis finds an answer to her loneliness in the
heady, passionate attentions of a handsome
young stockbroker. As a leading member of one
of Charleston's greatest military families, no
one is more surprised—or flattered—than she
by the affair. But Stephanie lives with the ter-
rible fear that her infidelity would be the last
straw to the Regis family, already broken by
one son's rejection of the military tradition so
proudly followed for generations.

Meanwhile, Stephanie's father-in-law, the
legendary ''General,'' is caught up in secrets
of his own—painful, shocking reminiscences
that emerge as he writes his memoirs. He is
unaware that the love and trust of neighbor
April Gossett might finally bring his youngest
son back into the Regis fold, *or* that a leak in
his other son's top-secret work may place the
lives of his entire family in danger. . . .

Watch for the next book
in the CHARLESTON series,
coming to you in April from Ivy Books